Galactic Empire Wars: Rebellion

Galactic Empire Wars Book 3

By
Raymond L. Weil
USA Today Best Selling Author

DEDICATION

To my wife Debra for all of her patience while I sat in front of my computer typing. It has always been my dream to become an author. I also want to thank my children for their support.

Galactic Empire Wars: Rebellion

Chapter One

It was a small, discreet star system huddled between two warring Empires, which would soon be witness to an event that would change the galaxy. Six planets and fourteen moons circled the small, yellowish-orange star with a small asteroid field between the fifth and sixth planets, both of which were small gas giants. The system's only habitable planet was .82 AU out from the system's primary and held a budding civilization just beginning to explore the planets in its own star system.

The Strell had long since found the Beltian system and added it to their Empire as a minor planet with an intermediate technological civilization. Due to its technology level and minimal resources, the Strell had only requested the Beltians furnish specific food products to the Empire. Twice each year, six large Strell cargo ships would come to the planet to have their holds filled with the designated agricultural products. Other than that, the planet was left to govern itself with strict instructions from the Strell not to attempt to venture out of their star system. To do so would result in disastrous consequences for the Beltians.

-

The Strell warfleet dropped out of Fold Space into the unsuspecting system. For six years, they'd been fighting a fierce war against the Kleese, who were attempting to smash the Strell Empire and add it to their own growing territory. The first hint the Strell had that the status quo between the two Empires had changed was when the Kleese attacked several of the inhabited worlds between the Empires. It had been followed up by a massive attack by the Kleese warrior caste, the Zaltule, on the Strell Empire itself.

The Zaltule were a dangerous and warlike caste, which the Strell had long believed, had died out. They'd paid for that false belief with the loss of millions of lives and nearly a quarter of their Empire. Now, a major portion of their remaining warships had been gathered to ambush an inbound Kleese fleet that would be entering the system shortly. If the fleet could be destroyed or forced to retreat, it would buy the time the Strell needed to rebuild their forces and push the Kleese back.

"All ships have dropped out of Fold Space," hissed Minor Den Leader Lish his tongue flicking forth. Lish was two meters tall, very thin, and his head resembled that of a large snake.

"We will wait here," ordered Den Leader Rith. His eyes, set wide on both sides of his head, narrowed to thin slits as he turned to gaze at the tactical screen.

The screen was covered in green icons, which represented the two thousand powerful Strell battlecruisers lying in wait for the inbound Kleese fleet. Rith's eyes could make out the different colors, though his ancestors in the dim past had only been able to see in black and white. The Strell had progressed far on the evolutionary scale from the time they had slithered on the ground until they'd developed arms and legs, which allowed them to build a technological civilization.

"We will not be favored in this battle," Lish spoke, the scales on his body seeming to ripple as he turned to face the Den Leader.

"If we lose, our Empire will surrender to the Kleese," Rith responded in a cold and nearly emotionless voice. "The Kleese will have demonstrated their superiority and won the right to lay claim to our Empire. The Dens will swear allegiance to the Kleese and become part of their realm."

Lish nodded in agreement. The Strell were a logical race and rather than suffer the total destruction of their Empire, they would surrender and serve the Kleese as willing vassals.

Several hours passed and the Strell battlecruisers waited. The ships were dark gray and nearly two kilometers long and one thousand meters in diameter. Their hulls were covered with small hatches covering sublight missile tubes. Numerous weapon turrets, which were pointed out toward empty space, waited on the enemy, who were expected to arrive shortly. Sensors reached out searching for an enemy that was nearly as ruthless and cold as the Strell and would show no mercy in battle. This would be a battle to the death until one side or the other had been completely annihilated.

Tens of thousands of Strell stood at their posts waiting to throw their deadly weapons at the Kleese. There was very little talking as the Strell were a cold-blooded species and showed very little emotion. Only the Queens in the great dens were emotional and they controlled the Empire. A Queen very seldom ventured into space, preferring to stay beneath the ground surrounded by thousands of Strell, who obeyed her every command.

The sensors continued to probe space and then the first Kleese warship dropped out of Fold Space. Instantly, warning alarms sounded in the waiting Strell fleet and their crews snapped suddenly to full vigilance. Their eyes narrowed and loud hissing noises echoed down the narrow corridors of their ships.

Den Leader Rith gazed at the tactical screen as Kleese warships appeared all around his fleet. Somehow, the Kleese had detected the ambush and adjusted their fleet formation accordingly. His tongue flicked out as he turned toward Lish. "All ships fire! We must destroy these den killers."

-

Kleese War Overlord Harmock gazed without compassion at the massive Strell fleet assembled before him. Harmock was an arachnid standing upon six legs. His upper torso was humanoid with two nearly black arms extending from the shoulders. The arms ended in a slim hand with seven long digits. A large triangular shaped head with multifaceted eyes took in the data the ship's sensors were recording. Harmock was the War Overlord of the Zaltule and he had come to end the war against the Strell and add their Empire to that of the Kleese.

"It is as we expected," Minor Overlord Gareth spoke from Hammock's side. "The Strell have gathered their remaining ships to oppose us. If we win this battle, their Empire will be ours."

Harmock was silent for a moment. Much had happened in the six years since his awakening by Xaltul, the Supreme Overlord of the Kleese race. The rest of the Zaltule had risen, the ancient shipyards had been reactivated, and new warships were in the process of being constructed. Now Harmock watched as the last of his four thousand disk ships dropped out of Fold Space. Each ship was dark black, three kilometers across, and one thousand meters thick. They were armed with heavy pulse fusion weapons, energy turrets, and antimatter sublight missiles. It was a force capable of crushing any opponent as the Strell were about to find out.

"For the Empire!" roared Harmock over the ship's com, which connected all of the Kleese ships. "Destroy them all!" His multifaceted eyes gazed with annoyance at the multitude of enemy before him.

Resistance to the Empire was not permitted. The Strell should have been conquered over a thousand years ago. Instead, the Council of Overlords had grown weary of the war against the Strell and had come to an agreement with the cold-blooded race. The war had ended and the Zaltule had gone into deep sleep to serve the Empire in the future. Now that day had arrived, and Harmock fully intended to conquer every species that stood between the Kleese and domination of the galaxy, even if it was necessary to make changes to the Council of Overlords. The Zaltule would never agree to go into deep sleep again, and it was only fitting that the first major threat to be dealt with were their old enemies, the Strell.

From Strell battlecruisers, thousands of metal hatches slid open and sublight missiles vanished from their tubes as they accelerated at one hundred gravities toward their designated targets. Inertial compensators were stressed as they were pushed to the limit to handle the sudden thrust of the sublight drives on the deadly missiles. Around the surrounded fleet, massive ten-megaton antimatter explosions blossomed into existence as they slammed into their targets.

Space flared in brilliant flashes of light as raw energy clawed at the powerful shields protecting the Kleese warships. Under the intense onslaught, more than a few shields faltered, allowing missiles to impact the vulnerable armored hulls. Across the Kleese formation, twenty ships died in massive fiery explosions as they were blown apart by antimatter energy.

However, the Kleese were firing back and they had a two to one advantage plus more powerful ships. A Strell battlecruiser's energy shield collapsed, allowing a Kleese pulse fusion beam to strike the top section of the ship. Massive sections of the hull were torn loose as the beam penetrated deep inside, setting off secondary explosions. Then a couple of twenty-megaton antimatter missiles struck the hull and two burning suns flashed into existence where the ship had been. Moments later, all that remained were glowing gases and a scattering of debris.

The Strell ships tenaciously held their positions as they poured heavy weapons fire into the surrounding Kleese fleet. As with the Zaltule ships, the Strell battlecruisers had been designed for war and could take a lot of punishment. More Kleese ships were blown apart from the furious onslaught as energy weapons and antimatter missiles penetrated faltering screens and smashed into the armored hulls. Across the Kleese formation, bright suns appeared where powerful warships had once been.

Kleese ships began to coordinate quickly and efficiently as they used their superior firepower against their ancient enemy. Strell ships began to die as the Kleese used their numerical superiority to overwhelm the Strell battlecruisers. Two or three Kleese ships would join together and pummel an opposing battlecruiser until there was nothing left but a drifting hulk or burning debris. Once the ship was out of action, the Kleese vessels would shift their fire to the next ship.

Den Leader Rith felt his flagship shake violently and listened impassively as damage reports began to come in from across the ship. Six compartments had been opened to space, secondary Engineering had been destroyed, sixteen missile tubes were nonfunctioning, and twenty percent of the ship's energy weapons were gone.

"We are severely damaged," hissed Lish, his forked tongue waving in anguish. "The Kleese outnumber us and are destroying our ships."

"It is as I feared," replied Den Leader Rith his snakelike head turning toward his second in command. "The Zaltule cannot be defeated, at least not by us. Too long have we allowed our military to become weak due to a lack of enemies, now we are paying for that oversight."

"We thought the Zaltule were gone," Lish responded. "It is the primary reason the Queens agreed to a truce in the original war with the Kleese. The Kleese Council of Overlords promised they would do away with the warrior caste."

"We were tricked," Rith responded his eyes becoming very narrow slits. "The Kleese used subterfuge to fool our Queens, and now we will pay the ultimate price for that grievous error in trusting their council."

On one of the main viewscreens, a Kleese battlecruiser was burning. Even as Rith watched, a series of antimatter explosions finished the ship off. If the Strell only had more warships, the Kleese could be defeated, but they were too heavily outnumbered. They would die for their Queens; it was far better than having a Kleese obedience collar placed around one's neck.

The ship shook violently again and the lights went out. The emergency lighting came on, but the command crew were no longer working at their stations. All heads and eyes were focused on the Den Leader.

"Our energy shield is down," Lish reported as he listened to one of the assistant Den Leaders in Engineering. "Fusion reactors one and two have been compromised and have been taken offline. We have battery power for two hours of life support."

Rith looked slowly around the Command Center acknowledging his den mates. "I don't believe we will need life support shortly," he spoke calmly. His eyes narrowed into slits as he contemplated his impending death. "Our Empire ends today; we serve our Queens in death."

Rith never saw the four Kleese antimatter missiles that struck his flagship. Raw, uncontrolled energy flashed through the two-kilometer long vessel vaporizing metal and incinerating flesh. In a microsecond, the flagship ceased to be.

-

In space, the surviving Strell warships moved closer together for mutual support with their energy screens nearly touching. Their energy weapons were firing nonstop and they were launching sublight antimatter missiles in sprint mode. Space was lit up from the multitude of antimatter explosions. Occasionally a Kleese energy shield would fail and the hapless ship would instantly be attacked by dozens of Strell battlecruisers. When that happened, the disk ship would vanish in a series of fiery explosions, leaving glowing debris behind.

One of the other Den Leaders had taken command and formed what remained of the fleet into a compact globe formation to allow for maximum defensive support. The Strell had superior computers tied into their defensive systems, and many of the Kleese sublight antimatter missiles were being intercepted. Unfortunately, the Kleese were launching thousands in massive waves at the Strell formation and too many were getting through.

The commanding Den Leader recognized the inevitable and sent word back toward Strell space that the battle was lost and the fleet would not be returning. He informed the Queens to prepare themselves to receive the Zaltule and to surrender the Empire.

-

Harmock watched in deep satisfaction as the Strell fleet was steadily pushed back. Every minute, their globe formation was becoming smaller and smaller as more ships were eliminated. The

Strell formation was full of glowing suns, which indicated dying ships.

"They are defeated!" spoke Minor Overlord Gareth. "We have forced them back into a purely defensive position and their offensive weapons fire has greatly diminished."

"They are fools to resist the Empire," responded Harmock as he watched another ten Strell battlecruisers being torn apart on the viewscreens by Kleese pulse fusion beams. "This will be a great victory for the Zaltule."

"Then it will be time to return to the council," Gareth added his powerful arms folding across his dark chest. His triangular head focused on the Overlord. "It is time the Zaltule were better represented by the council."

"As we shall be," agreed Harmock. "But first we must finish this battle."

The black Kleese ships continue to press the Strell. Even with their numerical advantage and superior weapons, it takes time to destroy two thousand warships. Ship after ship died in blazing deaths as the Kleese eliminated them. Occasionally a Kleese shield would fail and the Strell would take revenge for their fallen den mates. The Strell formation was slowly becoming a cloud of glowing energy and drifting debris. Finally, the last Strell ship died in a blaze of light as over one hundred antimatter missiles blew it into oblivion.

"What were our losses?" demanded War Overlord Harmock. The battle was over and the Zaltule were victorious. It proved once more that the Kleese were the superior race in the galaxy and all others should be subservient.

"We lost four hundred and twelve ships," Gareth answered.

"Acceptable, considering the size of the victory," Harmock replied after a moment. "We will take six hours to repair our damage and then we'll set course back to our home system. It is time that I meet with the Council of Overlords. A new era has arrived for our Empire, and the Zaltule will lead our people to new victories and glory. There are members of the council that are weak and will resist the new order; they will need to be replaced. The ranks of the Zaltule will furnish new and stronger leadership for the council."

Six hours later, the Kleese warfleet entered Fold Space and left the small indiscreet star system far behind. From the second planet of the system, the Beltians had watched the entire battle on their primitive space sensors. They cringed in disbelief as the Strell warships were blasted into oblivion and wondered if the Strell would still come for the agricultural products the planet furnished. If not, then would the strange black disk ships, which had destroyed the Strell fleet, return instead? The Beltians had always believed the Strell were the supreme power in the galaxy, now that belief had been blown away. For the immediate future, they would look to the skies in fear; fear that the black disk ships would return and take the place of the Strell in making demands of the Beltians.

In the Great Hall of the Council of Overlords, a special meeting was being held by the twenty members of the Kleese council. Xatul, the Supreme Overlord, gazed with disdain at the worried members standing at the massive stone table. Word had just been received of the Zaltule's successful defeat of the main Strell battle fleet, which meant the Strell Empire was now a part of the Kleese domain. Already, several hundred thousand Zaltule warriors were on their way to the home worlds of the Strell. The Strell Queens would be fitted with metallic obedience collars to ensure there would be no future rebellion to Kleese rule.

"No conscripts are being sent to the Strell Empire?" Keluth asked in a voice showing great concern. "I'm not comfortable with the Zaltule having complete control in this matter."

"Nor am I," added Overlord Hymtal. "The Zaltule are assuming too much authority in our Empire and using far more resources than necessary. Already, control of many valuable star systems have been taken from the council. The Zaltule are using these systems to rebuild their war machine."

"The use of conscripts has been a cheap and efficient method for us to expand the Empire for generations," stated Raluth as he addressed the council. "The Zaltule go through resources as if they are water. Many of the planets we control are being strained to supply the war materials the Zaltule are demanding. It's been necessary to send large numbers of conscripts as well as Kleese to keep these worlds in line. We must restrain   the Zaltule before the Council of Overlords finds itself in a weakened position due to a lessening of power. The more power the Zaltule seize, the more Kleese look to them for guidance. Very soon, the Zaltule will be the ultimate power and authority in our Empire unless we do something."

Xatul remained silent. Hammock was on his way back with his warfleet and Xatul was nearly certain the Zaltule leader would demand a greater representation on the council. Most likely, the Zaltule leader would want several of his people to take over key positions. He wondered cynically just how many of the other Overlords realized that.

Bixutl stood next to the large stone table gazing at the other council members. For untold eons, the Council of Overlords had represented the most powerful Kleese in the Empire. Advancement on the council was done through open challenges, and if the council agreed the challenge was legitimate, then a battle to the death was arranged. If the challenger won, they would take over the council position of the slain Overlord. It ensured the council was controlled by only the most powerful and ruthless of the Kleese.

There was little doubt in Bixutl's mind that if any of the Zaltule wanted a position upon the Council of Overlords there would be nothing they could do to prevent it. In recent weeks, with the war with the Strell coming to an end, Bixutl had taken precautions to ensure the Zaltule didn't challenge him for his spot on the council. He strongly suspected Xatul had done the same thing.

"Kaluse has requested an additional increase in special metals for ship construction at the Zaltule shipyards," Bixutl reported. Bixutl didn't mention he'd already ensured the necessary materials would be sent. It was part of his agreement with Kaluse to ensure Bixutl's continued status on the council.

"More warships!" grated out Raluth his multifaceted eyes looking around at the other arachnid council members. "We have our exploration ships, which have served us for centuries in taking over thousands of star systems; why do we need such a massive Zaltule warfleet?"

"I agree," Hymtal added in a cold and angry voice. "Our conscripts have served us well and now that the Strell have been defeated it's time for the Zaltule to go back to sleep. They are no longer needed!"

"I don't think it will be as simple as that," answered Xatul, rising to full height on his six legs and placing his hands upon the stone table. "The Zaltule will not return to deep sleep."

"Why not?" demanded Hymtal, challengingly. "They have served their purpose."

Xatul looked without emotion at the other council members, knowing what he was about to say would mean the deaths of a number of them when the Zaltule returned and demanded positions on the council. "The Zaltule were dying in their sleeping chambers."

"Dying?" uttered Raluth, looking with suspicion at Xatul. "What do you mean they were dying?"

"It began a number of years ago," Xatul responded. "I was notified by the garrison commander that the Zaltule were starting to die. Over the years, the number of deaths began to increase rapidly. In order to preserve the warrior caste, it would have been necessary to wake them even if the Strell hadn't become a threat."

Several council members shifted uneasily on their feet, realizing the potential threat the Zaltule could represent. A few began thinking about taking trips to the outer reaches of the Empire.

"Then the Zaltule are here to stay," Bixutl stated in a calm voice. He was pleased he had made the deal with Kaluse to supply metals to the shipyards.

"They will attack the nonaligned worlds," Raluth predicted in a cold voice. "The Zaltule will not allow any world to exist which doesn't obey the Empire."

"It would have had to happen eventually, anyway," spoke Bixutl, swinging his triangular head toward Raluth. "The nonaligned worlds become more powerful every year. Their advancements in science and technology have always posed a threat."

"Bixutl is correct," Xatul commented in a steady voice. "The nonaligned worlds will be the Zaltule's next target before they move out past the borders of the Empire in their conquests."

"Many Kleese will be opposed to such rapid expansion," Raluth spoke. "Our method of using exploration ships to find new worlds and then sending our conscripts to conquer them has worked well for centuries with little strain on our resources. It will no longer be so with the Zaltule."

"Many Kleese in the outer regions of our Empire have become weak," Xatul pointed out. "The Zaltule will not tolerate such weakness. I strongly suggest that if you want to preserve your council position you begin making preparations."

"We cannot fight the Zaltule," Martule replied in a cold and dark voice. "I fear the warrior caste may soon dominate this council."

Later, Xatul stood at a window looking out over the sole city on the planet. A cold wind was blowing and the sky was dark and threatening. The city ran the Empire and soon it would answer to the Zaltule. Several years back, Xatul made a deal with Harmock to ensure he would remain as the Supreme Overlord of the Kleese. Unfortunately, a number of the other Overlords on the council would soon die. This meant little to Xatul as the council had always favored the most powerful of the Kleese race.

The Zaltule would be the instrument Xatul used to ensure the continued dominance of the Kleese as the supreme race in the galaxy. Those that stood against the Kleese would either capitulate or be destroyed. It would also be necessary to drastically increase the number of conscripts taken to serve on newly conquered worlds. They would be needed to maintain control as the Empire was expanded. The warriors of the Zaltule were too valuable to serve as garrisons.

Thinking about the conscripts, Xatul wondered what had become of the Humans. At one time, they'd seemed to pose a threat to the Empire but they hadn't been heard from in a number of years. Perhaps it would be wise to send out an exploration cruiser to check on the Humans to see if they had died out or decided to stay inside their paltry little star system. They had served once as excellent conscripts. Perhaps if there were any survivors they could do so again.

Chapter Two

Second Lieutenant Ryan Nelson looked apprehensively at the small mountain in front of him. He was in one of the training domes on Centerpoint Station and wearing a Type Three battlesuit. He'd finished four years at the Officers' Academy inside the asteroid Vesta and two additional years of combat training. He was now in the process of learning how to handle one of the Type Three suits in a combat situation. Ryan was one of a handful of Human officers who had volunteered for a special operations program.

"Damn, that mountain's steep," complained Corporal Casey Hunter as she looked at the nearby peak. Casey was one of the Human clones that had also volunteered for this special project. She'd never been hesitant to volunteer and exceeded at everything she tried. Casey had dark brunette hair and hazel eyes along with a childlike innocence. "And we're supposed to make it to the top and press some type of button to turn off all of the hidden weapons." She turned her head to gaze curiously at Lieutenant Nelson.

"Yeah," Ryan said, grinning. He and Casey had gone through the Academy and combat training together. She was a very bright young woman approximately the same age as he was, though with the way the clones were grown it was difficult to ascertain their exact physical age.

"I spoke to others who have gone through this training," commented Private Rios from just behind the two officers. Rios was a Human from Luna City and had attended the fleet training center there. He spoke with just the barest hint of a Mexican accent. "No one has ever made it to the top in less than four attempts. Those damn hidden weapon emplacements supposedly pop up and start blasting away when you least expect it. The guys I talked to said the stun beams hurt like hell!"

Ryan nodded. His brother, Colonel Wade Nelson, had casually mentioned that this part of the training would be particularly difficult though he had only smiled knowingly when Ryan asked how he had done on the mountain drill.

"The drill has been modified slightly in recent years," Ryan said, recalling what he'd been told in the morning briefing by Major Winfrey. "The energy beams have been changed to stun guns that supposedly just sting and make your body feel as if it's on fire. The RG rounds have been adjusted so they just put dents in your armor rather than blow a hole completely through your arm or leg."

"Glad to hear that," Rios commented as he glanced down at the RG rifle he held in his metal arms. "This training is supposed to be for a special project. Either of you two have any idea what it is?"

"No," answered Ryan, shaking his head. "The brass wanted a well-trained group of marines and space force officers for this project."

"I've heard rumors it might involve the new Type Four battlesuits," ventured Corporal Hunter. "They're reportedly ready for trial deployment."

"I've heard those rumors for several years," Ryan replied with a frown. Everyone knew that the Human military research department, in conjunction with the Kiveans, was developing a new battlesuit. It was supposed to be a full generation ahead of the current Type Three battlesuit and meant to give them an edge in combat operations if they had to fight the Zaltule in a ground operation.

"Here comes the major," commented Casey as another Type Three battlesuit strolled purposely toward the waiting marines and fleet personnel.

Major Dylan Winfrey smiled to himself as he walked up to the twenty men and women in battlesuits waiting for him. Dylan had assumed the role of a trainer for the last few years as the active combat role for the marines had decreased considerably. Military operations against the Kleese had come to a stop with the advent of the Kleese-Strell war. His four platoons of British Special Forces were still active and currently assigned to Luna

City. This group would be particularly interesting as it was comprised of nearly half clones and the rest normal Human born. It was also made more intriguing since Colonel Nelson's younger brother was the platoon leader.

"Alright, volunteers," Dylan spoke with a slight British accent as he looked at the two lines of battlesuits. "You have volunteered for a special project the R&D boys have been working on. If you want to be a part of this, you have to make it to the top of Charring Mountain. Dylan turned and gestured toward the two thousand foot tall peak behind him. "There are hidden popup weapons on the slopes and other areas that are set to prevent your successful ascent. You should know the best any platoon has done in the years I've been here was to reach the summit on the fourth attempt. For that platoon, only three members were still active when the deactivation button was depressed."

The assembled platoon shifted uneasily on their metal feet. The ten-foot-tall nearly black battlesuits made one feel invincible, but Major Winfrey was making it quite clear the suits might not be as much protection as the wearers thought. They wondered nervously just what was waiting for them on the mountain and how painful this drill was going to be.

"The weapons on Charring are set to inflict pain," continued Winfrey, grimacing slightly recollecting his own experiences on the dreaded peak. "They will serve as a stark reminder of what it feels like to be shot by the enemy. For today's drill, you're allowed to use your RG rifles, energy cannons, and RG explosive rounds. Major suit explosive rounds are not permitted." Dylan paused and gazed intently at the assembled platoon though he knew they couldn't see his face through the visor of his battlesuit. "You're using live weapons. I don't want to see anyone injured or killed due to friendly fire. If someone is injured, the drill will continue and I will send appropriate medical personnel to handle the situation. Your battlesuits are capable of handling most medical emergencies until proper medical care can arrive."

Dylan paused as he slowly walked down the double line of assembled battlesuits. "You have six hours to make the ascent and press the red button on the pedestal on top of the summit of Charring Mountain. If time runs out, then you lose. Your time starts now!"

Ryan turned toward Corporal Hunter as his eyes shifted to the young woman. "I want two scouts out front with another two skirmish lines behind them. The scouts will be used to draw out the hidden weapons and hopefully we can annihilate them before they take the scouts out."

Casey nodded as she looked at the assembled soldiers. Mentally she thought about who best deserved to die first on the mountain. There was no doubt in her mind that the first two scouts wouldn't last long. When the hidden weapons disabled a battlesuit, it was considered a death. Then her eyes fell on Privates Alexander Parker and Lauren Adams. The two of them had gotten into a fight in the mess hall the night before arguing over who had the best RG target score. She grinned wickedly as she made her decision deciding this would be good punishment for the two.

"Parker, Adams the two of you have the point. Move out!" she ordered.

"Crap!" uttered Alexander, glaring at Lauren. "Now we're both going to get killed."

"Shut your mouth and let's go!" Lauren grated out.

If Parker hadn't grabbed her arm in the mess hall, she wouldn't have popped him in the jaw. There was no doubt in her mind that they were being punished for that incident, though it had felt good to see the shocked look on Alexander's face after she'd punched him.

The two set out holding their RG rifles at the ready. The rest of the platoon formed up into two ragged skirmish lines and began following close behind. In only a few moments, they entered the heavy woods that marked the beginning of Charring Mountain.

Ryan was watching the twenty green icons on his HUD in the helmet of his command battlesuit. Currently, all were undamaged and had begun the treacherous ascent up the mountain. The HUD showed the exact position of each battlesuit in relation to Ryan's position.

"Keep your eyes on the lookout for popups," he warned as he used the enhanced vision abilities of his suit to scan the terrain up ahead. All he could see were tall trees, brush, and boulders. "Adams, Parker use the trees for cover, try to stay out of open areas which make you an easy target."

"Easy for him to say," mumbled Parker over the private suit com he had established between his battlesuit and Adams. "I doubt if any of the weapons will target a command suit."

"Don't bet on it," Lauren responded as she slipped behind a large tree trunk to gaze up ahead. "I was told the popups don't distinguish between one type of suit and another." She had scarcely stepped behind the protection of the massive tree when she heard numerous projectiles impacting the bark. "Damn, there's an RG popup somewhere up ahead!"

"Stay behind the tree," Alexander ordered as he bent down behind a stony outcrop, which offered some protection. He used his suit's advanced sensors to quickly pinpoint the hidden weapon. The suit's sensors picked up the inbound rounds and traced their trajectory back to their point of origination. Alexander changed his com frequency back to the normal platoon one. "Popup RG weapon sixty meters up the mountain on the right side of that tree with the busted limb."

"Can you take it out with explosive rounds?" Corporal Hunter asked as she motioned for the troops in her skirmish line to go to the ground. A ten-foot tall battlesuit was not something easy to hide.

"Affirmative," Alexander replied as he switched his RG rifle to the indicated round. Taking careful aim, he placed two shells where he thought the popup was. Two resounding explosions threw debris up high into the air causing some rocks and dirt to slide down the mountain. A flash of fire and rising black smoke indicated the popup had been hit.

Alexander studied the impact point for a moment before being satisfied that the popup had been destroyed. "Weapon's been eliminated."

"Very well," Hunter replied as she stood back up. "Continue to move up the mountain. I suspect the higher up we go, the more weapons we'll come across. This isn't supposed to be easy." Casey began moving back up the slope using her suit's augmented vision optics to scan for possible weapons. She could feel herself breathing faster and knew her heart was racing.

For another hundred meters, everything was quiet, and then a pair of twin stunners popped up and fired, striking a battlesuit directly behind Private Parker. The soldier screamed in agony as the painful stunners immobilized his suit. The soldier then collapsed to the ground and lay still. On Ryan's HUD one of the twenty green icons switched to red.

"Stay alert!" Ryan warned as he gestured for everyone to hold their positions. "I want that ridge in front of us scanned. If you see anything, report it. We can't advance until that weapon is taken out."

For several minutes, the soldiers remained still using the sensors in their suits to scan the terrain ahead of them. A breeze was rustling the leaves in the trees and there was no other detectable movement. The embedded weapons were camouflaged so they would blend in with their surroundings.

"Up ahead and on our left flank sixty meters out," Corporal Hunter said as she saw a metallic glint with her enhanced optics. She quickly took aim with her RG rifle and laid six shells on and around the target. Two resounding explosions of flame indicated she had hit her targets. "Stunners eliminated."

"Move out!" Ryan called out. "Corporal Hunter, I want two more scouts out ahead of the first skirmish line and a slow, steady movement up the slope. Soldiers in the first skirmish line are to watch for any popup weapons that might be triggered by the scouts."

The soldiers continued to advance, for twenty minutes they moved slowly up the steep slope, stepping around boulders and towering trees. Every moment they expected more hidden weapons to announce their presence by firing RG rounds or stun beams, but all remained quiet. Everyone felt apprehensive, recalling the scream of pain from the soldier in the first stricken battlesuit. No one was anxious to join him.

"I don't like this," Alexander muttered as he stopped to look around a large boulder that barely hid his ten-foot tall battlesuit. "I feel like we're being set up."

"For once, I agree with you," Lauren answered as she paused in her advance to look over at Alexander. "It's like we're walking into a trap."

Corporal Hunter listened to the comments over her com, worried that the two might be right. This mountain was supposed to be nearly impossible to ascend. Up ahead something attracted her attention; was that movement by that large tree up ahead? She checked it with her scanners and detected nothing. She took a deep breath and used her optics to check the area, still nothing could be seen.

Moments later, six twin stunners and four RG cannons opened up on the ascending troops, firing at the first skirmish line and ignoring the four scouts.

Ryan heard two of his soldiers scream in pain and two more icons changed from green to red. "Take cover!" he yelled over the com as he threw himself behind a nearby boulder as several RG rounds struck the ground in his previous position.

"I'm hit!" Private Rios called out. "Damn RG round got me in the leg; it hurts like hell!"

Ryan saw Rios' suit icon turn from green to amber indicating damage. "Find those weapons emplacements and use explosive rounds to take them out! They've got us pinned down."

Ryan switched on his suit scanners trying to pinpoint the weapons, but nothing registered. He felt frustrated by his failure to ascertain where the attack was coming from. It made him realize the suits were not as all powerful and invulnerable as he had been led to believe. It would be necessary for him to reevaluate his strategy for conquering Charring.

Instantly, along the line of trees up ahead grenade like explosions began tearing into the steep slope throwing rocks, soil, plants, and even small trees up into the air. Some of the debris spilled down upon the forward skirmish line. After a minute, the explosions tapered off and it became quiet.

"I think we got them," Alexander reported as he stood up and stepped out into the open. Alexander braced himself, but nothing happened. "Yep, we got them."

Lauren only shook her head. "Don't step out into the open like that or you'll be the next casualty."

"Just keeping you safe, sweetheart," Alexander answered glibly on their private channel.

"I'll make you regret that comment," Lauren replied, icily.

Ryan stood back up and stepped away from the boulder. He glanced at his HUD, which now showed three red icons and four amber ones. Looking up the mountain, he knew they still had a long way to go to reach the summit. If this kept up, he would run out of soldiers long before then. He needed to come up with a better plan. He wondered just what it was that was causing the hidden weapon emplacements to activate. The most obvious were movement and heat sensors. Since the battlesuits were self-contained, the likelihood of it being heat that was triggering the popup weapons was minimal. The most obvious remaining method of detection was movement.

Looking up, Ryan watched the tall trees swaying in the wind. The dome was a controlled environment and could simulate almost any type of weather. He wondered what his brother would do in this situation. He knew his sibling had taken this training when he was being held captive by the Kleese. Wade had never told Ryan how many times it had taken him to reach the top. For several minutes, Ryan studied the terrain ahead and thought about the resources he had available. He could clear a path with explosive rounds, but he suspected they would run out well before they reached the summit. RG rounds were useless unless they could hit one of the emplaced weapons multiple times. That left the energy beam cannons that six of his remaining soldiers were carrying.

His eyes returned to the tall trees as an idea came to mind. "Corporal Hunter, I want our soldiers that have energy cannons to fire at the tops of the trees to bring some of the branches down. Perhaps it will cause the popups to respond." Ryan hoped if the embedded weapons were using motion sensors, the falling limbs might cause them to react.

Casey quickly passed on the orders as she scanned the trees up ahead. "Fire into the taller ones about ten meters up," she ordered. From what her sensors were reporting, some of the trees were as tall as twenty meters. "I want to see limbs falling and hitting the ground!"

A few moments later, first one and then the other five energy cannons opened fire. The energy cannons were large, bulky weapons and fired a beam of blue energy. The beams played across the upper sections of the trees, shearing limbs and trunks in two. Limbs began to fall and sure enough, four popup weapons made an appearance and began firing at the falling debris.

"Take out those weapons!" yelled Casey, seeing the red threat icons appear on her HUD. "Use suit explosives!" She felt the adrenaline flowing through her body as she fired several rounds at the popup weapons.

Instantly, upon the slope twenty grenade-like explosions smashed into the ground, throwing up dirt and other debris, which came raining down on the two lines of battlesuits. In four locations smoke drifted up into the air, indicating the destroyed weapon sites.

"Move up to that line of trees and we'll do it again," Ryan ordered over the general com frequency. "Scouts stay on the lookout. There's no guarantee this will work with all the weapons; some may not be responding to movement."

The four scouts moved carefully forward, using all the cover they could find. However, a ten-foot tall battlesuit was difficult to keep hidden. It was just too big a target.

Private Parker was the first to reach the trees and took up position behind the largest one he could find. Looking to his right, he could see the other scouts including Private Adams, who was on the far end of the four. "I don't see anything," he spoke softly as if he was afraid the embedded weapons would home in on the sound of his voice.

"I don't either," Lauren replied as she used her suit's sensors to scan the slope above them. There were several open spaces as well as numerous tall trees and brush. Popup weapons could be hidden anywhere.

Corporal Hunter was listening to the scouts and after a moment, felt the area immediately ahead was safe. "Move out," she ordered, standing up and beginning to move forward. "Keep your eyes open and watch your sensors."

Casey had turned up the sound in her helmet so she would hear even the quietest noises. She could hear the heavy footsteps of the battlesuits, the crunching of branches, and even the wind in the trees. A ten-foot tall one thousand pound battlesuit was nearly incapable of stealth.

They reached the next line of trees without being fired upon, and once again, Ryan had the soldiers carrying the energy cannons fire into the tops of the trees ahead of them. Once more, several popups made their presence known and were quickly eliminated. Ryan was beginning to feel more confident. If they could keep this up, they would make it to the top with the majority of the platoon. Perhaps Charring Mountain wasn't as difficult as everyone claimed.

In the dome's Command Center, Colonel Wade Nelson and Major Winfrey were watching the platoon's progress on several large viewscreens. Wade had come to the dome to watch his brother's first attempt at Charring Mountain. He'd made sure Ryan was not aware of his presence.

"Clever," Dylan commented impressed by the young lieutenant. "He's using the falling limbs to eliminate the embedded weapons."

"Ryan was always the clever one," Wade spoke with a grin. He was pleased to see how his brother was adapting to the drill. "If he keeps this up, he might just make it to the top."

"We don't want to make it too easy," Dylan said, folding his arms across his chest. He quickly passed on some new orders to the techs, who were operating and controlling the weapons upon Charring Mountain. "We'll switch off the motion sensors and use the metal of the suits for the weapons to home in on. No one makes it to the top of Charring the first time!"

Wade nodded his head in agreement. The purpose of the drill was to teach the soldiers in the battlesuits they were not invincible. Now he would be curious to see how Ryan reacted to this new change in the scenario. Wade settled back in his chair, knowing this drill was far from being over and was about to get much more interesting.

Ryan and his platoon had made it to the next grove of trees upon the slope. So far, his plan of using the falling limbs to activate the hidden popup weapons was working well. He hadn't lost another soldier and he was halfway to the top of Charring Mountain. He paused, taking in a deep breath and used his suit's sensors to scan the slope up above them. He knew the drill was being controlled down at the training base Command Center. Ryan strongly suspected his method of activating and destroying the embedded weapons wouldn't be allowed to continue all the way to the top of the mountain.

He watched intently as Corporal Hunter directed the next firing of their energy weapons, once again several popups appeared and were quickly eliminated. He let out a breath of relief as he stepped back out into the open and began moving up the steep slope.

The four forward scouts began advancing cautiously, followed by the two larger skirmish lines. They had only taken a few steps when six more hidden embedded weapons popped up and began firing.

"Take cover!" yelled Corporal Hunter as one of the scouts went down with their suit icon turning red. Around her, soldiers in their battlesuits darted for cover. While the battlesuits were large and even seemed cumbersome at times, they allowed a soldier to move extremely fast.

"What do we have?" demanded Ryan as he crouched down behind several boulders. He could hear the fire of RG rounds and the occasional zapping noise the stunners made.

"Six popups," Casey reported as she used her suit's advanced sensors to spot the weapons. "One hundred and ten meters further up the slope."

The fire from the popups was nonstop as they searched for targets. Two more battlesuit-encased soldiers went down with their icons turning to red in Ryan's HUD. Several others were showing amber from being struck by RG rounds.

"Privates Parker, Adams, Matheson can you take the weapons out?" demanded Casey as several RG rounds struck the ground near her. The three scouts were close enough they should be able to fire upon the weapon emplacements. The rest of the platoon was pretty well pinned downed.

"Yeah," Alexander answered as he looked cautiously around the tree he was hiding behind. "We can take them out, but I don't know if we'll survive."

"How bad can it hurt?" Lauren asked. Due to Alexander's comment earlier, she was really hoping that at some point in the drill he would get hit by a stun beam. "It can't be any worse than some of the other stuff we've been through."

"I just don't like the idea of lying immobile in this damn suit for several hours," muttered Alexander. Then looking over at Lauren and Matheson he nodded. "Now!"

All three remaining scouts stepped out from their hiding places and began firing RG explosive rounds at the targets. As soon as they stepped into the open, the weapon emplacements' sensors quickly targeted the three battlesuits. Alexander was instantly hit by several RG rounds in the shoulder and then two stun beams nailed him squarely in the chest. With a loud moan, he slid to the ground as his suit shut down except for life support.

Lauren didn't waste a moment worrying about Alexander as she fired RG explosive rounds in rapid succession at the emplacements. She managed to take three of them out before a stun beam struck her battlesuit, immobilizing it. She was amazed at the intense pain the beam generated. She felt as if a dozen wasps were all biting her at once. She regretted wanting Alexander to feel this type of pain even after what he'd said. Lauren fell to the ground and lay still, listening to the battle still going on around her. The stinging and burning sensation was gradually beginning to fade.

The remaining scout managed to take out two more emplacements before he too was struck by the remaining stunner. Moments later, the stunner was blown apart as Corporal Hunter hit it with an RG explosive round. She'd managed to move closer until the aggravating weapon was within her sights. Casey shook her head, looking at the scouts lying prone on the slope.

"Weapons eliminated," she reported over the general com frequency. "All scouts are down." She looked at Alexander and Lauren's still forms almost regretting choosing them as scouts. She hoped they'd learned their lesson.

Ryan nodded and ordered the rest of the surviving members of the platoon to move up to the area where the weapons had been destroyed. It was time to come up with a different strategy. He glanced at his HUD, seeing nine glaring red icons with another six showing as wounded. That was well over half his platoon. Charring Mountain was beginning to take control of the scenario.

"Guess that will slow them down," commented Dylan, glancing over at Wade with a chuckle.

"We'll see," Wade replied as he studied the viewscreens, wondering what Ryan would do now. It was a shame that Beth wasn't here to watch this. She was currently back home at Vesta working with General Bailey on some new upgrades to the asteroid's defenses. He knew she would've really enjoyed watching Ryan's first attempt at the mountain.

Ryan stood next to one of the destroyed weapon emplacements, realizing that the parameters had indeed been changed. The embedded emplacements were no longer using motion sensors to find their targets. They seemed to be homing in on the battlesuits.

"What now?" Corporal Hunter asked as she stepped over closer to the lieutenant. "I don't think the popups are responding to motion any longer."

"They've changed the programming on the weapon emplacements," Ryan said as he looked up at the steep slope ahead of them. "I think it's time we used more of our RG explosives. Gather the RG rifles from those that are down. We'll lay down an explosives' barrage in front of us and advance up the mountain as far as possible behind it. Order each of our soldiers to save four rounds for use on weapon emplacements. This is about to get down and dirty."

For the next thirty minutes, they moved steadily up the mountain, blasting a swath one hundred meters wide in front of them. Ryan moved his soldiers closer together toward the center of the cleared area to lessen the possibility of attacks from embedded weapons on the perimeter. He finally called a halt when Corporal Hunter indicated they had expended all the explosive rounds except those being kept back to take out the embedded weapons.

Looking ahead, Ryan guessed they only had three or four hundred meters to go to reach the summit. He let out a deep sigh as he gazed at the beckoning heights, which signified victory. He wondered how many others had made it this far on their first attempt.

"What now?" asked Corporal Hunter from Ryan's side where she was also gazing up the mountain. She hadn't expected to get this far.

"We use the energy weapons to clear us a path," he answered. While the energy weapons had a much shorter effective range than the RG explosive rounds, they should at least be able to get them further up the slope. "Spread our six energy weapons out along a line so we can clear a space one hundred meters wide."

"They won't last long at that kind of use," warned Casey. It sounded to her as if Ryan was getting desperate; she knew there was a lot of pressure on him due to who his brother was. "We might get another two hundred meters up the slope if we're lucky."

"That's two hundred meters closer to the top," Ryan answered as he thought over his options. "Once the energy weapons are drained of power, we'll stop and see what our next option needs to be."

Corporal Hunter quickly passed on the order and soon six powerful blue energy beams were playing across the ground in front of them, tearing up the soil and cutting down the large trees. The surviving members of the platoon walked slowly behind the soldiers with the energy weapons, their RG rifles held at the ready. Whenever an energy beam struck an embedded weapon emplacement it would explode, sending fire and smoke up into the air.

–

"Interesting," Wade said with a nod of approval. Ryan was using all of his resources to get closer to his target.

"That young shit head's going to make it yet," muttered Dylan, shaking his head. "He's come up with some inventive methods to take out the weapon emplacements."

"But not good enough," responded Wade, agreeing with Dylan's assessment. "His energy weapons will run out of power a good one hundred meters from the summit."

Dylan grinned wolfishly, his eyes glinting. "The closer he gets, the more overconfident he'll become. I have a special surprise waiting if he does indeed make it to the top of Charring."

–

28

Ryan watched disappointedly as the last energy beam sputtered and then faded out. He guessed they were still at least one hundred and fifty meters from the summit. There were fewer trees this high up on Charring Mountain and he could plainly see the summit beckoning as if mocking him. If he had to do this all over again, he would have equipped his soldiers with more energy weapons. With a heavy sigh, Ryan knew there was a good chance he might very well get that opportunity. No one had ever made it to the summit on their first attempt.

He looked around at the remaining ten soldiers in their battlesuits. Six of them showed as wounded and could only move at half speed. "We'll form four staggered lines of three and charge the top," he said at last, knowing the last line would only have two in it. "Only one of us has to reach the reset button to win this scenario."

"None of us may make it to the top," Corporal Hunter pointed out. She had no desire to be hit by one of those powerful stunners. She could still remember how loudly Private Parker had cried out when he had been hit.

"I know," answered Ryan, in a calm voice. "But no one expected us to make it this far. "Corporal Hunter, you'll be in the second group. Keep an eye on the slope in front of you; the popups should target the first group. You have to take them out with your remaining explosive rounds as quickly as possible. I'll see you at the top."

"You heard the lieutenant," bellowed Casey. "Form four lines and let's get moving. The sooner we reach the summit and press that button the sooner we can get off this damn mountain and get some chow!"

Ryan watched as Corporal Hunter formed up the remaining soldiers for the run at the summit. From her actions, no one would know she had been grown inside a glass nutrient case inside of Vesta. Casey acted perfectly human; she should after everything she'd been exposed to at the Academy. Even today, six years after the revelation of the cloning technology, many people still refused to accept the clones as real people.

"We're ready, Sir," Casey reported a few moments later.

"Let's do this, then," Ryan ordered evenly as he looked at his remaining soldiers. "Go as fast as we can and take out any weapon emplacements that pop up. It's only one hundred and fifty meters to the summit and victory."

"Let's go," ordered Casey, resolutely. She already felt as if a stunner had her in its sights. She shuddered slightly as the first three battlesuits took off at a run. She waited two seconds and then her group took off. They were quickly followed by the rest.

Stunners and RG cannons quickly opened up as they rose up out of the concealing ground. The first line of battlesuits quickly fell, but the second line managed to take out most of the weapons. They were nearly to the summit when even more weapons seemed to pop up all around them. The charge faltered as they attempted to take out all the weapons now firing at them. The battle grew more intense as some of the soldiers ran out of explosive rounds and had to switch to RG rounds, which were nearly ineffective against the popups.

Casey felt several painful RG rounds strike her suit armor and her icon in her HUD turned amber. She also felt her suit slow down as it registered the damage. A moment later, she felt the stinging sensation of a stunner. She felt like her skin was on fire and then her suit shut down as she fell face forward onto the rocky slope to lie perfectly still. Ryan owes me for this, she thought as she fought through the slowly fading pain.

Ryan saw Casey go down and grimaced. They'd been friends throughout most of the four years at the Academy and combat training, he knew she would make him pay for getting her shot. Shaking his head, he turned back to the task at hand. The other soldier with him had an undamaged battlesuit and both of them were sprinting toward the summit. A soldier in a battlesuit could move faster than an Olympic sprinter, much faster. Everyone in the lines ahead were down and Ryan and his other soldier were firing desperately at the popups that kept on appearing. Ryan saw his companion suddenly throw his metal arms up and collapse in pain as Ryan leaped forward to land on the summit.

Everything fell silent as Ryan looked around in amazement. There were no weapons in sight. He'd made it! Looking around, he saw a large metal pedestal with a small pylon on top of it about fifty meters away. On the pylon was a large red metal button. All he had to do was stroll over and press it, and the scenario would be over. He had won; his platoon had done the impossible on their first try! They had conquered Charring Mountain!

As Ryan walked over toward the pedestal four stunners suddenly rose up out of the ground in front of him and blasted him in the chest. Ryan nearly passed out from the intense pain. Should've known it wouldn't be this easy, he thought as his battlesuit struck the ground.

"Got him!" Dylan gloated with a laugh as he watched Ryan fall so tantalizing close to the pylon, which contained the red victory button. "No one beats Charring on their first attempt."

Wade nodded. Charring Mountain wasn't so much about victory as learning tactics and how to use the weapons the suits were equipped with. It also demonstrated very plainly that a battlesuit wasn't invincible. Ryan's platoon would be sore in the morning, but today they'd learned a valuable lesson. Even so, Wade had been very impressed by his younger brother. There was little doubt in Wade's mind that Ryan and most of his platoon would qualify for the special project they had signed up for. He just hoped Ryan was ready for what waited in his future.

Chapter Three

Colonel Wade Nelson stepped aboard the five hundred-meter battlecruiser Constellation. He was met by Commander Adamson as soon as he exited the small shuttle. Over the last few years, the rank structure in the fleet had been changed and simplified since on many operations there were both fleet personnel and marines involved as well as individuals from nearly every branch of the military services that had existed on Earth. For the fleet, the rank structure ran Fleet Admiral, Admiral, Commander, Captain, Lieutenant, Ensign, Petty Officer (first and second class), and Spaceman (first and second class). For the marines, the rank structure ran General, Lieutenant General, Colonel, Major, Captain, First Lieutenant, Second Lieutenant, Sergeant, Corporal, and Private.

"How was the drill?" asked Adamson, knowing that Wade had gone on board Centerpoint to watch his brother attempt Charring Mountain.

"As expected," Wade responded as the two began walking toward the ship's Command Center. "Ryan actually made it to the top but was taken out by the stunners guarding the reset pedestal. He did surprisingly well for his first attempt."

"I've never had to go through that drill," Adamson spoke as they took a turbo lift to the level where the Command Center was located. "Has anyone ever made it on their first try?"

"No," answered Wade, shaking his head. "The drill is set up to make it impossible to make it to the reset pedestal on the first or second attempt."

"A no win scenario," mused Adamson. "Do the marines participating in the drill know that?"

"No," Wade admitted. "The battlesuits are an awesome weapon for a marine to use. It makes you feel invulnerable and capable of achieving almost anything. What we want our recruits to understand is that while the suit greatly augments a marine's abilities, we're going up against enemies who have the ability to neutralize or destroy a battlesuit. Charring Mountain teaches them that."

Commander Adamson well understood that point. It was the same in the fleet; being in a powerful warship made you feel invincible until the Kleese show up with one six to ten times larger. Once that happens, your feeling of invincibility vanishes very quickly and a sense of reality sets in.

The door of the turbo lift opened and the two stepped out into the short corridor that led to the Command Center. As they approached the hatch, two heavily armed marines stepped forward to confirm their identities. After verifying who they were, one of the marines stepped over to the heavy metal hatch and opened it. If this had been a wartime situation, two marines in Type Two battlesuits would have been guarding the hatch. The Constellation had numerous corridors wide and tall enough to accommodate the battlesuits. All battlecruisers and light cruisers did now, though it had meant some major modifications in their designs. It had ensured boarders could be dispatched with a vengeance if it became necessary.

Once inside, the two went to the central command console. Wade looked up at the main viewscreen showing a view of space. Hundreds of unblinking stars were visible, reminding him just how small the solar system was in the overall scheme of things. On the main tactical screen, Wade could see the friendly green icons of the rest of Second Fleet. It consisted of six battlecruisers, sixteen light cruisers, and thirty-two assault ships. Currently, there were six fleets of this size in the solar system. In addition, there were another four hundred of the smaller, disk shaped assault ships scattered about the system on patrol or protecting different habitats.

"I wonder how much longer the Kleese-Strell war is going to last?" Adamson commented as he sat down in his command chair. He knew the war between the two Galactic Empires had kept the solar system safe from the Kleese for the last six years.

"Not much longer, I'm afraid," answered Wade with a look of worry on his face. "We're still sending out diplomatic missions to the nonaligned worlds warning them of the Zaltule and the danger they represent to the galaxy."

"Any success in bringing them over to our side?"

"Not yet," Wade admitted in a frustrated voice. "Several have expanded their fleets and increased planetary defenses, but they refuse to join with us against the Kleese. They feel their neutrality agreements with the Kleese should keep them safe, and they're hesitant about doing anything that might risk invalidating it."

"What do you think?" Adamson asked as the Constellation began moving away from the fleet. He looked over at Wade, curious to hear his answer.

"I don't think the neutrality agreements will mean anything to these Zaltule." Wade took a deep breath and watched the viewscreen, which was now showing Centerpoint Station. "I believe the Zaltule will attack the nonaligned worlds to gain their resources and technology."

"We could use some of those worlds on our side," Adamson said as he looked at the main viewscreen. The station was visibly becoming smaller as the Constellation accelerated away from it.

The station was one hundred and twenty kilometers across and twenty-four kilometers thick. It had been stolen from the Kleese and brought to the solar system. Without the station, most of the surviving Humans on Earth would have perished. The station had tremendous manufacturing capabilities as well as numerous ship construction bays.

"The Zaltule seem to have taken over the fighting for the Kleese Empire," continued Wade. "They're more heartless and far more dangerous than the regular Kleese. I didn't think that was possible, but everything is pointing toward that being true."

"Where did the Zaltule come from?" asked Adamson, arching his eyebrow. He knew Marken had mentioned that the Zaltule were a warrior caste from the Kleese past. Their sudden reemergence was a mystery.

"We don't know," answered Wade with a deep sigh. "I've spoken to Marken and he's suggested the possibility that the Zaltule were in deep sleep somewhere in the Empire. I just don't know if I believe that; we're talking about hundreds of thousands, perhaps millions of this warrior caste."

"It's a mystery," conceded Adamson as he gave the order for the Constellation to leave Second Fleet and head for Vesta. He wasn't anxious to face the Zaltule anytime soon.

As Wade watched, the station began to rapidly dwindle in size as the Constellation began piling on the acceleration with the ship's sublight drive. The screen switched to a view directly in front of the ship and for a moment, space seemed to shrink in on itself as the ship's Fold Space Drive was activated. The drive warped space directly in front of the ship, making the distance between two points shrink. The more power used to increase the warping effect, the faster a ship could travel.

"What will happen if the Zaltule attack the solar system in force?" Adamson asked as he thought about the forces they had available. "Can we stop them?"

There had been a massive buildup of the fleet using the construction facilities on Centerpoint as well as those inside Vesta. In the last few years, thousands of Human clones had joined the fleet to bring the crews up to their full complements.

"I don't know," answered Wade, truthfully. He'd spent numerous sleepless nights worrying over this. "We have the new ion cannons installed around all the habitats. We still have a hidden base at Jornada as well as the two we discovered in China. It won't be that easy for the Kleese to wipe us out."

Wade still recalled the stunned amazement everyone had felt when the Chinese had finally broken radio silence and requested supplies for their two hidden survival centers in Central China. Wade had gone down to visit the Chinese and tour their bases. The two Chinese survival centers had been built into the sides of several mountains in the Altun mountain range, which bordered the Qaidam Basin. It was a sparsely settled region and the Chinese had frantically used their military and civil engineers to drill two large tunnels into the mountains and set up twin survival centers after the Kleese missile had set off volcanoes and earthquakes across the globe. Each center, when finished, was capable of supporting 120,000 survivors and had supplies for three years. It was only when their supplies had run dangerously low that the Chinese had finally asked for help.

The Chinese had been made the offer of having a new habitat built in one of the asteroids but turned it down. They preferred to stay in their homeland, convinced that someday they would emerge and build a new China. A few Chinese had traveled to Centerpoint and even set up a diplomatic office there. Other than that, the Chinese were staying to themselves.

"I guess we'll see when they finally attack," Adamson replied as he leaned back and looked around the Command Center. "I understand President Randle is going to retire at the end of his current term."

"It looks that way," answered Wade. "The Federated Assembly has settled down and seems to be doing a good job representing the different habitats. The twelve members of the Federated Council are responsible men and women and have reached the point where they can be trusted to begin running things. President Randle has already turned a lot of the day to day operations of the government over to the council."

"Things will sure be different without President Randle leading us."

Wade nodded. He stood silently watching the main viewscreen, knowing they would be at Vesta shortly. Beth and he had been married four years back and both had elected to stay in the military. They'd decided not to have children right away, at least not until they knew how the conflict with the Kleese was going to turn out. He was also a little nervous about Ryan becoming a Space Marine. The new program Ryan had volunteered for did involve the new Type Four battlesuits. If and when the Kleese returned, Wade feared Ryan would be right in the middle of the most dangerous fighting. It was going to take him a while to get used to that thought.

Ryan was in the large food court in the center of Centerpoint Station. Over the last few years, it had been expanded and now almost anything one wanted could be found. There were even rumors of a black market operation where illegal pleasures and items could be purchased for the right price. There were nearly three hundred thousand Humans on the massive station. Many were part of the crew and others were a mixture of military, civilians, and a few entrepreneurs who were providing services for the station.

"You owe me for getting shot yesterday," Casey informed Ryan as they walked through the court taking in the sights. "How about Chinese food for a change?" The different aromas of cooking food present in the food court were making her feel ravenous. She also enjoyed spending time with Ryan as they'd been close friends for years.

Ryan let out a loud sigh. He and Casey had been friends since the early days of the Academy. He could still remember how innocent and naive she had been at first, particularly the first year or two. That was why all the clones spent their first two years of life inside Vesta under close supervision. It took them a while to assimilate how Humans interacted with one another and to be able to handle their emotions. Even now, on occasion, he had to explain things to Casey.

"There's a new one over there," she said, pointing excitedly. One of the things Casey enjoyed the most was trying out different styles of food. Only recently had she discovered Chinese, and she'd fallen in love with the different tastes and aromas.

Ryan nodded and they threaded their way through the crowd to the small restaurant Casey had spotted. She was right, this was a new one; it hadn't been here a few weeks back. Ryan liked the wide-open spaces of the food court. There were tables scattered about where one could sit and take his or her time eating. People came here from all of the different habitats; many came to the station to trade or pick up supplies. Numerous small cargo ships now traveled from habitat to habitat delivering products and other items necessary to make life inside the habitats as comfortable as possible.

Reaching the restaurant, they took a seat at a table along one wall where they had a little more privacy. Ryan watched with interest as Casey examined the menu critically for a food item she hadn't tried before. She was always wanting to try something new.

"This looks interesting," Casey said, pointing to the sweet and sour chicken on the menu. "I think I'll try that."

They waited for several moments and Ryan was starting to get a little impatient. He noticed the server who'd given them their menus wait on several other tables, taking their orders. That was strange, as Ryan and Casey had been seated a few minutes before these others.

As the server passed by their table, Ryan reached out and gently tapped his arm. "We're ready to order."

"One moment," the server replied before turning and rushing to the back of the restaurant to vanish through a door leading to the kitchen.

Ryan watched curiously as a larger man stepped through, followed by the server who was pointing toward their table.

"What's going on?" asked Casey, looking with confusion at Ryan. "Why won't they take our order?" She'd noticed how the server had been pointedly ignoring them but had been hesitant to mention it. There were still so many things about Humans she didn't fully understand. That was one reason she liked the military as it was a more structured environment with rules and regulations.

The large man stepped up next to their table and stared at Ryan with a narrow look in his eyes. "I'm the manager. I'm sorry, but we don't have any food for you."

"What do you mean?" asked Ryan, feeling suddenly suspicious. "The other customers in this restaurant are being served their food."

"I mean we don't serve her kind!" answered the man gruffly, pointing a finger at Casey. "We only serve real Humans."

Ryan felt his anger begin to stir. There were an uncomfortably large number of regular Humans, who hadn't accepted the clones into society even though it was the law. "What do you mean, her kind?" Ryan asked challengingly, his eyes narrowing sharply. His hand clenched into a fist as he struggled to control his rising anger.

"Clones!" the manager replied in a hard and cold voice. "You can eat here, but she'll have to leave."

Ryan let out a deep breath. Unfortunately, the Human clones were easy to spot. Their skin was unblemished and had an unusually youthful look. He closed his eyes and shook his head. This was something he'd not been expecting to encounter on Centerpoint. There were hundreds if not several thousand clones on the station every day.

"She has just as much of a right to eat here as anyone else," Ryan spoke evenly, staring into the man's unrelenting face. "The Federated Assembly has given clones the same rights and legal protection as every other Human."

"Not in my eyes," the man retorted, turning to gesture toward two burly looking men standing at the back of the restaurant. The two started walking toward the table. "You can leave peacefully or I'll have you thrown out."

"I don't think so," a male voice from behind them said.

Ryan turned in surprise, seeing Privates Rios, Parker, and Adams standing behind them. Private Parker had been the one to speak. "You're going to serve all of us or when we're through, you won't have much of a restaurant left."

"We're not afraid of the military," the manager uttered, his eyes flashing anger as his two men came up to stand behind him.

"Let's leave," Casey said with an odd look on her face. "A meal isn't worth fighting over." She knew this was her fault even though she didn't fully understand why.

Lauren stepped protectively over next to Casey. "You're just as Human as the rest of us," she said in a soft voice, her eyes glaring with anger. Lauren stepped closer to the manager, her body posture extremely threatening. "You'll take all of our orders or I'm going to smash your face in and my two friends will beat the hell out of your two bouncers. If we find anything wrong with our food, we'll come back and you won't like what we'll do. I can assure you it won't be pleasant as we'll bring more of our friends along with us!"

The manager looked at Lauren, not sure what to do. His face was flushed and he clearly recognized he'd lost control of the situation. He'd never been threatened by a woman like this before. He glanced at Parker and Rios, who were standing directly behind her with their fists clenched. Rios cracked his knuckles and took a step closer.

"We'll take your order," the manager spoke, tersely. The manager gestured to the server and then left, taking his two lackeys with him.

The server came over and all five of them placed their orders. Lauren ordered several different items off the menu just to further aggravate the manager. "We'll take our orders to go," she said as the server turned to leave. "I don't expect to wait too long!"

The three sat down at the table. "We saw you come in here and knew there would be trouble," Lauren explained as she looked around the restaurant. The other customers looked away or down at their food not wanting to meet her eyes. "I've heard several complaints about this restaurant from a few of the other clones."

"When we get back, I'll report this establishment to Major Winfrey," Ryan said still finding it hard to believe what had just happened. "Establishments like this won't be tolerated on Centerpoint."

"I don't know," Lauren replied with doubt in her eyes. "There's more of this going on than you know, Lieutenant. As more clones are admitted to society each year, people are becoming uneasy. A lot of people have this manager's feeling, but they keep it hidden."

"I think the manager might receive a fine, but it won't change his attitude," Alexander added.

"I didn't mean to cause a problem," stammered Casey, feeling unsure of herself. There were still so many things about regular Humans she had trouble comprehending at times.

"I know," Ryan responded in a reassuring voice.

He had been so focused on his career that he hadn't been that aware of the growing distrust regular people had for the Human clones. When he got the opportunity, this was something he wanted to talk to his older brother about. Wade was heavily involved in the cloning program. He was best friends with Marken, the head Kivean, who helped run the massive cloning center back on Vesta.

A few minutes later, they had their food and hastily exited the restaurant. Finding a table, the five of them sat down and began eating.

"This food is really good!" Lauren said, surprised. She had about three times more than she could eat. No matter, she was sure that Rios and Parker would help her finish it off.

"It is!" agreed Casey with a grin. She'd never tasted anything like this sweet and sour chicken. She took another bite, savoring the taste. "This chicken is delicious."

Ryan smiled; he was glad to see Casey enjoying her meal. He allowed himself to relax and took a deep breath. He didn't want to think about what a brawl in the restaurant would have done to his career. This was a situation he hadn't handled very well and he knew it. He was still going to speak to Major Winfrey about what had happened, and he was also going to mention it to Wade next time he had a chance to speak with his older brother.

Once the five of them finished their meal, they headed back toward the training dome. In two more days, they were going to try Charring Mountain once again. Ryan wanted to spend some time with his platoon discussing strategy and what they'd done wrong the first time. He was determined to beat that damn mountain on their next attempt even though he knew the odds were stacked heavily against him.

Wade watched with interest as the Constellation arrowed down toward the surface of Vesta. A massive airlock slid open, revealing a lighted entrance, which would take them to the massive spacedock deep inside the asteroid. Around the perimeter of the airlock, eight small particle beam cannons ensured there was no unauthorized entry. The helm officer brought the ship smoothly inside the tunnel, and they were soon traveling along its lighted length toward the spacedock.

"It's good to be back on Vesta," spoke Wade, looking forward to seeing Beth.

He'd been gone for several weeks consulting with General Mitchell and recently promoted Fleet Admiral Thomas Kelly about possible action against the Kleese. Kelly had been the former executive officer of the Constellation but had shown a knack for strategy and understanding space warfare. It hadn't taken him long to move up to commanding officer, then admiral, and now Fleet Admiral with the retirement of Fleet Admiral Kirby. Wade knew that Kirby had always felt uncomfortable in his command position. He'd heard that Kirby had gone back to prospecting in his old prospecting ship the Raven.

"Vesta is our mainstay," responded Adamson, turning toward Wade. "Everyone knows what Vesta did to save the Human race. If not for President Randle, none of us would be here today. It's going to be a sad day when he steps down as president."

Wade nodded his head in agreement, but it was time for the civilian government to take a more active role in managing the habitats and even the war. President Randle couldn't do that forever, nor would it be wise. However, there'd been talk of him taking on some type of advisory position to help guide the next president through all the pitfalls of managing a Human civilization scattered across the solar system

On the main viewscreen, another pair of large airlocks slid open and the Constellation entered the massive spacedock or, as some preferred to call it, a landing bay. The bay had been enlarged several times over the past few years. It was now eight kilometers in width, two kilometers in length and a full kilometer from floor to ceiling. Inside the bay, numerous ships could be seen in their berths, prospecting ships, cargo ships, passenger liners, and even a few battlecruisers. On the far end of the bay, three new battlecruisers were nearing completion.

"There're over two thousand Kiveans inside Vesta most of the time," commented Adamson, turning to look over at Wade. "We've come a long way since our rescue mission." He knew that many of the Kiveans were technicians or scientists helping in ship construction or research projects.

Wade nodded; the rescue mission Adamson was referring to was when they had taken a fleet to the Kiveans' home world to rescue what survivors they could after the Kleese used antimatter weapons on the surface of the planet to annihilate most of the population. They'd managed to save over seventy-five thousand Kiveans, many of them scientists, technicians, students, and their families. They were mostly living in two habitats inside a nearby asteroid where Marken had established the original Kivean habitat for the six thousand Kiveans that had escaped with Wade and General Mitchell from the trading station.

"The Kiveans have been a tremendous help with the cloning program," Wade commented. "They also serve as instructors at the Academy."

"Speaking of the clones, I heard there was some unrest in Luna City recently," Adamson spoke with a trace of concern showing on his face. "We still have a lot of people who don't like the cloning program; they feel we should have built up our military forces with Human volunteers."

"They simply weren't enough," Wade responded with a deep sigh. He was well aware of the unrest caused by the cloning program. He knew the latest survey showed that only thirty-two percent of the Human population agreed with producing the clones. "With only eighteen million survivors to pull personnel from, we couldn't have reached the numbers we needed to resist the Kleese. Even so, we've had a tremendous amount of volunteers from the civilian population."

"When the Kleese attack us again, the rest of the civilians will see the wisdom of creating the clones," responded Adamson, confidently.

Wade nodded; they all knew it was only a matter of time before the Kleese returned.

"What's next on your schedule?"

Wade allowed himself to smile. "I'm sure you're curious why the Constellation brought me back to Vesta instead of a shuttle."

"The thought did cross my mind," admitted Adamson, looking over at Wade.

"Give your crew some leave time," Wade suggested with a secretive look in his eyes. "They may not get another for quite some time."

Adamson nodded his eyes widening slightly. "I suspected something of that sort when I heard you were coming aboard. I don't suppose you can tell me where we're going?"

"No; at least not yet," Wade answered his eyes meeting those of the commander. "There are still a few details that need to be ironed out. Once everything's ready, I'll let you know what's going on."

Adamson nodded; he would begin making arrangements for his crew to take leave immediately. From past experiences with Colonel Nelson, he knew they could be gone from the solar system for quite some time. At least Vesta, with its large habitats, was the best place in the system to take leave.

-

Wade exited the Constellation to find a female marine major waiting impatiently for him. She walked up to Wade, put her arms possessively around him, and kissed him on the lips.

"About time you came home," Beth said, stepping back after the kiss and smiling. "Your parents have been asking about both you and Ryan."

"Ryan's doing fine," responded Wade, taking Beth's hand. "He just took his platoon up Charring."

"Really!" Beth spoke her eyes widening. "How far did he make it?" Both she and Wade had been trained by Marken when they had been Kleese conscripts. She recalled how difficult getting to the top of the mountain had been. It was the same dome they had trained in, though there'd been a lot of modifications done, including changes to Charring Mountain.

"All the way to the top," Wade said, feeling proud of Ryan's first attempt.

"He won the first time?" Beth said her eyes growing wide in disbelief.

"No, he died at the top," Wade answered with a laugh. "No one wins the first time."

Beth nodded. Charring Mountain was a tough lesson. She had seen marines get frustrated and never beat the mountain.

"How's your mom doing?"

"Better," Beth replied with a sigh. "She's moved into a retirement home where she can be professionally looked after. It's a really nice place with lots to do. Mom was hesitant at first but seems to be settling in." Then she looked deeply into Wade's eyes. "What did General Mitchell want?"

Wade let out a deep breath. He looked over where the two eight hundred-meter military transports were berthed. They were the biggest ships in the fleet and General Mitchell had placed them under his command.

"We have a new mission," Wade answered as he and Beth began to walk toward an airlock that would allow them to exit the bay. "We have several advance scouts which have reported back and the war between the Kleese and the Strell will soon be over if it isn't already." The fighting was taking place so far away it was impossible to get real-time information. Everything they had was months behind.

"Are the Kleese going to win?" asked Beth, growing concerned. It had been hoped that the two Empires would weaken one another to the point that they wouldn't be a serious threat anymore.

"It's those damn Zaltule," uttered Wade, shaking his head. "Their warships are more powerful than those of the Strell and they have superior numbers. The Strell have taken some horrific losses and Marken feels they'll have no choice but to surrender shortly rather than risk the destruction of any of their home worlds."

"Then the Kleese will come after us," Beth said, feeling a cold chill run down her back at the prospect of more of the massive disk ships coming to the solar system.

"No, Marken doesn't think so, at least not at first. He believes they'll go after the nonaligned worlds."

"Even with their neutrality agreement?"

"The Zaltule don't believe in neutrality," responded Wade, grimly. His eyes took on a more worried look. "The Zaltule believe you're either a part of the Kleese Empire or you're their enemies."

Beth stopped in mid-stride and looked back at the Constellation where some of her crew were exiting the hatches. Then she looked at her husband accusingly. "You're going to the nonaligned worlds," she said with dawning comprehension. "That's why you came back in the Constellation."

Wade was silent for a moment before confirming Beth's words. "We're going back," he corrected her. "We're going to some of the nearer nonaligned worlds; you and I and a very carefully handpicked group of marines. We'll be escorting several high-level diplomatic ships, which will be making a last ditch effort to bring as many of the nonaligned worlds as possible into an alliance with us."

"Will there be any combat?" Beth asked her eyes seeking Wade's. It had been years since any of the marines under her command fought in a battle.

"We're taking the Fire Fox and the Crimson Star," Wade answered solemnly in explanation. "If there is, we'll be prepared."

"What about warships?"

"A full fleet," Wade answered. "We're taking the Constellation, the three new battlecruisers, sixteen light cruisers, and two hundred of the latest disk assault ships."

"You expect us to fight a major battle," Beth said sharply her eyes widening at hearing how many assault ships would be going. "Are the Kleese that close to returning to this sector of space?"

"We think so," Wade said as they resumed walking and stepped through the airlock. "If the Kleese attack one of the nonaligned worlds in our sector of the galaxy we have a plan. It may only work once, but if it does we have a good chance of bringing a number of the nonaligned worlds into the Alliance."

"What if we can't bring them in?"

"Then we lose," Wade said in a softer voice. "By ourselves, we can't hope to stand up to the Zaltule in a galactic war; at least not yet. Many of those nonaligned worlds have a science and technology more advanced than the Kleese. You've seen some of that technology from the computer flash drive they gave us."

Beth nodded. The cloning technology, new ion cannons, and even better sensors and energy shields had come from the nonaligned worlds. There had also been some modifications to the Fold Space Drives to improve their efficiency to allow for greater speeds. The flash drive had been a gold mine of information and still was.

"How soon do we leave?" she asked. She still needed to make sure that her mother was settled in at the retirement home and could get by without her presence. She'd felt guilty about putting her there in the first place, though she knew it was for the best.

"Four weeks," Wade answered. "The new battlecruisers have to go through their space trials and some special weapons we've designed have to be finished. We also have to make some modifications to the Constellation." Wade stopped and turned toward his wife. "Beth, I didn't want you to go on this mission, but we can't risk this failing. We have to have our best people."

"I understand, Wade," she responded, taking his hand. "We're marines and we'll do whatever is necessary. Now, let's go home. I think we can find something more pleasant to do for a while. The war can wait until tomorrow."

Chapter Four

Nine thousand light years from Earth was the Kleese home world. The Kleese planet orbited a small K Class star, which was slightly cooler than Earth's. The sun was yellow-orange in color with twelve planets orbiting it, as well as several small fields of asteroids. The fourth planet was nearly devoid of life due to the early, turbulent years of the Kleese civilization and the wars they'd fought for planetary dominance. Hundreds of millions of Kleese had died, many in thermonuclear explosions or worse. Biological warfare, chemical warfare, every horror one could imagine had been unleashed upon the surface of the planet as the different castes fought to eliminate one another. The wars were harsh, with little or no mercy shown to the defeated.

Much of the planet had been laid to waste from the use of those brutal weapons. When the wars finally ended, only one faction of the Kleese race had survived. The others had all been eliminated and their deep underground nests destroyed. The Kleese were egg layers, and females laid multiple eggs in their nests, which were protected by the dominate males. Great pain had been taken by the winning faction to ensure all the nests of their enemies were destroyed to ensure no future competition for the limited living space left.

As the Kleese looked around their ruined world, they realized that it was no longer capable of sustaining a thriving civilization. They had been forced to turn to space as the ravaged surface of their planet was no longer capable of supporting what remained of their civilization. All forms of animal life had been decimated in the century's long wars. Virtually all the vegetation upon the planet had died out from the multiple nuclear winters that had covered much of the planet in kilometer thick layers of ice. The Kleese fled to space, knowing that to remain upon their home planet would ultimately mean their death. Only one city remained and it was from here the Kleese Council of Overlords ruled over their extensive Empire.

Xatul looked impassively across the massive stone table at Overlord Harmock, the leader of the Zaltule. There had been several changes on the council as had been expected with the return of the Zaltule from their triumphant victory over the Strell. Four Council Overlords had been challenged, and all four had lost in duels meeting their untimely deaths, as was tradition. Council duels were fought to the death to ensure that the defeated Overlord could not later return and attempt a second challenge. Such duels were frowned upon as they could keep the council in a constant state of flux. By fighting to the death, the council was always controlled by the most powerful members of the Kleese race and challenges were few and far between.

Advancement on the council was done through open challenges and if the council agreed the challenge was legitimate, then a battle to the death was arranged. If the challenger won, they would take over the council seat of the slain Overlord. In this case, the Zaltule had chosen four of the weaker Council Overlords, easily beating them in open combat.

Hymtal and three other Council Overlords had been eliminated and replaced by Darthu, Lackeln, Creedal, and Tintul all of the Zaltule. In addition, Overlord Harmock had taken the position of Supreme Military Commander of the Kleese, a position that was deemed equal to Xatul as the Supreme Overlord of the Kleese race.

"The war with the Strell is over," Harmock announced his thick, hairy arms folded across his powerful chest. His multifaceted eyes looked at the other Overlords as if seeking anyone who might dare challenge the changes that had come to the council.

"Then it is time for the Zaltule to return to sleep," suggested Raluth. "There are no further threats to the Empire; the Zaltule have done their duty."

"No!" roared Harmock his fierce gaze centering on Raluth in anger. "We were dying in the sleeping chambers; we will not return there. The Empire still has many enemies and as long as there are Zaltule, we will fight for the glory of our Empire."

"What enemies?" Raluth dared to ask. He wondered if he continued to ask questions whether a member of the Zaltule would challenge him to combat. He was a powerful Overlord, but the Zaltule were trained as warriors from birth.

"The nonaligned races, to begin with," answered Harmock, leaning forward and placing his two hands upon the table. His six legs stomped the hard stone floor of the council chamber noisily. "These races have been laughing at the Kleese, sitting behind the neutrality agreements they signed with this council."

"Most of those nonaligned worlds have a very high level of science and technology," Xatul began as he gazed directly at Harmock. He was not afraid of the Zaltule war leader. "It was decided war against them could result in serious losses to our exploration fleet. They were bypassed and the Empire continued to expand against the inferior races, which populate the majority of the galaxy. The nonaligned worlds serve a purpose in trading with the Empire and not interfering in our affairs. They furnish many high-tech products, which are not available on the more primitive worlds."

Xatul had arranged for one hundred and ten of their large exploration ships to be in orbit of the home planet when the Zaltule returned as a show of force. All of them were controlled by Xatul or those loyal to him. It was his insurance card so that he would remain as the Supreme Overlord of the Kleese. So far, Harmock had not indicated that he was going to challenge that.

Harmock turned toward Darthu, one of the Zaltule who had taken over a seat on the council. He was also very well versed in science. "How big a threat is the technology of these worlds?" He'd been impressed by Xatul's show of force with the exploration ships. It had shown him that at least for now, Xatul could remain as the Supreme Overlord. It would make the rest of the Kleese race more tolerant of the Zaltule if Xatul remained in power, at least for now.

"Several of them are very highly advanced," Darthu admitted. "They are unlike much of the primitive vermin that infests other worlds."

"We shall add their science to ours," declared Harmock, waving his hands at the council. "We'll take them one by one until they know the feel of an obedience collar around their necks. They'll serve and work for the Empire!"

"Their science and technology will be a boon to our military might," Darthu confirmed. "Once we have assimilated their science and applied their technology to Kleese warships, our warriors will be unstoppable."

Bixutl stood silently upon his six legs, listening. He was not in as powerful a position as Xatul. He'd made dealings with Kaluse, who had assured Bixutl he would be allowed to remain an Overlord as long as the Zaltule shipyards received the required materials needed to update and build new warships.

He wondered if he should mention the Humans. Nothing had been heard from them in years. The Humans had freed a large number of Kivean scientists and the Kiveans were one of the most advanced races known. If the Humans had that technology available to them, then the Zaltule might face a formidable enemy someday. The question was how Bixutl could use that knowledge to his advantage. The other Overlords seemed to have forgotten how dangerous the Humans had been, but Bixutl had not. Perhaps he should send one of his exploration ships out to check on the upstart race. It could be done discretely with the Zaltule none the wiser.

"This council is not as it was in the old days," stated Harmock, rising to his full height. "There are no races in the galaxy of equal stature with the Kleese and no warriors as powerful as the Zaltule. Many of the vermin races are unfit to even serve the Empire and should be exterminated."

"We have taken many conscripts from those vermin races," Martule spoke in disagreement. "They have made excellent fighters for our battlesuits and have allowed us to greatly expand the Empire. They also serve as occupation forces sparing us the necessity of using Kleese to hold the numerous worlds we have added to the Empire."

Harmock shifted his gaze toward Martule. "None of the vermin races will ever serve upon a Zaltule warship! You may continue to use these excrement species to expand the Empire against other vermin. The Zaltule will focus on adversaries more worthy of our warriors."

"When will you attack the first of the nonaligned worlds?" inquired Xatul, knowing he had no choice but to support Harmock in this. To do otherwise might endanger his position as the Supreme Overlord of the Kleese.

"Shortly," Harmock responded. "The warships of the Zaltule must be repaired from the damage inflicted by the Strell. Our strategists will begin to review which nonaligned worlds to strike first; this should not take long and these worlds will soon become a part of the Kleese Empire as they should have been all along."

Second Lieutenant Ryan Nelson stood at the base of Charring Mountain with his nineteen soldiers in battlesuits. Once they conquered the mountain then they could be called Space Marines. It was a daunting task ahead of them and one Ryan had dwelled on considerably since their previous defeat. He didn't intend to lose again.

"What's the plan?" Casey asked as she walked over to stand next to Ryan. She felt secure in her battlesuit and was anxious to get the drill started. She and Ryan had spent considerable time the night before discussing their previous attempt at Charring.

"We're going to try something different," answered Ryan, as he turned his battlesuit toward Casey. He'd spent several hours the previous night, after speaking with Casey, thinking about different strategies and what others before him might have tried.

To the casual observer, the ten-foot tall black battlesuits looked ominous and threatening. They were able to keep the soldier inside alive for over twelve hours on its own environmental and power systems. It also was capable of using its suit functions to treat major wounds and inject necessary chemicals into the wearer's body to allow them to continue to fight even if mortally injured.

"Only five of us will have RG rifles, everyone else will be carrying energy cannons."

"What?" stammered Casey her eyes growing wide in disbelief. "We'll never make it even close to the top without more RG rifles and their explosive rounds."

"Maybe," Ryan responded as he turned back toward the waiting mountain.

Looking up the heavily forested slope, he couldn't even tell where they'd gone up the mountain in their first assault. Everything had grown back or been replaced. He wasn't sure how the Kiveans did it, but the mountain looked as if it had never been touched.

"How do they do that?" asked Casey, guessing what Ryan was thinking.

She had come to know Ryan very well over the years they had been together and trusted his judgment. She knew there were several Kiveans around that kept the different training facilities on Centerpoint functional. She'd been around Kiveans at the Academy as well as immediately after coming out of the cloning facility and had a lot of respect for their science.

"I don't know, but we have to assume all the popups have been replaced and are probably in new locations."

Casey nodded; Ryan had always had a knack for solving problems as long as she had known him. As a clone, she had technically only experienced seven actual years of life.

"Let's go," Ryan ordered over the general com frequency as he glanced at the waiting battlesuits. "Two scouts ahead and we'll form six lines of three. Let's see if we can make it to the top this time."

"Here we go again," mumbled Alexander as he checked the energy cannon he was carrying. It had a full charge, but it was much bulkier than an RG rifle. Alexander had a propensity for the smaller weapon, but today that was not to be.

"Let's not get shot this time," Lauren suggested as the two took up their positions in front of the rest of the platoon. Lauren didn't know what they'd done wrong to keep drawing the position of scouts. Scouts tended to get shot first. She wondered if Corporal Hunter was still upset with her and Alexander. She'd hoped that after the scene at the Chinese restaurant the little incident in the mess hall would be forgiven.

Ryan watched Privates Parker and Adams move out. Since the two had served as scouts the first time around, he felt they'd be better prepared to spot popups. He needed any edge he could get, and he hoped the two privates would be able to give him one. He wondered what his parents would think if they could see him standing here at the base of Charring Mountain in a Type Three battlesuit. Ryan knew that his parents had hoped he would apply for the fleet and away from the marines. However, Ryan decided to follow in his brother's footsteps, and conquering Charring Mountain would put him well on the way to doing just that.

In the dome's Command Center, Major Winfrey smiled to himself as he saw Ryan begin sending his soldiers up Charring. He was curious as to why the second lieutenant had elected to take mostly energy weapons with him this time. The energy weapons would give out long before the lieutenant and his platoon made it to the top.

Dylan leaned back in his chair gazing at the multiple viewscreens on the wall, which afforded him an unobstructed view of all of Charring Mountain. Major Stevens would be joining him shortly, and Dylan was interested in hearing the majors take on the weapon mix that Ryan had chosen.

General Mitchell was meeting with newly promoted Fleet Admiral Thomas Kelly in his office to discuss potential action against the Kleese. He shuffled several papers around on his desk before finding the report he was searching for.

"The Kleese-Strell war is probably over," he announced, looking at the report in his hand and leaning back in his chair behind his desk.

"What will the Kleese do now?" Kelly asked with narrowed eyes. He knew if he were in charge of the Kleese fleet, he would repair the damage suffered in the war with the Strell and then go immediately back on the offensive.

"We're not sure, but we think they'll attempt to take out the nonaligned worlds."

"How many nonaligned worlds are there?" Kelly asked. He knew they were scattered throughout the Kleese Empire.

"Several hundred," Mitchell answered as he leaned forward and laid the report back down on his desk. "They'll probably start with the ones closest to their home world and gradually work their way outward toward us."

"Is there anything we can do to turn some of those nonaligned worlds to our side in this war? I've read reports from the Kiveans that some of those systems have some very advanced warships, particularly the one that gave us the ion cannons."

"Perhaps," replied Mitchell, recalling the plan that he and Colonel Nelson had come up with. It had been necessary to call in several Kiveans, including Marken, to come up with a workable option. "There are forty-two nonaligned worlds within two thousand light years of the solar system; we hope to get at least ten of them to join a new Alliance we're trying to form. The Kleese are just too powerful for us to fight alone."

"The fleet's ready," Kelly said. "All six fleets are now fully crewed and ready for combat operations. We have three more battlecruisers coming online this week and they'll begin their space trials shortly."

"That's one of the items I wanted to talk to you about," Mitchell said as his eyes focused on the Fleet Admiral. "I have other plans for those battlecruisers and the new light cruisers we just completed. I'm turning them over to Colonel Nelson for a special mission. Commander Adamson on the Constellation will be in command of the warships. There will also be a large number of assault ships going as well."

"So it's about to begin," Kelly said, taking in a deep fortifying breath. He suspected that General Mitchell wouldn't be committing that many ships to this mission unless he thought there was a good chance there would be combat.

"Yes," answered Mitchell with a heavy sigh.

"How many assault ships are you sending on this mission?

"Two hundred."

"Two hundred!" exclaimed Kelly his eyes bulging at the number.

"We feel it's necessary if the mission is to succeed."

"Are you certain you want Commander Adamson to command and not one of our fleet admirals?"

Mitchell looked at Kelly with a serious look in his eyes. "That's something else I wanted to talk to you about. Commander Adamson has performed admirably in all of the off world missions we've sent him on. I would like to see him promoted to the rank of admiral."

Kelly nodded; he'd been considering that promotion himself after reviewing all of the candidates in the fleet. Adamson was highly qualified, particularly after his missions to the trading station and the Kivean home world.

"Very well," Kelly replied with a smile spreading across his face. "We'll assign the Constellation permanently to Seventh Fleet as its new flagship." The original plans had been for all the new warships to be held in reserve to fill in for damaged or destroyed ships in the six regular fleets. Kelly knew they'd have to construct more ships to fill that role now.

"I think it's a wise move," Mitchell commented with a satisfied look upon his face. "There's a very good chance Seventh Fleet will have to fight a major engagement against the Kleese, most likely against the Zaltule themselves."

"Should we add another battlecruiser or two to his fleet?" asked Kelly, worriedly. All the other fleets had six battlecruisers assigned to them. Admiral Adamson had only four even though he would command far more assault ships.

"No," replied Mitchell, shaking his head. "We need to keep our six fleets at full strength just in case the Kleese strike here instead of the nonaligned worlds."

"You think that's likely?"

"It's a low probability," answered Mitchell, recalling what the military strategists and Kiveans believed. "Marken said his people think the probability is under twenty percent, particularly since we haven't launched any type of attack against the Kleese in recent years to draw their attention to us."

"Except for starting the Kleese-Strell war," replied Kelly with a frown. "If they ever find out we were responsible, they'll descend upon us with a vengeance."

"They won't find out," promised Mitchell, confidently. "There's no evidence we were ever involved."

Kelly nodded. After discussing a few more details with General Mitchell, he stood up and left the office. He needed to take care of the promotion of Commander Adamson to admiral as quickly as possible. He knew it would be pleasing to a number of people who'd already mentioned to him that Adamson was deserving of such a promotion, they just hadn't had a fleet for him. Now it appeared that they did.

Ryan grimaced as one of his soldiers fell and another icon turned a glaring red on his HUD. Eight down and twelve remaining and they were only halfway to the top of the damn mountain. "Grab Private Swen's energy weapon," he ordered as everyone waited to begin moving forward again. "Private Parker and Adams move up, but take your time. We're going the rest of the way in single file and we'll be stepping in each other's footsteps."

Lauren sent a confirming reply over her suit's com and began moving forward very slowly. Alexander was about four meters behind her, scanning to their left and right with his suit's sensors while Lauren used her energy weapon to burn a narrow path directly in front of them. She was burning a swath about twenty meters wide, and whenever her energy weapon's charge became exhausted, another energy cannon from one of their fallen comrades was passed forward.

Twice she narrowly missed being struck by stunners, and once several railgun rounds hit next to her metal encased feet, showering her with dirt. She took a deep, steadying breath and continued firing her energy cannon ahead of them. She moved it in a gentle arc, burning through everything. Trees, brush, and even the ground burned as the deadly blue beam annihilated everything before her. Occasionally a small explosion, a bright flash, and a pillar of rising dark smoke would indicate where the beam had struck a hidden popup weapon.

Behind her, Alexander had exchanged his energy cannon for an RG rifle and was using its explosive rounds on any popups that appeared on their flanks. Whenever he missed, it invariably meant another soldier would be hit by stunners or painful RG rounds. Alexander was trying his best not to miss!

Corporal Hunter was following closely behind the two scouts. She found it remarkable that neither had been hit since they were leading the platoon up the steep slope of the mountain. Like Private Parker, she was carrying an RG rifle set on explosive rounds and was watching intently for any hidden weapon emplacements Alexander might miss. So far, she'd taken out eight of the painful weapons, though she and Alexander had missed a few, which had resulted in them losing eight soldiers so far. Each was lying in a Type Three battlesuit behind them, immobile until the drill was over. Lieutenant Nelson made it a point of taking the fallen soldier's weapons each time one was hit.

Major Winfrey looked at the viewscreens, which were showing numerous views of Charring Mountain and the platoon of Type Three battlesuits that was slowly advancing toward the top. It was beginning to look as if Second Lieutenant Nelson was once again going to reach the summit. The latest computer estimates predicted he had just enough power in his energy weapons to get to the top. The question remaining was how many soldiers would he have left?

"Definitely Colonel Nelson's brother," commented Major Stevens with a grin. "The son-of-a-bitch is going to make it to the top of Charring on his second try."

"Looks that way," replied Dylan, thoughtfully. No one had ever made it to the top and deactivated the embedded weapons this quickly. At the moment, he didn't see how he could stop the young lieutenant. "He made it to the top on his first ascent, but the stunners around the pedestal took him out."

"I would never have thought of using the energy weapons that way," Mark went on impressed by what he was seeing. "They're clearing out a narrow path directly ahead, which means they only have to be on the lookout for the weapons on the perimeter. As soon as they pop up, their sensors detect them and they're using their RG rifles to take them out."

"Most of them," Dylan replied as he watched two more of the popups being destroyed. "The question is, how many soldiers will Nelson have left when he gets to the top? He'll also need an energy weapon or some explosive rounds to take out the stunners protecting the deactivation button."

"Are you going to let him win?" asked Mark, feeling curious.

"I don't think I can stop him," Dylan replied with a long sigh. "In all the scenarios we've run on Charring, no one has used energy weapons quite the way Lieutenant Nelson is. There's always been a propensity to use explosive rounds when advancing up the mountain."

"They provide the biggest bang for the buck and can clear a wide area," commented Mark, recalling his own attempts at Charring. Well did he recall just how painful the stunners felt; he grimaced and frowned at the recollection.

"What the new battlesuit recruits don't realize is that after each attempt we reduce the number of weapons slightly to gradually allow them to get higher up the mountain until on the fifth or sixth try they have a reasonable chance to make it," spoke Dylan as he watched another of Nelson's soldiers fall from a stun beam. The stunner was quickly taken out by an RG explosive round. "Lieutenant Nelson isn't quite playing by the rules."

"They volunteered for the new program," Mark said. "They're supposed to the toughest and the brightest. Also, in this war there are no rules."

"Think you can handle them?" asked Dylan, turning his head to look at Mark. "It's your program."

"The new Type Four battlesuits are ready to go; we just need the men and women to operate them."

Dylan nodded. The Type Fours were supposed to be far more deadly than the previous models. Earth's military scientists along with the Kiveans had spent several long years perfecting the suits to where they were now ready to be deployed. They would be needed in the war against the Kleese, particularly now that the Zaltule were a part of the mix. Dylan shifted his gaze back to the viewscreens. He was curious to see how this turned out.

-

Ryan groaned silently to himself as he saw Private Adams go down with an echoing cry of anguish over the suit's com. Lauren had been hit by an RG cannon, which had popped up on the right flank and opened fire on her before Private Parker could sight in his RG rifle and take it out with explosive rounds. Corporal Hunter made short work of the offending weapon as she blew it apart with an explosive round. On his HUD, he saw Lauren's green icon flash over to red. He gestured for the others to come to a halt as he checked to see who remained with him. He still had Private Parker, Corporal Hunter, Private Rios, and himself surviving. All were uninjured and the summit was less than one hundred meters above them.

"Weapons check!" Ryan called out.

He had a full magazine of RG rounds, but they were nearly useless against the popups. It was necessary to hit them dozens of time to inflict any appreciable damage and by then they would be returning fire, which was nearly impossible to avoid. He had six explosive rounds left.

"I'm out," Private Rios reported as he checked the readouts on his RG rifle.

"Four rounds left," Corporal Hunter responded.

"Ten percent charge on my energy cannon," Private Parker added. He had stepped forward and picked up Lauren's energy cannon as his RG rifle was empty of explosive rounds.

"Damn, I'm not sure that's enough," Ryan spoke as he considered their options. He looked at the steep slope ahead wondering just how many more popups there were. The ground was rocky with a few large boulders scattered about, some short bushes, and only a few trees. They would be highly visible the rest of the way.

"Let me go first," volunteered Rios. "I'll run up the slope as fast as I can. The rest of the hidden popups between here and the summit should try to take me out. Once they pop up you can destroy them, and that should get you to the summit."

"You'll get taken out," warned Ryan.

"It'll only hurt for a few moments," quipped Rios, trying to sound nonchalant.

He knew if he were hit by a stunner it would hurt like hell and there were bound to be a few surviving stunners between here and the summit. When he took off running, every embedded weapon left would target him and begin firing. He knew he wouldn't get far, but it would be worth it if it meant they could win.

Ryan was silent for a few moments as he considered their options. He knew what Private Rios had suggested was their best chance. It should cause most if not all of the remaining weapons to reveal themselves. He took a deep breath and then looked directly at Rios standing a few feet away in his battlesuit.

"Okay, Rios," Ryan finally said. "If you can get all the remaining weapons to fire on you, there'll be a steak dinner for you tonight in the mess hall."

"Medium-rare," Rios answered, grinning. He could already taste the steak; it almost made the pain he was about to go through worth it.

"Anytime, Rios," spoke Ryan. "Private Parker, save your energy weapon for the summit. Corporal Hunter and I will take out the remaining popups."

"I'm gone!" Rios shouted as he suddenly stood up to his full height and bounded up the steep slope. He took a deep breath and braced himself for the pain he knew was coming.

He hadn't gone more than twenty meters when the first RG rounds slammed into his suit, making his icon change from green to amber. He managed to stagger forward another ten meters before a pair of stunners struck him, sending his battlesuit tumbling to the ground.

Ryan and Casey were firing as rapidly as they could, taking out the remaining weapon emplacements. They couldn't afford to miss; each round had to count.

"I'm out," Casey called out as her RG rifle failed to fire on the last popup.

"So am I," Ryan yelled as he saw the stunner swiftly turning toward Casey. It suddenly exploded as Private Parker blew it away with a blue beam from his energy cannon.

"We should be clear to the summit," commented Private Parker as he walked over to Casey and handed her his energy weapon. "There's only one way to find out."

"Parker!" yelled Ryan as Alexander began running up the slope toward the summit.

Parker zigzagged but no weapons fired. When he reached the summit, he hunkered down behind a large boulder and looked back down toward Ryan and Casey. "I think we got all of them."

Casey shook her head. "We got lucky," she spoke as she began walking up the slope toward Parker. His actions and what Rios had done confused her as she still didn't fully understand why Humans acted as they did. She still had so much more to learn.

Ryan followed Casey up the slope and soon all three were crouched down behind the large boulder. Looking around it, Ryan could see the pedestal and the pylon, which held the tantalizing red button that would deactivate all the weapons on

Charring Mountain. If he could just push that damn button then they would never have to come up this infernal mountain again.

Casey handed the energy cannon back to Private Parker. "You're a better shot with this than I am," she explained. Casey took a deep breath and turned to face Ryan. "Private Rios had the right idea, and I volunteer to do the same thing. Once I step out onto the summit, the stunners around the pedestal should activate." Her eyes focused on Private Parker. "Alexander, don't miss!"

"I won't," promised Parker, nodding his head solemnly. "I'll take the stunners out."

"Casey, wait," Ryan said, reaching out his metal arm and touching her shoulder. "I should be the one doing this, you can press the button."

"No," replied Casey, shaking her head. "You're the commanding officer of our platoon; in a battle it will be essential that you survive. It has to be this way."

Casey tapped Alexander on the head and then standing up to her full ten-foot height, charged out onto the summit of Charring Mountain. Instantly, six popup stunners appeared, four around the pedestal and two twenty meters to the side. Casey went down almost immediately with a loud scream of anguish as she was hit with multiple stun beams. She lost consciousness instantly from the intense pain.

Alexander sighted carefully and calmly blew all six of the offending stunners to oblivion. When the last one was a pile of smoking wreckage, he looked down, seeing that his energy cannon still had a two percent charge.

"Stay here," ordered Ryan as he stood up. "If any more popups make an appearance take them out and then go push that damn red button!"

"Yes, Sir!" responded Alexander as he watched Ryan stand up and step out onto the summit.

Ryan walked determinedly toward the pedestal expecting to be hit by a stun beam at any moment. With surprise, he stepped up onto the pedestal, and then after looking around for a brief moment, he pressed firmly down on the red button. Instantly, a voice came over the com channel in his suit.

"Congratulations, Lieutenant Nelson," Major Winfrey said. "You have set a new record for conquering Charring Mountain. Your soldiers are now officially Space Marines!"

Ryan allowed himself to relax and breathe out a long sigh of relief. They would be celebrating in the barracks tonight. He looked around at Corporal Hunter's still form and Private Parker, who was stepping out onto the summit carrying his energy cannon. He was proud of his people; they'd done what was necessary to conquer Charring.

Major Winfrey looked over at Major Stevens. "Well, there's your first bunch; are you ready to start their training?"

"Damn right!" uttered Mark with a smile. "If they thought Charring was hard, just wait until they start the training for the new suits. It'll make Charring look like a newborn kitten."

Dylan nodded. He knew that tonight Second Lieutenant Nelson's people would be celebrating and feeling exhilarated over their victory. He would let them have their enjoyment; they deserved it. In a day or two, he would inform them of the new hell they had just qualified for.

Chapter Five

Newly promoted Admiral Karl Adamson stood in front of the mirror in his personal quarters admiring the admiral stars on his shoulders. He breathed out a long sigh as he realized just what the promotion meant. Fleet Admiral Kelly had informed him he was being promoted and placed in command of the newly created Seventh Fleet. He was due to meet with Colonel Nelson and Marken shortly to discuss the mission his newly formed fleet would be going on. Knowing Nelson and Marken as he did, Adamson was certain the mission would be full of danger and intrigue.

Straightening his shoulders, he exited his quarters and took the turbo lift, which would take him to the command level. Moments later, he stepped out and walked the short distance to the Command Center hatch. The two marines on duty looked at the newly promoted admiral, their eyes widening upon seeing the stars on his shoulders. Adamson was immediately allowed entry as one of the marines stepped inside.

"Admiral on deck!" the marine's powerful voice rang out.

Everyone jumped up from their consoles and turned, coming to rigid attention. Several allowed satisfied smiles to spread across their faces when they saw who the admiral was.

"As you were," spoke Adamson, feeling a little embarrassed by the crew's response. He had known most of these people for years.

"Congratulations," spoke Sandra Shepherd, the executive officer. Sandra had transferred over from the battlecruiser Phoenix several years back.

Adamson grinned as he reached into his shirt pocket and took out two small silver stars, which designated the rank of a ship commander. "You're the new commander of the Constellation, Sandra," Adamson said as he handed her the two stars with a twinkle in his eyes.

Sandra's eyes widened as she took the two small stars and gazed at them in awe. She'd always dreamed of becoming a ship commander. It was one of the reasons she had transferred over to the Constellation.

"I will treat her right, Sir," Sandra answered as she smartly saluted.

"Admiral," Colonel Nelson and Marken have arrived and are being escorted to briefing room two," Lieutenant Emma Travers reported from Communications.

"Commander Shepherd, if you will accompany me, maybe we can find out exactly what's going on and why Fleet Admiral Kelly has formed Seventh Fleet."

"Seventh Fleet?" asked Shepherd, looking confused. "I thought we only had six active fleets."

"I've been given command of the new Seventh Fleet, which will consist of the Constellation, the three new battlecruisers nearly completed here in the spacedock, sixteen light cruisers, and two hundred assault ships."

"Two hundred assault ships?" uttered Sandra, coming to a stop in the corridor and looking worriedly at the newly promoted admiral. "Are we going into combat?"

"I suspect so," Adamson replied in an even voice. "We'll know more when we speak with Colonel Nelson and Marken."

Wade watched as newly promoted Admiral Adamson and Commander Shepherd stepped into the briefing room. He'd suspected that Adamson would promote Shepherd to commander. She was an excellent choice and Wade had full confidence in her abilities.

"Congratulations on the promotion," Wade said, rising to his feet and walking over to shake Adamson's hand.

"It's well deserved after everything you've done for my people," added Marken as he also stood.

Marken was a Kivean. His skin was a light red and his arms were slightly longer than a normal Human's with long, narrow fingers on his hands. His face was humanoid with slender eyes, no eyebrows, a wide nose, and small ears. His most unusual feature was there was no hair at all upon his head.

As they all sat down, Adamson and Shepherd turned their attention to Colonel Nelson, curious to hear what he had to say about this mission they were going on. From the size of Seventh Fleet, they strongly suspected they were going deep into Kleese controlled space.

"I don't know if Fleet Admiral Kelly told you or not, but we strongly suspect the Kleese-Strell war is coming to a close if it isn't over with already."

"I don't suppose we got lucky and the Strell won?" asked Adamson, arching his eyebrow.

"No," replied Wade, shaking his head. "From all reports, the Kleese had the Strell outnumbered and outgunned. The Strell weren't expecting an attack from the Kleese and suffered some serious losses at the beginning of the war, which seriously hampered their ability to defend their Empire."

"So, where does that put us?"

"Seventh Fleet is going to escort several civilian diplomatic ships that will be traveling to some of the nearer nonaligned worlds to try to talk them into joining into an alliance with us," Wade explained. "We'll also be taking both of the marine transports as well as several supply ships."

"We're taking two hundred assault ships," mentioned Commander Shepherd, gazing intently at Colonel Nelson. Nelson had a reputation of always being where the heaviest fighting was. "Why so many?"

"Yes, we're taking a large complement of assault ships," Wade confirmed. "If the Kleese launch an attack on any of the nonaligned worlds we're seeking to add to the Alliance, we'll aid in their defense as a gesture to encourage all the nonaligned worlds in our sector of space to join."

"If we're talking about fighting the Zaltule, we could be looking at some serious ship losses," Adamson said his eyes narrowing sharply. "Those three kilometer disk ships of theirs are built for war and will not be easy to destroy."

His new fleet might not last long against the dangerous warrior caste of the Kleese. He well recalled what had happened when just six of the Zaltule warships attacked the solar system six years back.

"It will probably be the Zaltule you'll face if there is indeed combat," Marken spoke in a calm voice. "The Zaltule are the warriors of the Kleese and seem to have taken over the combat role for the Empire. During the time the Kleese were fighting the Strell, there has been very little expansion of their Empire in other areas."

"From our last combat with these Zaltule ships, our ship weapons and theirs are pretty evenly matched," Commander Shepherd said her eyes narrowing in thought. It worried her since they would only have four battlecruisers in the fleet.

"That may be true, but we've come to believe the six Zaltule ships that attacked our solar system were not being operated by the warrior caste but regular members of the Kleese race," Wade informed her. "We may not have won if the ships had been commanded by the Zaltule."

"Which means we're going to have a major problem on our hands if we have to fight Zaltule battlecruisers," Adamson reiterated with a frown.

"We may have a solution to that," Marken responded as he reached down in front of him and picked up two red folders. He handed one each to Admiral Adamson and Commander Shepherd.

"This is a new sublight missile developed by the Kivean scientists," Wade explained as Adamson and Shepherd opened up the folders and began looking through the contents.

"It's slightly larger than a normal sublight missile and contains six antimatter warheads," Marken explained. "Each warhead has a yield of twenty megatons and can be independently targeted."

"How did you get that many warheads inside the missile?" Commander Shepherd asked as she studied the design specs. "It doesn't seem to be that much larger than our standard sublight missiles."

"Miniaturization," Marken explained. "Our Kivean science plus some of the information from the computer drive furnished by the nonaligned worlds allowed us to drastically reduce the size of some of the missile's components without compromising the integrity of the missile. The three new battlecruisers and the sixteen light cruisers have all had their missile tubes modified to handle this new weapon."

"In addition, engineers will shortly begin upgrading the missile tubes on the Constellation," Wade added. He had already spoken to Ethan Hall about this and Ethan had assured him it could be done very quickly.

"When do we leave?" asked Adamson, leaning back and taking a deep breath. He had a feeling this was going to be a long and complicated mission. They always were when Nelson and Marken were involved.

"Four weeks," Wade answered. "You have that much time to get your fleet ready for combat." He leaned forward with a serious look upon his face. "We're going to be facing off against the Zaltule. Our new missiles should give us an advantage in the first engagement; we need to make sure it's decisive so we can buy the time we need to organize the Alliance."

"If any of the nonaligned worlds will join," interjected Shepherd with a worried frown. She wasn't certain any of the nonaligned worlds would make such a commitment.

"Surely with the threat the Kleese now represent they'll be more inclined to join the Alliance," suggested Adamson, glancing over at Sandra.

"They've refused to so far," Sandra was quick to point out. "Why should they change their minds now?"

"If they don't join then the Zaltule will over run those systems and add them to the Empire," Wade declared his eyes flashing with deadly seriousness. "We know some are supportive of our cause due to the computer drive they provided us as well as the warning about the impending attack from the Kleese they gave us years back. Some of those races will surely see the wisdom of joining us. That's why we're taking the fleet and making this final push to form the Alliance."

"We can only hope they see the wisdom of joining," Adamson said, drawing in a sharp breath. "How long will it take to make the modifications to the Constellation's missile tubes?"

"Six days," Marken answered. "A group of Kivean and Human technicians will start on it later today."

"Ethan Hall told me earlier that the three new battlecruisers will be ready for their trials in three more days," Wade added. "Their crews have already been selected and gone through extensive training."

"Most of those will be newbies," groaned Shepherd, shaking her head.

"We managed to transfer some experienced people also," Wade informed them. "Can you get them knocked into shape in time for us to leave in four weeks?"

"It'll be tough, but we can do additional training on the way to the nonaligned worlds," Adamson answered as he thought over what would be needed to bring the crews up to acceptable operational levels. "I'll schedule a meeting with their commanding officers for later today."

Later, Marken, Beth, and Wade toured the cloning facility. Over the years, it had grown into a massive complex as slightly over one hundred thousand clones a year were now being produced and imprinted with basic Human knowledge. It was also heavily guarded and admittance was restricted to authorized personnel only.

They were in an observation room where they could watch the new clones being awakened. Medical personnel, both Human and Kivean were in the room below dressed in sterile white gowns as they helped the new Humans take their first steps.

A dozen cloning chambers had been brought into the room and were in the process of being opened. Each chamber contained a fully grown clone and was filled with a gas that resembled a heavy fog. The gas was pumped out and then the top of the chamber was opened.

"They look so helpless," Beth murmured as she watched a female take her first hesitant steps and then look at the attending nurse with a pleased and excited look.

"I hate that they miss out on their childhood," added Wade, thinking about all of those childhood memories he treasured. They had helped to make and mold him into the person he was today. The clones missed out on that important aspect of life.

"We implant some basic memories about growing up," Marken informed them as he watched the awakening process going on in the room. He had lost track of how many awakenings he had attended over the last six years. Each day, nearly two hundred and seventy-five clones were awakened and processed.

"What's the failure rate?" asked Wade, shifting his gaze to Marken. He knew that not all awakenings were successful.

"Less than two percent," Marken answered in a sad voice. "For some reason, a small percentage of the clones won't take the imprinting process and their bodies fail as soon as we attempt the awakening process. Harnett is working on a solution, but she's still mystified by what's causing the problem."

Wade nodded, it was not common knowledge that nearly two thousand clones a year never awoke and their bodies had to be disposed of. If it were, the public outcry against the clones would only increase.

"What is the procedure once a clone has been successfully awakened?" Beth asked curiously, looking over at Marken. This was the first time she'd been allowed to watch the awakening process.

"For the first month, the clones stay with surrogate Human parents who help them with their emotional development. After the first month, they're transferred to a dormitory with twenty other clones where they're closely monitored. They go through classes taught by Humans and their Human surrogate parents stop by periodically to check up on them. After six months, they begin specialized schooling to prepare them to enter either the

Academy here on Vesta or the fleet training facility on the Moon."

"From the time they're awakened, how long before they're fully capable of taking over their military responsibilities?" Beth asked.

"Five years," Marken answered, promptly.

"How many decide not to join the military?"

Marken hesitated for a moment. "Actually a slightly larger percentage than we originally projected. Currently, nearly twelve percent of the clones elect to take civilian jobs, though most of those jobs do involve the military in some way."

Beth nodded; she had already been familiar with some of this from what Wade had told her in previous conversations. She knew Wade came to the cloning facility on occasion to check up on its progress as he had been instrumental in talking President Randle into instituting the program to begin with.

"The clones plus our regular Human volunteers are allowing us to greatly expand the fleet as well as our ground forces," Wade added as he watched another clone take its first hesitant steps. "Nearly one hundred and twenty thousand Human born volunteered for military duty last year and we expect about the same this year."

"Not bad out of eighteen million people," commented Beth, thoughtfully.

Wade watched as several more clones were awakened and processed. They seemed so innocent in their newborn state. He turned and looked over at Beth, who was watching the awakening process with keen interest.

"We're taking both the military troop transports," Wade informed her. They had some important decisions to make as far as personnel went. "I'm putting you in charge of the Fire Fox and Major Jeffries in charge of the Crimson Star. Both of you need to pick your command staffs and what marine companies the two of you want deployed on each ship. For this mission, the assault ships will only have a small complement of marines on board."

Beth turned her attention away from the awakening chamber to focus her eyes on Wade. "I want Captain Stern and Captain Foster's two companies for sure," she responded without a moment's hesitation. "I suspect Major Jeffries will want Captain Perry's company."

Wade nodded. He'd expected that. "We'll be gone from two to six months," he added in a softer voice. "You need to tell your mother, and I need to speak with my parents."

"What about Ryan?" asked Beth her eyes focusing intently on Wade. "Are you going to talk to him?" She knew her mother wouldn't be happy with her being gone for such an extended time, particularly after moving into the retirement center.

"Probably just a short message. When we return, he should be finished with his training and will be getting his first assignment."

Wade let out a deep breath. He knew Ryan would easily qualify in the Type Four suits; it also meant he would be getting some of the toughest and more dangerous assignments. The Type Four battlesuits were designed to take on armored members of the Kleese race, most likely the Zaltule.

Harnett and I will be accompanying you on this mission," Marken said his narrow eyes focusing on the two Humans. "There will also be ten other Kiveans going along to give support from a technical perspective as well as assisting in the negotiations. There are several Kiveans from our home world highly familiar with some of the races we'll be speaking to."

"Marken?" Beth said, inquiringly. "What do you think the odds are that some of the nonaligned worlds will join us?"

"We've pretty much determined which ones were involved with giving us the information on the computer drive as well as the nonaligned world ship that gave us the warning about the Kleese attack," he said slowly as he thought hard about the different races. "I'm certain we can turn six or seven of them to our cause, but we need more. The Kleese have an Empire to draw their resources from, whereas we will only have a few worlds."

"Unless we can sow discontent on more of the Kleese controlled planets," Wade pointed out. He had spoken in considerable length with General Mitchell about launching more clandestine attacks in an attempt to tie down some of the Kleese warfleet.

"What concerns me is what the Kleese and the Zaltule are up to now," Marken said his eyes showing worry. "They may start moving against some of the nonaligned worlds any day now, particularly those closer to the central part of their Empire."

Wade nodded; he knew they needed to get the mission launched as soon as possible. He was afraid they were rapidly running out of time.

Harmock winced as his flagship, the Warrior's Fire, was bracketed by multiple antimatter missiles. The ship's energy screen was showing stress as it glowed brightly under the mounting attack. Harmock stood upon the Command Pedestal of his flagship, gazing with rapt attention at the numerous viewscreens and tactical displays showing the fighting around the Warrior's Fire. He'd brought two hundred Zaltule warships to the Talt system to pacify the nonaligned world and bring it permanently into the grasp of the Empire. The Talts were a humanoid species with large yellow eyes and a very dark complexion.

His fleet had been met by sixty smaller warships, all with incredible weaponry. Twelve of his warships lay in ruin, split apart by some type of massive plasma round that smashed through a ship's energy screen and caused tremendous damage to the interior. Fortunately, the weapon took time to recharge or his fleet would have suffered far heavier losses.

"Firing primary pulse fusion beams," Minor Overlord Gareth reported as the Warrior's Fire unleashed twenty powerful fusion beams upon the nearest Talt ship.

The Talt ships were four hundred meters long and spindle-shaped. Their maneuvering ability was remarkable, making them even more difficult to hit. A pulse fusion beam needed a few seconds on target to inflict appreciable damage. The beams on a Zaltule warship were powered by dual fusion reactors and could project a massive amount of energy.

The Talt ship darted out of the way after only suffering a microsecond's worth of fire from the deadly beams. It spun around and a fiery red plasma bolt darted toward the Warrior's Fire. It struck the energy shield, clung to it, and then burned through, striking the ship's heavy armor and penetrating into the interior of the ship, setting off several large explosions.

Harmock felt his flagship shake violently and warning alarms began sounding. He cursed silently to himself, knowing his flagship had been seriously damaged.

"Secondary Engineering has been destroyed," Gareth reported nearly stumbling off the Command Pedestal as the ship shook violently. His six legs managed to keep him upright as he continued to study the data coming in on the damage done to the ship. "Fusion cannons seven, nine, and twelve have been destroyed. Energy beam turrets twenty, twenty-one, and thirty are no longer responding. We are streaming atmosphere and I'm locking down the damaged areas of the ship."

"I want our ships to attack in groups of four," Harmock ordered, infuriated that a lesser race would dare to damage his flagship. "Switch to sublight antimatter missiles and use volley fire upon these vermin. We'll see if their ships can dodge a hundred missiles coming toward them at sublight speeds."

The orders were quickly passed and the remaining Zaltule ships formed up into their designated groups. Once assembled, they began advancing toward the waiting enemy.

-

The Talt reformed their fleet and waited to see what the Kleese would do next. The Talt commander had hoped that if enough Zaltule ships were destroyed in the early part of the engagement the Kleese would decide to honor the neutrality agreement. Now the Talt commander was beginning to have his doubts. His greatest weapon was the plasma rounds and the speed of the Talt ships, but he was badly outnumbered.

With trepidation, he watched the Kleese warships form up into groups of four and begin advancing. He was outnumbered by nearly three to one, which would mean that each of his warships would have to engage a group of Zaltule ships. However, he would not play into the Zaltule's hands. If his fleet was to be destroyed and his world conquered by the Zaltule, then he would teach the Zaltule a lesson that might make them hesitant about attacking other nonaligned worlds.

The commander had already sent word back to his home planet that all the designs for the plasma weapon were to be destroyed as well as all military research. The plans for the highly maneuverable sublight drive his ships were equipped with were also to be destroyed. That type of advanced technology would not be allowed to fall into the hands of the dreaded Kleese.

"It is time," Commander Cribbs spoke, his large yellow eyes focusing on his second in command. "Send word to Commander Pasha that his mission is confirmed."

Sub Commander Leyen stepped over to Communications and quickly passed on the message to the ships hidden behind the home world and away from the Kleese sensor scans. Four ships waited in their world's shadow; there were two warships and a couple of large passenger ships. In the past few years, rumors had spread through the nonaligned worlds of a civilization far out on the edge of the Empire, which had dared to challenge the Kleese. These ships would be leaving in an attempt to find that world. The two largest ships contained scientists and their families who, if all else failed, would flee to the far edge of the galaxy to begin a new Talt civilization.

"Take us in," Cribbs ordered grimly, knowing there would be no surviving this battle. "All ships to attack in groups of three and hit the right quadrant of the Kleese formation."

-

Harmock watched as the Talt ships began shifting about and suddenly started accelerating toward one section of his fleet. He swiftly sent out new orders as he recognized what the Talt were attempting. He would wheel his other ships around and hit the

Talt from their flank as they hit his fleet formation. He would pin them between two walls of warships.

The two fleets closed and the Zaltule warships let loose with a barrage of antimatter missiles, their missiles far outranging the Talt's deadly plasma weapons. In the Talt formation, massive explosions danced across energy shields, overloading a number of them. Whenever that happened, the Talt ship vanished as antimatter energy annihilated it. Twelve ships quickly died and then the Kleese ships hit the flank of the Talt formation. More missiles were fired and sixteen additional Talt ships vanished in flashes of fiery death. Then the Talts were in range of the Kleese warships and their plasma weapons fired.

Balls of fiery orange-red plasma energy struck the three-kilometer Zaltule warships, burning through energy screens and impacting the armored hulls. Large sections of hull plating were blasted loose into space and then interior explosions caused even more damage. Eight Kleese warships were hit by multiple plasma rounds and died a quick death as the intense heat of the plasma killed the ships.

Harmock watched impassively as the icons representing the Zaltule warships dropped off the tactical screen. It would take a short amount of time for the Talt ships to recharge their weapons. While they were doing that, every ship in his fleet was firing sublight antimatter missiles in waves at the darting and dodging enemy ships. On one of the tactical screens, he watched as Talt ship after Talt ship met its fiery death.

-

Commander Cribbs grimaced as another one of his warships blew apart under the unrelenting attack of the Kleese. He was making them pay for every ship the Kleese were destroying, but he was too heavily outnumbered. They should never have trusted the Kleese to keep their word on the neutrality agreement. They should also have built up a much larger fleet to defend their world. Now they would pay for that lack of foresight with the loss of their freedom.

"We only have four ships left," Sub Commander Leyen reported as the flagship shuddered violently and the lights flickered. "Our plasma weapon is recharged."

"Fire it!" uttered Cribbs his yellow eyes focusing on his second in command. "Shortly we will go and join our ancestors."

Leyen nodded as the weapons officer fired the plasma weapon one last time.

On the main viewscreen, Cribbs and Leyen watched as their weapon impacted the screen of the nearest Kleese ship, burning through and striking the ship's armor. A massive explosion indicated the plasma round had struck something vital.

Before Leyen could say another word, a Kleese antimatter missile flashed through the ship's weakening shield and the Talt flagship ceased to be.

-

"Last enemy ship has been neutralized," Gareth reported his multifaceted eyes focusing on the War Overlord.

"What were our losses?" demanded Harmock, still finding it hard to believe a lower race such as the Talt could inflict such losses upon his fleet.

"Thirty vessels destroyed and another eighteen are reporting heavy damage," Gareth reported.

Harmock was beginning to understand why the Council of Overlords had left these worlds alone. "Move us into orbit around the Talt home planet and have our ground forces prepare to invade. "We'll take the capital city and all of the spaceports on the planet's surface."

"There's a large orbiting space station above the planet," Gareth added.

"We'll destroy it after we have searched it for any technology we may find of interest," proclaimed Harmock. "The Talt will no longer be allowed access to space. Have our scientists and technicians ready to board the station once we go into orbit."

Harmock had been surprised at the ferocity of the attack by the Talt ships. Back in the home system, new Zaltule warships were nearing completion. If the rest of the nonaligned worlds were as difficult to conquer as this one, they would be needed. The Talt would make useful servants to the Empire. It would be the new order of things; all races would be subservient to the Kleese. As long as they obeyed and provided a useful service they would be allowed to continue to exist; if found otherwise then the surface of the offending planet would be cleansed of all life.

Harmock gazed at the main viewscreen in the Command Center as they neared the Talt planet. For now, he would allow Xatul to continue to rule as head of the council. However, once Harmock had subdued all of the nonaligned worlds, he fully intended to take over command of the Council of Overlords and become the Supreme Leader of the Kleese race and Empire. An Empire ruled by the Zaltule that would someday control the entire galaxy.

Chapter Six

Ryan waited with some impatience outside the door to Major Stevens' office. It had been two days since his platoon had conquered Charring Mountain and it was strangely quiet inside the dome. There had been no drills or additional instructions though Ryan had taken his platoon out for routine physical training and a five-kilometer run.

Casey was sitting next to him fidgeting nervously with her hands in her lap. She knew this interview was going to be very important and she wanted to do her best. This was the hard part for her, running the platoon was much easier as she had a structured system in place set up by the military to go by; this was different.

"What do you think they'll ask us?" she spoke, looking over at Ryan expectantly. "I hope we all qualify for this special program, especially if it involves the new battlesuits."

"I'm sure we qualified," answered Ryan, trying to sound confident. He was feeling a little nervous also. If for some unknown reason he'd failed to qualify, he didn't know how he would be able to face his older brother.

The door to Major Stevens' office opened and Major Winfrey stepped out. He looked at the two young marines and then gestured for them to enter. "Major Stevens is ready to see you now."

Ryan glanced at Casey and then stood up and walked through the door. Casey followed close behind. Winfrey shut the door behind them but didn't enter.

They found themselves in a small well-organized office with a bookcase on one wall and numerous photos of various fleet ships on another. Major Stevens was sitting behind a large desk, looking at two files in manila folders he was holding in his hands.

Mark laid the two folders down and gazed curiously at the two young marines coming into his office. For that was what they were now that they had conquered Charring. They stopped in front of his desk and came to attention, both saluting.

Mark stood up, returned the salute, and gestured for the two to sit down in the comfortable chairs in front of his desk. "I want to congratulate the two of you on reaching the top of the mountain," he began as he sat back down. "I watched part of the drill and it was quite interesting. I'm curious, Lieutenant Nelson, as to why you decided to use primarily energy weapons in your assault upon Charring."

Wade took a deep breath as he thought over his reply. He wondered if this was a test of some kind. "Corporal Hunter and I talked about numerous strategies to use for getting to the summit," Ryan began to explain. "Everything we discussed seemed as if it would end in failure. There was just no way to get to the top of the mountain with enough of the platoon and working weapons left to allow us to win."

"Do you agree with that summation, Corporal Hunter?" asked Major Stevens as his eyes focused on the young woman.

"Yes, Sir," answered Casey, looking confused. "The more we studied different strategies, the more apparent it became that Charring was a no win situation. The scenario is designed so no one can possibly reach the reset button on top of the mountain."

"Why would that be the case? Why have a no win scenario?" Stevens asked, curious to hear her reply.

"The battlesuits give the occupants superior strength and speed," Casey began, looking over at Wade who nodded slightly. "You have enhanced vision optics and various sensors to help locate and eliminate the enemy. The suits are impervious to most types of weapons and allow you to carry a tremendous amount of firepower. In most situations, a marine wearing a battlesuit has nothing to fear from the opposition."

"But that's not the case on Charring," pointed out Stevens. "The RG rounds, while they won't penetrate the suit armor, still sting and the stunners are extremely painful."

"That's the point of Charring," Ryan interjected in a calm voice. "Charring is to teach us that the suits aren't as invulnerable as we're led to believe in our earlier training. We'll be going up against enemy combatants who have the weaponry to damage or even destroy a battlesuit. We need to learn caution and not to take the battlesuits for granted. Strategy must play a role in any scenario where there will be combat, and we should resist the temptation to just try to bull our way through the opposition."

"Then how did you manage to win?" Stevens asked his eyes looking penetratingly at Ryan. "You shouldn't have been able to win if it's a no win scenario."

"Sacrifice," Ryan answered with a deep sigh. "I calculated that if we cut a narrow swath up the mountain and used our weapons to clear out the popups on our flanks we just might be able to reach the top. Or at least a few of us would." Ryan hesitated, not sure if he wanted to explain the rest of the strategy he and Casey had come up with.

Mark was silent for a moment as he contemplated the lieutenant's words. "So, you decided to sacrifice members of your platoon to clear out the weapons on your flanks as you burned a narrow path up the mountain. Is that what you're telling me?" Mark looked coldly at Ryan.

"Yes, Sir," replied Ryan unabashedly, as he realized the major was too smart not to figure out what they had done. "It was the only way to win and I don't believe in losing, Sir."

"Did your soldiers know you were planning on sacrificing most of them to get to the top? Charring is supposed to be about adapting to the changing scenario to save lives, not to lose them."

"No," answered Ryan, uneasily. "We decided it was best not to tell them. We realized in this no win scenario that there was more emphasis being placed on learning strategy and trying to save lives; it wasn't designed to take intentional sacrifices into account. It was the only way we could beat the mountain and that's what we decided to do."

"You just barely made it to the top," Mark said as he leaned back in his chair and focused his steady eyes on Ryan. "If you had lost one more soldier or had taken one less energy weapon, you never would have made it and your sacrifices would have been in vain."

Ryan and Casey remained quiet. They didn't know if they were about to be reprimanded or what. It didn't sound as if the major was happy about what they had done. They knew in some ways, due to how the scenario on Charring was designed, they had technically cheated by refusing to play by the rules.

"This war we're in is a tough one," Mark said as his eyes focused on the two. He'd studied their files and been highly impressed. Ryan had graduated in the top ten percent of his class at the Academy on Vesta and could have been an officer in the fleet. Corporal Hunter had excelled as well, particularly in the science part of the curriculum. "We're vastly outnumbered by a race that thinks it's superior to us in every way. In their eyes, we're nothing more than vermin that needs to be wiped out. If we're going to win, we have to take risks and make sacrifices. That's what you did on Charring and I offer you my congratulations. While it wasn't what we were expecting, it was an innovative way to beat the mountain. I'm sure Major Winfrey will be modifying the scenario so this can't work a second time."

Mark opened the top drawer in his desk and took out a sheet of paper with a full lieutenant's insignia attached. "Second Lieutenant Ryan Nelson, effective today you are being promoted in rank to full lieutenant."

Ryan took the promotion paper and insignia and gazed at it in surprise. He hadn't been expecting this. "I guess this means we qualified for the special project we signed up for?"

"Yes," Mark replied his voice becoming much more serious. "Three other platoons will be joining you shortly in the training dome. As you have probably already guessed this training involves the new Type Four battlesuits. If we're going to beat the Kleese, we need every advantage we can possibly get and these suits will help to provide one. The training will be difficult and not everyone will make it through. For those that do, you'll be leading the fight against the Kleese to help ensure the survival of our race."

"So, we're staying in this dome?" asked Casey, surprised. She'd been assuming they would be moving to a different one for the advanced training.

"Yes," Mark answered as he stood up and walked over to the only window in the room. He looked out at Charring Mountain and then turned back around to face the two new Space Marines. "You will be pleased to know that you're not quite done with the mountain yet. Once you've become acclimated to the new suits, your platoon will once again have to reach the summit, only this time I can assure you the tactics you used this last time won't work."

Casey looked over at Ryan and sighed deeply. "I guess we're going to need a new strategy."

"Sounds like it," Ryan answered. He'd hoped to be through with Charring Mountain, but it looked as if it was once more waiting in his future.

Major Stevens watched as the two young marines left his office. He allowed himself to smile, knowing that Colonel Nelson would be pleased to find out that his younger brother had breezed through the first phase of the training. Wade and Mark had discussed Ryan's entry into the program in some depth.

This first company of Space Marines, once they had qualified in the Type Four suits, would be assigned immediately to a combat role to test them out against the Kleese. The survival rate of this first group wouldn't be too high as they would be pitted against the stiffest opposition that could be found. Wade had insisted that Ryan be treated like any other applicant and so far, Mark had made that happen. He'd ensure this group had the best training possible and the most powerful weapons they could handle. He would also be going into combat with them.

-

Colonel Wade Nelson was in the main Control Center inside of Vesta. The asteroid had four large habitats with nearly six million people, making it one of the largest concentrations of humanity left in the solar system.

"So, your brother qualified for the new battlesuits," commented President Mason Randle standing next to Wade.

"Yes, Sir," Wade answered. "He begins his training almost immediately."

"We're going to need men like him," Mason said as he looked across the busy Control Center.

It was strange not seeing Pamela Cairns around, but she'd retired to finish raising her family. Her son was now sixteen and she had a two-year-old that was occupying much of her time. She still put in an appearance now and then, but she had turned her work over to Jessica Lang.

"This war will be getting much more intense shortly," General Bailey added from where he was standing next to the military consoles listening to the two talk. He turned and walked over closer to Mason and Wade. "Fleet Admiral Kelly is ordering more fleet drills and General Mitchell is having additional ion cannons installed around all habitats. He's also issued orders to make sure all the deep bunkers are adequately stocked and for everyone to run some routine emergency drills."

"A necessary precaution," responded Mason, folding his arms across his chest. He looked over at Wade and continued. "A lot is riding on your mission, Colonel; we have to coerce some of those nonaligned worlds to come into our Alliance."

"We'll get it done," promised Wade, drawing in a sharp breath. "We won't come back until the Alliance is an actual fact."

"I know you will," Mason replied with a nod. "General Bailey, I'll be setting up some evacuation drills for Vesta in the next few days to practice getting our people down into the secure bunkers; I need you to coordinate the military part of the drill with the vice president. We'll be scheduling at least two additional drills that will involve all the habitats across the solar system."

Ralph Steward had come a long way since the council was originally formed and had now taken on the job of vice president. There was little doubt he would win the upcoming election and take over as president. Mason was satisfied that Steward would make an excellent choice and had no qualms about turning over the presidency to the talented politician.

"I'll contact him later today," Bailey responded with a nod. "I'll also have military personnel coordinate with the proper civilian authorities to check on the emergency supplies in the bunkers. They're reviewed routinely each year, but it never hurts to perform a more scrutinized inspection in case something was overlooked."

Mason looked around the Control Center one more time. Much had changed in the last six years, with the military presence growing considerably. Over a third of the people operating the numerous consoles now had some type of military training. Turning, he headed for the hatch. He was meeting Adrienne in the Viridian habitat for lunch and then they were going shopping to pick out some baby clothes. Adrienne was six months' pregnant and they were having a baby girl. They had decided, with Mason's decision not to run for another term, it was time to start a family.

A little later, Mason stepped out into the habitat. He paused as he gazed out over the remarkable world they had created inside the massive asteroid. It almost looked as if a part of Earth had been taken and placed within the surrounding rock. The habitat extended for kilometers, with verdant farmland on the periphery and a big, modern city running down its center. Large apartment buildings towered nearly forty stories and the city was full of green, as trees and parks were abundant. The city had been built with the aid of Kivean construction technology.

It took him a few more minutes to make it to the restaurant where he was meeting Adrienne. He also knew that his sister, Susan Kirby, was coming along. Susan was so excited to be helping. She'd screamed loudly with joy when they'd given her the news about Adrienne's pregnancy. The two girls, Candace and Karen had been thrilled also at the thought of a new cousin. It was still hard to accept that those two were now in high school and Karen would soon be graduating. Karen had already announced her intentions to study Kivean medical science and Harnett had agreed to help her in that endeavor.

Two security personnel were walking slightly behind Mason to ensure there were no incidents. Mason wasn't too concerned since crime inside Vesta was literally non-existent. He noticed a large sign in the window of one of the stores and stopped to examine it. A frown crossed his face as he read the words.

"NO CLONES ALLOWED. THIS STORE IS FOR HUMAN BORN ONLY!!!

"That sign wasn't there two days ago," one of the security guards commented. "Do you want us to have it removed?"

"No," Mason said, drawing in a sharp breath. "I'll bring this up to the council and see what they recommend." He didn't want to cause a scene and the cloning situation was a hot topic anyway with the civilian population. It was far wiser to let the council handle this.

Mason turned and began walking down the busy sidewalk toward the restaurant. He let out a deep sigh of disappointment. That sign wasn't the only one that had appeared recently. There were others scattered about as many people, even here inside Vesta, were against the cloning project.

Cheryl Robinson had launched numerous ad campaigns trying to change public opinion, but it had done very little to sway the masses. There had even been a few demonstrations against the clones, but nothing violent. They'd known from the beginning there would be problems when they instituted the program, but they'd greatly underestimated how opposed the average Human would be.

Reaching the restaurant, Mason went inside while his two security guards took up a protective stance near the entrance. They would make sure Mason and his family weren't bothered while they ate. In many ways, Mason would be glad to turn his presidency over to Steward. He'd carried so much on his shoulders since the original Kleese attack on Earth. Now all he wanted to do was raise his family.

-

Ryan stood with the rest of his platoon on the parade field of the training dome. Three other platoons had joined his and were waiting patiently for Major Stevens to put in an appearance. The minutes passed slowly by and the marines stood still, standing at attention in their respective formations. Ryan could hear a few marines starting to whisper to one another as they wondered how long they'd have to stand here waiting on the major.

"Look up," Corporal Hunter spoke in a quiet voice that held a hint of awe.

Ryan looked up and was startled to see what looked like a battlesuit descending down toward them. Ryan estimated it must be a good five hundred meters up in the air. His first thought was that the suit was falling and then he noticed controlled movements as the suit began to slow and finally landed nimbly directly in front of the assembled marines. It became very quiet as everyone's eyes focused on the battlesuit, wondering who its occupant was.

"As you were," Major Stevens's voice boomed from the suit. "This is a Type Four battlesuit. It's equipped with antigravity plates in the feet, which when used properly will allow limited flight." He then reached down and drew an Energy Lance from his waist, igniting it and moving the glowing blue rod through several impressive movements before bringing it down on a block of metal sitting in front of him, cleaving it in two. He then put the lance back in its protective sheath at his waist.

Ryan began examining the new Type Four battlesuit, realizing that it seemed smaller and more form fitting than the Type Three or Type Twos. He wondered if that meant it had fewer weapons and was more dependent on speed and maneuverability. The suit was black and gray with small red lights at the joints and other areas on the suit. It looked nimble and quick.

As if reading his mind, Major Stevens removed the RG rifle from his shoulder and aimed it at a nearby target on the firing range. He fired a short burst and the target exploded into hundreds of pieces. He then switched the rifle to a different setting and fired two explosive shells at another target, which was instantly obliterated.

"The new RG rifle has three different settings," he explained as he took several steps closer to the assembled marines cradling the rifle in his metal arms. "The first fires regular RG rounds, which you're all familiar with. The second fires explosive tipped RG rounds and the third fires regular explosive shells. All the rounds and shells have been greatly reduced in size, allowing the rifle to hold nearly double the amount of ammunition that a regular RG rifle holds."

He then turned to his side so everyone could see the twin tubes on the back of the suit. There was also a third and larger tube in the center.

"The suit does have two explosive round tubes on the back," Stevens continued in a lecturing tone. "However, instead of holding twenty shells each, these hold forty. Once again the size of the shells have been greatly reduced."

"What's that one in the middle?" asked Private Parker. He'd been looking closely at it and had no clue as to its purpose. It looked markedly different than the explosive shell tubes.

"That's our special surprise for the Kleese," Stevens replied in a much more serious tone. "The center tube contains four small nuclear tipped shells capable of leveling an area one hundred meters across. These shells are special developments of the Kivean military research department. They use fusion to create the nuclear reaction and leave very little radiation when they explode."

"We're going to be carrying nuclear weapons on our backs!" exclaimed Private Swen his eyes growing wide with concern. "What if one goes off accidentally? It would wipe out everyone around it!"

"They can't go off accidentally," Stevens said in a reassuring voice. "There have been some safeguards added to ensure marines can't be killed from friendly fire. The weapons also have to be activated from a neuro transmitter in the commanding officer's battlesuit."

"What's a neuro transmitter?" asked Casey, suddenly feeling nervous. She didn't like the sound of that.

"It's a small device inserted into the cerebral cortex of the brain to allow for direct control of weapons, sensors, communications, and other battlesuit functions just by thinking about what you want the suit to do. Everyone in the program will have one surgically implanted so as to be able to use the new suits."

The marines grew very silent as they wondered about what they'd volunteered for. Everyone had a language communication device implanted in their brains about the size of a pea; this had been done on their first day of training. This neuro transmitter sounded like something far more complicated and possibly painful.

"I can assure you the procedure is completely painless and once you become acclimated to the transmitter, you won't even know it's there," Stevens informed them. "You may experience a day or two of discomfort as your system adapts to the transmitter, but it will open up a whole new world of combat information and maximize the use of the new battlesuits. The suit will seem like a part of your body and will make the Type Three suits seem quite primitive."

"When would we have this surgery?" asked Ryan, wondering how many members of his platoon were having second thoughts.

"This afternoon," Stevens responded as he turned to gaze out over the assembled marines. "The surgeons are standing by and we can process all four platoons by the end of the evening."

"And it's absolutely safe?" questioned Private Swen with an uncertain look on his face. He didn't like the idea of having his brain operated on and another device inserted.

"Yes," Stevens answered. "I've had the surgery as well as my training staff. There is one more thing I want to say. This neural transmitter will make you and the Type Four battlesuits the most deadly fighting instrument the Human race has ever created. If we win the war against the Kleese, these suits and the marines operating them will play a major, if not the defining, role in that victory."

"Guess we're getting operated on," spoke Casey in a soft voice, glancing over at Ryan. "I really want this." The military was Casey's home and she was willing to do anything if it would make her a better marine.

"Guess so," responded Ryan still keeping his eyes on the major.

"I realize this is something a few of you may feel hesitation about doing," added Major Stevens. "You have two hours to decide if you want to be a part of this training. If you decide against it, all you have to do is report to my office. You'll be transferred back to a platoon who will be using the Type Three battlesuits and there will be no black mark on your military record."

There was a slight shuffling in the ranks as the marines looked around at each other wondering what everyone was thinking. A few looked distressed as if they didn't like what they had just heard.

"Two hours," Stevens spoke, evenly. He then turned and trotted off toward his office, which was on the far side of the parade grounds.

"Another piece of crap in my head," mumbled Alexander as he reached up and rubbed his hair.

"They probably won't shave all of your hair off," ribbed Lauren with a wolfish grin. "Just a patch right down the center."

Private Swen walked over to the two with a concerned frown on his face. "If this surgery turns me into a robot, just shoot me!"

"You could be a plaything for Lauren," Alexander spoke with a wide grin spreading across his face. "Just think; you could answer to her every whim. I bet she has a really good imagination, if you know what I mean."

Alexander let out a loud bellow as Lauren punched him in the stomach, driving the air out of his lungs. "The only plaything I want is you for a punching bag!"

"Sorry," Alexander spoke with a painful grimace. "I was only joking."

"Sometimes, you just don't know when to shut up!" Lauren turned and began walking toward the barracks. She thought it might be a good idea to get in some sack time before the surgery and she was still a little aggravated at Alexander.

Private Swen watched as Lauren headed away from them, and then he turned toward Private Parker. "You know, one of these days you're going to make her really mad and when you do she's going to tear your head off."

Alexander was silent for a moment as he watched Lauren leaving. "Lauren's a great marine," he said as he turned back to Private Swen. "I guess I just have a hard time admitting she's as good as me."

"Better in some things," Swen pointed out. "She'll make corporal before you do."

"Great!" muttered Alexander with a grimace. "Then my life will really be a nightmare."

Ryan was still talking to Casey about the impending surgery when he noticed two of the other platoon lieutenants walking over.

"Hello," the taller one spoke. "I'm Brice Felton."

"And I'm Autumn Guthrie," the blonde headed woman spoke.

"Wade Nelson and this is Corporal Casey Hunter."

"Didn't I see you at the Academy on Vesta?" Casey asked. She thought Brice had been in some of her classes; it was also obvious he was a clone.

"Possibly," Brice responded. "There were a lot of us in those classes."

"What do you think about this surgery?' asked Autumn, crossing her arms over her chest. "This is something way different than what I was expecting. It sounds as if our brains are being hardwired to the suits."

"It's a logical development," Casey said her eyes looking thoughtful. "We already have the translation device implanted in our heads and this won't be much different. It'll give us a direct connection to our battlesuits and should make our response times almost instantaneous."

"I can see where that would be useful in a battle," conceded Autumn.

"You're Colonel Nelson's brother, aren't you?" asked Brice. He'd seen the colonel on several occasions back on Vesta.

"Yes," Ryan answered. He let out a deep breath; everyone knew his brother and what he and Beth had done freeing the Kiveans from the Kleese and their subsequent battles.

"Did he say anything to you about the Type Four battlesuits?"

"No, not a thing," Ryan answered. "He wouldn't, anyway."

Brice nodded. "I've only heard the best about your brother, I'm glad to see we have a Nelson in this program."

Ryan felt surprised but nodded his head. "Do either of you think any of your marines will back out?"

"A few might," admitted Autumn as she could see several animatedly talking to each other and gesturing. "I think when we start talking about brain surgery and what it might imply as far as these suits go; a few might be hesitant about going on with the program."

"We can only wait and see," added Brice with a nod of agreement. "I guess we'll know in the morning.

Ryan looked around and saw that most of the assembled marines were gradually making their way toward the barracks and the mess hall.

"I think I'm going to go get something light to eat and talk to some of my platoon to see if they have any questions. I'd really like to see all of them enter the program; they're a good bunch."

"I believe we all feel that way about our platoons," Brice responded. "We probably should make ourselves available and the mess hall is as good as anywhere else."

"Then let's do it," Ryan said as he began walking across the parade grounds with the others following closely behind.

He hoped he was making the right decision. It sounded as if the Type Four battlesuits were going to be in the thick of the fighting, something he knew his parents wouldn't want to hear, particularly his mother. Both of his parents had encouraged him to join the fleet, but the marines and the battlesuits had been too big a temptation. He just hoped he wouldn't come to regret that decision.

Chapter Seven

Colonel Wade Nelson was in the Command Center of the battlecruiser Constellation as it pulled away from Vesta and moved out away from the asteroid field to join the rest of Seventh Fleet. As he watched Vesta gradually diminish on the viewscreen and then finally disappear, he let out a deep sigh. They were finally ready to start their mission and would soon be entering Fold Space to head for the first nonaligned world on their long list. He wondered what lay ahead for the fleet and the mission.

"Fleet is ready to initiate Fold Space entry upon your order," Commander Shepherd informed Admiral Adamson.

"We may be gone for a long time," commented Adamson from his position next to Wade where he too had been watching the viewscreens.

"This is an important mission," responded Wade, glancing over at the admiral. "There's a very good chance we'll be involved in some heavy combat, both on the ground and in space."

"We're going to remind the Kleese we're still around," Adamson pointed out. "This could be a very dangerous game we're playing, and we're going to be a long way from home if anything goes wrong."

"It's the hand we've been dealt," answered Wade, evenly.

On the viewscreen, the rest of the ships were coming into view. Overall, there were two hundred and twenty-six ships in the newly formed Seventh Fleet. This would be the largest and most powerful fleet ever to leave the solar system. It would definitely be a wakeup call to the Kleese once it was detected.

"We're moving into position between the Falcon and the Rampage," reported Lieutenant Percy Lash, who was sitting in front of the ship's primary sensor console. The Falcon and the Rampage were two of the three new battlecruisers assigned to Seventh Fleet; the third was the Firebolt.

"All ships stand by to enter Fold Space," Adamson ordered over the fleet com connecting to all ships. "Initiate two minute countdown on my mark." Adamson waited a few seconds and then spoke once more. "Mark!"

"Message from President Randle," Lieutenant Emma Travers reported from Communications. "He says good luck and he'll be waiting for good news."

"One minute to Fold Space Drive activation," spoke Lieutenant Jase Martin from the Helm. "All system functioning normally."

"Message from Fleet Admiral Kelly and General Mitchell," added Lieutenant Travers. "Message says 'good hunting'."

Adamson allowed himself to smile. The messages themselves served to indicate just how important everyone considered this mission to be.

"Fold Space Drive activation in ten seconds," Martin spoke in an even voice. "Five, Four, Three, Two, One, Activation!"

In Engineering, the Fold Space Drive began generating an energy field in front to the ship, warping the very fabric of space. In this area, the laws of physics were slightly different than in the normal Einstein Universe. The space directly in front of the ship was suddenly drawn in upon itself, making the distance between two points shrink substantially. The greater strain the Fold Space Drive put upon the space directly in front of the ship the greater the warping effect, allowing the ship to travel at speeds many multiples of the speed of light. To the casual observer, without the advanced sensors to detect the warping effect, it would seem as if the ship had just suddenly vanished as it exceeded light speed.

"All ships have made the transition into Fold Space," Commander Shepherd confirmed as she checked with several of the Command Center personnel.

"All ships reporting normal operations," Travers added as she listened to the multitude of messages coming in over her Communications console.

"Engineering reports Fold Space Drive operating within normal parameters," Commander Shepherd stated, satisfied that the ship was finally underway.

Wade glanced at the tactical screen showing a jumble of green icons, which designated the estimated location of fleet ships. At the speed they were traveling, the icons were only a computer-generated estimate of where the ships were in relation to the Constellation. Fortunately, one of the side effects of the Fold Space Drive was that no two ships could occupy the same point in space as the drive formed a small protective spatial bubble, which would repel an identical bubble or, in simpler terms, push it gently away. Of course no one was certain what the results of a head on collision would be. Scientists had been hesitant to attempt such a collision as several top Kivean space scientists had suggested it might result in an actual rip in space-time.

They were going nearly fifteen hundred light years, which was a flight time of approximately twenty days during which the fleet would drop out of Fold Space four times for routine maintenance checks. The new Fold Space Drives the ships were equipped with allowed for a cruising speed of nearly eighty light years per day, though the new battlecruisers were capable of slightly over ninety.

Looking at the green icons on the tactical screen, Wade wondered which one was the Fire Fox where Beth was. Beth and Major Jeffries were planning to work on battle simulations in case they had to drive the Kleese from one of the nonaligned worlds. Each time the fleet dropped out of Fold Space he planned on going over to the Fire Fox for a strategy meeting if time permitted. He also wanted to see his wife on occasion as this could be a long mission.

-

Ryan flexed his metal encased hand, still feeling awe at the sensations the suit generated within his mind. The Type Four battlesuit was eight feet tall and made out of a new type of composite material, which was stronger and lighter than that of the Type Three suits. It allowed for greater flexibility in movement that at times made the wearer almost forget he or she was encased inside one. In addition, the Type Four suit was capable of operating in full combat conditions for nearly twenty hours before needing to be recharged. In non-combat situations, the suit could keep its wearer alive for well over a week.

Ryan recalled the first time he'd put on the Type Four battlesuit. They went on the same as the Type Threes; the suits opened up in the front and you stepped backward into the suit and allowed it to seal up around you. Many marines felt a momentary sense of claustrophobia during that brief moment as the suit sealed off the outside world. Activating and controlling the suit was also much different and had taken some getting used to.

In the Type Fours, a microscopic wire entered the base of your neck and connected to the neuro transmitter inside the cortex. Ryan knew that on the back of his neck was a small insertion port protected by titanium about the size of a dime. The suit connected to the port and then sent a microscopic wire snaking along a miniscule titanium tunnel leading to the neuro transmitter buried deep inside Ryan's brain.

"All right, Lieutenant Nelson; you can come down now."

Ryan looked down at Sergeant Olivia Morris, who was helping him operate the antigravity repeller plates in the feet of his suit. For the last ten minutes, he'd been hovering in the air about ten meters above the ground. The antigravity plates generated a repelling force, which allowed the Type Four battlesuit a limited flying ability. It was something exceedingly difficult to control as Ryan and numerous others in his platoon had learned the hard way when they'd slammed into the ground on several occasions. There had even been a few broken limbs, but medical nanites had made quick repairs to the broken bones and tissue, getting the marines back into the training program within just a few days.

Ryan directed the suit back down, knowing that the suit's on board computer system would keep him balanced until his feet touched the parade grounds. He breathed a sigh of relief as he touched down and didn't stumble.

"You didn't crash this time," commented Casey, who'd been watching Ryan with interest. She was next in line after the lieutenant.

"It becomes more automatic with time, just like walking," spoke Sergeant Morris as she turned to face Corporal Hunter. She'd formerly been in Major Winfrey's British Special Forces group and volunteered for the initial Type Four training along with Captain Taylor. Now they were serving as instructors. "You have to learn to trust your neural implant. Just as when you walk or run you trust your body not to fall."

"I guess it's my turn," Casey spoke, uneasily.

She'd crashed violently into the ground several times and even dislocated her shoulder on her last attempt. Casey stepped forward, knowing many of her fellow platoon members were watching. She had to master this if she expected to lead them into battle.

"Remember, Corporal Hunter," Sergeant Morris spoke in a reassuring voice. "Just think about what you want to do and the neural implant will take care of the rest."

Casey took a deep breath, nodding her head. The neural transmitter was linked directly to the central computer of the battlesuit, which controlled all of the suit's intricate functions. She knew it was just a matter of trust.

Focusing her mind, Casey actuated the antigravity repeller units and felt herself lift slowly up off the ground. She could tell the suit was wobbly. She immediately put her arms out and began flailing about trying to keep her balance.

"Don't fight it," instructed Sergeant Morris, keeping a watchful eye on the corporal. "By moving your arms around you're fighting the suit's own attempts to keep you properly balanced."

Trying to calm her nerves, Casey lowered her arms to her side and felt the suit quickly stabilize. Remarkably, this reminded her of the first steps she'd taken after coming out of the cloning chamber back on Vesta. She recalled how the nurses had worked at keeping her calm and saying soothing words. Now it seemed Sergeant Morris was assuming that role teaching her to fly the Type Four battlesuit.

For the next ten minutes, the sergeant talked Casey through some simple flight maneuvers. There were smaller antigravity repeller units on the sides of her metal feet, which could cause the suit to move forward or backward. Forward wasn't so difficult, but backward was something else. Going backward Casey nearly slammed into the ground but managed to recover just in time to avoid a crash. Morris had Casey practice several more times moving backward until she was satisfied the corporal wouldn't hurt herself or anyone else. When the drill was finally over, Casey landed the suit, touching down lightly.

"Not bad," Ryan said with admiration. "In another few weeks, we'll all be flying around like birds."

"I think I'd prefer a Road Runner," uttered Casey, turning to face Ryan. "They spend most of their time on the ground."

"As will you," Sergeant Morris interjected. "You'll find by activating the repeller units at varying strengths, you can jump the battlesuit higher and farther. If you want to reach a rooftop, the repellers will help immensely. Flight should only be used as a last resort because it makes you plainly visible to the enemy, who will probably attempt to shoot you down."

Later, Ryan's platoon was in the mess hall eating their evening meal. One thing he could say about the marines, they had the best cooks in the military. He looked down at his plate, which held a sizable portion of meatloaf, mashed potatoes and gravy, and green beans. Several buttered dinner rolls were also over on the side.

"I don't know if I'll ever get used to flying," Casey moaned as she leaned back and gazed over at Ryan. "I guess I'm just afraid of falling."

"That's what we have medical facilities for," Private Adams said with a grin.

She'd witnessed several of Casey's spectacular crashes. Lauren had taken to flying like a duck to water and found it an exciting and fun experience. She could easily see where it could be used to give oneself a tactical advantage over an enemy.

"I hear we get to try Charring again in a few days," Private Parker voiced with a deep sigh. "I hate getting killed on that damn mountain!"

"Maybe we won't get killed this time," Private Swen spoke in a hopeful voice, looking over at Casey and Ryan hoping they would agree.

"They're not going to make it easy on us," Casey answered her hazel eyes looking at the others. "I'm afraid what we went through the first two times on Charring will seem like child's play compared to what they're going to put us through this time."

Lauren looked thoughtful and then nodded her head. "They want us to be the best possible. These new suits must cost a fortune and they expect us to learn how to use them to their maximum capability."

"It's going to be tough," Ryan admitted in between bites of his meatloaf. "I suspect we're going to see a lot of Charring Mountain and each time they're going to make the drill more difficult."

"They're not going to let us win," stated Lauren her eyes narrowing.

"Oh, we can win," answered Ryan, putting his fork down and leaning forward on his elbows. "They're just going to make it as difficult as possible. We have to learn how to use the new suits so we can make it to the top."

He looked down at the remaining food on his plate. It reminded him of the meals his mother cooked. It would be nice to get some leave once this training was over so he could return to Vesta and see his parents. He had received a short message from Wade mentioning that he was leaving on a mission and would be gone for several months. That could mean only one thing; his older brother had left on a mission outside the solar system. He wished he could have seen Wade one more time before he left. He had a few questions he would like to ask him; now they would have to wait.

"How long do you think this training will last?" asked Casey, looking across the table at Ryan.

"Six more weeks possibly," answered Ryan, thinking about the training schedule Major Winfrey and Major Stevens had discussed with him and the other lieutenants. "We have a lot to learn, and look how long the training took in the Type Two and Type Three suits."

Lauren nodded. "I get the impression they want to deploy us as soon as possible. It wouldn't surprise me if they have our first mission already in mind."

Ryan was silent. He wondered if that mission might have anything to do with whatever his brother was up to. Reaching for his tea, Ryan took a long drink as he thought about what uses the Type Four suits could be put to. The most likely seemed to be direct combat against the Kleese themselves. To the best of his knowledge, no one had ever fought a Kleese wearing a battlesuit. Ryan had a bad feeling that was about to change and they would get to experience it first hand.

Beth was in the Command Center of the Fire Fox along with Captains Foster and Stern. They were well on their way to their first drop out point and they had come to the Command Center to watch.

"Four hundred light years in five days," boasted Captain Trace Stockwell with a pleased look upon his face. "That's much better than the last time we left the solar system."

Beth had to agree. The last time she'd been on board the Fire Fox was when they had launched the rescue operation on the Kivean home world. There had been some brief heavy combat in that operation, and if they had to go into combat this time, she was glad to have the two officers standing beside her along.

"I checked out the new hover tanks," Captain Nicole Foster spoke, her eyes focused on the ship's main viewscreens. "We have eight of them on board and they have a powerful energy cannon as the main armament. The tanks have two secondary railgun cannons and dual explosive launchers. If we need some heavy firepower, they'll serve very well."

"They also have suit energy recharging stations built into them," Captain Stern added her deep blue eyes focusing on Major Williams. "They might come in useful in a long battle or a long term deployment."

"Let's hope it doesn't come to that," Beth responded. She had no desire to spend days cooped up inside a battlesuit.

"Dropping out of Fold Space in one minute," reported Ensign Patrick Walker.

"All stations are at Condition Two," reported Lieutenant Eugene Bryan. Eugene was the main sensor officer and also doubled as executive officer. The ship was at Condition Two as a standard precaution since they were dropping out of Fold Space into an unknown star system.

"Drop out!" called out Ensign Walker.

The main viewscreens seemed to shimmer and then the stars swam into sharp focus.

"Beginning sensor sweeps," added Lieutenant Bryan. "The rest of Seventh Fleet is dropping out."

"I have the flag," reported Ensign Janice Brill from Communications. "Admiral Adamson is giving us six hours to run system checks and do any necessary maintenance."

"Assault ships are moving into defensive positions around the fleet," spoke Lieutenant Bryan as he watched the numerous green icons now on his sensor screens beginning to shift around. "No hostile or unknown targets being detected within twenty light seconds. Long-range sensors are beginning scans."

"Looks as if we're in the clear," commented Captain Foster with a relieved look upon her face. She didn't mind combat but preferred it on the ground where she could control the situation. She felt helpless aboard a ship where all she could do was watch.

They waited a few more minutes until the long-range sensors indicated there were no detectable threats in sensor range.

Once that was confirmed, the ship was placed at Condition Three.

Beth nodded, pleased that so far the mission was going smoothly. "Let's head down to the barracks and get some additional training time in today."

Beth preferred to stay busy as it kept her mind off being apart from Wade as well as leaving her mother in the retirement center at Vesta. She greatly feared one day she would be gone on a long deployment to return and find that her mother had passed on.

"Sergeants Russell and Dawson will be glad to hear that," Nicole spoke with a wolfish grin on her face.

Russell and Dawson had both refused promotions to lieutenants as they felt more comfortable with their current rank. Russell and Dawson both had platoons they were in charge of, and there had been an intense rivalry between them for years. Nicole just enjoyed stoking the fire a little every once and a while.

As they made their way out of the Command Center, Beth took one last look at one of the viewscreens displaying the Constellation. She knew on their next Fold Space dropout that Wade was planning on coming over to the Fire Fox. For now, she needed to work off her pent up energy and the best way to do that was to run combat drills in battlesuits with some of her marines.

With a deep sigh, she stepped through the hatch and into the outside corridor. She reminded herself she had a meeting with Harnett later to discuss the treatment of injured marines in battlefield conditions. Harnett had been working on a way to use medical nanites in combat situations. Harnett was a brilliant Kivean doctor and had been instrumental in acquiring the production system for medical nanites on the trip to the nonaligned worlds' trading station six years back. She'd also helped set up the ultra modern hospitals and medical research centers inside Vesta. From what Wade had told her, President Randle's oldest niece was going to be tutored by Harnett personally.

Thinking about kids, Beth wondered when she and Wade should think about having some. They had discussed it, but they both wanted a better feel for how the war was going to go though the solar system did have some very powerful defenses now, particularly Vesta. Maybe when this deployment was over she would bring the subject up again. But for now, she needed to focus on getting her marines ready for combat.

Supreme Overlord Xatul looked over the assembled Council of Overlords. Including himself there were twenty Kleese represented, though four of those were members of the Zaltule. As a precaution, Xatul was keeping twenty of the large exploration ships above the home planet to ensure that Harmock didn't try to remove him from power.

"What are the latest reports from the Zaltule shipyards?" he demanded in a harsh and unforgiving voice.

"They're turning out new warships as required," Raluth answered his hard gaze meeting that of the Supreme Overlord. "Material shipments are being met and Minor Overlord Kaluse feels confident that he can meet all of War Overlord Harmock's fleet demands."

"Two new shipyards are even now being constructed," the Zaltule Overlord Darthu added in a cold voice. "Ships are being equipped with the most modern weapons known to our science. We're also in the process of updating some of our older vessels."

"What's the current size of the Zaltule fleet?" asked Bixutl. He placed his hands upon the stone table and leaned slightly forward. It seemed to him the Zaltule were becoming too powerful too quickly and it was only a matter of time before they demanded even more seats on the council.

"Six thousand two hundred vessels," answered Darthu, promptly. "War Overlord Harmock is seeking a fleet of ten thousand vessels to ensure our successful conquest of all races that might oppose our Empire."

"What about the Talt?" questioned Bixutl, recalling the report Darthu had delivered to the council a few days back.

"They inflicted considerable losses on War Overlord Harmock's fleet with their plasma weapons. They also possess a subspace drive that seems to be superior to ours. Have we located samples or the designs for either?"

"A minor setback," responded Darthu, evenly. "We have some of our top scientists and technicians on the Taltian home world searching for the secret of their plasma weapon as well as their subspace drive. From sensor scans taken by our warships, it's very probable that with a little more research our own scientists can duplicate both even if we can't find the blueprints."

"There are many more nonaligned worlds," spoke Martule, hesitantly. "Many will be as powerful as the Talt. What are Harmock's plans for dealing with them? We still have our exploration fleet as well as thousands of assault ships, which could be used to help the Zaltule subdue those worlds."

"The assault ships are infested with vermin!" spat the Zaltule Overlord Creedal. "The vermin you have taken for conscripts might be fine fighting uncivilized worlds, but not the nonaligned races. Those will suffer the wrath of the Zaltule and their leaders will know what it means to wear our collars of obedience."

Supreme Overlord Xatul remained silent as he contemplated Creedal's words. He wondered if the real reason to keep the exploration ships and the assault ships away was to ensure they didn't discover any new technology or scientific breakthroughs the nonaligned worlds possessed. Were the Zaltule trying to keep any procured advanced technology for themselves? It was a worrisome thought.

"I have also heard that the Zaltule Queens have been awakened and new nests have been created," spoke Overlord Syndat. Syndat didn't speak often during the council meetings, though he controlled three of the Empire's large trading stations as well as the fleets assigned to them.

"Is that true?" asked Xatul, feeling irritated. The Queens were not to have been awakened without his permission.

"Six of the ten Queens have been awakened," confirmed the Zaltule Overlord Tintul. "We dared not take the risk of any of them dying in the sleeping chambers. If there are any signs of failure in any of the remaining four, they will also be awakened."

"Where are the nests located?" demanded Xatul his voice echoing across the chamber. "They were not to be awakened without my knowledge." Xatul leaned forward, his six legs rattling the floor and his multifaceted eyes focused intently on Tintul.

"It was decided that due to the combat losses suffered from fighting the Strell and now what looks like possibly more projected casualties in subduing these nonaligned worlds, the lost warriors of the Zaltule must be replaced."

Xatul was silent wondering if this was a direct challenge to his authority. There were only a few Zaltule warriors in the immediate area and he had forces of his own he could call upon. He wondered if he should execute all four of the Zaltule Overlords as an example of what it meant to go against the wishes of the Supreme Overlord of the Kleese.

"I will take you to the new nests," Tintul spoke quickly, realizing the danger he'd just placed himself and the others in. While some of the overlords at the council table were weak, that did not apply to the Supreme Overlord. In many ways, he was like a Zaltule. "We would be honored to introduce you to our Queens."

"I may indeed take you up on that," Xatul replied as he gazed coldly at Tintul. "What are the current attack plans of War Overlord Harmock?"

"We will be attacking the nonaligned worlds with six fleets of five hundred vessels," answered Darthu. "With those numbers, we will easily outnumber any opposition we may come across and limit our losses in battle. War Overlord Harmock estimates he will have subjugated all of the nonaligned worlds within the year."

"Then we'll move out into the rest of the galaxy," Zaltule Overlord Lackeln spoke. "Our new fleets will be ready and we'll begin expanding the Empire in earnest."

"It may be necessary with so many new worlds coming into the Empire to make more use of the vermin conscripts," added Darthu. "Zaltule warriors will not be used as occupiers for worlds infested with primitive vermin. On worlds where the vermin infestation is too great or hopelessly primitive, the planet's surfaces will be cleansed."

"Very well," Xatul said as he pondered the coming attack upon the nonaligned worlds. He'd always known that at some point in time the free alien species would have to be brought under Kleese control. For now, he would allow Harmock to do as he pleased in the war. "Keep me informed of all developments."

"As you command, Supreme Overlord," Darthu responded.

Bixutl had listened to the exchange with interest. There was little doubt in his mind that once the Zaltule Queens were established and new young were being hatched the numbers of the warrior caste would swell rapidly. They would grow fast enough that in a relatively short time they might begin to replace other Kleese throughout the Empire. Someday, the entire Empire might be nothing but Zaltule. Somehow, he had to find a way to slow the Zaltule down. Once again, his thoughts turned to the Humans. He'd sent an exploration ship toward their system and it should be arriving there in the next few weeks. Perhaps then he would know if he had a weapon he could use to control the warrior caste.

Chapter Eight

Harmock gazed without mercy at the destruction his fleet was inflicting upon the nonaligned world's fleet that had dared to oppose the Zaltule. On the main viewscreen a long, needle-shaped spacecraft burned as massive holes were driven through its hull, igniting the atmosphere within. The needle ship was nearly one thousand meters in length and had been equipped with heavy energy beams as its main armament.

"Additional ships are in route from the planet's surface," Jalridd the Zaltule at the main sensor console reported as a warning alarm began sounding.

"They launched from the surface of the planet?" asked Harmock, wanting to make sure he had understood correctly. A ship the size of these needle warships should not be able to land or be launched from a planet.

"Yes," Minor Overlord Gareth spoke as he turned toward Harmock. "Evidently the Ralathe use some form of powerful antigravity repellers to allow their ships to land upon their world. It's possible the construction facilities for their spacecraft are also located on the surface."

"Make capturing those facilities a priority," ordered Harmock, wanting to capture the technology. He could see how useful it would be in landing ground forces. "How many more needle ships did they launch?"

"Forty-three," answered Jalridd as he studied the information coming in on the ship's powerful sensors. Even as he spoke, the tactical screen was being updated.

"The ships were launched from three major space complexes on the planet," Gareth added as he adjusted a viewscreen to show a close up of the Ralathe home world.

The planet Ralathe was a semi-arid world with much of its surface covered in deserts. However, a wide swath around the planet's equator was covered in verdant vegetation indicating a living and healthy planet. The Ralathians had their cities on the edges of this green band. A large number of rivers snaked across the surface around the cities and into the tropical area where numerous massive blue lakes could be seen.

"Move us toward the planet," ordered Harmock. "We'll engage these last warships and then subjugate the planet. By this time tomorrow, the leaders of this world as well as their major scientists will wear the collars of obedience."

"As you command," Gareth responded.

The forty-three Ralathian warships formed up into a loose cone formation and advanced resolutely toward the inbound Zaltule warfleet. Already the four outer defense squadrons had been crushed by the superior numbers of the Kleese. FTL transmissions were already being sent to other nonaligned worlds warning them of the Kleese transgression. It was rapidly becoming clear that the long-standing neutrality agreements, signed by the Kleese ages ago, were no longer being honored.

The Ralathian ships' activated their powerful energy shields and targeting sensors reached out, locking onto multiple targets. After a quick discussion between commanders, it was decided to target only ten inbound Kleese warships at a time. After the first ten were destroyed, they would target the next ten and so on. It had taken longer to deploy these ships as special weapons had been brought from the secret armories to be loaded into the ships' missile tubes. It had been hoped these missiles would never have to be used as their destructive power was truly frightening.

Upon the slim hulls of the Ralathian ships, armored hatches slid open and sublight missiles were readied. The special warheads on these missiles seemed to glow with a mysterious energy. From all forty-three ships, missiles flashed away as the order was given to fire. Each ship fired two missiles at their targets, knowing it was necessary for only one to get through to do its deadly work.

Kleese computers managed to locate and destroy twenty-two of the inbound missiles but the rest struck their targets, lighting up the Kleese fleet with an eerie light.

Harmock watched in unbridled anger as ten of his battlecruisers burned from a mysterious blue energy eating away at the hulls of the ships, changing the hull material into a strange reddish glowing substance. The missiles had exploded against the energy screens of the Zaltule ships and then streamers of blue energy had darted through, attacking the armored hulls.

"What is it?" he demanded, turning toward Gareth for an explanation.

"We don't know," answered Gareth, as he queried other ships and even a few of the Zaltule scientists aboard the Warrior's Fire. "No one has ever seen anything like this before. The energy seems to be eating away at the very hulls of our ships and changing it into something else."

"But what's it changing it into?" demanded Harmock, seeing that one of his warships was now completely covered and its hull was glowing a dull red as if it had a life of its own. The viewscreen suddenly darkened as a tremendous flash lit up space.

"The sensors are showing a massive energy release!" Jalridd warned as the Warrior's Fire began to vibrate violently. Warning alarms began sounding, indicating some compartments on the massive battlecruiser had been compromised. "From the readings we're receiving, the ship's hull was converted to energy and then exploded as it became too unstable. Initial readings indicate a blast in the four hundred to five hundred-megaton range."

Even as he spoke, several more Zaltule warships detonated. Warning alarms continued to sound in the Command Center as damage reports started to come in.

"Target those ships!" roared Harmock as ten additional ships were struck by the Ralathian's deadly weapon. "Hit them with everything we have!"

Hundreds of pulse fusion beams flicked out to strike the Ralathian ships' energy screens. Sublight missile after missile began launching in sprint mode as a panicked Zaltule fleet fought for their very lives. Resistance such as they were now seeing had not been expected. The weapon the Ralathians were using was a nightmare weapon the Kleese energy shields seemed powerless to stop.

In the Ralathian fleet, first one and then two defending battlecruisers blew apart as Zaltule energy beams and antimatter missiles tore brutally into the ships. The Kleese were attacking with desperation and a vengeance. Ralathian ships began to die faster and the space around them was aglow with energy weapons fire and detonating antimatter warheads.

The Ralathians were now on their third group of Kleese warships as their deadly missiles delivered their warheads, which exploded on contact with the energy shields and from which tendrils of blue reached down to leach onto the vulnerable hull armor. Where the blue writhing energy touched, the metal seemed to melt away and reform into a dimly glowing red sludge. When enough of the hull had been converted, a chain reaction began blowing the ship to oblivion as hundreds of megatons of uncontrolled energy were released.

In order to reduce the damage to the Zaltule battlecruisers Harmock had ordered them to open up the fleet formation, putting more distance between ships. On the main viewscreen, he watched as the space occupied by the Ralathian ships began to look like the fiery heart of a burning star. It was aglow with exploding antimatter missiles and blue pulse fusion beams.

The Warrior's Fire had moved back toward the rear of the Kleese formation to ensure its survival. Harmock stamped his six legs restlessly as he watched the last few Ralathian ships die under the onslaught of hundreds of pulse fusion beams and antimatter missiles.

"The last Ralathian ship has been destroyed," reported Minor Overlord Gareth as he checked the tactical screen.

On the main viewscreen, the Ralathian fleet had been turned into glowing plasma and drifting areas of burning gas, which was rapidly beginning to fade. Shortly, there would be no sign that forty-three needle-shaped battlecruisers had met their destruction in that small area of space.

"What were our losses?" demanded Harmock, knowing that once again he had lost more ships than had been projected.

"Forty-eight destroyed and twenty-seven others damaged," Gareth responded as he studied the information from the battle. "We lost most of our warships in this last attack when the Ralathians used their new weapon."

"When our warriors descend to the surface, I want a priority made in finding the secret to this weapon we just faced. Our energy screens seemed to be useless against the missiles they launched at us. If the rest of their ships, which we destroyed earlier had been equipped with the same type of missile we might very well have been forced to withdraw."

"It will be a priority," confirmed Gareth. "This weapon could be highly useful to our fleet if we ever encounter a powerful enemy, particularly since it seems to be able to penetrate an energy screen."

Harmock remained silent. Both of the two nonaligned worlds they'd attacked had inflicted far more losses upon the Zaltule fleet than Harmock had believed possible. He wondered what else lay ahead for his fleets as they continued to bring the nonaligned worlds into the Empire. It might be necessary for him to reevaluate his timeline for conquering the nonaligned worlds.

"As much as I hate to say it, the Council of Overlords might have been correct in signing a neutrality agreement with these worlds," uttered Harmock, looking over at Gareth. "The ships of the Zaltule are designed for war and our caste is trained as warriors. Exploration ships and assault vessels would have suffered far more losses and may not have been able to conquer the two systems."

"They should have awakened us sooner," spoke Gareth his multifaceted eyes focusing on the War Overlord. "They let the nonaligned worlds grow too strong and now the Zaltule will have to pay the price for that tactical error with our blood."

"It will not happen again," declared Harmock. "The Zaltule will never return to the sleep chambers, and once the Queens are established in their new nests and the first hatchings begin, we will take over more of the council."

"The council should be controlled by the Zaltule," suggested Gareth.

"It will be, in time," confirmed Harmock. "For now it has a purpose to serve until we can greatly increase our numbers. While that happens, we will continue to subdue the nonaligned worlds and prepare to expand beyond the borders of our Empire."

"To the edge of the galaxy," spoke Gareth, rising up to his full height upon his six legs. "The galaxy will be ours!"

"Yes," agreed Harmock. "Someday the Kleese Empire will reach from one edge of our galaxy to the other. There is no power that will be able to stop us."

-

Ryan took a deep breath as he stood behind a large tree trunk halfway up Charring Mountain. This was the twentieth time he'd led his platoon up the mountain in the last thirty days. So far, he had made it to the top four times. Each time he did, their next assault on the mountain met even more embedded weapons. On top of that, the mountain was now seeded with a minefield that made just moving about on the steep slopes a challenge. The mines wouldn't damage a battlesuit, but they would toss you up in the air making you an easy target for a long-range stunner. Ryan also suspected the intensity of the stunners had been increased since marines who had been hit multiple times claimed the pain was more intense each time. He knew from his own experience it seemed to be so.

"When do we get some rec time?" muttered Private Parker from where he was standing behind a jagged boulder. He looked over at Private Adams, who was twenty meters away and lying in a hole left from an exploding mine.

"When we reach the top again," replied Lauren in exasperation. They all needed some rec time, but Alexander didn't need to remind them of it constantly.

Before Alexander could make a reply, Major Winfrey's voice suddenly interrupted the drill. "Drill is over," Winfrey spoke in a commanding voice. "Lieutenant Nelson, move your platoon to the armory and get a full load out for your weapons."

"What's up?" Ryan asked as he stepped out from behind the tree trunk. He noticed that all the suits in his HUD that had been showing amber or red had suddenly turned back to green.

"We have four unidentified ships that have just dropped out of Fold Space close to Mars. General Mitchell has placed the military at Condition Two with Mars at Condition One."

"We're on our way," Ryan answered as he motioned for his platoon to follow him down.

"Are they Kleese?" Casey asked worriedly as she trotted over close to Ryan. "Do you think they'll want to use us to try to take those ships?"

"We won't know until we get to the armory," Ryan replied as he stepped around a shattered tree stump. "I just wonder why there are only four ships. If this was an attack they would've used a much larger force."

"A probe perhaps," suggested Casey. She'd spent a lot of time going over the past battles fought in the solar system. She felt suddenly nervous and her stomach weak knowing they might shortly be going into battle. She didn't want Ryan to know how queasy she was feeling.

A few minutes later, they were standing in front of the small armory, which held the weapons and munitions for their training dome. Major Winfrey, Major Stevens, Captain Taylor, and Sergeant Morris were there waiting for them. All were in Type Four battlesuits.

"Arm up," ordered Major Winfrey. "The other three platoons have already and are on their way to their assignments. "RG rifles only with class one explosive shells. You'll also need to take your Energy Lances."

Ryan nodded; the class one explosive shells had the explosive force of a regular grenade while the class twos were much more powerful. The class twos were too dangerous to use inside Centerpoint.

"What's our assignment, Sir?" asked Ryan as he picked up several RG mags. He slammed a fresh one into his rifle and placed a spare in the holder in his armor. He took down his Energy Lance and attached it to his suit, seeing a light flash on in his HUD indicating it was connected to the suit's power supply and ready for use.

"The Command Center," Major Stevens informed him. "Take your platoon and guard the two adjoining corridors as well as the main one that runs directly in front of the hatch. I want four of your best people on guard ensuring there is no unauthorized admittance to the Command Center until this crisis is over."

A few moments later, Ryan saw that everyone in his platoon was properly armed. "Let's move it, people," he commanded as he set out toward the main hatch to the training dome.

Casey fell in line behind Ryan and noticed Captain Taylor and Sergeant Morris were bringing up the rear. If they were going, this was indeed a serious situation. Casey could feel her heart hammering in her chest; she just hoped she didn't disappoint Ryan.

General Mitchell was inside the Command Center pacing in front of the main viewscreens. He glanced up impatiently at the large tactical screen, seeing Second Fleet beginning to pull away from Mars and heading out toward the four inbound unknowns.

"Admiral Sanders reports he's twenty minutes away from rendezvous with the unknowns," reported General Pittman, who was sitting behind the command console on the Command Pedestal. "There have been no attempts at communication from them."

"Fleet Admiral Kelly has placed First Fleet at Condition One and is moving it out past the Moon in case the unknowns get past Admiral Sanders."

"Sir," interrupted Captain Jennifer Owens. "I have Skagern on the com and he says it's urgent that he speaks with you."

"Put him on," Mitchell said, cocking his eyebrow. Skagern was a Kivean and Marken's second in command. He wondered if this involved the unknown ships.

"General Mitchell," Skagern began in an excited voice. "We've made contact with the four unknown ships that have dropped out of Fold Space near Mars. They are Taltian and are requesting asylum. Their commander has told us that the Zaltule have conquered their system and destroyed their fleet."

"Is that a nonaligned world?" asked Mitchell his eyes widening at the ramifications if the Kleese were already attacking nonaligned systems. The name didn't sound familiar.

"Yes," Skagern replied. "It's very near the center of the Kleese Empire and is one of the oldest nonaligned worlds. Their commander has said that if you accept his request for asylum he is willing to provide you with some valuable military technology."

"What types of ships does he have with him?" Mitchell asked as a viewscreen suddenly began showing two spindle-shaped vessels and two additional ones that were bulkier and looked more like cargo or passenger ships. The transmission was coming from an orbiting Mars satellite.

"Two warships and two passenger ships," Skagern answered and then continued in an earnest voice. "Their commander has described a plasma weapon which is capable of destroying Zaltule warships as well as a highly advanced sublight drive. I plead with you to offer them asylum. This could go a long way in convincing the other nonaligned worlds to join our cause."

"Inform their commander to lower their ships' energy shields and depower their weapons," General Mitchell stated in a firm voice. "Once we have confirmed that has been done, Admiral Sanders will establish contact and we will proceed from there. Inform them that I am sending out a civilian negotiating team to discuss possible asylum."

"Immediately," Skagern responded in a calmer voice. "This could be the break we need to form the Alliance."

Mitchell turned to General Pittman. "Contact President Randle and apprise him of the situation. We'll dispatch a battlecruiser to pick up the negotiating team and I want you to go along to represent the military. Also, pick up Gerald Lawson on your way. He's a military weapons specialist and can verify if what these Taltians' claim about this plasma weapon is true or not."

"Yes, Sir," Pittman replied as he stood up and prepared to leave the Command Center.

Mitchell shifted his gaze back to the viewscreen showing the spindle-shaped ships. He let out a heavy sigh of relief, knowing that most likely combat had been avoided. He was curious to meet the Talts and find out just what type of allies they would be as well as what had happened to their world.

Commander Pasha allowed himself to relax once the Kiveans confirmed that the Humans were willing to talk and would probably grant them asylum. The Kiveans had even gone on to say that once the Humans agreed they would be willing to help the Talts construct a habitat that would be acceptable to their race.

"The Human fleet has stopped its advance," reported Sub Commander Kith. "Their admiral has requested we remain at this position until their negotiators arrive. He's also asked if there is anything we require in the way of aid."

"We have the results from the long-range scans," reported the ship's sensor operator. "Their world has been destroyed by the Kleese as we'd heard, however, it seems they have spread out across the system. That red planet ahead has a large population. We're detecting what appear to be ion cannons on the surface."

"Ion cannons?" Commander Pasha uttered in shock, his large yellow eyes growing wide. "That's very advanced indeed." His own race had experimented with ion cannons but could never find a sufficient power source to make them a practical weapon. He hoped he would be given the opportunity in the future to inspect one of the cannons.

"As rumored, there is also a Kleese trading station in orbit between the Human's home world and its moon," added Kith. "The moon is very large and has numerous artificial habitats on its surface. There's also a tremendous amount of ship traffic in the system. Many of the ships we're detecting appear to be civilian, but a large number are definitely military."

"Then let us hope they grant us asylum and are an honorable people," Pasha replied his eyes shifting to his second in command. The survival of his people now rested with these mysterious Humans.

Counting the two passenger liners and both his warships, he'd brought five thousand Taltians to this system. He hoped it was enough to begin their civilization anew since he strongly suspected he would never see the Talt home world again.

President Mason Randal stood in the Control Center inside Vesta, gazing in deep thought at the viewscreen showing one of the Talt spindle-shaped battlecruisers. He'd spoken to General Pittman earlier and an assault ship with several civilian negotiators was already on its way to meet the inbound battlecruiser.

"Skagern said the Talts are a humanoid species," uttered General Bailey with a skeptical look upon his face.

"He told me the same thing," replied Mason, folding his arms across his chest as he gazed speculatively at the spindle ships. "We know from what the Kiveans have told us there are a lot of different species out in the galaxy. Don't forget the Kleese are similar to tarantulas except for their upper body."

"Do our negotiators know what they're getting into?"

"Yes," answered Mason. "Fortunately Skagern found several Kiveans who've had past dealings with the Talts and two of them volunteered to accompany our negotiators."

"I wonder how much more of this we'll see as the Zaltule attack additional unaligned worlds?" questioned Bailey. "We may need to set up a special department to deal with alien refugees."

"It's a possibility," admitted Mason as he thought about the ramifications of allowing even more alien species into the solar system. He wasn't sure how the general public would feel about that, particularly considering how they felt about the clones.

"How's Adrienne doing?' asked Bailey, knowing she was in the last stages of pregnancy.

"Miserable," answered Mason with a tired smile. He'd never known women could be so demanding until his wife became pregnant. Between the cravings and requests for backrubs, it had been a wonderful and trying experience so far.

"It will be a much different world that our children grow up in," Bailey commented as his eyes shifted back to the viewscreen. "There may come a day when alien races are quite common in our solar system."

"If the Alliance pans out, that's a good possibility," spoke Mason, wondering what his child's life was going to be like. Would their daughter be going to school with children whose parents had lived beneath other stars? Only time would tell.

Chapter Nine

Wade let out a deep breath of frustration as he stepped aboard the shuttle that would take him back up to the Distant Star in high orbit around the nonaligned world of Lanolth. Lanolth was very similar to what Earth once was, with large oceans, white ice caps on the poles, and a warm to hot equatorial zone. It was also heavily populated with a population of nearly five billion. Lanolth was the fourth planet out from the system's sun with two small moons orbiting it. Both of the rocky moons had large habitats sprawling across their surfaces where another two hundred million Lanolthians lived and worked. There were twelve planets in the system and numerous mining and scientific posts existed on almost all of them.

As Wade sat down, he looked across at Hyram Blake, the chief negotiator, who was based on the large passenger liner. "How can they be so stubborn?" he asked, shaking his head in disbelief. "Don't they know if they do nothing, the Kleese will come to this system and put obedience collars around their necks?"

"They know," Hyram answered with a tired smile. He'd spent many long hours in negotiations with the Lanolthians. "They want an Alliance; the problem is the civilian population is so used to centuries of peace with the Kleese that the idea of actually going to war with them is nearly incomprehensible."

"What are we going to do?" inquired Wade, feeling that they were at a stalemate. "We need this Alliance if we want to fight the Kleese."

"There are some things going on behind the scenes," Hyram confessed in a quieter voice. "The Lanolthians have been secretly increasing the size of their fleet and nearly every one of their major cities sits inside a ring of ion cannons. The Kleese would have a very difficult time taking the planet."

"What!" Wade exclaimed his eyes widening in disbelief. "I didn't see any signs of ion cannons."

He had visited several of the Lanolthians' major cities while down on the planet's surface. Their architecture was amazing and all of their buildings had a simple, aesthetic beauty. At no time had he seen any evidence of defensive or offensive weapons; an ion cannon wasn't something easy to conceal.

"They're well hidden," answered Hyram. "From what we've been able to gather from our research into the flash drive given to us by the nonaligned worlds, Lanolth is where the designs for the ion cannons came from. It was also one of their ships which left the message in our solar system about the impending Kleese attack six years ago."

Wade leaned back and shook his head, not quite understanding what he was hearing. "Are you telling me the Lanolthian government has been preparing for war against the Kleese in secret and keeping it from their people?"

"Precisely," Hyram answered with a nod. He reached into the inside pocket of his suit jacket and pulled out a set of papers, which he handed to Wade. "This document has been signed by the Lanolthian ruling council, and they have agreed to join the Alliance on the day the Kleese attack any nonaligned world within five hundred light years of Lanolth."

Wade took the document and looking through it, saw in amazement that it was indeed signed. "Then we have the first member of the Alliance," he spoke in awe his eyes lighting up at the ramifications.

"It's much more than that," continued Hyram, drawing in a sharp breath. "From what the Lanolthian leaders have told me, there were six more worlds, plus the Lanolthians, responsible for the information on the flash drive. They have assured me that the other six will become part of the Alliance once the Kleese attack. Not only that, but all six have been preparing in secret for that day once they heard about the Zaltule attack upon the Strell. Most have doubled the size of their defensive fleets, though many of the new ships are hidden inside construction bays or deep within secret asteroid bases. They were fearful that if the Kleese discovered the buildup it would cause the neutrality agreements they'd all signed to become void immediately."

"Seven star systems will be a significant boost in forming the Alliance, but we need more," responded Wade, handing the document back to Hyram, who placed it securely back inside his suit pocket.

"I know," Hyram said, leaning back and staring at Wade. "Much of the discussions my team and I've had with the Lanolthian ruling council have been about other nonaligned worlds that might rally to our cause when the Kleese reveal their true intentions. The Lanolthians have given us a list of fourteen more worlds they feel might come into the Alliance with the proper inducements."

"What kind of inducements?"

"The Lanolthian Council feels if we offer those worlds ion cannons for defense it will go a long way to bringing them over to our side. They have agreed to supply the designs for a basic cannon if we agree."

"You said inducements," Wade pointed out suspiciously. "What else do they want?"

"Space Marines," Hyram spoke in an even voice his eyes seeking out Wade's. "All of these worlds can fight from a spacecraft where computers control the weapons, but hand-to-hand combat against the Kleese, particularly the Zaltule, is beyond them. We would need to offer to provide sufficient numbers of Space Marines in Type Two or Type Three battlesuits to handle any physical invasion of these worlds."

"I suppose the Lanolthians and the other six nonaligned worlds involved with the flash drive want Space Marines also?" asked Wade.

"Yes," responded Hyram, letting out a deep breath. He cocked his eyebrow and glanced out the viewport next to him. The shuttle was already out of the planet's atmosphere and well on its way back to the Distant Star. Then he shifted his eyes back to Wade. "Can we do that?"

"I don't know," answered Wade, truthfully. "I would need to speak to General Mitchell as well as President Randle. "It might be necessary for us to expand the clone program to get the necessary numbers."

"How many could we deploy immediately if it becomes necessary?" asked Hyram. "It may be what makes or breaks the Alliance."

Wade was silent for a moment as he ran the numbers through his head. "We have forty thousand Space Marines currently in our solar system," he answered, pursing his lips in thought. "We could possibly deploy twenty thousand of them to the Alliance without compromising our own security."

Hyram nodded, his eyes narrowing slightly. "I hope that's enough."

"It'd better be," Wade said, folding his arms across his chest and leaning back in his seat as he mulled over all this implied. "It will take a while to train more."

"We may need to provide a demonstration of our ability to fight the Zaltule on the ground," added Hyram, worriedly. The Lanolthians had indicated the other races would want proof that the Humans could defeat the Zaltule in combat.

Wade closed his eyes in consternation as he realized what Hyram was suggesting. There was only one group of Space Marines being trained to fight the Zaltule in armed combat, and that was Major Steven's Space Marine company, of which Ryan was a member. With a cold chill, Wade wished he'd spent more time trying to talk Ryan out of becoming a Space Marine. Now his brother might be going into battle with an enemy, which was more frightening than most could imagine. How was he ever going to explain this to his parents?

-

Beth looked over at Harnett and sighed heavily. "You want to add medical nanites to the Type Three battlesuits to handle extreme injuries?"

"Yes," replied Harnett, nodding her head. She was Marken's lifemate as well as a highly trained physician. "They would be injected in the same manner as the other medicines the suits are capable of providing."

"What to you think, Marken?" asked Beth, looking over at the other Kivean. She had witnessed just how powerful the nanites were at healing severe wounds. Punctured skin and contusions could heal in just minutes and bones could be mended at astonishing speeds.

"It will be simple enough to add to the suits," Marken answered with a thoughtful look in his eyes. "It'll take some minor programming of the suit's central computer and some small modifications, but I don't see why it wouldn't work."

"If a marine gets severely injured in a battle, this will give them a much better chance to survive," Harnett spoke her voice sounding hopeful. "We could save lives with this technology."

"How long would it take to modify the suits?" Beth asked. The medical nanites had always made her a little bit nervous. Having microscopic robots injected into one's blood system gave her a cold chill, but she understood the necessity.

"A technician could modify a suit in less than an hour," Marken replied.

"Alright, I'll agree to a trial," Beth said after a moment. "Can you modify all the Type Three battlesuits in Captain Stern and Captain Foster's companies?"

"I believe so," responded Marken, cocking his head slightly. "The Fire Fox has the necessary technicians and we can start immediately. "We should be able to make the necessary changes to the suits in a little over forty-eight hours."

"Make it so," Beth said, reaching a decision. "If we go into combat on this mission I want to give my people every chance possible to survive."

-

After Beth left the small conference room, Harnett turned to her lifemate. "Are we doing the right thing?"

"If it'll save lives, then yes," Marken answered.

"I know it's the right thing to do," responded Harnett, sounding a little nervous. "The computer in a battlesuit is not a medical computer; we can only program it to react to a limited number of possible injuries. I worry about what might happen if the suit's computer can't decide what to do about injuries it's not programmed for."

"We'll cross that road when we come to it," Marken said, reaching out and taking Harnett's hand. "The Humans have come so far since we first met them and now they're forming an Alliance to fight the Kleese. We must do everything we can to ensure they survive, even if we have to take a few risks."

Harnett nodded; so many of her friends were Human. She was even going to take President Mason's niece, Karen, as an apprentice and teach her Kivean medical technology and methods. "You're right," she answered, releasing Marken's hand and standing up. Let's go get something to eat, I'm famished."

Marken laughed and nodded his head. That was one thing he missed on these long-term space missions. Harnett was an excellent cook and he really enjoyed the meals she prepared for them when they were at home. At least they were together, and their guest quarters were quite spacious for a warship.

-

Admiral Adamson was sitting behind the command console on the Constellation drumming his fingers on the armrest of his command chair. For three weeks, the fleet had been motionless, holding its position in a small brown dwarf system as the two passenger liners traveled from system to system visiting the different nonaligned worlds in this sector of space.

"Sensors are still showing no unknown contacts," reported Lieutenant Lash as the last sensor sweep was completed. For those three weeks, the sensors had been absent of any contacts other than those of Seventh Fleet.

"I don't like letting those two passenger liners go off on their own like this," Commander Shepherd commented as she walked back from Communications. "What if a Kleese ships finds one of them?"

"It's a risk," admitted Adamson, shifting his gaze to Sandra. "But if we were to go with them, the Kleese would readily recognize our warships. We sent four assault ships along with each passenger liner as protection. If they're spotted, the assumption will be that they're Kleese ships. The assault ships are standing by on the outskirts of the system the liners are in and can go to their aid very quickly if needed."

"Assault ships won't last long against a Kleese exploration ship or a Zaltule warship," Sandra was quick to point out. "We should have sent a light cruiser or two along."

"They'll be fine," Adamson assured her. "At the first sign of the Kleese the captains of both liners know they're to enter Fold Space and get out of the system."

Sandra was silent as she gazed at the tactical screen showing the green icons that represented Seventh Fleet. "I just have a bad feeling about this," she confessed.

"Women's intuition," suggested Admiral Adamson.

"Call it what you want," answered Sandra, turning back around to face the admiral. "I just don't think all of us will be going home."

-

Wade watched the main viewscreen as the Distant Star dropped out of Fold Space into the Nalton system. This was one of the worlds that was questionable about joining the Alliance. The Lanolthians were pretty confident that if the Naltons joined the Alliance several other nonaligned worlds would follow their example.

"Hostile ships detected!" called out Mace Sutton, the sensor operator. "Two Kleese assault ships at thirty light seconds."

Looking at the tactical screen, Wade saw two icons suddenly flare up and turn red. "Continue on our present course," he ordered. "Don't act as if anything is wrong."

"What are Kleese assault ships doing here?" questioned Captain Julian Rios. The Distant Star wasn't armed but did have a powerful energy screen, which could be activated if need be.

"Picking up a squadron of Nalton warships accelerating out to intercept them," added Sutton.

"Move us farther away from the assault ships and continue toward the Nalton home planet," ordered Wade, drawing in a sharp breath. "We'll watch how this plays out. Captain Rios, be prepared to jump the ship back into Fold Space if it becomes too dangerous to hang around here. I'm not sure what's going on. This may be some type of regular inspection the Kleese do."

"The Fold Space Drive will be ready," Captain Rios promised as he went over to talk to Dash Stahls at the Helm.

"The Lanolthians did mention that Kleese assault ships come into their system on occasion to ensure they're not violating the terms of the neutrality agreement," commented Hyram from where he was standing slightly behind Wade. "Council President Raytol mentioned the Kleese make inspections about twice a year."

"Hopefully, that's what this is," Wade said as he watched the tactical screen, which showed even more ship icons across the system.

"Picking up quite a few cargo ships as well as a number of other nonaligned world ships in the system," Sutton spoke as his sensors worked to categorize the numerous icons appearing on the sensor screens. As soon as they were identified, he switched them over to the ship's tactical screen. The Lanolthians had provided a ship database on many of the nonaligned worlds in this sector as well as several of the surrounding ones.

Wade nodded. He knew that the nonaligned worlds traded with each other on a regular basis, though what they could trade was strictly limited by the Kleese. Any new items had to be approved by the Kleese on the nonaligned worlds' trading station.

"What type of warships do the Naltons have?" asked Hyram, glancing over at Wade. The Lanolthians hadn't said too much about the warships the other nonaligned worlds possessed.

"I don't know," answered Wade, looking over at Mace Sutton. "How large are those Nalton ships that are rendezvousing with the two Kleese assault ships?"

"Eight hundred meters in length and two hundred meters in diameter," replied Sutton. "The ships are nearly perfect cylinders.

I can't tell from here what type of weapons they're equipped with."

"Those are big ships," Hyram said, impressed. The fleet's own battlecruisers were only five hundred meters in length.

"You mentioned that the Lanolthian President felt pretty confident we could bring the Naltons into the Alliance," spoke Wade, turning and shifting his gaze to Hyram. "What do we have to offer the Naltons?"

Hyram sighed deeply and looked down at the deck before raising his eyes to gaze at Wade. "Probably a demonstration of what our Type Three battlesuits are capable of," he said uneasily. "The ships of the Naltons are highly computerized and almost capable of fighting a battle without the crew raising a hand, but they're very weak in combat troops. Crime on Nalton is virtually nonexistent and they have a very small police force, considering the size of their population. From what President Raytol told me, their actual ground troops total less than one hundred thousand and none of them has ever seen actual combat. They're mostly used for ceremonial purposes."

"I fear that's going to be the case with many of the nonaligned worlds," sighed Wade. "They're all highly advanced and peace has existed on their worlds for centuries. It's surprising they've resisted the Kleese for so long."

"It's the technology on their warships," Hyram responded. "Their weapons are equal to those of the Kleese and in some cases surpass what the Kleese have on their assault and exploration ships. The Kleese were hesitant to take the losses they would've suffered in bringing the nonaligned worlds into their Empire."

"That assumption no longer exists due to the Zaltule," Wade murmured with a slight nod. "The Zaltule's ships are designed for war and they seem intent on bringing the nonaligned worlds, as well as everyone else, into the Empire."

Hyram nodded his head in agreement and then spoke. "The nonaligned worlds are capable of fighting; they've just forgotten how."

"Then we'll have to teach them," Wade said, decisively. He felt apprehensive as he realized the mammoth task ahead of them. Twenty thousand Space Marines in battlesuits might not be enough.

As the Distant Star continued toward the planet, Wade kept a watchful eye on the tactical screen. Most passenger liners didn't have an advanced tactical screen in the Command Center; normally they just depended on their sensor screens. However, due to the missions the Distant Star had been sent out on over the years, an up to date military tactical screen had been added.

The Nalton ships rendezvoused with the two Kleese assault ships. There were eight Nalton battlecruisers in the squadron as it decelerated and then came to a stop in relation to the Kleese ships. After a few minutes, the squadron took up positions around the assault ships and began escorting them toward Nalton.

"Looks as if we're going to have company in orbit," said Captain Rios, unhappily. "I was hoping they would take a few sensor scans and then leave."

"Not our luck," responded Wade, folding his arms across his chest. "Try to stay as far away from them as possible while we're in orbit. Once they're satisfied the neutrality agreement is still being honored they should leave."

"If the Naltons don't turn us in," muttered Dash Stahls at the Helm.

"Just be ready to activate our energy screen," Wade replied. "It'll hold up long enough against two assault ships to allow us to activate the Fold Space Drive and escape."

"They won't turn us in," predicted Hyram, confidently. "They assured the Lanolthians they would guarantee our safety while we're in the system conducting negotiations."

"Only thing is they didn't expect to have two Kleese assault ships here at the same time," Captain Rios interjected with deep concern etched on his face. "Don't forget that a sublight missile could be launched and strike us before we could raise our energy shield."

"They have to open a missile hatch first," Wade said, understanding the captain's concern. "If we see one open, activate the shield and get us the hell out of here."

"I'll monitor their missile hatches closely," Sutton promised as he turned and adjusted the ship's sensors. "If they open a hatch, I'll know about it."

As the Distant Star neared the planet, they were contacted by the Nalton's equivalent of space control and assigned an orbit. The Naltons had been expecting them and no one on board was surprised when they were placed in an orbit far away from the two Kleese assault ships. They also noticed several squadrons of Nalton battlecruisers take up positions almost nonchalantly between the Human ship and the Kleese.

"I have a message on a tight beam instructing us to stay in the assigned orbit and not to launch any shuttles at this time," Anne Norman reported from Communications. "They expect the Kleese to be departing in a few hours and then we can send a shuttle down."

"Very well," answered Captain Rios, sitting down in his command chair. He wouldn't be leaving the Command Center until the two Kleese ships were safely out of the system.

Wade looked at several viewscreens, showing views of the planet. He recalled what he knew about the Nalton home planet and star system from the briefing he'd received earlier from Marken and Admiral Adamson. Nalton was a heavily forested planet covered with small, deep lakes and snaking aquamarine rivers. The population of the planet was slightly over four billion and there was no orbiting moon.

Nalton was the third planet out from the system's primary and slightly smaller than Earth. There were eight planets in the system with planets four and five having a large number of orbiting moons as well as a massive asteroid field between them. The Naltons had a number of large domed habitats and mining operations on the moons with nearly three hundred million Naltons living upon them. There was also a robust mining operation in the asteroids where much of the system's refined metals came from.

As Wade settled down to wait, he wondered how Ryan's combat training was going. By now, Ryan was well into it and would be nearing the final, grueling tests. Wade was deeply concerned that before this current mission was over his brother would be joining them. He hoped not, but if the nonaligned worlds wanted a demonstration as to whether the Humans could stand up to the Zaltule in armed combat on the ground there was a high likelihood that Ryan and his company would soon be on their way.

Wade let out a heavy sigh of worry. Ryan was old enough to look out for himself, but Wade still felt responsible since he was the oldest. However, he didn't know what he could do to help protect his younger brother in what was to come. He wished he could talk to Beth about his concerns, but she was far away with the rest of Seventh Fleet. Looking at the viewscreens and the blue-green world they displayed, Wade couldn't help but notice how peaceful everything looked. Wade had a haunted feeling that very soon all that was going to change and not for the better.

Chapter Ten

Wade was standing on a firing range just outside one of the Naltons' small military bases. A viewing stand had been set up and over two hundred Naltons were seated, waiting for the demonstration to begin. The majority of them were in the Nalton military with a few important government officials there to observe as well.

For nearly four days, Hyram Blake and his team of negotiators had been holding high-level talks with the Nalton government and military as well as several other nonaligned worlds, which had sent representatives. Hyram hadn't been aware that three other nonaligned worlds would be represented and had been burning the midnight oil to get everything set up for this demonstration.

"Well, this should be interesting," commented Sergeant Russell in his South Chicago accent, looking at the packed viewing stand.

"Just don't blow them up instead of the target," drawled Sergeant Dawson, who was standing next to him. Dawson was from the Midwest and had a slight southern drawl when he spoke.

Wade and the two sergeants were all wearing their Type Three battlesuits waiting for the signal from Hyram for the demonstration to begin. Hyram was currently addressing the spectators as to what they were about to see. Once they'd learned that the Naltons and the other three races wanted to see a demonstration of Humans in battlesuits, Wade had requested that the Fire Fox be sent to the Nalton system. The large troop transport was currently waiting just outside the system with two light cruisers as escorts. Sergeants Russell and Dawson had been sent ahead in a shuttle for the demonstration.

Even as Wade watched, Hyram seemed to finish his presentation and turned to face him. He waved his arms, indicating that the demonstration could begin.

"Alright, Sergeants," Wade said over his suit com. "We have twenty remote controlled vehicles that will be coming over that rise a thousand meters away. There are also forty popup weapon emplacements, which will appear between the vehicles and us. They're not armed, but the drill is to see how rapidly we can annihilate the attacking force and the popups. Sergeant Russell, you're carrying an energy cannon so your first priority is the popups. Sergeant Dawson, you'll assist with annihilating the popups with explosive rounds from your RG rifle. I'll focus on the vehicles with my suit explosive rounds. This shouldn't take long."

"Yes, Sir," Sergeant Dawson answered. "Let's make this look impressive!"

"Piece of cake," added Sergeant Russell as he removed his energy cannon from his shoulder to cradle it in his arms. "Just say when."

Wade turned to face the small rise and waited expectantly. He didn't have long to wait as twenty small remote controlled tanks suddenly rolled over the hill. They were slightly larger than a mid-sized car but they appeared to be heavily armored. They had one turret with a medium-sized cannon affixed.

At the same time as the tanks rolled over the rise, forty embedded popup weapons rose up from the ground with their guns swiveling to lock on the three battlesuits. It was an excellent job of synchronization.

"Fire!" commanded Wade. His suit sensors immediately locked upon the tanks and began assigning targets. Before he could fire a round, one of the tanks fired and an explosion threw him violently to the ground.

"What the hell?" yelled Dawson as flying rock and dirt fell on him. He was already firing his RG rifle at the popups as quickly as he could. Several vanished as the grenade-like explosives tore them apart. "I thought they were supposed to be unarmed!"

Wade staggered back to his feet and began firing off suit explosive rounds as rapidly as he could. "Change of plans," Wade called out, feeling pissed off. The tanks weren't supposed to have been armed with live rounds. "Sergeant Russell, switch to suit explosives and help me clear out those tanks."

Immediately, massive explosions began to roll across the advancing line of tanks. Even as several exploded and were destroyed from the explosives fire, two more fired at the three Humans. Sergeant Dawson screamed as an explosion hurled him violently up into the air, causing him to come crashing down to the ground. On Wade's HUD, Sergeant Dawson's green icon switched to amber.

"Report!" yelled Wade as he frantically fired explosive rounds as rapidly as possible. Already, in the line of tanks, six of them were burning and five others were lying on their sides. Even as he watched two more were hit by Sergeant Russell.

"Leg's busted," Dawson groaned as he staggered back upright. He immediately began blowing the popups apart as he fired round after explosive round from his RG rifle.

Wade nodded; he knew Dawson's suit would be injecting him with meds including painkillers. Several more explosions went off close to them, showering them with debris, but the three kept up an unrelenting fire of explosive rounds. In another few seconds, the target range became quiet as the last target was blown apart. Smoke drifted everywhere and a number of the small tanks were on fire. Where the popups had been, small craters indicated their destruction.

Wade turned around to see where Hyram was. The negotiator was about to get a piece of Wade's mind over this demonstration. The tanks were supposed to have been unarmed and Hyram hadn't briefed Wade that the demonstration had been changed. As his eyes focused on Hyram, he could see the man was standing in front of several nonaligned world members gesturing with his hands and pointing at the burning tanks. Even from here, Wade could tell that Hyram was deeply upset. Wade decided it was best not to say anything at the moment. They would discuss it when they returned to the Distant Star.

"How are you feeling, Dawson?" asked Wade, turning toward the sergeant.

"Fine," Dawson replied. "The pain meds have kicked in and I'm pretty sure the suit's already injected me with medical nanites to fix my leg."

"Medical Nanites?" asked Wade, sounding confused. "I didn't know Harnett was ready to try those out yet in the suits."

Russell laughed. "We're the guinea pigs," he said, walking over to stand next to Dawson. He could see that Dawson's right suit leg had a good-sized dent in it. "Or I should say Sergeant Dawson here is the first guinea pig."

Before Wade could say anything else, Hyram came striding over to where the three were standing. He stopped and looked up at the towering battlesuits with an aggravated look in his eyes.

"Colonel Nelson, I'm extremely sorry about this demonstration. The Naltons have expressed their deep regret over the use of explosives. They assured me that the tanks were set to fire their rounds to go off in close proximity to you and not to strike you directly. They felt this would be more impressive to the other three races that were observing the exercise. I didn't know this change had been made until the drill began. I hope none of you were hurt."

"We got through it," replied Wade, evenly.

Hyram glanced over at Sergeant Dawson's suit and his eyes widened when he saw the huge dent in the suit's leg armor. "Are you alright?"

"Fine," replied Dawson, feeling a little giddy from the meds.

"Sergeants Dawson and Russell need to get back up to the Fire Fox," Wade said. He wanted Dawson in the ship's infirmary as quickly as possible so his leg could be checked out.

"Fine," Hyram answered with a nod. "Colonel Nelson, if you'll come with me, several of the military people as well as a few of the government officials would like to see your battlesuit up close."

"Are they going to join the Alliance?" asked Wade, hoping the drill hadn't been a waste of time. He was still feeling aggravated at one of his men being injured.

"I think so," replied Hyram, nodding his head. "They seemed quite impressed with the demonstration and I think after you answer a few questions, they'll feel well satisfied in our ability to defend their planets from a ground attack by the Zaltule."

Wade nodded. He quickly ordered the two sergeants to return to the shuttle and head back to the Fire Fox. However, in the back of his mind he wondered if the tanks had actually been programmed to miss. Several of those rounds, particularly the one that had injured Sergeant Dawson, had come uncomfortably close.

-

Harmock watched as the Warrior's Fire's weapons lit up the energy shield of the nonaligned world's battlecruiser, causing cascades of glowing energy to erupt. This was the fourth nonaligned system he'd attacked in the past three weeks and its defenders were putting up a stiff resistance.

"Send a message to the reserve fleet to strike the enemy force from the rear," Harmock ordered as the flagship shook slightly from inbound weapons fire impacting upon the ship's energy screen.

Recently, he had ordered that all Zaltule attacking fleets would have a reserve force of two hundred vessels accompanying them to be used if the nonaligned system they were attacking was heavily defended. He'd reduced his attacking fleets to four to ensure he had enough reserve ships for support. After each attack, any ship losses suffered by the main fleet would be replaced by ships from the reserve. A message was then sent back to the main Zaltule fleet stationed at the Zaltule shipyards to send replacements to the reserve force to bring it back up to strength.

"Message sent," replied Dalock from Communications.

"Reserve force should be in position in twenty minutes," added Minor Overlord Gareth.

On the main viewscreen, a Delton battlecruiser exploded in a fiery release of energy as several Kleese antimatter missiles penetrated its weakened energy screen, annihilating the vessel. The Delton battlecruisers were slim vessels nearly seven hundred meters in length and were equipped with some type of primary energy beam, which could be fired from the nose of the ships. It was far more powerful than the energy beams the Zaltule had at their disposal.

"These nonaligned worlds are truly a threat to the Empire," Gareth commented as the Delton ship the Warrior's Fire was attacking finally succumbed as several energy beams flashed through its battered shield. Several large sections of hull material were blasted loose, then two twenty-megaton antimatter missiles struck the hull and the Delton ship ceased to be.

The battle was raging along a front nearly two million kilometers long. Two hundred and twelve Delton ships were fighting stubbornly against five hundred of the Zaltule disk ships, attempting to keep them away from their home world. Occasionally, several of the Deltons' ravishing beams of energy would penetrate a Kleese shield, blasting massive holes into the stricken ship and setting off secondary explosions. Already, twelve Zaltule warships had been destroyed and a number of others heavily damaged from the energy beams. In return, the Deltons had lost forty of their vessels.

"They will only be a threat to the Empire if they become united, and that is not going to happen," Harmock spoke in a harsh voice. "The Kleese are the superior race in the galaxy and the Zaltule are the warriors. It will be through us that the Kleese Empire will someday stretch across the galaxy."

"As it should be," Gareth replied as the Warrior's Fire moved on to its next target. Looking around the Command Center, he saw that the twenty Kleese at the ship's control consoles were focused on their duties. The Zaltule lived for combat, and the air in the Command Center was intense as the command crew fought the ship to bring glory and victory to the Kleese Empire.

The battle in space raged on, with neither side pulling back. For every Zaltule warship the Deltons managed to destroy, they lost two of their own. The Deltons' energy screens were better and their energy beams more deadly, but the Zaltule battlecruisers were just too large. It was taking six or more strikes by energy beams to disable or destroy one. The sheer number of weapons the Kleese were able to target upon the defending Delton ships were just too much for their powerful energy shields to bear. Shield after shield was being blasted down, exposing the vulnerable armored hulls to the Kleese weapons.

The Deltons were a small race, standing slightly more than a meter in height. Their bodies were humanoid with large round eyes that could see in the dark. They were of slim stature and highly dependent upon their computers to operate their warships. In the early years of their civilization, the Deltons had been a savage and warlike people, but those years were far behind them.

"Ship 247-886 has been destroyed," reported the Delton in front of the flagship's sensors.

"We will not be able to hold our line much longer," commented Baylith, who was second in command. He turned his large eyes to the Fleet Commander. "We are losing too many ships."

"Long-range detectors have located a second Kleese fleet inbound via Fold Space," reported the sensor operator. "They will be within attack range shortly."

"We're too heavily outnumbered for any hope of victory," Baylith spoke with great sadness in his voice. He knew that soon the Kleese would be landing on their world and placing their obedience collars around his people's necks.

Fleet Commander Achlyn thought about his options. If his fleet were destroyed then any hope of a free Delton race would be gone. He must preserve his fleet and hope that someday he could perhaps return and drive the Kleese from his world. "Is the evacuation fleet prepared?"

"Yes," the communications officer reported. "They're awaiting your orders."

"Tell them to initiate the plan; we'll meet them at the rendezvous with what ships we can," ordered Achlyn, letting out a deep breath. By activating the plan, he was telling the leaders of his world that there was no hope for victory.

"As you command," the communications officer reported. He quickly sent the necessary messages, knowing that any hope of setting foot back on their home planet was now gone.

For weeks, they'd been preparing for the Kleese attack after hearing of what was happening to other nonaligned worlds. They'd known it was only a short matter of time before the Kleese came to their system to bring it forcibly into the Empire. Achlyn did not intend to wear a Kleese collar of obedience now or ever. He would die with his fleet first if it became necessary. However, the Delton High Assembly had crafted another plan, one that gave them hope for the future. They'd gathered all of their passenger and many of their cargo ships and placed inside them all that was needed to continue the Delton civilization. It would be Achlyn's responsibility to escort them out of the Kleese Empire and find a new world in a distant section of the galaxy.

For several more minutes, the battle raged, and then the communications officer turned toward Achlyn. "Evacuation fleet has entered Fold Space and is safely away."

"Ships 189-779 and 121-768 have been destroyed," the sensor operator reported. Examining the tactical screen, he knew over half of the fleet was now nothing more than glowing debris.

"We have many ships that are heavily damaged," Baylith reported, his large eyes focusing on the commander. "They will not be able to withdraw."

Achlyn nodded in understanding. "Order all ships with functioning Fold Space Drives to implement withdrawal plan Delton-221 and rendezvous at the emergency coordinates. All other ships are to cover our withdrawal."

The orders were quickly passed and eighty-seven Delton battlecruisers suddenly spun about on their axis and accelerated away from the surprised Zaltule battlecruisers. They continued to gather speed and then activated their Fold Space Drives, altering course to take them safely out of the system.

-

"They're fleeing!" roared Gareth as he saw the red threat icons that represented the Delton battlecruisers pull away from the battle and then enter Fold Space.

"We'll worry about them later," Harmock spoke in a hard and cold voice. "For now we must destroy the ships that can't escape." Looking at the tactical screen, Harmock could still see nearly forty Delton battlecruisers continuing to attack his fleet. With their reduced numbers, they wouldn't last long against the Zaltule.

For long minutes, Harmock watched impassively as the remaining Delton ships were hunted down and destroyed. None attempted to flee but fought until their ships were blown apart. Harmock stood quietly as he thought about the ships, which had escaped. That had been unexpected and now he had the aggravating prospect of having to hunt them down and destroy them. It might take thousands of vessels to find that small of a fleet in the myriad of stars that encompassed the Empire. With a slight feeling of resignation, he knew he would have to call upon the Council of Overlords and request the Empire's exploration ships and assault ships be put to the task. It might take a while, but they would eventually find the missing Delton ships.

-

Fleet Commander Achlyn watched tensely as his flagship exited Fold Space. The star system they had entered was a red giant, and they were far from the system's primary. It was in this system the evacuation fleet was supposed to be waiting.

"Contacts!" reported the sensor operator as numerous green icons began filling the tactical screen.

Achlyn watched the screen, feeling relieved that the evacuation fleet had made it to the rendezvous point along with a sizable portion of his military fleet. "Give me a status on the ships that are here," he ordered. "Including our battlecruisers."

"Eighty-seven battlecruisers, sixteen passenger liners, and twenty-eight cargo ships," replied the sensor operator promptly.

Achlyn nodded. That was all the ships that had been equipped with modern Fold Space Drives and included in the evacuation. The passenger liners were large vessels, nearly one thousand meters in length, and quite luxurious. They'd been used by Deltons primarily interested in taking lengthy vacations to other nonaligned worlds. Each passenger liner held over two thousand civilians. Many of them were scientists, technicians, and even farmers who would be needed to raise crops on a new world. The cargo ships contained supplies and the materials necessary to help establish a new Delton civilization. Each cargo ship held several hundred more civilians plus their crews. In all, not counting the battlecruisers, nearly forty-five thousand civilians had made it to the rendezvous coordinates.

"Where to now?" asked Baylith. "I don't think we should stay in this system too long. The Kleese will be searching for us shortly."

"To some of the outer nonaligned worlds," responded Achlyn, turning to face his second officer. "We must warn them of what the Kleese are doing before we flee the Empire. Some of them might want to send evacuation fleets along with us."

"It will be a long voyage," Baylith commented his large dark eyes growing even wider. "The civilians might not like being inside the ships for such an extended period of time."

"They will adapt," Achlyn answered. "We will spend six hours here to allow our warships to make necessary repairs to the damage they suffered in the battle. Once repairs have been made, we'll enter Fold Space and head outward toward the far reaches of the Empire. Perhaps by warning other nonaligned worlds, they will be better prepared when the Kleese come for them."

Harmock glared with rage at the four Delton leaders in front of him. Each wore a metallic obedience collar and had been defiant in their answers when asked about where the Delton warships had gone. Harmock stepped over and took a small black box from the hands of one of his fellow Kleese. He saw the fear suddenly grow in the Deltons' large eyes as they recognized what the box was. It had been explained to them earlier when the obedience collars had been placed around their necks.

The Deltons looked at each other nervously and then back at the terrifying Kleese. There were six of the spider-like Zaltule in the audience chamber. Just gazing upon them was a frightening experience, sending cold chills through the four leaders.

"You will answer!" Harmock snarled as he pressed one of the buttons.

A resounding explosion rang out in the chamber as the head of one of the Deltons was blown off, showering the other three with blood. They cringed as they saw their fellow leader fall lifeless to the floor, his body still pumping blood, which was spilling out onto the ornate tiles. They looked back in terror at the Kleese that towered over them.

"How many ships were in the fleet?" demanded Harmock, stepping closer and gesturing toward the black box he still held in his hand. "I will continue to blow your heads off until someone talks. If you refuse, then I will start on your families, including your offspring."

The three looked at one another, knowing there were too many Deltons who knew about the evacuation fleet. Even if they said nothing, the Kleese would eventually learn of the fleet. Fortunately, the rendezvous coordinates were only known to the ship commanders and they were long gone.

"We sent an evacuation fleet of forty-four ships away from our world," one of them confessed his large eyes wide with fear, knowing his answer probably meant his death. He then looked up at the Zaltule leader with defiance replacing the fear. "They're going out of the Empire where you will never find them!"

Harmock eyed the three, feeling defiled at having to deal with a lower race even though it was a nonaligned world rich in science and technology. "You should have answered my question sooner," he spoke as he adjusted the black box and pressed the button again. Three more explosions rang out as the remaining leaders fell lifeless to the floor.

"That's more ships we'll have to find," spoke Gareth his voice showing aggravation.

"They should be together," commented Harmock as he turned away from the dead Deltons. "Their warships and civilian ships are bound to have joined up. When we find one ship, we'll find all of them."

Harmock left the chamber, his multifaceted eyes gazing about. Zaltule warriors were fanning out across the planet, eliminating resistance and placing the collars of obedience on all Delton leaders and their scientists. Soon the planet would be completely compliant and another cog in the growing Kleese Empire. As soon as he returned to his flagship, he would be sending a message to the Council of Overlords. They had some ships to find and he expected the council to cooperate fully or he would be forced to add more of the Zaltule to its governing body.

Ryan stood once more upon the summit of Charring Mountain, only this time over seventy percent of his platoon stood with him. Over the past weeks, they'd learned how to use the Type Four suits to spot the hidden weapons on Charring and to take them out before they could fire. The suits now felt like a second skin and for the most part, Ryan couldn't even tell he was wearing one. Even the neural implant now seemed like a natural extension of his senses.

"That was easy," Casey spoke as she looked at the upraised pedestal and the waiting red button on the pylon, which would signal victory. "Surely this will mark the end of our training."

"Possibly," conceded Ryan with a nod. He walked over to the pedestal followed by his platoon and stepping up onto the platform, pressed the red button on the pylon one more time.

"Drill is over," Major Stevens announced over their suit coms. "Everyone report to the parade grounds for an announcement."

"I wonder what that's about?" asked Private Parker. This was the first time a drill had ended that they had been told to report to the parade grounds. He wondered if they had done something wrong.

"Guess we'll find out when we get there," Private Adams responded as she turned around and began walking toward the steep slope that led back down from the summit.

Lauren hoped this signified that their training was over, though she felt apprehensive about where they might be deployed. The training over the last few weeks had been intense and physically exerting. The platoon had been forced to push the new battlesuits to the limit as they learned to respond instinctively to changing battlefield conditions. The biggest part of the training was learning to trust the neural implants and use them in conjunction with the suit's weapons to assess and annihilate an opponent.

Ryan and Casey followed the platoon back down the mountain as their thoughts dwelled on the weeks of intensive training they'd been through. Both had been shot by stunners numerous times and felt the impact of RG rounds bouncing off their suits. They had learned to use caution and stealth to accomplish their objectives and come to realize that a marine in a Type Four battlesuit was far more dangerous than one in a Type Three.

Reaching the parade grounds, Ryan had his platoon line up in formation and then they stood waiting for Major Stevens. With surprise, he saw both Major Stevens and Major Winfrey walking toward them, followed by Captain Taylor and Sergeant Morris. The four weren't wearing battlesuits but were dressed in their normal Space Marine uniforms.

"Congratulations," Major Stevens' voice rang out as he gazed at the assembled platoon. "You're the first platoon to complete combat training in the Type Four battlesuits. We expect the other three platoons to finish their training over the next few days."

"You will be deploying immediately," Major Winfrey continued as his eyes swept over the platoon. "A new troop transport has been constructed for your deployment. Over a month ago, a mission was sent to the nonaligned worlds in an attempt to bring them into an Alliance our government is attempting to form. This Alliance is essential if we hope to successfully fight the Kleese. Your transport will be sent to assist in possible combat operations against Kleese ground forces, most likely their warrior caste the Zaltule."

This announcement caused the marines to shift about uneasily at the prospect of fighting the legendary Zaltule they'd heard so much about. Several looked at each other and then their attention returned to Major Winfrey.

"You will not be going alone as four hundred other Space Marines in Type Three battlesuits have also been assigned to the transport," he added. "This transport has been specifically constructed to take you into a hostile combat environment, go into orbit, and then land you at your target. It's crucial we show these possible Alliance worlds that we have the capability to fight the Kleese on the ground and drive them from a world."

"I knew it," muttered Alexander, shaking his head. "We're going to fight the Zaltule and we're going to die."

"No, we're not," answered Lauren. She was glad that Alexander was on their private frequency where the others couldn't hear. "We're going to kick their butts; that's what we've been trained to do."

"I hope you're right," replied Alexander, falling silent. Too often in the scenarios they'd fought on Charring Mountain he'd been one of the lead scouts and had been killed so often he had lost count.

"I am right!" Lauren said, loudly. "Now, listen to what the Major is saying." She was hoping to hear more information as to what they might soon be facing.

Ryan listened to Major Stevens and Major Winfrey as they continued to talk. There was no doubt in his mind they were being deployed to where his brother had gone. Ryan suspected very shortly he would be seeing Wade again. He just hoped they both returned from this mission; it would devastate their parents if something happened to one or both of them. Ryan was determined to make sure that didn't occur. He glanced over at Casey, glad she was at his side. Casey was his closest friend and he knew that as long as the two of them were together, they could get through anything the Kleese might throw at them.

Casey listened to Major Steven's talk about their upcoming deployment. She felt nervous, knowing that they would shortly be going into combat. As a clone, she'd only known seven years of life. It had been a fantastic experience and she had no desire to see it end. She'd worked as hard as possible, even putting in extra time at the practice ranges making sure she could handle the Type Four suit.

Casey had passed up on several rec opportunities just so she could improve her combat skills. She wondered now if she should've taken advantage of one or two of those opportunities as she might not get anymore soon. There was still so much about being Human she wanted to learn, and she was depending on Wade to teach her. She knew that a few things were probably off limits, at least for now. A smile spread across her face as she thought about Wade and what she hoped for in the future. She felt her face flush and then forced herself to focus on Major Stevens. Some things could definitely wait until later.

Chapter Eleven

Ryan and Casey stepped out of the large lunar shuttle along with a number of other members of their platoon. They'd been given seventy-two hours leave and decided to spend it at Luna City.

"Have you ever been here before?" Casey asked, excited at the prospect of seeing something new. Other than Vesta and Centerpoint, she hadn't traveled to any of the other habitats scattered across the system.

"A couple of times," Ryan answered as they followed the crowd to the check in stations at the airlocks that led to the city proper. "Once with my parents and another time my brother brought me here to show me the fleet training facility." Ryan knew that was Wade's last attempt to direct him toward the fleet instead of the Space Marines.

"It's like most other habitats," Private Juan Rios commented from just behind them. Rios was from Luna City. "You have to be careful in Luna City, though. A lot of trade from all over the system comes through here, and there are some unscrupulous people who will buy and sell almost anything if there's profit in it. Luna City has had to increase the size of its police force to keep the black market under control."

"Why not eliminate it?" asked Casey, feeling confused. "If it's a problem, why does it still exist?"

"It serves a purpose," Juan answered with a frown on his face. "Sometimes there are things which can only be found on the black market; even the government occasionally procures items there."

"Where does the stuff on the black market come from?" asked Casey, wondering who would sell anything to these profiteers.

"From Earth," Ryan said as they reached one of the lines of people waiting to be cleared for entry into Luna City. "There are still small ships sneaking down to Earth in search of anything that could be traded or sold on the black market. I've heard there are several prospecting ships that routinely make illicit runs down to the surface."

After passing through the check in station, the group stepped out into Luna City. The city itself was covered with a transparent dome, which stretched ten kilometers across with a center height of two kilometers. A light energy screen protected the dome from meteor impacts. Even if the dome were compromised, the energy screen would ensure the protective atmosphere stayed in place while repairs were made. The landscape was covered with tall skyscrapers and green parks reaching from one edge of the dome to the other.

"How many people live here?" asked Casey her eyes filled with wonder. Some of the buildings she was looking at must be fifty or sixty stories tall. They were the highest she'd ever seen. Not even Vesta had buildings this tall.

Juan grinned, noticing how excited Casey was at seeing his home. "There are dozens of habitats that make up Luna City," he said in explanation. "Nearly seven million people live here on the Moon. This habitat we're in comprises the original one, which was greatly expanded when the new dome was added by the Kiveans."

"I want to do some shopping," Lauren announced as she looked around at the others. "I have several months' pay that needs to be spent. I could use some new shoes and a few other things."

"Shopping sounds interesting," Casey said, curious to see the Luna City shops. Being closer to Earth and the ongoing salvage operations, there were products available here that couldn't be found anywhere else.

"I wouldn't mind doing some shopping," commented Private Mary Hatterson, wanting to be included. Mary was another clone and this was also her first trip to Luna City.

"Okay," Lauren replied, pleased she wouldn't be going alone. She'd been to Luna City before and knew where the best clothing shops were located. "Why don't we split up and meet later at a restaurant?"

"The Chinese Luna Express might be a good one," Juan suggested. "It has really good Chinese food and my cousin knows the owner." Juan had been fortunate that when he had been evacuated to Luna City to find that he had an older first cousin that had survived.

"Sounds like a plan to me," Lauren said in agreement.

"Let's do it," Ryan said. "What say we meet at the restaurant in five hours? That should give everyone time to do what they want."

He wanted to go astro gliding to see if it was as exciting as everyone said it was. It had originally been one of the main tourist draws to Luna City prior to the original Kleese attack. There was a large park with a high cliff where one could be equipped with artificial wings and leap off into the open air. The area was kept at Luna normal gravity to allow one to experience what it felt like to fly.

The group split up, with Lauren leading the women toward the shopping district while Juan led the men toward the Astro Park. Around them, the city seemed to buzz with the muted voices of excited people and the sounds of a busy city.

-

Lauren was trying on her tenth pair of shoes with Casey and Mary watching with interest. She currently had on a pair of black high-heeled boots that came up nearly to her knees.

"I don't understand," Casey said in confusion. "As high as those heels are, those boots are going to be very difficult to walk in. They don't seem very practical."

Lauren giggled and looked at Casey knowingly. "It's the look," she explained. "Men like women in high heels and these will really catch their eyes."

"Sex!" Mary blurted out in sudden understanding. "It's all about getting men to want to take you to bed."

"Sort of," Lauren responded with a grin as she slid down the zippers on the boots so she could take them off. "Sometir men need to be enticed and sometimes it's just fun to do some harmless flirting. Plus, I look really good in these boots. I think I'll buy this pair."

"I guess I just don't understand," Casey said, feeling confused. She folded her arms across her chest and looked at Lauren. All her clothes were pretty simple; she either wore her military uniforms or when off duty a pair of pants and a colorful blouse. The emphasis that normal Humans put on sex still bewildered her.

"Excuse me, ladies," a male voice spoke from just behind them.

Looking up, they saw the store clerk that had been helping Lauren. He had a concerned look upon his face.

"I couldn't help noticing that two of you are clones. It might be wise if you stayed inside the store for awhile."

"Stay in the store?" Lauren repeated her eyes focusing sharply on the clerk. "Why?"

"I'm afraid you picked a bad time to come to the downtown shops," he began, sounding embarrassed. "There's a demonstration going on down the street at one of the government buildings. While it's supposed to be a peaceful demonstration, for your own safety I would recommend staying inside."

"What type of demonstration?" asked Casey, feeling curious.

The clerk let out a deep breath and then spoke again. "It's a demonstration against clones," he said. "There are a lot of people in Luna City that feel too many clones are being created and that the process should either be slowed down or eliminated. They also feel that clones shouldn't have the same rights as a regular Human. Some of the people are very vocal in their views, and I wouldn't want to see any of you get caught up in it."

The three women walked over to the large window at the front of the store and looked out. They could see a large crowd had assembled at a building several blocks away. Many of the people in the crowd were holding signs and others were chanting. "NO MORE CLONES! NO MORE CLONES!"

"Does this happen very often?" asked Lauren, turning back toward the clerk who had followed them to the window.

"Several times a week," he replied with a long sigh. "Whenever it does my business generally comes to a stop. It makes people afraid to come downtown to the shops."

Casey was trying to read some of the signs. She could see several that read, "CLONES ARE NOT HUMAN!" and others that said, "NO RIGHTS FOR CLONES!"

"Do people really feel that badly toward us?" Casey asked the clerk, feeling stunned at what she was seeing. She couldn't help but think about the incident in the Chinese restaurant on Centerpoint a while back.

"Some do and others don't," he answered. "I think many are afraid that someday the clones will replace regular Humans."

"What do you think?" Mary asked her eyes focusing on the clerk.

"People are people," he replied, shrugging his shoulders. "To me it doesn't matter if they're born from Human parents or come from a cloning tank. Now if you ladies wouldn't mind stepping away from the window, I have some more shoes you might be interested in."

Ryan had just leaped off the tall lunar cliff for the third time. The feeling of flying was exhilarating. Gliding high up in the air, feeling the warm air in his face as he made gentle sweeping circles in the light lunar gravity was fantastic. The pair of wings he was wearing were ten feet across and gave him just enough lift to allow him to glide in the gentle air currents. He wore a control belt that ensured he stayed in control of the wings. If he became unbalanced, the control belt would quickly take over control of the wings until he was in stable flight again. So far, that had only happened once when he descended too fast.

"This is great!" yelled Alexander as he swooped by, catching the wind currents with his wings.

Ryan had to agree. He thought flying in the battlesuits had been fun, once he had gotten the hang of it. However, nothing compared to what he was now experiencing. He wished he and Wade had come here when they came to Luna City. From this height, he could look out over the park and into part of the city itself. The scurrying people looked like ants, and in the distance, he could see what looked like some kind of disturbance. He could see police vehicles rushing toward one section of the city with their lights flashing and now he could hear their sirens. He wondered if there had been an accident.

A few minutes later, they were all safely back down on the ground. Checking the time, they noticed it was nearly time to go meet the girls. Reaching the edge of the park, Juan flagged down a cab and gave directions to the restaurant. The electric powered vehicle quickly moved off, turning onto a main street and headed into the city.

"What were all the sirens about earlier?" Ryan asked the driver.

"Clone riot," the man replied stone faced. "There was a demonstration at one of the government buildings where a number of clones work. It got a little violent and the police had to move in to break it up."

"Does that happen often?" asked Ryan, wondering how close the riot was to the shops the girls had gone off to.

"It doesn't turn violent often," the cab driver answered. "But recently, the demonstrations have been getting larger and more out of control. If something isn't done soon, this whole clone thing is going to get out of hand and people are going to start getting hurt."

"What do you think about the clones?" Alexander asked.

"They're grown in tanks so they're not Human," the cab driver answered definitively. "They may have their place in the military to save Human lives, but they shouldn't be allowed to take jobs regular Humans can do."

Alexander started to reply, but Ryan caught his eyes and shook his head. He decided it was best if they remained silent. No point in getting the cab driver aggravated. Ryan leaned back in his seat and thought over what the cab driver had said. It was becoming more obvious to him every day that the public's feeling against the clones was getting worse. The problem was he didn't see what could be done to change their minds.

Xatul stood in front of the Kleese Council of Overlords listening to the current dispute. The warrior caste was demanding more resources be allocated to their ship building program and that contingents of Zaltule warriors be placed on all of the trading stations.

"The trading stations will remain under our control," spoke Raluth in a cold and hard voice.

"I operate three stations," Syndat spoke in a loud voice. "I will not turn over control of the stations to the Zaltule!"

"Control is inconsequential as long as there are members of the warrior caste on board for security reasons," Creedal responded.

"Those trading stations represent massive investments by some of us here on this council," Martule spoke his eyes focusing on the four Zaltule Overlords. "They will not be turned over to the warrior caste."

"We do not wish control," Darthu responded in an impassionate voice. "As we strike more of the nonaligned worlds there is a danger that the trading stations may be targeted. We only wish to ensure their safety."

"We will agree to a small security force of the warrior caste," Xatul spoke in a commanding voice, reaching a decision. "Our own security forces on the stations should be sufficient to resist any attack by the nonaligned worlds, though I doubt if any such attack will take place."

Bixutl remained silent. So far, no one had mentioned to the Zaltule that such an attack had taken place years ago when the Humans managed to take control of a trading station and fly it through Fold Space to their star system where it still remained. Two days previously, he had received a report from the exploration ship he'd sent to check on the Humans. An assault ship had managed to slip into the extreme outer reaches of the system and take sensor scans. The Humans were still there and stronger than ever.

The question now was how Bixutl could use that information to his advantage. At some point in time, the Zaltule were bound to learn of the Humans and what they'd done. He wondered what their reaction would be to that information. So far, the other council Overlords had remained silent about the Humans either believing their threat had faded away or fearful of what the Zaltule response would be if they learned a trading station had been lost to an inferior race.

Bixutl turned his attention to the Supreme Overlord, wondering if he could use the information he now possessed to remove Xatul from his esteemed position and seize it for himself.

"We will provide the warrior caste with the materials it needs to produce more warships," Xatul said, looking across the council.

He didn't mention that he'd already sent out orders for more exploration ships to be built as well. While he didn't expect there to be armed conflict between the Zaltule and the rest of the Kleese, it never hurt to ensure he had the forces necessary to reign in the warrior caste if need be.

"What of new weapons?" demanded Raluth, turning toward the Zaltule Overlords.

"We have some promising technology we've procured from several of the nonaligned worlds that have recently been brought into the Empire," Darthu responded, evenly. "Our scientists are still evaluating its potential to be used as weapons."

"Will you be sharing that technology with the rest of the council?" asked Martule.

"In time," answered Darthu. "There is much research yet to be done."

Bixutl nodded to himself. The Zaltule were stalling. It was evident to him that the warrior caste didn't intend to share any advanced weaponry they might procure from the nonaligned worlds. He wondered why Xatul wasn't objecting more stringently.

"I have heard some disturbing rumors coming from Sector Eleven of our Empire," Keluth ventured in a carefully controlled voice. "One of our trading stations has reported someone is trying to organize an Alliance of nonaligned worlds to resist the Zaltule."

"An Alliance!" roared Lackeln his multifaceted eyes focusing sharply on the Kleese Overlord. "Who is trying to organize this Alliance?"

"That is unknown," replied Keluth, trying to stay calm. "It was reported by some conscripts who overheard several members of one of the nonaligned worlds discussing it."

"The nonaligned worlds cannot be allowed to form an Alliance against us," spoke Xatul in a commanding voice. "With their science and technology they could pose an imminent threat to the Empire."

"I will send word to Overlord Harmock immediately," stated Darthu. "It might be necessary to send a Zaltule fleet to crush this budding Alliance before it becomes a reality."

"A wise decision," Xatul replied.

He strongly suspected that if someone was trying to organize the nonaligned worlds into an Alliance, it had to be the Humans. He wished now that he had sent an exploration ship to check up on that upstart race. By not doing so, he might have endangered his position as Supreme Overlord.

Ryan and his platoon were aboard the newly constructed troop assault ship Defender. Ryan had been amazed when he'd first seen the massive warship, for a warship was what the Defender was. The troop assault ship was one thousand meters in length, two hundred meters in width, and one hundred and eighty meters in height. It had the firepower of a battlecruiser, including a particle beam cannon in the bow as well as two heavy KEW cannons. If the ship had to fight, it could hold its own in combat.

Even more importantly, the ship had eighty Space Marines trained in the use of the new Type Four battlesuits and another four hundred trained in the use of the Type Threes. There were also eight of the new hover tanks in the main cargo hold to be used if heavier firepower was needed on the ground.

"She's quite a ship," commented Casey as they stood in a small observation room waiting for the ship to depart. The observation room had a number of massive titanium reinforced viewports that stretched from one end of the room to the other. When in battle, combat armor would slide down to cover them.

In the distance, Ryan could see one of the light cruisers moving into screening position between the Defender and Centerpoint Station. He knew that four light cruisers and eight assault ships had been assigned as escorts for the Defender. A sizable force, which made him feel secure if they encountered any problems on their trip to the nonaligned worlds where Seventh Fleet awaited.

"Do you think we'll see combat?" asked Casey, turning her eyes toward Ryan.

"I'm sure of it," Ryan answered. "I don't think they would be sending out this force if they didn't believe it would be needed." Ryan knew that Major Stevens was currently in the Command Center where he would be observing their entry into Fold Space. Only Major Winfrey had stayed behind to begin training the next group of recruits for the Type Four suits.

Casey looked around. A few other marines were also in the observation room, anxiously waiting for the ship to begin accelerating away from Centerpoint. Even as Casey watched, the ship started moving and the station began to fall away. Without thinking, she reached out and took Ryan's hand, waiting anxiously for the ship to jump into Fold Space. She didn't have long to wait as the stars suddenly seemed to blur and then returned to normal. She knew that the ship was now traveling at many times the speed of light. Glancing down at her hand, she felt embarrassed as she realized what she had done. She released Ryan's comforting hand and focused on the sea of stars outside of the viewport as if nothing had happened.

Ryan had been surprised when Casey had taken his hand but assumed it was due to her nervousness about entering Fold

Space. They were on their way, and in three weeks would be rendezvousing with Seventh Fleet. He wondered what Wade would say when he found out that Ryan was aboard the Defender. He just hoped his brother would be as supportive and understanding as he'd always been.

Supreme War Overlord Harmock felt growing rage inside of him at the most recent report from the Council of Overlords. Somehow, word had reached the council that a number of nonaligned worlds in sector eleven were discussing forming an Alliance to stand up to the Zaltule. He looked up at one of the viewscreens showing the Delton home world, which was now firmly under Kleese control. Every leader and all important scientists now wore the Kleese collars of obedience.

"This Alliance must not be allowed to come into existence," spoke Minor Overlord Gareth, rising to his full height and gazing at Harmock. "The nonaligned worlds we have thus far conquered were difficult enough without a group of them joining together for their common defense."

"They may have higher levels of science and technology, but they are still inferior races when compared to the Kleese or our own warrior caste," uttered Harmock, folding his powerful dark arms across his chest. His triangular shaped head shifted until he was looking directly at his second in command. "We will gather a fleet and set out immediately for sector eleven. Once there, we will find these worlds and crush their feeble attempt to form an Alliance against the Empire."

"We may have to pull ships from the other attacking fleets to make up for our losses and the damage some of our battlecruisers took during the battle with the Deltons," pointed out Gareth.

"The Deltons!" roared Harmock still aggravated that a large number of Delton warships and civilian ships had managed to escape his grasp.

Dozens of Delton leaders and military personnel had suffered the consequences of failing to reveal to their Zaltule

Overlords where the ships had gone. The black boxes which controlled the collars of obedience had been used a surprisingly large number of times but yielded no results. Zaltule battlecruisers had been sent to many of the nearby systems, but no signs had been found of the missing ships.

"Pull the ships we need from the attacking fleets," ordered Harmock, coldly. "They can requisition replacements from our home systems. Once the necessary ships arrive here, we'll set out toward sector eleven and see if these rumors of a possible Alliance are true."

"It will take us fifty-four days to reach sector eleven from here," reported one of the Zaltule warriors operating the navigation controls.

"Fifty-four days during which they can make preparations against us," warned Gareth as he thought of what it might mean to go up against a group of heavily armed nonaligned worlds that had the necessary time to prepare for the arrival of the Zaltule.

"It will make no difference," spoke Harmock in a dark and menacing voice. "They will be crushed just the same and know what it means to wear our collars of obedience. They'll just be brought into the Empire sooner than originally planned."

"It will be done," Gareth responded as he turned and descended from the Command Pedestal and walked over on his six legs to the primary Communications console. It would be necessary to contact several of the attacking fleets for the needed ships.

Harmock gazed around the Command Center, satisfied that his fellow warriors were performing their jobs efficiently. He also wondered about the problem in sector eleven and if there wasn't something else going on the council was keeping from him. His thoughts turned dark at the consequences to the Council of Overlords if he found that to be true. If the council were hiding a secret, then on his return he would implement sufficient changes to the council to ensure the Zaltule had complete control over it as well as the Empire.

Chapter Twelve

General Mitchell was meeting with Fleet Admiral Kelly and Commander Pasha of the Talts. Also sitting in on the meeting were Gerald Lawson, the military weapons specialist, as well as Skagern, who had flown in from the Kivean asteroid.

"How effective is this plasma weapon?" asked Kelly, looking over at Lawson. "Is it worth installing on our ships?"

"It's highly effective at close range," Lawson replied in an earnest voice. He'd spent considerable time speaking with several Talt weapons scientists and even been allowed aboard one of the two Talt battlecruisers for a weapons demonstration.

"How hard would the plasma cannons be to install on our battlecruisers?" asked Kelly. Anything that was effective against the Kleese he wanted on his ships.

"I would suggest installing only one cannon on a battlecruiser as the equipment needed is a little cumbersome, though the Kiveans believe they can use micro engineering to reduce it to a more manageable size," answered Lawson. "The cannon would need approximately forty seconds to recharge before it could fire a second round."

"I've spoken to a number of our scientists and technicians," Skagern added his eyes focusing on Fleet Admiral Kelly. "They feel they can have a workable design ready for our battlecruisers within two months."

"Commander Pasha, if you had to fight the Zaltule again, what changes would you make to any fleet under your command?" asked Kelly. The Talts had fought literally to the last ship and had managed to destroy a number of the large Zaltule battlecruisers.

"We needed larger ships," Pasha stated his large yellow eyes focusing on the Fleet Admiral. "Our ships didn't have sufficient weapons to push the Kleese back. Their ships are three kilometers in width and nearly every square meter of their hulls are covered with some type of offensive or defensive armament. I have noticed that your own battlecruisers are only slightly larger than ours."

"How much larger do our ships need to be in order to be able to adequately defend against the Zaltule?" asked General Mitchell, leaning forward in his chair. One of the reasons for the size of the fleet's battlecruisers and light cruisers were crew constraints. Until the clone program began, they just didn't have the crews for larger warships.

"One thousand meters," answered Skagern, promptly. The Kivean had spent considerable time discussing this with Lawson, the Talts, and several Kivean weapons specialists. "If we build new battlecruisers one thousand meters in length we can arm them sufficiently to easily handle a Zaltule warship."

"That's double the size of our current ships," commented Kelly with a frown. That would require much larger crews and an obvious increase in the cloning program.

"With the plasma weapons and particle beams we'll have a decisive advantage against the Kleese in a standup battle," Skagern pointed out. "We need larger ships to be able to take the punishment being handed out by the Zaltule warships."

"We can build them at the Vesta spacedock," Lawson suggested. "It would only take some minor modifications to the construction docks to handle the larger ships. We did build the Defender there."

General Mitchell nodded. The Defender was one thousand meters so he knew that it could be done. "What about other modifications? We currently have a mission off to the nonaligned worlds; they may return with more suggestions for upgrades to our ships."

"It's a possibility," conceded Skagern. "I would suggest we work on a design with what we currently have, and it can be modified once the mission returns. We already have a base design from building the Defender."

"We can have a completed ship design within two months," promised Lawson as he narrowed his eyes in thought. "If there are no major changes, we could go to production in three."

"What would be the estimated construction time?" asked Kelly, wondering if they would have to make up a new category for these larger ships.

"I would suggest we build four at a time," spoke Skagern in a serious tone. "There is room in the Vesta spacedock for that type of construction operation, and we could have the first battle group done in six months."

"My own scientists and technicians will be pleased to assist," put forth Commander Pasha. "It's possible we may have some construction techniques which could speed up the building of the ships. My people were very heavy into automated construction."

General Mitchell nodded his head in agreement. "I'll need to speak to President Randle as well as Sean Miller and Ethan Hall. The final decision will be up to the president and the Federated Council, but I believe they'll follow my recommendation. I want to go ahead and begin preparation for this new grade of warship, and as soon as I receive formal approval we'll begin allocating assets to get construction started."

"I think it's a wise decision," replied Skagern with a nod of his head.

"How is your new habitat coming?" General Mitchell asked Commander Pasha. He knew the Kiveans had been helping the Talts build a habitat in a nearby asteroid.

"It's nearly complete," Pasha responded with a pleased smile. "Our people will begin moving off the ships in another two weeks."

"I understand some of your people have visited the Kiveans' habitats," added Kelly. He knew the architecture the Kiveans used was quite remarkable. Many people who'd been inside the two habitats the Kiveans had built inside their asteroid remarked how the two cities resembled something out of a fairy tale.

"Yes," Pasha answered his large eyes shifting to Fleet Admiral Kelly. "We have been rotating our people, allowing them some time off the ships. Our civilians are not used to long space voyages and were getting restless."

"I can understand that," commented Lawson. Just flying the relatively short distances in the solar system made him feel nervous.

"My people and I are grateful for what the Kiveans and your people have done for us."

"We're all in this together against the Kleese," General Mitchell said. "I suspect your race won't be the only one we find fleeing the Empire. There will be others."

Wade looked over at Beth, who was lying in the bed next to him. He reached out and ran his hand softly over her cheek. She blinked her eyes and they opened. She stretched, yawned, and pulled the blanket up under her chin.

"Tell me it's not time to get up," she said, sleepily.

Wade laughed and placed his hand under the blanket until he was holding her breast. "It was you that kept us up late last night."

Beth giggled and moved Wade's hand as she sat up. "Yeah, and if I let you have your way, we'll never make it to our meeting this morning."

Wade sighed and swung his legs out of bed. "Let me take a quick shower and then you can get ready."

"A long, hot bath sounds good," Beth spoke as she snuggled back down in the bed, watching Wade walk across the room toward the bathroom. They were on the Distant Star and the passenger liner actually had bathtubs in the suites. On the troop transport there were showers but very little privacy. It was something the marines had gotten used to.

Two hours later, after eating a light breakfast, they stepped into one of the ship's conference rooms where the meeting was being held. Marken, Harnett, Hyram Blake, and Admiral Adamson were already there.

"The troop assault ship Defender arrived in the Lanolth system yesterday," Adamson informed them. "The Defender has a full company of marines trained in the new Type Four battlesuits." Adamson's eyes then shifted directly to Wade. "Your brother is in charge of one of the platoons with the rank of full lieutenant. From what Major Stevens told me, Ryan did an outstanding job in the drills. He even conquered Charring Mountain on his second attempt."

"What?" blurted out Beth her eyes widening in disbelief. "No one conquers Charring on their second try!"

"Lieutenant Nelson did," Adamson said with a grin. "He must take after you, Wade."

Wade nodded. He didn't know what to say. He only knew that his brother most likely would be going in harm's way very shortly.

"I'm glad the transport's arrived," Wade replied. He then looked over at Hyram. "What's the latest word on the Alliance?"

"Four confirmed worlds with signed documents pledging mutual support," he responded with a pleased smile. "We have another five which are leaning toward joining the Alliance and seven more that are still indecisive."

"What are they waiting on?" demanded Admiral Adamson, shaking his head and cocking his eyebrow. "Don't they know the Alliance is their only hope of remaining free of the Kleese Empire?"

"They know," answered Hyram. "They've just been at peace for so long that going to war is a foreign thought to them."

"But they all have defensive fleets and weapons," pointed out Adamson, feeling confused. "They wouldn't have those if they thought they weren't necessary."

"They have very powerful warships and defenses," agreed Hyram, recalling some of the talks with representatives of those worlds. "I think they're still unsure we can actually protect them. Once we prove that, then I think the majority of them will join."

"So we wait on the Kleese to attack," commented Wade with a frown.

"It's the only way," Marken said with a sigh. "I just hope our fleet is powerful enough to stop whatever the Kleese send our way."

There was a knock on the door and an ensign opened it and stepped inside, looking at Admiral Adamson. "We've just had a report from the Lanolthians that a nonaligned world's refugee fleet has dropped out of Fold Space in the Kales System. They're requesting we send some ships to meet with the refugee fleet."

"How large a refugee fleet?" asked Hyram, standing up.

"It's one hundred and thirty-one vessels," the ensign replied. Then, in an excited voice, he continued. "But it has eighty-seven large battlecruisers with it as an escort."

"Eighty-seven battlecruisers," echoed Admiral Adamson his eyes widening. He looked over at Hyram. "I think we need to talk to these people."

"I agree," Hyram responded. "How far is the Kales system from here?"

"Sixty-two light years," answered Marken, promptly. "We can be there in less than a day."

"Send a message to the Lanolthians that we're sending some ships to the Kales System to meet with the refugee fleet," ordered Admiral Adamson. "Anyone that has eighty-seven battlecruisers we need to talk to."

"If we can get these refugees to tell the nonaligned worlds what the Kleese did to their world, it might just be the kick start we need to get more of them to join," stated Hyram as he weighed the possibilities.

"Did the Lanolthians say what nonaligned world this refugee fleet came from?" asked Harnett, feeling curious and gazing at the ensign for an answer.

"Deltons," the ensign replied. "They said the fleet was Deltons."

"Have you ever heard of them?" asked Wade, looking questioningly at Marken and Harnett.

"No," answered Marken, shaking his head. "But the other Kiveans we brought with us might have. "We'll have to check."

"Let us know what you find out," directed Adamson. "Now let's decide what ships need to go to this meeting."

-

Supreme War Overlord Harmock gazed with satisfaction at the numerous green icons on the Warrior's Fire's tactical screen. The fleet had dropped out of Fold Space for routine systems' checks and would soon be continuing on their way toward sector eleven. Seven hundred large green icons were spread out over the screen designating the Zaltule warships.

"We'll stop at sector eleven's trading station before we engage any of the nonaligned worlds in that area," Harmock announced. By stopping there, he might be able to glean valuable tactical information about the possible Alliance being formed in the sector.

"I've heard that the trading stations on the periphery of the Empire are rather loosely run," commented Gareth. He shifted his six legs upon the Command Pedestal and looked down at one of the control consoles. "The Kleese who operate these outer stations are far enough away from the Council of Overlords that consequences for their actions or failure to act is of little concern to them."

"That will change now that the Zaltule have taken an active role in expanding our Empire," spoke Harmock, decisively. "Many Kleese have forgotten the way of our warriors and grown soft in this new Empire the council has created. All that is about to change; it is one of the reasons I want Zaltule security detachments assigned to all of the trading stations. We'll implement the old ways and assert more control over the races that use our stations for trade."

"What about the conscripts the stations use in their conquests of other worlds in their sectors?" asked Gareth as he turned back away from the console. "We're talking about thousands of worlds these stations help to control and though the conscripts come from inferior species, they free up innumerable Kleese from having to serve as occupation forces on many of those worlds."

"They have their use," admitted Harmock with distaste. "Someday, when the numbers of the Zaltule have increased sufficiently, there will be no need for these conscripts. I loathe the fact that inferior species walk the corridors of our assault ships and exploration ships."

"It's another three days' travel in Fold Space to reach the trading station," Gareth reported.

"We'll perform an inspection while we're there," Harmock announced, sharply. "We'll remind the Kleese upon the station the importance of staying true to the ways of the Kleese. If they have grown too soft, they'll be eliminated. There is no room in the Empire for the weak or those who refuse to aid in the expansion of the Empire."

"It is necessary," agreed Gareth. "The weak must be removed."

"Set course for the trading station," ordered Harmock. "We leave as soon as all ships are finished with their systems' checks."

Three days later, Harmock gazed in confusion at the tactical screen before him. They had dropped out of Fold Space where the trading station was supposed to be, but all that surrounded them was empty space. There was no sign of the station or any Kleese ships.

"Where is the station?" demanded Harmock in a cold voice as he stared at the Zaltule in front of the battlecruiser's sensors.

"This is the location listed in the database for our trade station," Jalridd responded. "I have run long-range sensor sweeps, and there is no sign of the station. I am picking up what appears to be ship debris but not near enough to account for the station."

"Something's not right," Gareth spoke. "Trading stations are not moved once they've been set in place."

"Send out some of our ships to the nearer worlds under Kleese control," ordered Harmock as he gazed at the tactical screen. All that was showing were Zaltule battlecruisers. "Find and bring back an exploration ship; I want to know what happened to the station."

Harmock watched as his orders were swiftly carried out. He had a feeling he was shortly going to learn what the council had been hiding from him and a suspicion he would not be pleased.

Two days later, a Kleese exploration ship dropped out of Fold Space along with two Zaltule battlecruisers serving as escorts. The twelve thousand meter disk ship came to a stop just on the outskirts of the Zaltule warfleet.

"We're receiving a message from the Minor Overlord in charge of one of the two escorting battlecruisers," Dalock reported from Communications. "It seems as if the commander of the exploration ship refused to come to meet us at first. Our two battlecruisers had to threaten to destroy the ship before the Kleese in command agreed to our requests for a meeting."

"They know something," Gareth commented his multifaceted eyes focusing on the War Overlord. "Something bad has happened here and they're fearful of us learning what it was."

"Order the Kleese command crew of the exploration ship to report to the Warrior's Fire immediately," commanded Harmock. "I want to know what they're hiding!"

Two hours later, Harmock gazed impassively at the disemboweled body of the Kleese commander of the exploration ship. It had been necessary to employ methods, which were distasteful even to the Zaltule to get the Kleese commander to talk.

"It's incomprehensible that an inferior race could capture and take a Kleese trading station," spoke Gareth still finding it hard to believe what the Kleese commander had told them.

"It's much worse than that," Harmock spoke in a hard voice. "These same Humans removed many of the Kivean scientists and their families from Kivea. The Kiveans are one of the most advanced worlds in the Empire; so advanced they were allowed a semblance of autonomy."

"Not anymore," spoke Gareth. "The Council of Overlords ordered the surface of Kivea to be carpet bombed with antimatter missiles. Nothing lives upon the planet now."

"The Humans have fought several battles against Kleese ships and have been victorious in every case," added Harmock.

"It may just be a coincidence, but the advent of the Humans is close to the same time the Strell started attacking our worlds in the neutral zone."

"Too much of a coincidence," stated Harmock as he thought about the recent war with the Strell. "The Strell claimed from the very beginning that we attacked them first with our assault ships."

"The Humans would have had assault ships from the trading station," pointed out Gareth. "They could have masqueraded as us and instigated the Strell into attacking our worlds."

"Then when the Strell attacked the planets in the neutral zone which were under our control, we of course retaliated and the war began," added Harmock in realization at how masterful the Humans had played the two Empires against one another. "It all makes sense from a tactical viewpoint."

"Can the Humans be that intelligent?" asked Gareth, doubtfully.

"Intelligence might not be the right question," Harmock said as he weighed over in his mind what he'd learned in the last several hours. "The Humans were taken to serve as conscripts at first because of their aggressiveness. Their world was annihilated to ensure that they would never become a threat."

"This Alliance being formed against us," Gareth said as he shifted about upon his six legs. "Could the Humans be behind it?"

"Very likely," Harmock responded. "They're preparing to fight a war against us and are attempting to rally the nonaligned worlds into an Alliance. After the planet buster launched at their world, their surviving population has to be minuscule compared to what it once was. They just don't have the numbers to fight us alone."

"If we stop this Alliance then the Humans would be powerless to prevent us from conquering their system," added Gareth.

"We won't conquer it, we'll destroy it," spoke Harmock, sharply. "Prepare the fleet; we leave for the first nonaligned world immediately. We'll crush this budding Alliance and then move on to destroy the Humans. Once that's been done, we'll return to the home worlds. The Kleese Council of Overlords has some explaining to do."

"Perhaps it's time that the Zaltule take over the council," suggested Gareth.

"You may be right," conceded Harmock in a cold and hard voice. "At the very least, more Zaltule will be included on the council."

"The time of the Zaltule has arrived," proclaimed Gareth with satisfaction in his voice.

"But first we must deal with these upstart Humans and this Alliance," spoke Harmock, turning his eyes toward the tactical screen. "Prepare the fleet for battle and stand by to jump into Fold Space. It's time we showed the nonaligned worlds and the Humans the full might of the Zaltule!"

Chapter Thirteen

The negotiations with the Deltons had gone surprisingly well, with both sides feeling mutually satisfied at what had been accomplished. The Deltons seemed relieved to find a force willing to fight the Kleese, and the Humans were pleased to receive the promised assistance of so many Delton battlecruisers.

Wade leaned back in his chair and gazed at Hyram, Admiral Adamson, and Marken. The negotiations had been intense, with both sides asking a lot of questions and for detailed explanations. "So we have a tentative agreement?"

"Yes," answered Hyram, nodding his head enthusiastically. "Fleet Commander Achlyn has requested asylum in the solar system for his people. In return, he will remain with forty of his battlecruisers to reinforce Seventh Fleet and will send the rest of his ships on to Centerpoint. Once there, they will complete the negotiations with the Federated Council."

"I think Fleet Admiral Kelly and General Mitchell will be quite pleased when they realize they'll have another forty-seven battlecruisers that can be used to protect the solar system," commented Admiral Adamson as his eyes looked across the table at the others. "From what Fleet Commander Achlyn has shown me of his warships' capabilities, the main energy beams the ships are equipped with are quite impressive."

"They are forty percent more powerful than those we currently use," responded Marken, recalling how surprised he and the other Kiveans had been when shown the amount of energy the Delton weapons were capable of projecting. "They have found a method to tighten the focus of the beam, thereby reducing dispersion. Once we have the time to study the technology with some of their engineers, we should have no problem adding the technology to our existing energy beam systems."

"The technology some of these nonaligned worlds have is astonishing," commented Admiral Adamson, shaking his head in wonder.

"Fleet Commander Achlyn also seems to be quite receptive to the idea of building a habitat inside an asteroid protected by our ion cannons," added Hyram as he shuffled through a stack of papers in front of him. "There are approximately forty-five thousand civilian survivors chosen for their refugee fleet. The survivors come from nearly every aspect of Deltonian life. I've spoken to physicists, medical specialists, and even farmers. They were quite prepared to set up a colony outside of known space."

"It should make setting up a new habitat for the Deltons much easier," Marken added, his narrow eyes looking thoughtful. "Their initial plans were to warn the outer nonaligned worlds about the Kleese and then proceed to the distant regions of the galaxy to create a new world."

"They were desperate to escape the grasp of the Kleese," said Wade, nodding his head in understanding.

"Why did they decide to side with us?" asked Admiral Adamson, raising his eyebrows.

"They wish to see their home world freed someday," answered Hyram, letting out a deep breath. "If the Alliance is successful in stopping the Kleese then there is a possibility that eventually the Delton home world could be freed from the grasp of the Empire. If they proceeded to the galaxy's edge, then any hope of that would have been exceedingly dim."

"The Deltons have pledged forty battlecruisers to our cause," Wade pointed out as he looked intently at the others. "That will greatly increase the firepower of Seventh Fleet. What are the other Alliance worlds willing to commit?"

"Several more worlds have signed documents," Hyram spoke with a pleased glint in his eyes. "When the Deltons spoke to a number of potential Alliance delegates we summoned, you could see the shock in their eyes as they realized what the Zaltule were up to. I think many were refusing to believe the Kleese would not honor the neutrality agreements. Now that view has shifted, and we could see even more worlds move our way in the next few weeks."

"What worries me is what the Kleese will do next," spoke Admiral Adamson with a look of grave concern spreading across his face. "We've been conducting these negotiations for quite some time, and I worry that word of an Alliance being formed against them might reach the Kleese home world. If that were to happen, they could move against us immediately. It's what I would do."

Wade was silent as he weighed Adamson's words. He was in full agreement that if the Kleese were to learn of the Alliance they would move to destroy it before it became a dangerous reality. It put even more pressure on Admiral Adamson and Hyram to have a major Alliance fleet ready when that time finally did arrive.

"Hyram, we need ship commitments from the other races and we need them now," Wade spoke in a grim voice as he leaned back and crossed his arms over his chest. "Make them understand the future of their worlds is at stake. When the Kleese finally attack, we must be able to drive them off and inflict paralyzing casualties to their attacking fleet. If we can to that, it should buy us the time we need to finish organizing the Alliance and setting up more powerful defenses to protect Alliance worlds. Just one squadron from each prospective Alliance world would help."

Hyram nodded, knowing what Wade was suggesting would require some long hours of negotiating. "I think they'll agree," he said, leaning forward and staring at the colonel. "I think if we ask for an initial commitment of at least one full battlecruiser squadron from each world which has signed an Alliance agreement, we could come up with a sizable number of ships to reinforce Seventh Fleet and still leave them enough to defend their worlds."

"Do it quickly," suggested Adamson, sharply. "I fear we're rapidly running out of time."

"I know the Kleese," Marken said in a low voice as he recalled all the years his people had been subservient to the cruel and heartless alien species. "If they believe the nonaligned worlds are mounting a rebellion to resist being forced into the Empire, they will attack immediately and hard. They'll wish to make an example out of a potential Alliance world in order to frighten others away from joining. They may use antimatter missiles on its cities to put fear into the others." Marken felt deeply concerned, recalling how the Kleese had used antimatter missiles to destroy his home world.

Wade nodded. He could well remember how his own encounters with the arachnid species had been. The Kleese cared for no one except other Kleese; all other races were inferior and they had no remorse removing individuals or entire species, which might oppose them. Too many times, he had witnessed Kleese using their black box control devices to detonate explosive collars on conscripts with which they were displeased.

"Inform all the current Alliance worlds as well as those that are still indecisive that we're expecting a Kleese attack shortly," Wade said after a few moments of thought. "If they want to retain their freedom, we need their ships."

"I will do as you ask," Hyram stated as he stood up and gathered the scattered folders lying on the conference table.

After Hyram left, Admiral Adamson looked over at Wade and Marken. "How much time do we have?"

Wade let out a heavy sigh and only shook his head, shifting his glance questioningly over to Marken.

"There's a good chance the Kleese are searching for the Deltons," he spoke in a concerned voice. "They will be highly upset some warships and civilian ships escaped their original attack. We also haven't exactly been secretive about forming our Alliance. Several worlds we approached were very abrupt in demanding we leave their system and not return. It's possible one or more of these worlds could have sent a message to the nearest Kleese ship in the hope they could trade the information for a continuation of their neutrality agreement."

"A month at the outside," Wade said his eyes narrowing as he thought about how long it would take the Kleese to organize a major fleet and send it toward the nonaligned worlds. "I need to speak to Hyram and see if some of the nonaligned worlds would be willing to place pickets in some of the systems between us and the direction the Kleese will come from."

"They could use some of their cargo ships," suggested Adamson with a thoughtful look. "If we could have a few days' warning before the Kleese arrive at their destination, we could have the fleet ready to meet them."

"Assume the Kleese are traveling at seventy to one hundred light years per day, it won't be very easy for a cargo ship to detect them," Marken was quick to point out. "The cargo ship would have to be in a system the Kleese stop in to do systems' checks."

"But they might," responded Adamson, knowing the odds of detecting the Kleese fleet wasn't very great. "I think it's worth the attempt."

Wade stood up and looked at the other two. "I'll notify the Defender and our other two troop ships to stand by," he said evenly, not betraying the worry he felt at sending his brother's ship into combat. "If the Kleese beat us to the system they plan to attack, we might have to drive them off the surface of the planet."

"Wade," interrupted Adamson before the colonel could leave. "I think we should make an attempt to capture several Zaltule. Live prisoners could give us a wealth of tactical information."

Wade froze when he heard Adamson's suggestion. To Wade the only good Kleese was a dead one. He let out a deep breath before replying. "I'll make the suggestion to Major Stevens, but with the stipulation that it must be done without risking significant harm to his marines."

"I can accept that," responded Adamson, evenly.

As Wade left the room, he felt a cold chill at what Ryan and his platoon might have to do. To fight the Kleese in armed combat was one thing, but to capture one might be asking the impossible. He needed to talk to Beth about this. While he wouldn't be down on the planet, Beth would and she could help keep Ryan out of trouble. She'd fought the Kleese in combat and Ryan hadn't.

Ryan and Casey were standing at one of the large viewports gazing out, mesmerized at the peaceful blue-green planet that seemed to be floating in space. The planet was surrounded by a myriad of stars, which seemed to beckon to them with their steady, unblinking light. A large space station orbited the planet where numerous cargo ships and trading vessels were continually coming and going. Farther out the planet's two small moons orbited.

"It's a beautiful world," Casey said as she gazed at the planet. She could see several large oceans and wide swaths of green around the equator where tropical jungles existed.

"It's much like Earth used to be," Ryan said, longingly. It seemed like ages since he and his family had fled Phoenix and gone to Vesta. He could well remember the rafting trips they'd taken on the Colorado River and camping out in the mountains. Those were things of the past, as nothing like that existed in any of the new habitats. So much had been lost when the Kleese attacked Earth.

"What's that?" asked Casey, pointing to a large star that seemed to be moving. Then, looking more intently, she saw it was a full formation. She quickly counted and saw that there were ten objects that were moving.

"Lanolthian battlecruisers," Ryan answered as he gazed at the points of light. "I heard two battle groups are being assigned as an escort for the Defender when we move out and then they'll join Seventh Fleet once we reach our destination."

From what Major Stevens had said, he knew the Lanolthian battlecruisers were eight hundred meters in length and one hundred and fifty meters wide, being almost cigar shaped. They had very powerful energy shields and were equipped with heavy ion cannons on the bow for offense as well as energy weapon batteries. The ships were also capable of launching antimatter sublight missiles.

"Are the Lanolthians the ones who gave us the secret to the ion cannons we're installing all over the solar system?" asked Casey her hazel eyes widening.

"I don't know, but I'm guessing so," Ryan answered as he continued to watch the distant ships.

"Lieutenant," a voice called from behind them. Turning, Ryan saw Privates Parker, Adams, Rios, Hatterson, and Swen come into the room.

"Major Stevens is looking for you," Alexander said, coming to a stop next to one of the viewports and looking out. "He said if we found you you're to report for a briefing at 1600."

"Did he mention what it was about?" asked Ryan, looking down at his watch and seeing he had about an hour before the meeting was scheduled to begin.

"No," replied Alexander, shaking his head. "He just asked us to find you."

"Gosh, that's a beautiful world," Mary said as her eyes focused on the jewel of a planet. "Was that what Earth used to be like?" she asked, glancing over at Ryan her eyes growing wide. Since Mary was a clone, she'd never seen Earth before the Kleese attack devastated the planet.

"Yes," Juan answered with sadness in his eyes. "My home was in Austin, Texas where I lived with my uncle. My parents ran a small business just across the border in Mexico. My mother was a dress maker and made the most beautiful dresses, but my parents wanted me to attend school in America so I could receive a good education."

"Did your parents manage to escape?" asked Mary in a quiet voice. She couldn't recall Juan ever mentioning his family before.

"No," Juan replied, shaking his head slowly at the memories. "When the attack came, things became so bad so fast that I couldn't make the long trip from Austin to my parents' home village. When I last spoke to my dad, he begged me to get to a place of safety. My uncle put me on board a bus going to the evacuation center in Texas, saying he would join me there, but I never saw him again either."

Ryan was silent. Juan's story was one that had been told repeatedly by hundreds of thousands of refugees. The Kleese attack upon Earth had left tens of thousands of orphaned children and even more families whose loved ones didn't survive the horrors of that first year after the attack.

"From the stories I read, the survival camps were not pleasant places to be," spoke up Casey, recalling some of what she had read at the Academy.

"No, they weren't," Rios answered with a haunted look in his eyes. "We were always cold and never knew if we would have food for the next day. It's something I don't want to ever experience again."

"That's why we're out here," Ryan interjected. His eyes looked over the small group of marines. Most of them he could call friends, though he knew it wasn't wise to get too close to individuals in your command. "We're going to show the Kleese they never should have come to our solar system or this part of the galaxy."

"I'm ready to kill some spiders," Alexander spoke in a boisterous voice. "I understand the best way to kill a Kleese is to cut its head off with an Energy Lance." Alexander made a swinging motion like he was holding a lance, sweeping it through the air.

"Just so you don't cut yourself," cautioned Lauren with an enigmatic grin. "Don't forget that Kleese battle armor will probably be impervious to an Energy Lance anyway. You might want to use an energy cannon to burn their heads off."

"Either way, I'm going to kill them," boasted Alexander in a confident voice.

"They need to die," agreed Rios. "They are a cruel and evil race."

"We'll probably be going into battle shortly, isn't that right, Lieutenant?" asked Mary with concern in her eyes. Her face was so innocent and lacking any blemishes or birthmarks.

"Probably," Ryan responded. "I'd better go get changed and head to my meeting. I'll let you know if anything has come up."

Ryan put on a fresh uniform and made his way through the large ship until he reached one of the briefing rooms. Stepping inside, he paused and his eyes grew wide when he saw who was standing there. "Beth!" spoke Ryan, feeling stunned and then, recovering his composure, he quickly spoke again. "Major Williams."

"Sit down, Lieutenant," Major Stevens said, trying his best not to laugh at the young lieutenant's reaction to seeing his brother's wife. "Major Williams has come to brief us on an important matter, one that may be exceptionally difficult to accomplish."

"We'll do whatever is necessary, Sir," Ryan responded as he took the indicated seat at the small conference table. "My platoon is ready for combat."

Beth looked over at Ryan, very pleased with what she saw. He was in excellent shape and seemed to be carrying himself with an air of authority. "Admiral Adamson has suggested a slight change of tactics," she began. "After Colonel Nelson, myself, and a few others reviewed the admiral's request we decided it might be an excellent idea for the war effort."

Ryan looked confused. He wondered if Beth was talking about some type of guerilla action on the Kleese controlled planets. He knew it was an option the High Command had been considering. The Type Four suits would be ideal for such a commitment.

"We want you to capture a Zaltule," Beth said evenly her eyes focusing intently on Ryan. "More than one would be even better."

"What?" Ryan blurted out his eyes growing wide in shock. "How do we capture a Zaltule?" Ryan felt numb at the suggestion. The Zaltule were the warrior caste of the Kleese and would not be easy to take into custody.

"We expect the Kleese to attack one of the nearby nonaligned worlds sometime in the next month," Major Stevens announced as he leaned back and rubbed his forehead with his right hand. He knew this mission wasn't going to be easy. Hell, it sounded downright impossible.

"When they do, they will undoubtedly land ground forces upon the planet," continued Beth, knowing she was asking a lot of Ryan. "We'll make a heavy duty stun rifle available to several of your marines that should, when at its highest setting, knock out a Zaltule even if they're wearing a battlesuit."

"How close will we have to get?" asked Ryan, suspecting he wasn't going to like the answer. He strongly suspected the Zaltule wouldn't exactly be standing still waiting to be stunned.

"Within knife throwing range," replied Beth in a lower voice. Looking at Ryan, he reminded her so much of Wade when she'd first met him. She wasn't happy about sending Ryan and his platoon into this type of danger.

"What kind of support will we have?"

"I'll be going down with the four platoons in the Type Four suits," replied Major Stevens. "We'll deploy all of our hover tanks if the fighting looks intense as well as the four hundred marines in Type Three suits who are aboard the Defender."

"This will be a difficult mission to accomplish," stated Beth evenly, taking a deep breath. "From the reports of their war with the Strell, the Zaltule caste are fierce warriors. I'll be coming down also with all of my marines from the Fire Fox. Many of them have experience fighting the Kleese."

"But not warriors of the Zaltule caste," responded Ryan, gravely.

"No, not the Zaltule," Beth admitted her eyes focused on Ryan.

"Colonel Nelson will command the operation from orbit aboard the Defender, while Major Williams will be in overall charge on the ground," Stevens said. "Colonel Nelson will be transferring over sometime in the next week. He's still trying to finish up some negotiations."

They spent a few more minutes discussing the upcoming operation and what was expected of Ryan's marines. Once satisfied they had gone over what was necessary, Major Stevens excused himself and left Beth and Ryan alone.

"So, you conquered Charring on your second attempt," commented Beth with a relaxing smile.

"Yes," stammered Ryan. He hadn't expected Beth to know that. "How?"

"How did we know?" Beth responded with a pleased look that she had surprised the young lieutenant. "Your brother was keeping a close watch on you. He's extremely proud of how well you did in your training. He was even there in the dome Command Center watching your first attempt at Charring."

"Thanks, I guess," answered Ryan, feeling embarrassed. He hadn't suspected Wade had been at the training dome watching.

"Ryan," spoke Beth in a more serious tone. Leaning forward in her chair, she placed her hands on the hard surface of the conference table. "This mission is going to be extremely dangerous; there's a good chance that some of the marines in your platoon might not make it back."

"I understand that," answered Ryan, taking a deep breath. "It's what we were trained for."

"This won't be like training," Beth quickly pointed out. "A mistake out here and someone dies; I've seen it too often."

Ryan was silent for a long moment and then focused his eyes on Beth. "What advice can you give me?"

Beth nodded. She was pleased Ryan had asked that question. It showed he wasn't so caught up in his new position and the power of the Type Four suits to understand he didn't know everything.

"Be cautious but don't hesitate once you've made a decision," she spoke in a firm voice. "Make sure your marines know you're in charge and looking out for them."

"I have a good group of marines," Ryan responded. It made him uneasy thinking he might lose some of them on this mission. "I trust them to do whatever is necessary."

"One more thing, Ryan," Beth said her tone a little softer. "If you get into trouble or find you're in a situation you can't handle, don't hesitate to call for help. Major Stevens, myself, and others will be close by. In this operation, we're there to support you."

"It's not going to be easy to capture a Zaltule, is it?"

"No," Beth answered with a sigh. "It's not. We're not even sure if it's possible."

Ryan was silent as he thought over what his sister-in-law had just told him. For their first mission, his platoon had drawn a bad hand, but he was determined to make it a winning one. "We'll do it," Ryan finally said. "We'll capture a Zaltule."

Beth allowed herself to smile. Ryan even sounded like his older brother. She just hoped they all made it back safely from this mission.

The first three-kilometer Zaltule battlecruiser dropped out of Fold Space followed almost instantly by seven hundred more. In just a matter of a few seconds, space was full of the massive and deadly black warships.

"Status," barked Harmock as he stepped on top of the Command Pedestal, which gave him an unrestricted view of the Command Center.

"All ships have dropped out of Fold Space," reported Gareth from where he was standing next to the large sensor console. "All ship commanders are reporting normal flight operations."

Harmock stood silently as his gaze focused on the large tactical screen, full of the myriad of green icons, which represented his fleet. Since learning of the theft of the trading station, his fleet had stopped in several other inhabited systems controlled by the Kleese Empire. The more he learned about these Humans, the angrier he'd gotten at the Kleese Council of Overlords. For six years, the council had done nothing. They'd allowed an inferior race control of a Kleese possession without making additional efforts to recover it. To Harmock such actions were irresponsible and even treasonous.

What was even worse were the capabilities of the station itself. There was no doubt the Humans had learned how to operate the station, particularly since they had such a large number of Kiveans under their control. Harmock wondered what type of threat the Humans were using to control the Kiveans. He doubted if the Kiveans would work for them voluntarily.

"All ships have seventy hours to perform system's checks and prepare for battle," Harmock spoke in a cold and nearly emotionless voice. "Once all systems have been checked we will enter Fold Space and attack our target system."

"The system of Pradel is only two hundred light years distant," commented Jalridd from the sensor console. "It has six planets, two of which are inhabited. The second planet out from the system's star is the home world."

"Reports from some of the traders we spoke to in the last two systems we stopped in seem to confirm an Alliance is being formed against us and the Humans are behind it," added Gareth. "This Human threat has been allowed to simmer far too long."

"Yes," replied Harmock as his multifaceted eyes focused on his second in command. "The council in many ways has failed its duty with the handling of this upstart race. We'll take care of annihilating that problem, but when we return to the council world, there will be some major changes. The Council Overlords must learn not to keep secrets from the Zaltule."

Harmock left the Command Center to make a tour of his flagship. He knew that back home on several specially selected worlds, the Zaltule Queens would be laying their first clutches of eggs. Soon new Zaltule warriors would begin to emerge to take their rightful places in the Empire. Within a few years, the Zaltule numbers would swell to their ancient levels and they would sweep across the galaxy, crushing everyone who stood in their way. Harmock also knew that at that glorious moment, he would take over as the Supreme Overlord of the Kleese race.

On the other side of the system, a small Nalton cargo ship rose up out of the atmosphere of the planet it had been hiding in. In just moments, the ship accelerated and jumped into Fold

Space. The communications gear on board could reach nearly one hundred light years. It would take the small ship six valuable hours to reach the necessary range to be able to contact one of the nonaligned worlds, which was considering joining the Alliance. From there, word would be sent back to Lanolth and the waiting Human fleet.

Chapter Fourteen

The Warrior's Fire dropped out of Fold Space into the Pradel System and instantly went to full combat alert. Klaxons sounded and lights flashed as the Zaltule crew prepared for combat. Other battlecruisers began showing up around the flagship until the full seven hundred warships were present. They rapidly moved about into a compact defensive formation as their short-range and long-range sensors began reaching out scanning the system for potential hostile contacts.

"No hostile contacts within twenty light minutes," reported Jalridd as the first sensor scans began coming in. "Picking up a few cargo ships, but no warships."

"Hold the fleet at its current position," ordered Harmock, rising up to his full height on his six legs. "This is a nonaligned world and we know they have warships to defend their two worlds. I want to know where they are!"

The three-kilometer wide disk ships continued to hold motionless, their energy screens fully powered and weapons searching space for any hint of a hostile ship. The long-range sensors reached farther into the system and finally began picking up the Pradelians' battlecruisers. They were all together in a loose formation halfway between the second and third planets.

"Seventy-two ships," reported Jalridd as the red threat icons began appearing on the primary tactical screen. "They seem to be holding at their current position and have made no movement since we detected them."

"They might not know we're here yet," suggested Gareth as he studied the tactical screen.

"They know we're here," Harmock spoke in his cold and hard voice. "The cargo ships would have detected us and reported our presence as soon as we dropped out of Fold Space."

"Why are they waiting?" asked Gareth.

"They want us to make the first move," answered Harmock, taking several steps forward on the Command Pedestal. "Move the fleet toward them on our sublight drives and let's see if we can provoke a response. Keep our sensors focused on those warships; I want to know as much about them as possible before we initiate combat."

Gareth quickly activated the ship-to-ship communicator. "All battlecruisers proceed ahead at one third power on sublight engines. Standard defensive formation with the flagship at the center until further notice."

The seven hundred Zaltule warships instantly began accelerating and adjusted their course to intercept the waiting Pradelian ships. Metal hatch covers slid open, revealing waiting sublight antimatter missiles, and energy turrets rotated until they were focused in the direction of the fleet's travel. The heavy pulse fusion weapons were charged with energy and readied to fire upon command.

Aboard the Constellation, Admiral Adamson watched the Kleese ships intently as they began moving toward the waiting Pradel battlecruisers. Seventh Fleet had arrived just a few hours previously after receiving a frantic warning about the approach of the Zaltule fleet. After receiving the message from the Nalton cargo ship, they'd decided the Kleese were going to attack one of three nonaligned worlds. The Naltons and the Lanolthians had been adamant that Pradel would be the world under fire from the Zaltule. Pradel was a highly civilized world with a major colony on their third planet and even served as a trading hub for several of the nearer nonaligned worlds.

"They were right," spoke Commander Shepherd as she watched the tactical screen. "The Kleese are right on time."

"Make sure we keep our power output at a minimum," ordered Adamson, feeling his heart beating faster at the thought of combat. "We don't want the Kleese to know we're here until they're heavily engaged with the defending Pradel warships. I also don't want to use the new missiles unless absolutely necessary."

"All ships are operating at minimal power levels," Sandra assured the admiral. "They understand we need to remain undetected and to use regular twenty-megaton missiles unless otherwise ordered."

Adamson nodded as he allowed his gaze to play over his command crew. All were busy at their stations as if this was just a normal duty shift. Adamson let out a deep breath. He knew that a victory in the coming battle meant the Alliance would become a reality. A loss and everything they'd worked so hard for would fall apart. If he could win this battle without revealing the new six-warhead antimatter missile R&D had designed, it would give the Human ships a tactical advantage in future battles. However, if it became necessary to deploy the missiles to ensure victory, he wouldn't hesitate.

On one of the viewscreens, the troop assault ship Defender was displayed. At one thousand meters, the ship was very impressive and perhaps the most powerful ship in the fleet. She had heavier energy screens, thicker battle armor, and the weighty weapons of a battlecruiser. Colonel Nelson had left the Constellation and taken a shuttle over to the Defender just before they departed the Lanolthian System.

"The Pradelians are on the move," reported Commander Shepherd as the green icons on the tactical screen representing the nonaligned world's ships began to change positions. "They're moving to just outside the orbit of the third planet to intercept the Kleese before they can target Ryerson." Ryerson was the name of the other inhabited planet in the system and held slightly over one billion inhabitants.

"Kleese ships have jumped into Fold Space," called out Lieutenant Lash as the Kleese ships suddenly began moving rapidly toward the Pradelian battlecruisers.

"All ships go to full power," ordered Admiral Adamson over the com, which linked him to all of his ship commanders. "Standby to enter Fold Space upon my command." He knew the Kleese couldn't detect his ships as most long-range sensors didn't function well in Fold Space.

"Dropping out of Fold Space," reported Minor Overlord Gareth as the viewscreens on the Warrior's Fire began to clear and show the space around the ship.

"Pradelian ships are at extreme combat range," added Jalridd as the tactical screen began to light up with red threat icons.

"Close the range," Harmock ordered as he prepared himself for battle. "Detach twenty ships to begin the invasion of Ryerson."

"Orders have been passed to the indicated ships," spoke Gareth. He watched on the tactical screen as the small force broke off from the fleet and accelerated toward the planet.

"What's the latest status on the Pradelian battlecruisers?"

"The ships are one thousand meters in length and two hundred meters in diameter," answered Jalridd, promptly. "They are of standard cylinder shape with what appear to be numerous energy weapons and open hatches indicating missile tubes."

"A formidable warship," uttered Gareth. "Except they are dealing with the Zaltule and they shall soon learn their ships are not nearly as powerful as they believe."

"Weapons have locked on the nearer Pradelian ships," reported Salten from his weapons console. The Kleese all stood at their battle stations, as their form was not made for sitting. "Ready to fire."

"Overlord!" spoke one of the Kleese at another sensor panel. "I am detecting a spatial disturbance approaching from our rear."

"What type of disturbance?" demanded Harmock, feeling alarmed.

"It's a Fold Space disturbance approaching us at a high rate of speed."

"All ships come to a stop," Harmock ordered. "Prepare defenses for a massed antimatter attack!"

He wasn't a fool, and as the Supreme War Overlord of the Kleese and particularly the Zaltule, he was wise enough to spot a trap. It was obvious now that the Pradelian battlecruisers had been acting as a lure to draw his fleet into combat so these unknowns behind him could hit his fleet at the worst possible moment. The trap had almost worked. If not for the Zaltule at one of the sensor stations spotting the spatial disturbance, the inbound ships would have hit the Zaltule battlecruisers when they were fully engaged with the Pradelians.

Harmock began hurriedly adjusting his fleet formation as he realized he would soon be facing an attack from two directions. It would make maneuvering difficult.

"Unknowns are dropping out of Fold Space," Gareth reported his multifaceted eyes focused intently on the tactical screen, which was lighting up with numerous red threat icons.

"Numbers!" demanded Harmock his eyes seeking the tactical screen for more information.

"Nearly four hundred ships," uttered Jalridd as the information came over his sensor screens. "I'm detecting at least eight different ship types."

"The Alliance!" spoke Gareth as he turned toward Harmock. "This must be the Alliance we've heard about."

"Inbound weapons fire!" reported Jalridd.

"Return fire!" ordered Harmock in a hard voice. "We will destroy this Alliance here and now." He was confident his seven hundred ships could withstand this attack and complete its objective.

"Overlord," interjected Jalridd. "I am detecting two hundred Kleese assault ships in the attacking fleet."

"Assault ships?" questioned Gareth, feeling confused. Could a faction of the Kleese race be helping this Alliance?

"It's the Humans," answered Harmock without hesitation. "They have the trading station and could easily build assault ships for their own use. These Humans are a clever enemy indeed."

Admiral Adamson felt grim satisfaction in the knowledge they had trapped the Zaltule fleet between his forces and the Pradelian battlecruisers. Now he had to destroy it.

"Particle beam firing," spoke Lieutenant Kali Summers from Tactical.

"All ships are engaging," added Commander Shepherd as the viewscreen showed a Waltarn battlecruiser firing its massive KEW cannon at a Kleese battlecruiser.

Sandra knew from her earlier briefing that the Waltarn's cannon fired a ten thousand kilogram shell at twenty percent the speed of light. She was curious to see its effect upon a Zaltule battlecruiser. She was quickly rewarded when the screen lit up with light as the KEW round impacted a Zaltule energy screen, tore through, and then ripped into the hull, causing a massive explosion as its kinetic energy was released. When the glow faded, all that was left of the enemy battlecruiser were two shattered and burning sections."

"Now that's a railgun," uttered Lieutenant Summers with a jealous smile. "I want one."

On the viewscreen, other Alliance ships were now engaging the Zaltule and it was quickly becoming apparent that the combined Alliance fleet had a decisive edge in advanced weapons. Zaltule battlecruisers were being blown apart in rapid succession as powerful energy beams, pulse fusion beams, particle beams, and antimatter missiles battered down their energy shields.

Harmock's gaze turned cold and deadly as he watched another of his warships being destroyed on one of the Command Center's multiple viewscreens. These Alliance ships were all equipped with very advanced weapons as well as powerful energy shields.

"Overlord," spoke Gareth, addressing the military commander. "We are detecting Delton ships in this attacking fleet as well."

"Deltons?" uttered Harmock his gaze shifting to his second in command. "They must have fled to this sector and rallied the nonaligned worlds here to their defense."

"At least now we know where they went."

"The Pradelian ships are advancing and beginning to attack," warned Jalridd from his sensor console.

"Order all ships to intensify their weapons fire; we must destroy this Alliance before it becomes a major threat to the Empire!" ordered Harmock in a grim voice. He pointed one of his dark arms at a viewscreen showing an Alliance warship. "Focus our fire on that ship and destroy it."

-

In space, the opposing fleets were now so close to one another that very few weapons were missing or being intercepted by defensive systems. The Zaltule had the larger warships and could take greater punishment while the Alliance ships had the superior weapons. A group of ten Human two hundred-meter assault ships simultaneously fired their particle beam cannons at one of the Kleese battlecruisers. The beams struck the energy shield, causing cascades of glowing energy to erupt before penetrating and striking the ship's heavily armored hull. Ten massive explosions tore into the ship, ripping off large sections of hull plating before penetrating deeper inside and setting off secondary explosions. With a massive flash of light, the Zaltule battlecruiser disintegrated.

Each segment of the Alliance fleet was operating with some autonomy as there'd not been time to set up a rigid fleet coordination system. The Nalton battlecruisers were advancing in a compact formation, firing off their high intensity energy weapons at the Kleese ships ahead. The space between the two fleets was alive with the flashes of energy beams, pulse fusion beams, and the occasional detonation of a sublight antimatter missile.

Two Zaltule battlecruisers suddenly blew apart as Tureen 40-megaton sublight missiles flashed through weakened screens, leaving glowing fireballs to mark their passing.

-

"What was that?" demanded Harmock as the viewscreens momentarily dimmed from the sudden glare of the multiple explosions.

"Antimatter missiles," answered Jalridd, feeling shaken. "Sensors indicate explosions in the 40-megaton range."

"That's impossible," responded Harmock in a hard voice. "Antimatter becomes too unstable in amounts larger than what is used in our own twenty-megaton warheads."

"Evidently at least one of the Alliance races has found a way to keep it stable," commented Gareth as he studied the sensors, confirming what Jalridd had reported. "We're also detecting ion beams and massive KEW rounds being fired."

The Warrior's Fire suddenly shook violently and warning alarms began sounding. A Kleese rushed to silence the alarms and then reported to Harmock. "Secondary power system has been compromised; maneuvering ability has been reduced by twenty percent. There is also a sixty-meter hole in the outer hull, which extends down through twenty decks. There are multiple fires in adjoining areas."

"Get the fires under control," commanded Harmock, harshly. "If necessary, seal off the damaged areas and flush the air. Fires can't burn without oxygen. What about our combat ability?"

"We lost two pulse fusion cannons, four energy gun turrets, and two missile tubes," answered Salten. "All other weapons are functioning normally."

"Continue the attack," ordered Harmock. "We have the numerical advantage; we must eliminate this Alliance fleet." Harmock gazed at the tactical screen, swiftly calculating the odds of a Zaltule victory. At the moment, neither side had a clear advantage.

The light cruiser Artemis was having a rough time against the two Kleese battlecruisers attacking it. Antimatter missiles were stressing the energy screen, causing it to flicker in near failure.

"Status!" barked Commander Manning as a shower of sparks exploded across the Command Center from a shorted out console. The air was becoming thick with smoke and crewmembers were coughing heavily as they reached for and placed breathing masks over their faces so they could continue to function.

"Energy screen is at fifteen percent," Lieutenant Barkley responded with a desperate tone in his voice. "Engineering reports fusion two is down and we're operating entirely on the primary fusion plant. They've got it redlined trying to pump more power into the shields."

The ship shuddered violently and the lights in the Command Center went out, only to be replaced by dim emergency lighting. The ship continued to shake as if it was coming apart.

"Primary fusion plant is down," gasped Barkley his eyes turning pale as he glanced desperately at the commander. "We're running on batteries. Energy screen is at two percent."

"Then this is it," spoke Commander Manning as he looked calmly at his command crew. "It's been a privilege to serve as your commanding officer."

Before he could say another word, the world turned white as three Kleese antimatter missiles vaporized the ship.

-

"Light cruiser Artemis is down," reported Lieutenant Lash. "Assault ships 432, 475, 515, 562, and 601 are down." Lash knew those ships had names but calling out the numbers was easier and faster.

"The Falcon is being hard pressed," reported Commander Shepherd. She was in constant contact with the other battlecruisers so she could coordinate her own ship's attacks with theirs. "Commander Melvin reports his energy shield is down to forty percent."

"Order the light cruisers Scout and Argonaut to reinforce the Falcon," ordered Admiral Adamson.

They were losing ships, all the Alliance fleets were, but if Adamson was reading the tactical screen correctly, the Kleese were losing ships at a much faster rate. The tide of the battle was beginning to shift toward the Alliance. He had to keep up the pressure on the Kleese even if it meant more ship losses.

Fleet Commander Achlyn watched grimly from his Delton flagship as another of his battlecruisers died in the burning hellfire of multiple antimatter explosions. It was the third of his battlecruisers to die since the battle began. He also knew it wouldn't be the last.

"The Senchell was a valiant ship," commented Second Commander Baylith as he watched the hellfire die away on one of the ship's viewscreens, leaving a glowing gas field and a scattering of debris behind. He felt a hollow feeling inside knowing more of his people had just died. Delton ships were identified by numbers, but they all had names as well.

Achlyn nodded in agreement. His large round eyes were focused on the ship's tactical screen as his ships continued to press the attack against the hated Zaltule. With grim satisfaction, he saw another Kleese warship die under his fleets' heavy energy weapons fire.

"We're winning!" cried Baylith as he studied the various reports coming in from across the Alliance fleet. "The Zaltule are losing ships at over a two to one rate."

"Superior weapons," stated Achlyn, pleased that the tables had finally been turned on the evil Zaltule. "For once they will know the pain of defeat." He was glad now that he had agreed to join the Alliance the Humans were trying to put together against the Zaltule. He'd already taken note of the diversity in the weapons technology each used; almost every nonaligned world had technology, which was unique. If the Humans could hold this Alliance together, there still might be hope for the future.

"Press the attack," Achlyn ordered his large eyes narrowing. "It's time the Kleese learn what it means to die!"

"Battlecruiser Rampage is under heavy attack," reported Commander Shepherd. "They've lost one of their fusion power plants and thirty percent of their weapons are offline."

"Move us closer to them," ordered Admiral Adamson, not wanting to lose one of his valuable battlecruisers. "Have the light cruisers Ajax and Odin move in with us."

"We won't make it," Sandra said with a disheartened look in her eyes as she shook her head. She gestured toward one of the viewscreens where the Rampage was under heavy attack.

As Adamson shifted his gaze to the indicated viewscreen, he saw a brilliant explosion and the bow of the battlecruiser disintegrated before his eyes. The ship attempted a sharp turn trying to bring her secondary weapons to bear on the attacking Zaltule battlecruisers, but before the turn was completed, the ship vanished in a giant fireball as an antimatter missile detonated in her heart.

"Battlecruiser Rampage is down," reported Lieutenant Lash in an even voice as he fought down his emotions at the loss of so many Human lives. Lash knew that nearly seven hundred Humans had just died.

Admiral Adamson let out a deep and ragged breath. He momentarily closed his eyes and then reopened them. "They died in a just cause," he said as he looked into the eyes of his shocked command crew. "Now let's finish this battle."

-

On the main viewscreen, Harmock had watched an Alliance battlecruiser die. They'd determined that the ship was a Human one and it had been very difficult to kill.

"The Human battlecruisers are very powerful," stated Minor Overlord Gareth as the Warrior's Fire trembled from weapons fire impacting the ship's armored hull. "They have extremely strong energy screens as well as that infuriating particle beam weapon, which seems to pass easily through our ship's shields."

"This battle is lost," uttered Harmock as he studied the tactical screen noting two more icons representing Zaltule warships flicker and then disappear. "Our fleet is not powerful enough to stand up to these advanced weapons, not in the numbers were facing now."

"It's the fault of the Council of Overlords for letting these worlds develop such weapons to begin with," pointed out Gareth.

"They were lax in their duty to the Empire," agreed Harmock. "When we return to the home world, there will be some immediate changes."

"Then we're returning?"

"Yes," Harmock responded as his multifaceted eyes took stock of the tactical situation. "This Alliance is dangerous, but if we cut off its head it will collapse in upon itself."

"The Humans?"

"Yes," answered Harmock as he thought of a strategy to neutralize this new Alliance. "We shall return to the homeward, address the problems with the Council of Overlords, and then return with a fleet large enough to annihilate the Humans and what remains of their star system."

"It is a wise decision," Gareth spoke in agreement.

"Ready the fleet for departure," ordered Harmock. He'd already lost far more ships than expected. There was no point in sacrificing more in a losing situation.

"What about the ships in orbit over Ryerson?"

Harmock studied the tactical screen briefly and then shook his head. "Order them to begin picking up the ground forces immediately. They have fifteen minutes and then we execute our jump into Fold Space."

"They won't be able to extricate all of the ground forces in that short of a time period," warned Gareth. "Some will be left behind."

"Those that remain will bring glory to the Empire," Harmock answered in a dispassionate voice. "They know their duties as warriors."

"I will pass on the orders," replied Gareth.

Harmock turned his attention back to the tactical screen. He still had a battle to fight as he organized his fleet's withdrawal. His multifaceted eyes focused on a viewscreen showing a close up of one of the Human battlecruisers. Even as he watched, a bright blue beam of light flashed forth, spearing through a Zaltule battlecruiser's energy screen and setting off a massive explosion. A large section of the ship's hull could be seen drifting off into space. The Human ship then fired two antimatter missiles through the weakened screen, destroying the ship.

Harmock felt suddenly uncertain about the Empire. These Humans were an unknown. They had revolted against the Kleese, escaped the trading station, then returned and stole the trading station. Later, they defeated a Kleese fleet in their home system and then gone on a rescue mission to Kivea where they had rescued a number of prominent Kivean scientists, and then returned home to defeat a major Kleese fleet once more.

Were the Humans a greater menace to the Empire than what he had originally thought? When he returned to the home world, he fully intended to speak with other Kleese who had dealt with the Humans first hand, if any could be found. There would also be more changes to the council. By allowing the Humans to survive, the council had shown itself to be weak and incompetent; Harmock fully intended to change that. Now he needed to extricate his fleet before he lost too many more ships.

-

Admiral Adamson watched as the twenty Kleese warships over Ryerson suddenly broke orbit and accelerated away toward open space. In a matter of only a few minutes, they had accelerated sufficiently and jumped into Fold Space.

"Kleese fleet is disengaging," reported Commander Shepherd as she studied the tactical screen. She could see the Kleese ships trying to put some distance between them and the different Alliance warships.

"All ships continue to press the attack," ordered Adamson over the com, which connected him to all of the individual ship commanders. "We want to inflict as much damage as possible on this Kleese fleet to ensure it doesn't return." He leaned forward in his command chair, studying the tactical screen intently. With satisfaction, he saw a number of ships closing the gaps between them and the withdrawing Kleese.

-

The light cruisers Warspite and Sultan closed with a Kleese battlecruiser that had already suffered some damage. A major section of its armored hull plating had been blasted away and a thousand-meter wide crater was carved deep into the top section of the disk.

"Its energy shield is fluctuating," Commander Bolton of the Warspite communicated to Commander Atkins on the Sultan.

"Then let's finish it off," Atkins replied as his light cruiser activated its particle beam cannon.

A bright blue beam of light flashed out, smashing through the weakened Zaltule energy shield and slamming into the side of the disk ship, setting off a colossal explosion. It was quickly followed by a second particle beam from the Warspite.

-

"Two Human ships are engaging us," the Zaltule in front of the sensors reported.

"What's the status of our ship?" demanded Maltkel from the Command Pedestal.

"Fold Space Drive has been destroyed, sublight drive is functioning at forty percent," reported the Zaltule at Damage Control. "We've lost sixty percent of our ship's weapons, and we have major fires burning in most areas. Our energy screen will only last for another few minutes."

"Fire every antimatter missile we can at the nearest Human ship," Maltkel ordered. He was a commander of the Zaltule and while his ship might be doomed, he could at least take one of the accursed Human ships with him.

From the Zaltule battlecruiser, twenty antimatter missiles flashed out from its remaining missile tubes to impact the energy screen of the Sultan.

-

"Energy shield is failing!" screamed Ensign Sherry Wild from Damage Control as she was hurled painfully against her restraining straps.

The Sultan shook violently and then seemed to be shoved hard to one side as if struck by a giant iron fist. Several consoles in the Command Center blew out, sending cascades of brilliant sparks across the room. Screams of pain and cries of fright could be heard throughout the ship.

In Engineering, Chief Engineer Barker turned pale as the primary fusion reactor began to shake in its mountings. "Evacuate Engineering," he ordered as he saw the reactor itself beginning to glow, indicating a possible meltdown was taking place inside. The magnetic containment fields must be failing.

"The hatches are locked down!" screamed Spaceman First Class Jones. "There are fires on the other side!"

A dozen crewmembers looked expectantly at Barker, waiting for his orders. Surely, the chief engineer would know what to do.

Barker looked frantically around, knowing they were trapped. He looked down at one of the gauges, which showed the internal temperature of the fusion reactor and turned pale, seeing that it was redlined as far as the dial would go. He looked up at the reactor just in time to see its side melt away. In an instant, everyone in Engineering was incinerated as the reactor's tremendous heat was released

"Containment breach," screamed Ensign Wild as her damage control board lit up with red lights. "Engineering is gone!"

Commander Atkins looked around his Command Center. It was full of smoke and several crewmembers were lying on the deck, either dead or unconscious. With a heavy sigh, he knew the rest of them would shortly be joining them.

-

Aboard the Warspite, Commander Bolton recoiled as the viewscreen showing the Sultan suddenly filled with light, which was quickly reduced as the viewscreen adjusted itself.

"Sultan is down," reported the ensign at the sensors.

"Fire antimatter missiles at the Zaltule battlecruiser," commanded Bolton, grimly. "The least we can do for the Sultan is to finish off that Kleese ship."

From the Warspite, a spread of antimatter missiles flashed away to impact against the battered hull of the Zaltule battlecruiser. Six brilliant explosions of antimatter energy marked the end of the enemy ship.

"Kleese battlecruiser is down," the ensign at the sensor console confirmed.

"Find us another target," ordered Bolton. He knew they would mourn the fallen later.

"Kleese ships are entering Fold Space," reported Lieutenant Lash.

"All stragglers have been eliminated," added Commander Shepherd a minute later, as the last damaged Zaltule battlecruiser was blown apart by a Lanolthian ship.

Admiral Adamson let out a long and deep breath. He allowed himself to relax as he studied the tactical screen. It had been a brief and bloody battle, with both sides taking major losses. However, they had driven off the Kleese and at least had a victory.

"How many of them did we get?"

"We took out two hundred and thirteen of their battlecruisers," reported Sandra as she studied information on a computer screen near her.

"Seventh Fleet losses?"

"They were heavy," Sandra confirmed in a grim voice. "We lost one battlecruiser, six light cruisers, and eighty-seven assault ships."

"What about our allies?"

"They lost ships also," Sandra replied as she looked up more information. "Fifty-two confirmed losses, all battlecruisers."

Adamson winced, but considering the number of Kleese ships destroyed, it was to be expected. "Contact Colonel Nelson and inform him to proceed to Ryerson and begin troop landings. "I'm assigning the battlecruiser Firebolt to help provide support if needed." He knew the Defender had her own small escort fleet consisting of four light cruisers and eight assault ships.

Delton Fleet Commander Achlyn looked at the tactical screen in satisfaction. The Kleese fleet had been driven off and the Humans were moving their troop assault ships into position to finish off any Zaltule that remained on the surface of Ryerson.

"The Humans are indeed a threat to the Kleese," spoke Second Commander Baylith. "They handled themselves well in the battle."

"How many ships did we lose?" asked Achlyn, knowing every Delton ship lost was irreplaceable.

"Twelve," reported Baylith in an even voice. "Another six require considerable repair before they can enter Fold Space."

"We have the time," replied Achlyn. "I believe this battle will show many nonaligned worlds the importance of joining the Alliance the Humans are trying to form. We'll do everything in our power to help them and perhaps someday we can return to our home world and drive off the Kleese. The Humans have given us hope."

-

Aboard the troop assault ship Defender, Colonel Nelson gazed at the main viewscreen as they approached Ryerson. He knew down in the flight bay his brother was preparing to enter a drop ship and go down to the planet to fight the Zaltule. Wade wished he was going along to keep his brother safe, but Ryan had chosen this life and Wade had to trust his brother to do his job.

It also concerned him that Beth would be down on the surface also. The two people most important to him were going to be in harm's way and all he could do was stand in the Command Center of the Defender and watch. He just prayed nothing went wrong.

Chapter Fifteen

Colonel Nelson was sitting in one of the twin command chairs in the Command Center of the Troop Assault Ship Defender. Next to him was Commander Greer, who was busy directing the coming troop deployment. Looking around the busy Command Center, Wade noted that it was very similar to a regular battlecruiser except Communications and Tactical both had extra people. There were four people in front of Communications and two extra at Tactical. He knew this was to better coordinate fire missions with the ground as well as to stay in communication with various marine units.

"Five minutes until drop," announced Captain Alicia Damon, the executive officer, from where she was standing next to the large sensor console.

"What's the latest estimate of Kleese warriors still on the surface?" asked Wade as he looked at one of the viewscreens focused on the blue-green planet below.

"Unknown," answered Commander Greer, glancing over at Wade. "We know they hold the planet's main spaceport as well as part of the capital city, but estimates of actual numbers are sketchy."

"We have contact with some of their government officials," added Captain Damon, looking over toward Communications. "But they haven't been able to tell us much."

Wade nodded. He knew from initial reports on the ground, the capital city was in the process of being hastily evacuated. It wasn't an orderly evacuation as the populace was fleeing into the countryside to escape the Kleese as well as the fighting that was soon to commence. Several assault ships had been sent down for flyovers of the two soon to be contested areas. Energy weapons fire and several missiles had met them, forcing the two disk ships to retreat.

"The Fire Fox will be dropping the same time as us," added Commander Greer. On one of the viewscreens, the Fire Fox floated in space waiting to begin the operation.

"I intend to use the Defender's railgun batteries to clear out any heavy Kleese troop concentrations," Wade informed the commander. "We do want to hold damage to the spaceport and city to a minimum if at all possible."

He had discussed this with Beth and Major Stevens. As soon as both were down on the surface, they would send scouts ahead to search for key defensive positions for the Defender to take out. These were Zaltule warriors they were going up against and Wade had no doubt they would be extremely dangerous. This would be the first time Humans had gone up against a well trained Kleese ground force.

"Our railgun batteries are on standby," replied Greer. He knew the ship's railguns could take out nearly any planetary target. The ship's sixteen railgun batteries had been designed specifically for assaulting a planet.

"Three minutes until drop," spoke Captain Damon, tonelessly.

She was busily speaking to the ship's flight bay operations center to ensure the drop went smoothly. They would be sending down ten regular drop ships and two of the larger cargo drop ships. The cargo drop ships would each hold a full platoon as well as two of the Defender's eight hover tanks. Subsequent drops would deliver the remaining four tanks.

Ryan's platoon was in one of the cargo drop ships waiting patiently for the operation to begin. Each marine was encased in a Type Four battlesuit and sitting along the two walls, waiting expectantly for the drop. This would be the first time any of them had gone down in a drop ship.

"Damn, this is nerve wracking," moaned Private Parker as he shifted slightly in his seat."

"Look at it this way," commented Private Adams. "You're finally going to get a chance to kill some Kleese."

"We're supposed to capture one," complained Alexander, gazing down at the large stun rifle he was carrying. He wished he were carrying an RG rifle or even an energy cannon. At least he had his Energy Lance fastened to his waist. "How am I going to kill one with this?"

"Stun one and then stomp on its head with your big feet," spoke Private Rios with his slight Mexican accent. "That should work."

"One minute until drop," spoke Sergeant Olivia Morris.

Olivia looked around the group of marines knowing that none, other than her, had seen actual combat. That was one of the reasons Major Stevens had assigned her to First Platoon. As a member of Major Winfrey's British Special Forces group, she'd seen a lot of combat, both on Earth as well as in space.

"I'm scared," Casey said in a low voice from where she was sitting next to Ryan. She looked over at her friend and confident, but his face was hidden by his helmet. No part of a marine's body was left uncovered by the Type Four suits. "What if I screw up?"

"We're all feeling nervous," Ryan responded. He could feel butterflies in his own stomach. There was a lot riding on this mission and he didn't want to let Beth or his brother down. "We've had the training; all we have to do is follow what we've been taught." He tried to sound more reassuring than he felt.

Casey nodded and tried to calm her breathing. She could feel her heart beating rapidly and she was sweating even though the suit was trying to keep her cool. The air temperature inside the suit was a comfortable 72 degrees. Glancing around, she wondered how many of the others felt as she did.

"Drop!" called out Sergeant Morris as the drop ship suddenly began to move. "This'll be a little bit rough."

Casey felt suddenly queasy as the ship dropped straight down toward the planet's surface. She could hear the air buffeting the hull as the small ship entered the planet's atmosphere making a whistling noise.

"They're not going to be shooting at us as we go down, are they?" asked Alexander, sounding suddenly worried. He knew the drop ships and cargo drop ships were too small to have protective energy screens, though they did have a thick covering of battle armor.

"If they do, you'll never know it," Lauren replied between clenched lips as the small drop ship rocked violently as it plummeted through the upper levels of the planet's atmosphere. "There will just be a bright light and that will be it."

"Crap," moaned Alexander as he gripped his stun rifle tighter.

"Vaya con Dios," spoke Private Rios as he made a crossing motion with his left hand. His right hand held his rifle.

"Well, I'm not ready to go, yet," responded Private Swen as the drop ship continued to shake. "I met this cute redhead on our last leave and I plan on seeing her again."

"I'm sure she's waiting on you," responded Private Hatterson, shaking her head. She couldn't believe Swen could be thinking about women in this situation. It just showed there was so much more she needed to learn about Humans.

"When we deploy, set up a defensive perimeter around the drop ship," Sergeant Morris ordered. "Once the hover tanks have been unloaded we can move out toward our objective."

"The cargo drop ship will be returning to the Defender," Ryan added. "Sergeant Morris has been through this type of operation before, so listen to her!"

The vibrating seemed to lesson as the drop ship leveled out in the lower atmosphere. The small airfoils on the ship helped to stabilize their flight and soon the heavy buffeting of the planet's atmosphere seemed to go away.

"Standby for insertion!" called out Sergeant Morris as she felt the ship suddenly drop straight down.

The ship came to a jarring halt and the rear hatch slid open as a metal ramp extended out to touch the ground.

"Move out!" ordered Ryan as he stood and made for the open hatch gripping his RG rifle.

The platoon hurriedly descended the ramp and took up a defensive stance around the grounded cargo drop ship. After a couple of minutes, the two hover tanks came floating down the ramp and moved out a hundred meters away from the ship.

"Form up in a staggered line on either side of the tanks," ordered Corporal Hunter. Casey quickly made her way to the tanks, taking up a position on the right side of the two. "No sign of hostile contact."

Checking her HUD, she could see twenty-one glowing green icons. With a thought to her neural implant, she activated the suit's enhanced vision optics. In moments, she was studying the terrain up ahead in close detail. A few buildings and a wide paved road were all that she could see. The road led directly to the spaceport, which was their objective. She knew that on their flanks more drop ships were coming down, delivering the other three platoons with Type Four suits.

Ryan was standing behind the two tanks talking with Sergeant Morris. A noise behind him drew his attention and turning, he watched as the cargo drop ship took off and accelerated rapidly up into the air.

"Ride's gone," muttered Private Parker as he watched the small ship rapidly disappear.

"It'll be back," answered Lauren pensively as she took stock of their surroundings. At the moment, there didn't seem to be anything threatening.

"Scouts ahead," ordered Ryan, taking a deep breath. It was time to get this operation started. "We'll advance in a staggered line with the two tanks in the center." Ryan knew that the tanks had extremely sensitive targeting sensors, which would be continuously searching out threats. The small tanks held a three-person crew.

Ryan looked down at his metal encased hands. It was strange to be able to feel the wind blowing against his arms and the sun shining down on his armor. The neural implant sent messages directly into the areas of his brain that controlled the senses. The suit felt alive and as he walked, he could feel and sense everything as if he wasn't even wearing a battlesuit.

Flexing his right hand Ryan made it into a fist, feeling the metal fingers digging into his palm. Even after all of this time, the suit was amazing. Turning up his hearing, he could hear the footsteps of his marines and the distant sound of other drop ships taking off. By now, the first set of drops should all be down. Lieutenant Felton's platoon was on their right flank and Lieutenant Guthrie's was to their left. Major Stevens was behind them with the fourth platoon, which would be serving in a reinforcing role if needed.

"Everyone stay sharp," called out Sergeant Morris.

Privates Parker and Adams were now one hundred meters ahead of the rest of the platoon and moving cautiously forward. They'd landed on the outskirts of the spaceport where a few trees and several small buildings afforded them some semblance of cover. They made it a point to stay off the road as it made them easy targets.

"Where are they?" uttered Alexander as he peered around a large tree trunk, looking for any sign of a Zaltule warrior. He shuddered slightly, thinking about the giant spiders that were waiting for him.

"I don't know," responded Lauren, uneasily. It just seemed too quiet.

She paused and used her enhanced optics to scan the beginning of the spaceport just ahead of them. She could see a large area covered in blastcrete with numerous buildings. There were several cargo ships and perhaps even a passenger ship parked on the pads. However, everywhere she looked there was no movement.

"Corporal, I don't like this," Lauren reported over her com. "I don't see anything that could be a threat and there's no movement anywhere on the spaceport that I can see."

"Be careful," Casey cautioned as she moved up to just behind the two scouts and gestured for the rest of the platoon to come to a halt.

"We'll hold here for a few minutes until the other platoons are in position," ordered Ryan, feeling tense. Something just didn't seem right. Why were the Zaltule allowing them to advance without any resistance? There had been no weapons fire from anywhere. He couldn't hear any birds; the wind was light, and even the insects seemed strangely quiet.

"Maybe they've left," suggested Alexander, hopefully.

"They're here," Sergeant Morris stated in an even voice. "I can feel it in my bones. They may be trying to draw us in closer before attacking. Remember, these are Zaltule warriors and they are trained for fighting. They won't rush us like regular conscripts do." Morris well recalled how the Kleese sent their conscripts out in literal suicide waves to crush opposition. Conscript casualties were inconsequential to the Kleese.

Ryan contacted the two hover tanks over his com. "Launch two drones and let's see what they can detect."

Both hover tanks had four small drones they could launch which could scan an enemy's position and relay the information back to the tank it was launched from. Ryan stepped over to one of the tanks and set his neural implant to receive data from the two drones.

From each tank a small drone, about twenty inches in diameter, exited a small hatch and darted silently up into the clear blue sky. After reaching one hundred meters in height, they flew swiftly toward the nearby spaceport and were soon circling above its buildings and the few ships on the pads.

Ryan was getting a bird's eye view from the drones, but nowhere was there any evidence of any Kleese. There were no fortifications, no military vehicles, and no movement. The no movement part worried Ryan as there should have at least been some indication of movement from the Kleese. Shaking his head, Ryan ordered the tank crews to keep the drones circling and to notify him of any developments.

Beth let out a deep breath as her two companies of Space Marines took up attack positions just on the outskirts of the spaceport. Captain Stern and her company were to her right and

Captain Foster's company was directly in front of her and to the left.

"I don't like this, Major," Captain Stern commented as she gazed ahead at the quiet spaceport. "Where are the Zaltule?"

"Lieutenant Nelson launched several drones and they recorded no movement anywhere on the spaceport," Captain Foster added. She patted her RG rifle, which she'd set on explosive rounds. She still enjoyed blowing things up.

"Everyone's in position," Beth responded as she checked the HUD in her command suit. All the glowing icons were still green and the last drop ship had taken off to return to the ships in orbit. It had been over six years since she'd last seen combat. Taking a deep breath, Beth prepared herself for what was ahead.

She had five hundred Space Marines on the ground supported by twelve hover tanks. Major Stevens was on their left flank with all eighty of his marines in their Type Four battlesuits. She was curious to see the new suits in action.

Beth activated her long-range transmitter, which put her in contact with her husband up on the Defender. "Wade, there's no evidence of any Kleese at the spaceport; could they have gone somewhere else?" She waited tensely for Wade's response. She knew he would be checking the Defender's sensors.

"No," he replied after a moment. "Beth, they have to be there. We've been scanning the spaceport with the ship's sensors and we're detecting a lot of power readings, but we can't tell if they're Kleese or part of the spaceport's infrastructure."

"Maybe they all got off the planet," Beth suggested.

"No, we know that didn't happen," Wade responded. "We've established contact with the planet's government and they are insistent some Zaltule warriors remain. They claim there are some in the capital city, but the majority are holed up at the spaceport."

"They must be in the buildings, then," spoke Beth, sharply. "We'll have to go in and drag them out."

"I think they want you on the blastcrete," answered Wade, pensively. "Don't forget Beth, these are professional warriors. They won't be easy to take down and won't make mistakes."

"We could use the tanks to take out all the major structures," suggested Beth. She knew that would be the safest and easiest method to eliminate the Kleese. "Or even our suit explosive rounds."

"No," Wade sighed. "We want to cause as little damage to the spaceport as possible. We would like these people as allies."

"What if they won't come out of the buildings?" Beth asked. "We could lose a lot of marines if we have to go inside to get them."

"If we see the Kleese are too heavily entrenched, we'll use the Defender's railguns to clear them out," Wade replied after a moment. "I don't want to, but I also don't want to suffer a lot of casualties to save a few buildings. We need to get them out of the buildings if possible."

"Then we do it the hard way," Beth answered as she shifted her RG rifle in her hands. "We go in and try to lure them out."

"Use the hover tanks to take them out, if possible," Wade ordered. "I want to hold casualties down to a minimum."

"We'll try," answered Beth. She closed the circuit and switched over to the general com channel for all the marines taking part in the attack. "Scouts ahead, I want a full squad backing up each scout. The rest of us will advance in staggered formation along with the tanks. Move out!"

-

"Crap," muttered Private Parker as he moved out and walked toward the edge of the blastcrete, which designated the beginning of the spaceport.

"Don't get your ass killed," cautioned Lauren as she moved from behind her tree, walking twenty meters to the left of Alexander. "Remember, if you see a Zaltule, stun him and then report to the lieutenant."

Behind them, two five man squads followed in a staggered line ready to support the two scouts if need be. Everyone was using their enhanced vision, hearing, and their suit's sensors to scan for any signs of the enemy.

Ryan was walking between the two tanks and a little behind keeping his eyes open. He was breathing faster and he could tell his nerves were on edge. Looking ahead, he saw the scouts were stepping out onto the blastcrete followed by the two supporting squads. At any moment, he expected firing to break out.

Casey took a deep breath as she reached the blastcrete. She was behind the two squads trying to keep an eye on everyone and everything. Gazing at the blastcrete up ahead, she noticed several areas, which were badly tarnished. Before she could say anything, six popup weapons rose up from the tarnished areas and swung their barrels toward the advancing marines.

"Down!" screamed Casey as she threw herself to the hard, unforgiving surface. Even in her battlesuit, she felt the pain of the landing.

The popups fired and one of the hover tanks exploded in a fiery blast as it was struck by some type of explosive round. The other tank quickly responded, firing its energy cannon at the nearest popup, blowing it apart. Two others were quickly eliminated by explosive rounds fire from RG rifles. However, the others were firing explosive rounds at the pinned down marines in rapid succession.

Ryan felt himself picked up and thrown violently to the ground as an explosive round hit the spot where he had been recently standing. He tumbled and flung himself prone, raising his head up just high enough to see what was happening. On his HUD, he saw two icons turn amber and another red. He felt nauseous, knowing he had just lost his first marine. He knew if not for the tough composite armor of the suits many more would have been lost. Looking at the hover tank, he saw Sergeant Morris standing behind it, firing her RG rifle calmly at the popups.

The hover tank quickly targeted another popup and blew it away as the marines finished off the other two. Then quiet reigned briefly, only to be suddenly interrupted by the sound of other explosions going off on both their flanks. Other marine companies were coming under attack.

"Lieutenant Nelson," came Major Steven's voice over the command channel. "Report!"

"I lost one hover tank, one marine killed, and two injured," responded Ryan as he stood up, looking around. "We've eliminated the popup weapons in front of us." There were about a dozen small smoking craters nearby from the Zaltule weapons fire.

"They came out of areas of the blastcrete that were extremely tarnished," Casey added. "I don't see anything else like that in front of us."

"Hold your remaining hover tank at the edge of the spaceport," Major Steven's ordered. "Lieutenant Felton lost one also as well as three more marines KIA."

For several more minutes, Ryan held his marines in their current position until the firing around them died down and came to a stop. When there were no more sounds of explosions, Ryan assumed the other units had annihilated the popup weapons in their areas. It made him wonder what other surprises the Zaltule had waiting for them.

"Resume the advance," Major Williams announced over the command channel. "Scouts ahead and stay vigilant."

"Move out," ordered Ryan as he began moving toward the blastcrete.

"Just like God Damn Charring Mountain," mumbled Alexander as he stood up and looked over at Lauren.

"You're still alive," Lauren was quick to point out as she moved out further onto the blastcrete. "If this were Charring, you would be lying face down in the dirt!"

She felt highly exposed as there was no cover close by. Even though she was encased in an eight-foot tall battlesuit, she still felt vulnerable. Lauren held her RG rifle at the ready, looking for any signs of movement.

"Only because those damn popups fired at the hover tanks and the marines behind us," retorted Alexander. Too often he'd been hit by stunners on Charring Mountain and he knew how lucky both he and Lauren were to still be alive. They had been the closest to the Zaltule popups.

Just behind them, Casey and the two squads with her stepped farther out onto the spaceport. Looking to the flanks, she could see other marines from other units appearing.

"Spread out," spoke Casey, gesturing to the marines in the two squads to increase their spacing.

A few moments later, Ryan reached the blastcrete and ordered the hover tank to come to a stop. He also ordered the marines still with him to take up covering positions around the tank.

"Keep an eye on those buildings and the ships," he ordered as he used his vision optics to inspect the spaceport. There were numerous large hangers and other buildings scattered about on the blastcrete as well as several tall communications towers.

"I still don't see anything," spoke Sergeant Morris. She had taken up a firing position behind a large tree right next to the blastcrete.

Inside the Spaceport Operations Center, Minor War Overlord Braton glared in anger at the reports coming in to him. His Zaltule warriors had been too far into the city to be able to withdraw with the fleet. Now he was faced with incoming Humans in Type Three Battlesuits and some other smaller suit he was not familiar with.

"All popups have been eliminated," reported Caltill his chief aide. "The enemy continues to advance."

"These are the Humans we have heard so much about," Braton responded in a cold voice. "Their fleet commands the orbital approaches and we will not be rescued."

"Then we will die as Zaltule warriors," spoke Caltill with a nod. "It is the way of the warrior caste."

"But we'll take many of them with us," Braton replied as he studied several viewscreens in the Operations Center, which showed the approaching Humans. "Inform our warriors to open fire."

Suddenly, from over a dozen buildings, Kleese began firing from windows, doorways, and openings they'd made in the walls. Beams of energy and high-powered RG rounds struck the inbound marines, killing many of them.

"Take cover!" yelled Casey as she felt her suit impacted in the leg by an RG round. It hurt like hell, but her suit damage display indicated it was still intact. Looking about, she saw a small vehicle close by and darted toward it. Other marines were going prone on the ground and beginning to return fire.

Ryan quickly assessed the situation, not liking the vulnerable position his marines were in. While the Type Four battlesuits were superior to the Type Threes, in this type of situation they couldn't be used as they were designed. "Take out those weapons emplacements with your railgun cannons," he ordered the tank crew. He knew they had been cautioned about damaging the buildings, but his marines were under fire. He would worry about the repercussions later.

Instantly, the hover tank began firing railgun rounds in rapid succession at the buildings. The tank's central computer could detect inbound weapons fire and redirect the tank's twin railguns to return fire along the same trajectory.

Casey was hunched down behind the small vehicle firing explosive RG rounds at the buildings. Her suit was identifying potential targets and she was firing nearly nonstop. Around her, other marines were doing the same, occasionally changing position when enemy fire came too close.

Watching the battle carefully, Ryan realized quickly that not all of the Zaltule had started firing at the same time. Many had waited and as their fellow warriors were taken down were stepping in to keep up the deadly fire on the marines. Once fire from one location was eliminated, it would start back up somewhere else. On his HUD, he saw another icon turn a glaring red.

"They've pretty well got us pinned down," spoke Sergeant Morris as she fired at an open doorway in a building where she though she had seen some movement.

-

Beth was standing behind a small building with Sergeant Russell and a full squad of marines. On her HUD, she could see over twenty red icons and close to thirty amber ones. Whatever weapons the Kleese were using, they were quite effective against her marines.

With a sharp breath, she activated her long-range com. "Wade, we're under heavy fire from the buildings. The Kleese aren't coming out and we're taking heavy casualties."

"We see," Wade replied from the Defender. "Don't allow your marines to advance. We've pinpointed where the heaviest fire is originating from and are preparing to take the building out with ship weapons. I spoke to a head government official a few moments ago, and he has given us permission to use whatever force is necessary to remove the Kleese."

-

Up in the Defender, the crew prepared to fire the ship's planetary railguns.

"Ready to fire," reported Captain Damon. She was standing next to Lieutenant Craig Coleman at Tactical.

Wade nodded at Commander Greer, indicating for him to initiate the firing order. He just hoped there were no marine casualties caused from the hellfire they were about to rain down upon the spaceport. Most of the buildings were made of heavy metal and they were designating two rounds for each one. He hoped Beth was far enough back. He knew she preferred to be in the thick of things so there was no doubt in his mind she was on the spaceport somewhere.

"Fire!" ordered Commander Greer.

The large planetary bombardment railgun turrets locked onto their assigned targets and then eight of them fired twin shells into the planet's atmosphere. They lit up space like a fiery meteor but were traveling much faster. Down through the atmosphere they hurtled to impact the planet's surface.

Beth knew what to expect as she had seen railgun fire used against the Kleese Communications Center on one of her earlier missions. Suddenly, in front of her, massive explosions shook the blastcrete as huge sections of the buildings blew outward and multiple concussion waves traveled across the spaceport, rattling the remaining structures. Rising black smoke and fire indicated where the rounds had struck.

"Move up!" she ordered. "We need to hit them while they're still unorganized from the railgun strike."

Beth stepped out from around the small building holding her RG rifle at the ready. Sergeant Russell and his squad were with her as they moved rapidly across the blastcrete toward the burning buildings.

Minor War Overlord Braton stared out the thick, protective windows of the Operations Center at the destroyed buildings his warriors had been in. He let out a deep breath of frustration at how the Humans had used railgun strikes from orbit to obliterate the majority of his forces. This was a tactic the Zaltule used occasionally when an enemy was too concentrated to take out in a frontal assault.

"We are defeated!" spoke Caltill in anguish as he watched the Humans advance on the viewscreens.

Looking out the windows, he could see hundreds of battlesuit encased Humans advancing toward them. Only a scattering of defensive fire rang out from the few Zaltule warriors who'd survived the bombardment from space.

"Prepare yourself," commanded Braton as he closed the helmet on his Type Three battlesuit and picked up his RG rifle from where it had been lying on a control console. "The Humans will be here shortly."

"Vermin!" spat Caltill as he picked up his energy cannon. "How can we be defeated by vermin?"

Braton looked out the windows and only shook his head. While it had always been true that there were no other races in the known galaxy equal to the Zaltule in battle, he was beginning to wonder. These Humans seemed to be different and they were advancing toward him with such confidence. Was it possible they'd finally met a warrior race equal to the Zaltule? Braton found that thought hard to believe, but how else could one explain the Human victories?

Ryan had moved his marines up and formed his platoon into a long skirmish line as they quickly advanced toward the burning buildings. The other two Type Four platoons were on his immediate flanks. His lone remaining hover tank was just behind the skirmish line, swinging its energy cannon threatening back and forth seeking targets of opportunity. Occasionally the cannon would fire, obliterating a Kleese, who had dared to attempt to fire on the advancing marines.

Looking around, Ryan noticed they were quickly outdistancing their support troops on both flanks in the Type Three suits. The Type Fours were much more flexible and allowed for a greater freedom of movement as well as increased speed. As they neared the burning buildings, he saw marines from the three advancing Type Four platoons take to the air, leaping on top of buildings and other structures to give them a better view of the battlefield.

Taking a deep breath, Ryan raised his RG rifle and fired two explosive rounds into an open doorway where he thought he'd detected movement. A battlesuit encased Kleese stumbled out and fell to the ground.

"We need prisoners," Ryan spoke over his unit's com channel.

Lauren looked over at Alexander, who had stopped next to a tall tower. "You heard the lieutenant," she spoke over their private com channel.

"Yeah, I heard him," muttered Alexander as he activated the flight repellers in his feet and leaped up into the air.

He set back down halfway up the tower on a small platform, which was just large enough for him to stand on. Now I'm a sitting duck, he thought as he began inspecting the buildings around him with his enhanced vision. He checked each building one by one, not finding any potential targets. Then he looked at a building only one hundred meters away that was covered in large windows. Must be some type of control tower, he decided.

Alexander froze as he detected what looked like movement inside. Ramping up his vision, he gazed intently at the windows. Sure enough, he could see two Kleese in battlesuits looking out at the advancing marines. Both looked to be armed. Taking a deep breath, he raised his stun rifle and flipped off the safety. Aiming at the first target, he sighted carefully and pulled the trigger. With excited satisfaction, he saw the target go down. Before he could fire off his second shot one of the windows exploded outward and railgun rounds began to impact the tower around him. Then an explosive round hit, destroying the platform he was standing on. In desperation, he fired several stun rifle shots toward the shattered window as he felt himself falling toward the ground far below.

Beth gazed around at the burning buildings and the dead Zaltule around her. The Zaltule had fought to the end, never offering to surrender. Even now, a few Zaltule were still sniping at her marines as they combed the burning buildings and other structures.

"That looks like a control tower of some sort," Sergeant Russell said, pointing toward a nearby structure. "It seems to be pretty well intact."

"Looking at the structure, Beth could see several marines in the Type Four suits going inside. "Let's follow them," she ordered. "We can make that our command center until we're satisfied we've eliminated all the enemy."

Looking at her HUD, Beth saw with relief that Ryan's glowing green icon was still unchanged. She knew which icon was Ryan's and had been watching it intently throughout the entire battle. The lieutenant's platoon had also been the first one to reach the center of the spaceport with the other three Type Four platoons close behind. Marines from the four platoons had taken up positions on top of buildings and towers to cover the advancing marines in the Type Three suits. Beth strongly suspected when this was over with, the Type Fours would have a very high kill ratio, much higher than the Type Threes. She also noticed that Ryan's icon indicated he'd entered the supposed control tower.

Ryan and Casey were climbing a wide set of stairs, which led to the main, level of the Operations Center. Privates Matheson, Hatterson, and Swen were with them. Everyone had their weapons ready, though they could hear no sounds, which might indicate others were in the building. Reaching the main level, they found a heavy metal door in front of them. Private Matheson reached forward and pushed the door open as the others rushed in with their weapons ready.

"About time you made it," Alexander said from where he was sitting on top of a prostrate Kleese. Another was nearby and Lauren had her RG rifle pointed in its direction.

Ryan immediately noticed Private Parker's right leg seemed to be buckled and his suit looked singed. "Are they alive?"

"Yeah," Alexander replied with satisfaction in his voice. "They're alive, though this one I'm sitting on blew me off the tower platform I was standing on."

"Are you injured?" asked Ryan, looking at his HUD and seeing Parker's icon was now amber.

"Broke both of my legs," Alexander answered. "The suit's injected meds so I feel fine, Private Adams helped me get up the stairs."

Before Ryan could say anything else, he saw a marine in a command suit step into the room and quickly survey the situation. With surprise, he realized it was Beth.

"Are they alive?" she asked, seeing the two Kleese.

"Yes, they're alive," replied Ryan. "Private Parker got both of them with his stunner."

Beth quickly turned her suit's sensors on the two Kleese, detecting emanations of life. The sensors only worked at extremely close range. She gestured to two of the marines who had entered with her. "Keep your stunners focused on those two Zaltule. If they even twitch, stun them again. R&D thinks the stun effects should last about two hours on a Kleese, but we've never had a live one to try it out on."

"Good job, Private Parker," Beth spoke over the platoon frequency. "You'll get a commendation for this."

Alexander nodded, allowing himself to smile. The painkillers were really taking over and everything was starting to get hazy.

"Major Stevens is on his way up," added Beth, looking over at Ryan. "I want your platoon to escort these two Kleese up to the Defender. I'll have a cargo drop ship down shortly."

Ryan nodded, his first trial by combat was over and he'd survived. Looking over at Casey, he knew she must feel extremely relieved also. This had been nothing like Charring Mountain, and he now realized why Charring was so hard. It was to teach marines how to survive.

Wade finally allowed himself to relax. He'd just received the latest reports from Beth as well as Major Stevens. The spaceport was secure and they were doing a final sweep for any Zaltule, who might have been missed. They'd taken a lot of casualties but secured their prizes. Two Zaltule had been captured and from the reports, one of the two might actually be a Zaltule Minor Overlord. Both were still unconscious and their suits had been removed as a precaution.

"There is still some minor fighting in the city," Commander Greer reported as he listened to communications coming in from the surface. "I'm being told they should be wrapping up that part of the operation within the next hour."

Wade nodded as he looked at the main viewscreen, which was showing a magnified view of the spaceport. Much of the spaceport was still covered in smoke and a few of the building were burning. He was pleased that it had been members of his brother's platoon who had captured the two Kleese. Even more important to him, both Beth and Ryan were unharmed. He let out a deep breath and leaned back in his command chair. They'd accomplished their mission. Two Kleese had been captured, the Zaltule would shortly be eliminated on the planet below, and they had defeated the Kleese warfleet. There was no doubt in Wade's mind that now the Alliance would come into being. For the first time, Wade felt optimism for the future. They now had a fighting chance against the Kleese.

Chapter Sixteen

Xatul looked across the massive stone table at the other gathered Overlords. His multifaceted eyes studied each of the nineteen individuals at the table, weighing their strengths and liabilities. He knew his days as the Supreme Overlord of the Kleese race might be numbered unless drastic action was taken. Harmock was on his way back to the home world with his battered fleet and from the messages he'd sent ahead, the Warrior Overlord was highly angry with the Kleese Council of Overlords.

"Why were we not told of these Humans earlier?" demanded Darthu the Zaltule Overlord, who was also Harmock's military science advisor. "How can a race of vermin do what they have done to the Kleese race?"

"Many of the Kleese in the outer regions of the Empire are weak and have failed in their service to the Empire," began Martule, fearing his life would soon be in jeopardy. "They failed to deal adequately with the Humans when they first appeared as a threat."

"Excuses!" spat Darthu, glaring at Overlord Martule and stamping his six feet upon the cold stone floor of the council chambers. "All Kleese are born to serve our race and to advance the Empire. We are the most powerful and intelligent race in the galaxy. None should be able to stand up against our ships, let alone take a trading station!"

Martule fell silent, knowing there was nothing more he could say. All he could do was to wait for more Zaltule to arrive, knowing at least one would challenge him for his right to be on the Council of Overlords. There was no point attempting to flee; the Zaltule would only hunt him down. He would stay, fight the duel, and probably die.

"The Zaltule have been asleep for over a thousand years," stated Xatul evenly his eyes focused directly on Darthu. "Much has changed in that time and the Empire has grown. There has been no major threat to our race in all of those years."

"Except the Humans," spoke Tintul, darkly. "The great Council of Overlords has failed the Kleese race by allowing this inferior species to live after they stole one of our trading stations. They should have been hunted down and annihilated to the last member of their vermin species."

"That was attempted," Xatul responded in a cold voice. He leaned forward, placing his hands upon the surface of the table. "It would have been done except the Strell attacked some of our worlds in the neutral zone and it became necessary to awaken the Zaltule. Don't make me come to regret that decision."

"You dare to threaten me?" challenged Tintul, rising up to his full height. "I am a Zaltule and superior in battle to all but other members of my caste."

Xatul nodded at the two guards standing at the heavy wooden doors to the council chambers. The doors immediately swung open, allowing half a dozen heavily armed Kleese in Type Three battlesuits to enter. They quickly surrounded the four Zaltule standing at the council table.

"What is this?" demanded Darthu his eyes focusing sharply on the Supreme Overlord. "Why have you summoned armed Kleese into our presence?"

"I will not allow the Zaltule to dominate this council," spoke Xatul in an authoritative voice. "You Zaltule have dared to challenge my authority as Supreme Overlord of the Kleese race. For that, you shall die." Xatul nodded at the six Kleese in battlesuits who drew their Energy Lances.

In moments, three of the Zaltule lay upon the floor minus their heads, their life giving blood spreading across the council chamber's floor. Only Darthu remained standing with an Energy Lance held against his throat.

Xatul strode around the council table until he stood close to Darthu. "For now, you will be allowed to live. Know full well that guards of my choosing protect the council area. There are fifty exploration ships in orbit with their full complement of assault ships. All are crewed by members of the Kleese race who are loyal to me."

"What are you saying?" asked Darthu keenly aware of the deadly blade at his throat.

"Those of us in this room directly control hundreds of explorations ships as well as thousands of assault vessels," explained Xatul. "We also control all of the trading stations and have placed extra Kleese guards of our choosing upon every one of them."

"We do not want to fight a civil war against other Kleese," spoke Darthu as he thought over what Xatul had said. "What are your demands?" He knew that while the Zaltule had a powerful fleet, it would be difficult to defeat all of the exploration ships and assault vessels the Council of Overlords had at its command.

"I will allow the Zaltule to have four seats upon the council," Xatul answered. "No more Zaltule queens shall be awakened unless their lives are in danger due to the sleeping disease in the chambers. The Zaltule will bring the nonaligned worlds into the Empire and once that has been accomplished, will continue to expand the Empire out into the galaxy. They will continue to serve as the warrior caste under the command of the Council of Overlords."

Darthu was silent as he thought over what the Supreme Overlord was demanding. His actions today indicated he had the strength and willpower to continue to rule the Kleese race, at least for now. Sometime in the future, when the number of Zaltule in the Empire had grown substantially, then would come the time to challenge for control of the council, not now.

"Very well," Darthu answered. "I will pass on your demands to our Military Overlord and recommend that he accept them."

Xatul nodded at the armed guard holding the Energy Lance to Darthu's throat. The guard withdrew the weapon, deactivating it and returning it to his waist.

"I will spare your life," Xatul said in a cold and hard voice. "Now leave us and send word to Harmock of the changes on the council and that he is to send three other Zaltule to fill in these empty Overlord positions."

"It will be done," Darthu responded respectfully as he turned and left the chambers. He was wise enough to know not to show any disrespect or his head would end up on the council chamber's floor.

"Remove these bodies," commanded Xatul to the guards. "We have additional council business to conduct."

Through all of this Bixutl had remained silent. Xatul's actions had changed everything. Now every member of the Council of Overlords was committed to what he'd just decreed. Bixutl knew that any aspirations he had of ever becoming the Supreme Overlord of the Kleese race had just vanished.

-

General Mitchell was meeting with General Pittman, Fleet Admiral Kelly, Colonel Nelson, Marken, Gerald Lawson, and Hyram Blake in his office on Centerpoint Station. They were discussing the recent operation in the Pradel System and the establishing of the Alliance.

"Fourteen worlds," confirmed Hyram Blake with a tired smile. "All of them have pledged mutual support and increased their ship building."

"Seventh Fleet is currently in the Lanolthian System and will remain there as the key element in the new Alliance fleet being formed," added Wade. The troop transport Crimson Star had remained with Seventh Fleet to provide marine support if needed. The Fire Fox and the Defender had returned to the solar system along with one of the passenger liners.

"How large a fleet will it be?" asked Fleet Admiral Kelly. He wished it wasn't necessary to keep Seventh Fleet in Alliance space, but he understood the importance of what they were attempting to do.

"Each Alliance world has pledged two full squadrons for the fleet," answered Hyram. "That's two hundred and eighty battlecruisers with new construction planned to eventually bring the fleet up to five hundred ships."

"That's a powerful force when added to Seventh Fleet," commented General Pittman. "How soon do we need to begin deploying marines?"

"The fourteen Alliance worlds have requested one thousand marines in Type Two or Type Three battlesuits for each world," answered Hyram his eyes shifting to General Pittman. They'll be stationed near the capital cities and the main spaceports."

General Mitchell was silent for a moment as he thought about the logistics of deploying so many Space Marines away from the solar system and keeping them supplied; then he looked over at Marken. "How long would it take to build two more Defender class assault transports?"

"Eight months if we can build them at Vesta," answered Marken, promptly. "The first four of the new battlecruisers will be done in three and a half months, and once they're completed we can concentrate on the two new troop assault ships. I'll have to speak with Ethan Hall and Sean Miller to confirm that."

Mitchell nodded. He knew that many Kivean technicians were currently working in the large spacedock inside of Vesta on ship construction and other projects, including the cloning program. They were also still in the process of upgrading all of their current battlecruisers and light cruisers to handle the new multiple warhead sublight antimatter missiles.

"What about new weapons from the Talts and the Deltons?" asked Fleet Admiral Kelly. He knew that Gerald Lawson had been meeting with representatives of the two races trying to iron out the specifics of adding their weapons to the new battlecruisers.

"We've worked out the designs necessary to add the Talt plasma weapon to our new ships," confirmed Lawson, looking down at several sheets of paper on the table in front of him. We're also considering modifying the Delton energy beam weapons to use them on our assault ships."

"Why not on our light cruisers and battlecruisers?" asked General Mitchell.

"Our particle beam cannons are more effective," answered Lawson. "However, on the assault ships these new energy weapons will be just as powerful as the smaller particle beams they're currently equipped with and will nearly double their firepower."

"We need a different classification for these new battlecruisers," commented Fleet Admiral Kelly. "They're twice the size of our regular battlecruisers."

"Battleships?" suggested General Pittman.

"How about dreadnoughts?" added General Mitchell, looking thoughtful.

"Our Alliance worlds still call their ships battlecruisers," commented Wade, looking around the group. "A few of them have battlecruisers that are one thousand meters in length."

"How about just heavy battlecruiser?" suggested Fleet Admiral Kelly. "It's the simplest. Perhaps someday we'll build really massive ships that will be worthy of the names battleships or dreadnoughts."

"Sounds like a winner to me," commented General Mitchell with a nod. Then, turning toward Marken, he asked another question. "How are our guests coming along?"

"Both the Talts and the Deltons seem happy with what we're doing for them," Marken responded. "Commander Pasha and Fleet Commander Achlyn have been very forthcoming in offering whatever advanced technologies they have to help in the war effort."

"The Deltons are a surprising species," added Gerald Lawson with an enigmatic smile. "They're only about a meter in height with large eyes and they're very slim. They remind me of the little aliens we used to read about in UFO abduction stories."

"Which makes the size of their warships surprising," spoke Fleet Admiral Kelly. "Their battlecruisers are seven hundred meters in length."

"Their ships are highly computerized," Gerald Lawson informed the group. "I visited one the other day and had to be careful walking down the corridors so I wouldn't bump my head. I was very impressed by the tech they use on their vessels."

The meeting continued for several more hours before Wade excused himself to go check on Major Winfrey's latest recruits. Marken joined him as he also wasn't needed for what the others were currently discussing.

"How's Harnett?" asked Wade as they walked through the station toward a nearby transit tube.

"Glad to be home," Marken answered with a pleased smile. "President Randle's wife had her baby while we were gone and Harnett's been spending a lot of time at Vesta pampering it."

"Why don't you and Harnett have children?" Wade asked as they boarded a transit shuttle to take them to the training dome.

Marken sighed heavily and his narrow eyes took on a look of sadness. "The Kleese are very strict about breeding on their stations," he said in a forlorn voice. "They decided that Harnett should not have any children so she was operated on to ensure that would never happen."

"I'm sorry," Wade said, wishing he had never asked the question.

"It's okay," Marken said with a wry smile. "We've accepted that children are not in our future. At least with all the families we rescued from Kivea there are a lot of young ones inside the habitats. Their laughing and playfulness makes life much more pleasant."

The shuttle came to a stop and the two exited, walking the short distance to the training dome. Going inside, they were soon standing in the dome's Command Center watching the latest batch of recruits on Charring Mountain.

"I heard Ryan's platoon captured two Zaltule," spoke Major Winfrey as he turned his gaze away from the viewscreens. The current trainees in Type Four battlesuits were only halfway up the mountain and had already lost all but three of their number, including their commanding officer.

"How's our current batch of recruits?" asked Wade. He'd been impressed with the reports he had received of the Type

Four suits in action. Beth had also spent some time giving him her opinion of the new battlesuits.

"We just graduated a second company and have started the training scenarios for the third," answered Dylan, gesturing toward the viewscreens.

Shifting his gaze toward the screens, Wade was just in time to see popup stunners take out the last three members of the platoon currently assailing the mountain.

"Looks as if they have a lot to learn," commented Wade, recalling the trying times he'd experienced going up the mountain when they were captives of the Kleese. Marken had been in charge of their training during that tumultuous time and more than one marine had died on the treacherous slopes.

"They'll learn," Dylan replied.

He had spoken to Sergeant Morris earlier and she'd been very forthcoming in her evaluation of how Major Steven's marines had done on Ryerson. After a long discussion, Dylan had decided to change the training slightly to take into account what the marines had encountered in their attack on the Zaltule positions.

"We're going to need them," stated Wade, nodding his head. "These Zaltule are tough to bring down."

"Where are the two Zaltule captives?" Dylan asked.

"At Vesta," answered Wade, shifting his gaze back to the major. "We didn't want them on Centerpoint and Vesta has the best security system. General Bailey has constructed some special holding cells for the two.'"

"Are they talking yet?"

"No," answered Wade, shaking his head. "Not a word."

"They'll talk," Marken said with a long frown on his face. "I'm going to personally speak to them when we get to Vesta. I think they'll talk to a Kivean."

"So, you're going back to Vesta?"

"Yes," Wade answered. "Beth has already gone and Ryan is visiting our parents."

Dylan nodded; he had no surviving family members other than the marines in his Special Forces unit who had been with him at the survival camp in the UK. He was like so many others who'd been left with no surviving kin. Many people were still dealing with depression and the suicide rate amongst the survivors was still high.

"When you see Lieutenant Nelson, tell him no one has beaten his record on Charring yet."

"I will," promised Wade, smiling. "I'm sure he'll be pleased to hear that."

-

Casey sat uneasily in Ryan's parent's home on one of the soft couches. Ryan was beside her busily talking to his mom and dad about the training they had gone through at Centerpoint and only briefly describing the fighting on Ryerson.

"I just wish you weren't in the marines," his mom said in a worried voice. "I would've felt better if you had gone into the fleet."

"Ryan is an excellent marine," Casey said defensively, then wished she'd stayed quiet. Ryan's mom had said very little to her since they arrived. Casey wondered if it was because she was a clone.

"I'm sure he is," Jonathan answered with a gentle smile. "From what I've heard from Wade, you both are pretty good."

"I just don't know if we should be provoking these aliens like this," Ryan's mom said, shaking her head. "They've left us alone for over six years, why go and try to stir up a hornet's nest?"

"They were coming back eventually," Ryan explained in a softer voice. He knew his mother didn't care for the war and only wanted them to be left alone. "We did it to keep them away."

"Maybe," his mother replied with doubt in her voice.

"You're mother's just worried about you and Wade," Jonathan explained. "She's always been."

"I'm going to start supper," Ryan's mother said, standing up and smoothing down her long skirt. "We're having fried chicken and mashed potatoes."

Ryan watched his mother go into the kitchen and noticed she hadn't even glanced at Casey. "I'll be back shortly," he said as he stood up and headed to the kitchen.

"I understand you and Ryan met at the Academy," Jonathan said in a pleasant voice.

"Yes," answered Casey, feeling more relaxed in Jonathan's company. He certainly seemed to be trying to act friendly. "We had many classes together and were even at the fleet training faculty on the Moon for two years before we joined the marines."

"You like Ryan, don't you?"

Casey felt her face flush and then nodded. "I think the world of him; he's my best friend."

Jonathan nodded; he'd seen the looks she cast at Ryan on occasion. There was no doubt in his mind that he might very well be looking at his future daughter-in-law. "I hope everything works out well for you. "I'm sure you've noticed my wife hasn't spoken much."

Casey let out a sigh and nodded. "I assume it's because I'm a clone."

"I'm afraid you're right," Jonathan replied with a slight frown. "Wade and I have spoken a lot about the cloning program, and I understand you're just as Human as I am. It's something that might take my wife a while to get used to."

"I understand," Casey replied. "I think I'll go and see if she needs help with supper. I do know a little about cooking."

Casey stood up and walked to the kitchen door, as she neared it she could hear Ryan and his mother arguing.

"She's a clone!" Ryan's mother said dismissively. "She's not real!"

"Casey is just as real as you or I," Ryan answered in an aggravated voice.

"She was grown in a tank! How can she be real?"

"Mom, Casey is a wonderful person once you get to know her."

"I can't believe you brought one of those things into our house."

Ryan just shook his head, not sure what to say.

Casey backed away from the kitchen door and turned to find Jonathan standing behind her.

"I'm sorry you had to hear that," he said in an embarrassed voice.

"I think it's best if I leave," Casey said, feeling crushed. "Tell Ryan I'll call him later."

Casey turned and quickly left the house as the tears began to flow from her eyes. How could she and Ryan ever have a future if his mom felt the way she did? Of course, Ryan and she had never discussed a future; it was something she'd started thinking seriously about after speaking with Lauren and Mary. Casey knew that Lauren was somewhere on Vesta visiting her parents. She really needed someone to talk to and Lauren was the only one she could think of.

Ryan stepped out of the kitchen feeling flustered. How could his mother feel that way considering all the conversations with Wade about the clones? It was beyond his understanding. Looking around the living room, he noticed Casey was missing. He looked at his father, who was standing at the front door with a pensive look on his face.

"Where's Casey?" Ryan asked. He'd really wanted her to meet his parents.

"She left," answered Jonathan, dropping his shoulders. "She overheard your mother and you talking. I'm pretty sure she was crying when she went out the door."

"Did she say where she was going?" asked Ryan, growing concerned and feeling intensely aggravated at his mother.

"She said she would call later," Jonathan answered. "Ryan, she's a really sweet girl. When you see her, please tell her I said that."

Ryan nodded; all he could do now was wait for Casey to call. Vesta was too large a place to go off on a search for one person.

President Mason Randle stood in the Vesta Spacedock with General Bailey, Ralph Steward, Commander Pasha, Sean Miller, Ethan Hall, and Skagern. In one more month, the general elections would be held and Mason fully expected Steward to take over as president of the solar system. Mason would continue to serve in a secondary role of advisor, but much of the day-to-day work and decisions would then be Steward's responsibility. In many ways, Mason was ready to relinquish his authority. He had a new daughter at home, and he was looking forward to watching her grow up.

Around them, the spacedock was humming with activity as dockworkers unloaded cargo vessels and reloaded others. A number of the small, fifty-meter long prospector ships were being worked on as well as a slew of other vessels. The main hub of activity was around the four new heavy battlecruisers being constructed.

"Impressive," Commander Pasha commented. Commander Pasha was of the same size and build as a regular Human though he was of dark complexion with large, yellow eyes about double the normal size.

"All four of the new cruisers will have a plasma cannon on them," spoke Ethan. "In addition, there will be two heavy particle beam cannons on the bow as well as two enlarged KEW cannons. There will be an additional eight particle beam turrets on the main hull plus our standard weapons. The armor is twenty percent thicker and the energy screens will be the most powerful we've every built."

"What abut the new multi warhead sublight missiles?" asked General Bailey.

"The ships will have twenty-four expanded missile tubes all capable of handling the new missile," replied Ethan.

"I understand the Tureens joined the Alliance and have a forty-megaton antimatter warhead on their missiles," spoke Pasha. "Are they willing to share the technology which makes antimatter in that quantity stable?"

"We're currently in negotiations with them about that," answered Steward. "We're hoping by the time the heavy battlecruisers are finished we'll have the design specifications."

Pasha nodded. These Humans were becoming worthy allies. While overall their technology was far behind the Tarn's, it was obvious the Kiveans had succeeded in introducing a number of their more advanced technologies. That was very evident here in the spacedock where some very advanced construction methods were being used.

"Is your new habitat acceptable?" Mason asked. He fully intended to visit the Tarn's habitat before the elections.

"More than satisfactory," Pasha answered with a pleased smile. "The Kiveans have worked wonders building a new world for us inside our asteroid. In many ways it reminds us of home, which is good."

"We spent some time studying the history of your world you provided us," Skagern explained. "We tried to make your new home as esthetically pleasing as possible."

"You have succeeded," Pasha replied. "My people are most pleased with what you have done for us."

"General Mitchell wants two more Defender class troop assault ships built once the battlecruisers are finished," General Bailey said, looking over at Sean and Ethan. "Can we do that?"

"I heard," replied Sean, looking thoughtful. "We're already requisitioning the material we'll need. As soon as the battlecruisers are finished and out of the dock, we'll begin."

Mason looked around the dock and let out a heavy sigh. Years ago, the spacedock had been much smaller and his pet project, the exploration cruiser Phoenix, had resided here. He'd planned to take the ship on the solar system's first interstellar flight. The Kleese attack changed all of that, and now the Phoenix was a battlecruiser and the flagship of Second Fleet under the command of Admiral Sanders. The Kleese attack had wrecked the dreams of countless millions.

Later tonight, his sister Susan and her two teenage daughters were coming over to the house. Harnett would be there and he strongly suspected Karen would be asking the Kivean when she could begin her studies. Harnett had promised to teach Karen Kivean medical practices and technologies. There was no doubt in Mason's mind that someday his niece would be a fine doctor.

He turned his attention back to the group around him. Ralph Steward was asking some detailed questions about the cost of building the two new Defender type ships. It would be necessary to discuss this with the Federated Assembly, but he didn't see any problems with getting the approval for the two ships. Currently, defense spending was taking up nearly sixty percent of the solar system's budget, but everyone understood the necessity of protecting it from another Kleese attack. Mason allowed himself to smile as he listened to Steward. The man would make a good president and Mason was looking forward to semi-retirement. He knew Adrienne was also looking forward to Mason spending more time at home with her and their new daughter.

-

Casey was at Lauren's parents' home explaining to her what had happened. She'd walked around for nearly an hour crying before finally making her way to the New Eden habitat where Lauren's parents lived.

"I'm sorry, Casey," Lauren said, feeling dreadful about what Ryan's mom had said. Lauren knew that, unfortunately, many people felt that way. "Have you told Ryan how you feel about him?" They were sitting on Lauren's bed in her room.

"No!" stammered Casey her face flushing. "How can I?"

"Men need to be told sometimes," Lauren said, taking Casey's hand and gently squeezing it. "Sometimes they don't see the obvious. That's also why a man never asks for directions; the woman always has to."

"I'm not sure he feels the same way I do," Casey said, feeling unsure of herself.

"He does," Lauren assured her with a knowing smile. "I've seen the way he looks at you."

"Lauren," Casey began not quite sure how to say what she wanted. "There's still a lot about being Human I don't fully understand."

Lauren laughed and nodded. "I get that," she said. "Sex and men have always been a problem for women, and I can see how it would be even more confusing to a clone."

"So what do I do?" Casey asked with her hazel eyes looking intently at Lauren.

"I'll help you," Lauren promised. "This could be a lot of fun. First thing, go ahead and call Ryan; I'm sure he's worried about you. Tell him you're staying with me and we'll meet him for lunch tomorrow. It'll be you, Ryan, me, and Alexander."

"Alexander?" asked Casey with a confused look in her eyes.

"Yeah, Alexander," responded Lauren, shaking her head. "I made the mistake of telling him I would go out with him if he actually succeeded in stunning a Kleese with that giant stun gun he was carrying. I never really expected him to succeed."

"Does Alexander like you that well?" Casey asked as she picked up her phone to call Ryan. To her the two always seemed to be arguing.

"Maybe," Lauren replied with an impish look in her eyes. "I'm sure all he wants is to get inside my pants, but that's a long ways from happening."

"I don't understand," Casey said as she pressed the send button to call Ryan.

Lauren giggled. "Don't worry, Casey. I'm sure someday you will."

-

The next day, Ryan made his way to the Italian restaurant the girls had chosen to eat at. He suspected Casey was once more exploring different foods and he knew she liked Italian. That was a good sign as it indicated she had gotten over her shock from what his mother had said the previous evening.

Stepping inside, he found the others already there waiting for him at a side booth, which provided more privacy. He noticed Alexander was sitting next to Lauren so he sat down next to Casey.

"Hi," he said with friendly smile. He saw with surprise that Casey was wearing a short skirt and a very tight blouse, which dipped just low enough to show a hint of cleavage. Glancing at Lauren, he noticed a satisfied smirk on her face and knew she'd helped Casey pick out the clothes she was wearing. Casey normally dressed very conservative.

"We were just discussing what we would be doing once our leave is up," commented Alexander, looking curiously at Ryan, hoping for an answer.

"Don't know," answered Ryan, as he picked up the menu and began looking over it. "Major Stevens hinted we might be assigned to some of the new Alliance worlds on a temporary basis. He said he would know more when we returned to Centerpoint."

"I wouldn't mind staying here in the solar system for a while," commented Lauren her light green eyes focusing on Ryan.

"We might," Ryan responded. "At least until more marines are trained in the Type Four battlesuits."

"Ryan, I'm sorry about leaving so abruptly last night," Casey said in a soft voice.

"It's okay," Ryan said. "I wasn't expecting my mother to react that way, particularly since my brother has been so heavily involved with the cloning project. My mother said to tell you she's sorry and if you want to come back to the house she fine with it. You can stay in the spare bedroom."

"Your father must have spoken to her," Casey said. She'd really liked Jonathan.

"Yeah," Ryan answered with a nod of his head. "I believe they had a very long talk last night, and my dad can be very persuasive when he wants to be."

"I think it will be better if I stay with Lauren for now," Casey said. "I don't want to make your mother feel uncomfortable."

"There's a lot I can teach Casey if she stays with me," Lauren said with an enigmatic smile. "We're going shopping tomorrow to pick out some new clothes for her; she dresses way too conservatively most of the time when she's out on leave. She has a very nice figure, and I told her she should be showing it off."

Ryan was silent; he felt a little pique of jealousy at the thought of other men looking at Casey that way. The thought startled him; he'd always liked Casey, but now he was beginning to wonder if those feelings ran much deeper than he had believed.

The four ate their meal and continued to talk as they ordered dessert. Ryan's eyes kept moving unconsciously toward Casey anytime she spoke. He was highly aware of their legs touching beneath the table and how much he liked it. He also noticed she didn't move her leg away. He knew that Wade and Beth had served together, their closeness had eventually developed into love, and they were now happily married. Was it possible he and Casey were destined to go down the same route? He kept his thoughts to himself; he wasn't sure how Casey felt. He did know that this was a relationship he wanted to explore and see where it led.

Casey was well aware of the attention Ryan was paying her and his occasional glances at the tight blouse she was wearing. Lauren had threatened to tell Ryan how Casey felt about him if she didn't dress as Lauren wanted. She was acutely away of Ryan's leg touching hers and the silent thrill that simple touch caused. She saw Lauren watching her from across the table with a knowing smile. Yes, there was definitely a lot that Lauren could teach her. Ryan didn't know it yet, but his future was suddenly about to become much more interesting.

-

Marken stood outside the special detention center, which held the two Kleese. With him were four Space Marines in Type Three battlesuits who would provide security.

"Are you sure this is wise?" asked Sergeant Reynolds, looking over at Marken. The red-skinned Kivean looked small next to the ten foot tall metal encased Humans.

"It's a necessity," answered Marken, taking a deep breath. "These two Kleese are Zaltule, members of the warrior caste. If I can get them to speak, their attitude will tell us much."

"They haven't spoken since they were brought here," Reynolds said. "Their cells are monitored continuously and they won't even recognize our presence when we take them food and water."

"Open the door," ordered Marken, preparing himself for this confrontation. For most of his life, the Kleese had been his masters and they were the destroyers of his planet. Thanks to the Kleese, he and Harnett would never have any children. Marken felt no sympathy for the two Kleese captives and the plight they now found themselves in.

Sergeant Reynolds gave a signal and the heavy metal door slid open. Stepping inside, Marken gazed at the large Kleese manacled to the steel column in the center of the room. The four marines followed Marken inside and the door slid shut behind then. All four took up positions against the wall with their armored hands resting on their Energy Lances, the only weapons they carried.

"I am Marken of the Kivean race."

The Zaltule shifted his gaze away from the armored Humans to the Kivean standing in front of him. For the vermin Humans he had no use, but the Kivean was from a race of great scientists who had served the Kleese for generations. The Kiveans were not vermin, but they were still inferior.

"I am Minor War Overlord Braton of the Zaltule," he spoke in a cold and hard voice. "Release me and I will make sure your death is swift and painless."

"You will not be released," Marken said in an even voice, feeling a chill run down his back. It had been over seven years since he'd last spoken to a Kleese. "Your continued well being depends upon your willingness to answer my questions."

"Your threat is meaningless," Braton responded. "I am a Zaltule, a member of the warrior caste. Soon my brethren will descend upon this world and free me. When that happens, all of you will die. Why do you associate yourself with these vermin? You are from a world that long served the Empire. You could serve the Empire again if you agree to leave these Humans."

"The Humans are my friends," responded Marken, stepping closer to the bound Zaltule. "When will the Zaltule attack and with how many ships?"

"Soon," answered Braton his multifaceted eyes focusing on Marken. "Our fleet will come in such numbers as to crush your pitiful Alliance. It is the destiny of the Kleese and the Zaltule to rule the galaxy and all inferior races will be subservient to our will."

"We will resist," spoke Marken.

"Then you will die," stated Braton. "This conversation is over. I will not speak to you again."

Marken nodded, the conversation had gone about as he had expected. The Zaltule would not reveal any detailed military information. However, the Zaltule had been very adamant about his race attacking the Alliance with overwhelming force. He doubted if it had been exaggerating.

Turning, he motioned for the marines to open the door.

"Damn tarantula," spoke Sergeant Reynolds as they stepped outside and he resealed the door. Later, he would take the Zaltule back to its cell. "Do you want to speak to the other one?"

"No," Marken answered. "I doubt if the other will speak at all."

He would let General Mitchell know the results of his interrogation. He would tell the general to expect a Kleese attack with a major fleet, probably much larger than the one faced at Pradel. As Marken made his way to the Control Center to contact the general, he wondered if he had done the right thing all those years ago. He and his fellow conspirators had set the Humans upon this path. The known galaxy was about to be consumed in a deadly war for survival. He just wished he knew how all of this would end.

Chapter Seventeen

Harmock gazed in anger at the tactical screen on the front wall of the Command Center of his flagship. He stood upon the Command Pedestal gazing at the one hundred and ten large red threat icons orbiting the distant planet. However, what was more disturbing were the three thousand small red threat icons also in orbit.

"It seems our Supreme Overlord was not bluffing," spoke Harmock, his triangular shaped head turning to face Gareth.

"Will they actually fire on us?" asked Gareth, dubiously. "We are the Zaltule, surely they will back down."

"They are Kleese and desire to hold onto their positions of power," Harmock responded in a hard voice. "Xatul has done the same thing I would have done if our roles were reversed. In many ways, he has reaffirmed my faith in the Kleese race."

"We're supposed to send three more Zaltule to the council chambers to represent us," added Gareth. "Darthu was very specific in his instructions as to that point."

"I have chosen three warriors," responded Harmock, folding his large black arms over his powerful chest. "I will also send a personal message to Xatul assuring him the warrior caste accepts him as the Supreme Overlord of the Kleese."

"The Zaltule should rule," spoke Gareth, harshly. "It is our right!"

"In time," responded Harmock. "When our numbers are large enough and the fleet has been greatly expanded, our time will come."

Harmock also wanted to speak to Xatul about these Humans. He wasn't foolish enough to go down to the surface and enter the council chambers, not after what Darthu had told him had occurred there. He would stay aboard the Warrior's Fire and use the communications equipment. While it was distasteful to speak to another Overlord in that manner, it was the expedient and safe thing to do.

Two weeks later, Harmock looked at the many viewscreens in the Command Center. They were in orbit around the largest of the new shipyards that had been built to provide new Zaltule warships. His flagship had just completed some necessary repairs and updates in one of the numerous repair and construction bays, which covered the massive structure. Kaluse had personally overseen the work being done to the Warrior's Fire and assured the War Overlord the ship was more powerful than before.

"The fleet is gathering," reported Minor Overlord Gareth. "It will shortly be time for us to begin our journey to the Human system."

"One thousand ships," Harmock responded as he looked at the numerous three kilometer disk ships that were showing on the viewscreens. "All of these ships have been updated and have the newest weapons and reinforced energy screens. We will crush these Human vermin, and once that has been done this pitiful Alliance of theirs will crumble."

"We will eliminate every member of this upstart race," Gareth spoke his multifaceted eyes growing wider. "Humans will be a thing of the past and an abject lesson to others who might dare to oppose us."

"With the destruction of the Humans, the other nonaligned worlds will quickly fall into line and become part of the Empire," Harmock predicted. "We'll solidify our hold upon the Empire and then perhaps it will be time to return and deal with the council."

"The warriors from the first hatchings should be ready by then," added Gareth. "They will add greatly to our numbers."

Harmock nodded. Xatul could rule for now, but someday that would change and Harmock would take his place as the Supreme Overlord of the Kleese. His eyes returned to the main viewscreen where a squadron of black warships was maneuvering into position near the flagship. Soon the Humans would know the wrath of the Zaltule.

Fleet Admiral Kelly was aboard the Armageddon watching as the first of the four new heavy battlecruisers exited the large airlock on Vesta that led to the spacedock. After six long months, his four new warships were finally finished.

"They're huge!" spoke Commander Kevin Makita as he watched the Star Fury begin to climb up into orbit.

"The most powerful ships we've ever built," Thomas replied as he gazed at the new warship. "They will add a lot of firepower to our fleet."

"Eighth Fleet," stated Makita. "There was a time when I never expected to see that."

"Admiral Madison Layton will be the commander of Eighth Fleet," added Kelly as he watched the next heavy battlecruiser exited the airlock. This one was the London and the two behind it were the New York and the Freedom.

"We're assigning twenty Delton battlecruisers, twenty-four light cruisers, and forty assault ships to the fleet," Kelly informed Makita. "This fleet will be our heavy hitter."

"I've also given Fleet Commander Achlyn command of Ninth Fleet. It will consist of the remaining fifty-five Delton battlecruisers as well as eighty assault ships. Achlyn is used to commanding a large fleet and I believe he is fully capable of handling Ninth Fleet."

"It will be interesting to see the Delton battlecruisers in combat," Commander Makita said. "With the new technology we've received from the Alliance we've greatly enhanced their energy shields and they now have the new multi warhead antimatter missiles."

"With forty-megaton warheads," grinned Thomas. "I imagine that will be quite a shock to the Kleese if they ever attack us here in the solar system again."

Makita was silent for a moment before turning and looking intently at the Fleet Admiral. "What do you think the chances are of another attack?"

"One hundred percent," responded Thomas, arching his eyebrows in concern. "I'm surprised they haven't already. Our

Kleese captive was very adamant that the Zaltule will soon attack us after what happened at Pradel."

On the main viewscreen, the four heavy battlecruisers had now moved into a diamond formation and were ready to commence their shakedown cruise. They would spend a week in the solar system, checking out weapons systems before taking a short trip to Alpha Centauri and back. If everything checked out then the Delton battlecruisers, the light cruisers, and the assault ships would join them and Eighth Fleet would officially come into being.

Fleet Admiral Kelly leaned back in his command chair with a heavy sigh. "We've spent years beefing up the defenses in the solar system," he said, addressing Makita. "I've seen the reports from the battle in the Pradel system. If the Zaltule had been willing to risk losing most of their fleet, they could have seriously damaged the Alliance fleet, possibly even destroyed it. It's obvious from the battle footage I've watched that they were taken my surprise by the forces committed to defending the system. That won't be the case next time."

"Other than the Strell, the Kleese have never fought a determined enemy," said Makita.

"Well, they have one now," Thomas responded.

Makita gazed at one of the viewscreens showing Vesta. "It's strange knowing Mason Randle is no longer president. If not for him, none of us would be here."

"President Steward will be an excellent leader," replied Thomas. He also felt great sadness at Randle stepping down. "I spoke to President Randle several times and he indicated Steward is fully capable of filling his shoes."

On the main viewscreen, the four heavy battlecruisers began to move off and away from Vesta. Thomas watched them, feeling a little jealous. He could've taken one of the ships as his new flagship but felt keeping the four powerful vessels together was the prudent thing to do. Those four ships were designed with one purpose in mind, to be able to destroy Kleese warships.

"Take us back to Centerpoint," he ordered as the new battlecruisers dwindled on the viewscreen until they finally disappeared. "I need to meet with General Mitchell about the upcoming war games we have planned." He watched another viewscreen as Vesta slowly receded. His job as Fleet Admiral never ended. There was so much to do to ensure the system stayed safe. He just prayed they were ready when the Kleese did attack again.

-

Major Stevens had just returned from the Moon where he'd been visiting with his old friend Captain Samuel Griffith. Sam was in charge of a full marine company in Type Two battlesuits assigned to defend one of the major domed habitats. It'd been a pleasant visit getting to see Sam, his wife Margaret, and their three kids. Being with them for a few days made the war seem so far away. It reminded him that it was still possible to live a normal and productive life.

Reaching the training dome, he entered and soon made his way to the Command Center where he knew he would find Major Winfrey. As he expected, the major was busy watching another platoon work their way slowly up Charring Mountain.

"How many does that make?" he asked, sitting down next to Dylan.

"Once this group is finished training, we'll have five full companies ready to deploy."

Even as Mark watched the multiple viewscreens, which showed every view imaginable of Charring Mountain, three of the metal encased marines were knocked down by popup stunners.

"Must be a new group," he commented.

"Only their second week of training," Dylan informed him as he reached forward and changed the settings on some of the popups. Since Ryan had conquered Charring on his second attempt, he'd made certain no one else could duplicate the stunt that Ryan had pulled off.

"I'm taking two companies with me to Lanolth next week," Mark said. "The Defender and Crimson Star are being deployed and we're going to make a tour of the current Alliance worlds to demonstrate the capabilities of our Space Marines. Hyram Blake is going along in the Distant Star with a large contingent of negotiators. They're hoping the show of force will help to encourage several other worlds to join the Alliance. A number have been invited to attend the demonstrations."

"I hope you're successful," responded Dylan, looking away from the viewscreens. The platoon was moving up the steep slope again and it would be another minute or two before they reached the next set of popups. "Fourteen systems plus us isn't a lot to stand up against the entire Kleese Empire.

"It's enough to give them pause," replied Mark, glancing over at Dylan. "If we can build up the Alliance strong enough there is some hope the Kleese might come to a new agreement, which would leave us in peace. At least Marken believes it's possible."

"The Kiveans always seem to have a positive attitude toward things," Dylan stated as he turned his gaze back to the viewscreens. Any moment now and the next set of popups would fire on the advancing marines.

"Their technology saved a lot of lives when they first came to the solar system," Mark stated as he saw the marines on the viewscreen leap for cover as the popups opened fire.

Dylan nodded. He wondered what future history would say about these times. He just hoped there was a future history. Looking at the screens, he saw two more marines go down. With a wicked smile, he leaned forward and changed the popup settings once more.

Ryan was watching the happy look on Casey's face as she floated on twin wings in the gentle warm air of Luna City. The group had gone astro gliding and had already spent several hours experiencing the wondrous feeling of flying through the air. Rios swooped by Ryan with a slight wave of his hand as he dove down and then drifted back up on the artificial thermals, which the park generated. Rios was by far the most talented at this sport and could stay in the air the longest.

For the last few months, Ryan had gone out with Casey a number of times but always with Lauren and Alexander tagging along. Ryan strongly suspected Lauren was ensuring Casey didn't get lost in her new found femininity. The girls were always going clothes shopping and Ryan couldn't get over how gorgeous Casey looked in some of the outfits Lauren picked out for her. He also suspected Lauren was being careful to make sure Casey didn't get carried away with her newly discovered female charms. Today, Mary had come along and Ryan wasn't too surprised to see she was dressed a little more risqué than normal. No doubt the result of Lauren's influence on the female clones in his platoon.

Ryan caught a thermal and floated back up. He was rapidly getting the hang of astro gliding and was really enjoying the afternoon. Looking down, he saw both Casey and Mary were going in for a landing. The girls were probably getting a little tired

"You need to switch to the intermediate level of wings," called out Rios as he flew by. He did a quick dive and then shot nearly straight up before leveling out a few dozen meters away.

Ryan knew Rios was wearing a pro set of wings that one could only get after passing rigorous tests by the instructors who operated the Astro Park. Each level of wings gave the wearer more control and the ability to do more maneuvers. Looking down, Ryan saw Casey and Mary had removed their wings and seemed to be arguing with several men who had walked up to them. He didn't like the look of things and quickly adjusted his flight path to take him to the ground.

He had nearly reached the ground when he saw one of the two men push Casey, knocking her down. Ryan was unbuckling the harness to his wings as soon as his feet touched the grass of the Astro Park. He heard a swishing noise behind him and saw both Lauren and Alexander were also coming in for a landing.

Ryan dropped his wings and rushed over to where Casey was lying on the thick grass. "What's going on here!" he demanded, reaching for Casey's hand and helping her up.

"Well, what do we have here?" sneered the larger of the two men. "Another cloney lover? Can't find yourself a real woman?"

"Maybe there's something about a female clone we don't know about," suggested the other slimmer man. "Maybe we should take her with us and find out."

"I think you need to leave," Ryan said, stepping between Casey and the two men. Mary had retreated back to where Lauren and Alexander were standing.

"Get out of our way," the large man demanded his eyes narrowing. "Let's see what type of woman you have there and if all the parts are like a real woman's."

Without thinking, Ryan swung his fist at the smirking man's face, connecting just below the chin. The blow lifted the man up and he collapsed on the ground. His hand went to his chin with a look of disbelief spreading across his face.

"The two of you had better leave!" Lauren said, striding up with Mary and Alexander close behind. "If you don't, we'll make sure you spend the next few months in the hospital."

The man staggered to his feet and backed away. "Damn clone lovers," he muttered as he turned and left with his friend.

Ryan watched the two men walk off and get into a ground vehicle, which sped away into Luna City. "Are you okay, Casey?" he asked his voice filled with concern as he turned to look at her.

"I'm fine," Casey replied as she brushed some grass and dirt off her clothes. "I just wasn't expecting them to act that way."

"This protest against cloning is getting worse all the time," Alexander stated with a frown. "Just last week they had an actual riot at Mars Central and over a dozen people were injured."

"We need to be cautious when we go out," suggested Ryan, looking around at the group. Rios and Swen had both landed and joined them.

"Maybe we should begin wearing our uniforms when we're on leave," suggested Mary, still looking shaken up from the ordeal. "Surely they wouldn't bother someone in a military uniform."

"They might," Rios said with a disgusted look on his face. "I think Ryan is right; we should go out as a group just for safety reasons."

"Maybe this clone thing will be settled by the time we return from our next deployment," added Ryan, hoping it was so. It seemed as if every week now, the demonstrations against the cloning program were becoming more widespread. In a way, he was glad their platoon was leaving on the Defender the following week to go back to the Alliance.

"I hope so," Lauren said. "Let's go get something to eat, I'm starving!"

Ryan was in Major Steven's office the next day taking an ass chewing. They'd returned from Luna City early that morning. He knew he deserved the griping out and remained silent as the reaming continued.

"You hit a civilian!" roared Stevens, shaking his head in anger. "He filed charges, and it was all that I could do to get them dropped. What were you thinking, striking the man?"

Mark looked at Ryan, not expecting an answer. He'd already talked to the other marines that had been there and fully understood what had happened. In many ways, he didn't blame Ryan for what he'd done; hell, he might have done the same thing if he had been there. However, you couldn't have military personnel going around assaulting civilians even if the reason was justified.

"All of you should have turned around and just left," Mark said with an aggravated frown. "You're confined to base until we deploy next week."

"Yes, Sir," responded Ryan, feeling embarrassed over the situation.

"Lieutenant Nelson, do you have feelings for Corporal Hunter?"

Ryan hesitated and then nodded. "Yes, Sir." He knew there was no point hiding that fact from the major.

Mark was silent as he gazed thoughtfully at the young lieutenant. "In our new military, the rules about fraternization have been markedly changed. If I see it begin to affect the moral of the platoon I'll have no choice but to transfer one of you to another unit, do you understand, Lieutenant?"

"Yes, Sir," Ryan answered, not wanting either of them to be transferred. "It won't interfere with our duties, I promise that."

"Very well," Mark said, leaning back in his chair and gazing at Lieutenant Nelson. "We deploy next week and this time we'll have two full companies of Space Marines certified in the Type Four battlesuits. Is your platoon ready for this mission?"

"Yes, Sir," Ryan responded. "We won't let you down."

"Make sure you don't," Mark replied. "Now, go back to your platoon, I'm sure they're all curious as to what your punishment is. Tell them they're fortunate that all of them aren't restricted to base."

"Yes, Sir," Ryan responded as he stood up and saluted the major. He turned and quickly left the office relieved he'd gotten off so easily. He knew it could have been much worse.

Going back to the barracks, he saw most of the platoon was gathered outside, standing around. It was obvious they'd been keeping an eye on Major Steven's office.

"What happened?" Casey asked relieved to see Ryan still had his lieutenant stripes.

"Restricted to base until we deploy," he replied. Then, with a weak smile, he said. "It could have been worse."

"That bastard had it coming," stated Alexander, clenching his fist. "If you hadn't hit him, I would've!"

"We can't let civilians get to us," spoke Ryan, shaking his head at Alexander. "I let that happen and now I'm paying the consequences. If any of you go out on leave the next few days, I would prefer to see at least a group of six to ensure nothing gets out of hand."

"We should probably wear our military uniforms as well," Lauren added. "It can't hurt and might keep some of the malcontents away from us."

Everyone nodded their heads and then turned and went inside the barracks. Ryan remained outside with Casey, Lauren, and Alexander. "We deploy Monday," he told them. "From what Major Stevens told me we'll be gone for at least four months."

"Long deployment," Lauren said, nodding her head in thought. "I need to call my parents and let them know I'll be gone for a while."

"I'm sure a lot of us need to make some calls," Ryan replied. He knew he needed to call his own parents and Wade. He hoped Wade hadn't heard about the ruckus with the civilian.

"I'll go tell the rest of the platoon," Casey said as she and Alexander turned and went into the barracks.

"Ryan," Lauren said in a quieter voice. She'd gone to calling the lieutenant by his first name whenever they were alone or in their small group. "You know that Casey is head over heels in love with you, don't you?"

Ryan was silent, not knowing what to say. He knew his feelings for Casey were quite strong; it was good to hear she felt the same way.

"Casey still has a lot to learn about being Human," Lauren said in a serious tone. "Love is a very powerful emotion; make sure you don't ever hurt her. If you do, I'll make what you did to that civilian seem amateurish."

Ryan nodded as Lauren spun about and went inside the barracks. He was glad she was around. While Lauren might be a spitfire most of the time, she had a good head on her shoulders and was becoming a good friend as well.

Major Stevens was standing at his window watching the barracks. Tomorrow he had some promotions to announce. Lieutenant Nelson's platoon still needed some officers. Inside his desk were three promotions. Corporal Hunter was being promoted to sergeant and Privates Parker and Adams were both being promoted to corporal. Turning away from the window, he went back to his desk. He wanted to call Sam and let him know he would be out of touch for a while.

Harmock looked at the tactical screen as the Warrior's Fire dropped out of Fold Space. A full thousand Zaltule battlecruisers were in the fleet he was taking to the Human's solar system. In four more weeks, they would be there and shortly afterward, the Humans would be no more.

"The reserve fleet should be two weeks behind us," commented Minor Overlord Gareth.

"Five hundred more ships," Harmock said. "Once we have crushed the Humans and repaired our battle damage, we'll combine our fleet with the reserve and proceed immediately to the nonaligned worlds which have joined this Alliance. I expect when they hear we have annihilated the Humans they will capitulate very quickly. They'll have no desire to meet our warships in combat."

"The Zaltule are the supreme warriors," spoke Gareth, confidently. "We will show the Humans what it means to truly fight the warrior caste."

"Victory will be ours," agreed Harmock.

He knew once the Humans and the Alliance were crushed, he needed to begin thinking about dealing with the Council of Overlords. Xatul was now his greatest enemy in the Empire and somehow would have to be eliminated. Perhaps it would be wise to allow several more hatchings to occur. With the swelled numbers of new Zaltule, the council wouldn't dare refuse the demands of the warrior caste. Harmock knew it was only a matter of time until he became the Supreme Overlord of the Kleese race.

Chapter Eighteen

Mason Randle was enjoying a restful day at home with his family. His wife Adrienne was sitting on the couch holding their infant daughter and he was watching the latest news on the vid screen. Mason was still adjusting to being a regular person without any pressing obligations. For years, he'd made decisions, which determined the survival of the Human race. Now that was over and he was going to enjoy his semi-retirement. The biggest decision he had to make today was what type of steak he was going to cook out on the grill.

"How's Steward doing as president?" asked Adrienne, shifting Lara over to her other arm. She enjoyed being a mother and didn't miss her old days of being the First Lady or before that, Mason's secretary. Her deep blue eyes focused on her husband as she gently rocked back and forth.

"Great," replied Mason, turning off the vid screen. The news today was the same general run of the mill stuff. "He's settled right in and everything's running fine. He may not even need my advice." Before he could say anything else, alarms started sounding and warning sirens began going off in Smithfield.

"What's happening?" asked Adrienne, looking frightened and putting both arms protectively around Lara.

Mason switched the vid screen back on to see President Steward with a grave look on his face. He felt a cold chill run down his back, recognizing the look.

"All habitats are going to Condition One," announced Steward in an even voice. "There is no reason to panic. I am asking everyone to go to the emergency shelters and take only one bag per person. A large Kleese fleet has entered the solar system and is poised to attack. Our own forces are gathering to repel them, and we expect to be fully successful in defending the solar system as well as all of the habitats. We have several hours before the Kleese approach, so we have time for an orderly evacuation to the shelters. Once again, I ask you to remain calm. Marines in battlesuits are being deployed as a security measure. Don't be frightened at seeing them; they are there for your protection."

Mason's cell phone started ringing and he knew instinctively who was going to be on the other end. Picking it up, he said hello.

"Mason, this is Drake. I'm in the Control Center and they want you down here; I've called Pamela also. This looks as if it's going to be a serious situation."

"Give me a few minutes," replied Mason, drawing in a deep breath. He turned his phone off and looked over at Adrienne, who was standing next to the couch with Lara. "Call Susan and have her and the girls come over here; our shelter beneath the house will be sufficient. Don't come back out until you hear from me."

"This is going to be bad, isn't it, Mason? Do you have to go?" She knew what the call had been about. She wanted Mason to stay with her and Lara; after all, he was no longer president.

"They need me," Mason answered with a deep sigh. "I've been through this before and Steward may need my advice. I don't know how bad it's going to be, but I don't think the Kleese would attack unless they thought they had a reasonable chance of success. Our defenses here at Vesta are the most powerful in the solar system, I can't see them getting inside and we have plenty of marines to defend the habitats and the spacedock."

"Be careful, Mason," Adrienne implored as she picked up her cell phone to call Susan. "We'll be waiting for you."

Harmock gazed at the tactical screen as the first long-range scans began to come back. He'd studied the previous battles in this system and had already determined his two main targets. The fourth planet had a large colony of Humans on it and the stolen trading station was in orbit around the third.

"Designate the trading station as our priority target and the fourth planet as the secondary target," Harmock ordered in a cold and impassionate voice. "Overlord Tetus will command the fleet attacking the secondary target with three hundred warships. The rest of the fleet will proceed and take possession of our trading station."

"Our sensors are detecting a large number of ships in the system," Jalridd reported. "Both Human and Delton."

"So this is where the Deltons fled," commented Harmock his multifaceted eyes focusing on Jalridd. "Then this is where they shall die. Once we have destroyed their warships we shall hunt down every space vessel and search every world, moon, and asteroid. When we leave, there will be nothing left living in this star system."

"Should we advance in Fold Space?" asked Gareth, wanting to engage the Humans and Deltons as quickly as possible. It was time to exterminate these vermin. He moved closer to one of the command consoles, his six legs making clicking noises as he stepped across the metal deck.

"No," spoke Harmock. "We shall advance slowly so as to give us time to study their defenses. Even though this is a vermin race they have demonstrated they have the ability to be very dangerous."

The Kleese fleet broke up into two sections with one heading for the fourth planet and the other toward the trading station. As the two fleets advanced, sensors reached out attempting to gather every bit of tactical information possible. Harmock didn't intend to let these upstart Humans take his fleets by surprise.

General Mitchell and General Pittman were in the Command Center of Centerpoint Station, watching the Kleese battlecruisers. Their eyes widened as they saw the fleet split in two.

"One fleet is going to Mars and the other is coming toward us," reported Lieutenant Bryan Vail at the main sensor console.

"They seem pretty confident," commented General Pittman, shifting his gaze to General Mitchell.

"They want their trading station back," Mitchell said his eyes narrowing sharply. "I want all marines deployed in their battlesuits immediately. If they want the station back, that suggests a boarding action. I also want all civilians moved to the protected areas at the station's center." That area was the former Kleese living quarters and had been converted into a set of heavily armored bunkers. "Make the announcement all security doors will be sealed just prior to actual combat."

That should at least slow the Kleese down as the heavily armored doors would be difficult to get through. This was something Mitchell had added to Centerpoint. Originally, the station had a number of emergency doors, which would close automatically to prevent a loss of atmospheric pressure to the station. Those had been torn out and heavy armored doors installed in their place.

"Lieutenant Arnold, get Fleet Admiral Kelly on the com," ordered Mitchell as he leaned back in his command chair and gazed at the main tactical display. Hundreds of green icons were vanishing. Those were passenger liners, cargo ships, and prospector ships, which were cutting their power and going dark. Until the all clear was sounded those ships would only be operating their life support systems and at minimal power usage.

"I have Fleet Admiral Kelly on the com," Lieutenant Brenda Arnold reported from Communications.

Mitchell activated his com to speak to the Fleet Admiral. "It looks as if we have visitors," he said in a calm voice.

"We see them," Kelly answered. "It looks as if they're dividing their fleet up into two sections. From the looks of it, Mars and either the Moon or Centerpoint are the targets."

"I'm guessing Centerpoint," Mitchell responded in a grave voice. "President Steward has already issued a Condition One proclamation for the entire system."

"The Kleese don't seem to be in a big hurry," added Kelly. "I would guess they want to study our defenses as they come in."

"Well, they can't detect the ion cannons until we power them up," Mitchell said. "Every habitat in the system is sitting inside a ring of those."

"What about a planet buster?" asked Kelly, worriedly. "Could they launch one?"

"We can intercept it," answered Mitchell, confidently. "From what the Kiveans have told us a planet buster is too large to be fitted with a sublight drive. If they launch one, we can shoot it down. That's another reason we have so many energy weapons installed to support the ion cannons. The ion cannons will take care of long-range stuff as well as offense and the energy turrets will be used to knock down any missiles. With the new computer system, the Kiveans have assured us they can even take out a sublight missile if the launch range is great enough."

"I guess we'll find out," Kelly replied. "Any orders as to the deployment of the fleet?"

"That's up to you," Mitchell responded. "You're the Fleet Admiral and I'll defer to your judgment as to deployment."

"Then I guess I'd better get to moving my fleets around," Kelly responded. "Good luck, General."

"Good hunting, Admiral," Mitchell answered as he cut the connection.

"What about Holbrook Station?" asked Colonel Angus Robertson. Robertson was the operations officer and third in command of the station.

"Order it evacuated except for military personnel," Mitchell said with a frown. "If the Kleese get in close enough, it probably won't survive. I want the military members of the crew in suits and ready to evacuate to the escape pods if necessary. Also, begin launching all assault ships currently in the flight bays; we're going to need everything we have for this battle."

-

Mason made it to the Control Center just as Pamela did. As they stepped through the reinforced armored hatch, they saw the room was a beehive of frantic activity.

"I was hoping I wouldn't have to experience this again," spoke Pamela as she looked around.

"Mason," President Steward said, walking over and shaking the former president's hand. "I'm glad you're here. I may need your advice."

"What do we have?"

"One thousand Zaltule battlecruisers," General Bailey answered from where he was standing behind the military consoles. "Pamela, can you help get all the asteroid mining operations shut down? Some of them aren't cooperating very well."

"I'll get on it," Pamela said as she headed for the large communications console. "She knew those miners felt safe in their asteroids, but for their protection they needed to shut down and get inside their ships or secure facilities. Some would have to have their brows beat to comply and she knew just how to do that.

"All the liners and cargo ships have shut down," Jessica Lang reported from the main control console where she was sitting. "Even the Raven has gone silent."

Mason nodded. His sister's husband, Michael Kirby, was in command of the Raven.

"We're still in the process of getting everyone into the secure bunkers," Drake Thomason added from where he was speaking over a com unit to the security personnel responsible for the bunkers. "We need another hour to get everyone to safety."

"We should have that," General Bailey said, gesturing toward the big tactical screen. "The Kleese aren't headed our way, at least not yet."

"What about the spacedock?" Mason asked. The spacedock was the primary entry to Smithfield and the other habitats. If they could hold the spacedock, it would deny the Kleese entry to the habitats.

"I've got four companies of Space Marines in Type Two and Three battlesuits already headed that way," Bailey responded. "At the moment, we're keeping our weapons systems on standby mode to avoid the Kleese detecting them. I don't want them to realize how heavily defended Vesta is or we could become a major target rather quickly."

Mason nodded and took a deep breath. All they could do was prepare and watch the tactical screen. From the safety of Vesta, they would observe the dueling fleets fight for the survival of the Human race. Mason looked at the massive number of red threat icons on the screen; he'd never seen anything like that before. There was no way of knowing how this battle would end. He just hoped he would be able to hold his infant daughter in his arms when it was over.

Over Mars, Admiral Sanders and Second Fleet prepared to meet the oncoming Kleese warships. On his right flank was Fourth Fleet commanded by Admiral Rivers and on his left was Third Fleet commanded by Admiral Johnson. That gave him seventeen battlecruisers, forty-eight light cruisers, and ninety-six assault ships to stop a fleet of three hundred Zaltule warships. He saw only one real chance for victory.

The Kleese didn't know about the improved shields or the multi warhead antimatter missiles the battlecruisers and light cruisers were equipped with. He would meet the enemy, fire one, possibly two volleys of missiles and then drop down closer to the planet to allow the numerous ion cannons on the surface to fire upon the Kleese fleet. That should even things up, or at least he hoped it would. He just hoped the defensive energy turrets on the planet could cope with the return fire.

"Contact Governor Scott and inform him to make sure everyone is into the deep shelters," he ordered his communications officer. "This is going to get hairy for a while and the surface may get hit."

"Sending the message," the communications offered replied as he contacted Mars Central and informed them of the admiral's orders.

"Also, put me in contact with General Sanchez, he needs to know what's expected of the ion cannons."

Admiral Sanders leaned back, contemplating his battle plan. The enemy just had too many damn ships! They always seemed to have the numerical advantage. Well, this time there would be some surprises, and if everything worked as he hoped the Kleese attack would fail.

-

Fleet Admiral Kelly looked at the tactical screen at his assembled fleets. He had First Fleet, Fifth Fleet, Sixth Fleet, Eighth Fleet, and Ninth Fleet to defend the Moon and Centerpoint Station. Overall, he had four heavy battlecruisers, eighteen regular battlecruisers, seventy-two light cruisers, two hundred and sixteen assault ships, and seventy-five Delton battlecruisers. There were also another ninety-five assault ships protecting Centerpoint Station.

"All ships are in position," reported Commander Makita. "Fleet Commander Achlyn says his forces are ready to engage the Kleese."

"We'll hit them with our new missiles, first," Kelly said as he weighed his options.

"All ships are at Condition One and marines are at their security posts," added Makita from his command console. "We're as ready as we're going to get."

"Twenty minutes until weapons range," Lieutenant Fullerton reported her hazel eyes focusing on the admiral.

"I want the first strike," spoke Kelly, looking over at Lieutenant Marsten at Tactical. "All ships will fire a full spread of the new missiles upon my order. Then we'll advance and engage the Kleese."

-

Colonel Wade Nelson was standing next to Beth, waiting tensely for orders. They were both encased in Type Three battlesuits and two companies of marines were waiting with them. Marines had been dispersed to various sections of the massive station to await the Kleese attack.

"We're within ten minutes of all primary docking collars on this side of the station," commented Wade, looking over at Beth.

He wished he could see her face, but the heavy protective helmet of the battlesuit hid everything, even her eyes.

Beth nodded. She knew due to the size of the Kleese battlecruisers they would have to use the collars to dock to the station and then board. A platoon of marines was stationed at each docking station waiting to see what happened. If the Kleese succeeded in boarding, then she and Wade would take their marines to help repel the Kleese. Or at least that was the plan. Major Winfrey was doing the same on the other side of the station with several companies. Other marines were defending the flight bays and additional high-risk areas of the massive station.

"At least Ryan will miss this," Beth said, knowing that was a relief to Wade. The Defender was still in transit to Lanolth.

"Did you manage to speak to your mother?" Wade asked. He knew Beth had tried to send a message before communications were shut down.

"No," she answered, pensively. "I didn't make it in time. By now she's in the deep shelter close to the retirement center."

"I'm sure she'll be fine," Wade said, reassuringly. He knew his parents would also be safe in one of the heavily reinforced bunkers. Even if the habitats in Vesta were penetrated and lost their atmospheres, the bunkers would remain safe.

"Maybe the fleet will keep them away from Centerpoint," Beth said.

"This station is heavily armed," Wade reminded her. "Even if the Kleese get past the fleet, the station's weapons might prove an insurmountable obstacle."

"I hope so," Beth responded. She clenched her fist, thinking she was getting too old for this. When this was over, maybe it was time for her to speak to Wade about having children. It would be easy enough to get reassigned permanently to Centerpoint or even Vesta.

Wade took a deep breath, feeling the growing anxiety of going into battle. Beth was a good marine and excellent in combat, but sometimes bad things happened even to the best.

Harmock gazed in anticipation at the main tactical display. Both his fleet and War Overlord Tetus' fleet were coordinating their attacks to hit the Humans at the same precise moment. This battle would be quick and very destructive to the waiting Human forces. It would serve as an abject lesson to the nonaligned worlds not to oppose the Kleese.

"The Humans and Deltons have less than five hundred ships to oppose us and many of those are assault ships," reported Minor Overlord Gareth as he studied the tactical screen.

"We will take some losses, but our fleet will prevail," predicted Harmock. "It's disturbing the Humans have so many ships. The trading station should never have been allowed to remain in their hands."

"That will be remedied shortly," Gareth responded. "Our warriors are ready to board the station and bring it back under our control. We will annihilate all the vermin currently on board."

"As it should be," Harmock replied in a cold voice. "They will die for the transgressions they have committed against our race."

"Extreme weapons range," reported Salten from the weapons console. "Target locks confirmed."

-

"Fire!" ordered Fleet Admiral Kelly, seeing the green target lights glowing on the tactical console.

He leaned forward, gripping the armrests on his command chair. What would happen when the new multi warhead antimatter missiles struck the Kleese shields? Six forty-megaton explosions should have a devastating effect, particularly when delivered within microseconds of one another. They had been fortunate in acquiring the new antimatter technology in time to allow the R&D people to equip many of the multi warhead missiles with the more powerful antimatter charges.

"Firing," replied Lieutenant Edmonson as fourteen sublight missiles darted away from the Armageddon.

In all, nearly one thousand of the new missiles exited the missile tubes of the Human and Delton warships to strike the

Kleese shields. The attack was unexpected as the new technology made the missiles difficult to shoot down. Even so, the Kleese defensive computers located and destroyed three hundred and seven with intense energy weapons fire before the rest impacted Kleese energy shields.

Fleet Admiral Kelly saw the viewscreens in the Command Center suddenly glow with a severe brightness before the filters automatically kicked in, reducing the light.

"Impact," reported Lieutenant Fullerton.

When the screens cleared, Admiral Kelly was stunned to see the effects of the missile strike on the Kleese ships. Everywhere he looked, he saw debris and burning warships.

"We hurt them!" yelled Makita, jubilantly. "They never expected that. The new missiles blew right through their shields!"

"Kleese ships are returning fire," reported Fullerton as his sensors lit up with inbound weapons fire. "Missiles, pulse fusion beams, and energy weapons!"

"Close the range!" ordered Harmock stunned at the damage the Humans and Deltons had inflicted on his fleet. For several moments, the entire Kleese fleet had been lit up by the fury of the exploding warheads. "Their sublight missiles can't lock on if we get within minimal combat range."

"Ours won't, either," stated Gareth as he looked at the carnage the Humans and Deltons had wreaked on the Kleese fleet. "Those warheads were in the forty-megaton range." Looking at the viewscreens, he could see several Kleese battlecruisers with large sections blasted out of their hulls and others, which had been reduced to nothing more than scattering debris and glowing gases. They could not afford to fight a missile duel with the Humans.

"We have an advantage in energy weapons and pulse fusion beams," Harmock informed his second in command. "This battle will now become ship-to-ship and we'll crush the Human and Delton fleets." This would be a new kind of combat. Instead of firing their weapons from hundreds of kilometers away, they would close to within twenty or thirty kilometers.

The Warrior's Fire trembled as a Human pulse fusion beams struck the ship's energy screen. It was shortly followed by warning alarms as a particle beam flashed through the screen, blasting into a section of the flagship's hull.

Around the Warrior's fire, other ships were heavily damaged or had been destroyed by multiple missile hits, but the Kleese still had enough warships to handle the combined Human and Delton fleets and they fully intended to do just that.

The Kleese fleet accelerated ahead, including the damaged ones, to quickly close the range with the Human and Delton fleets. A few more of the deadly missiles impacted, blowing another dozen Kleese battlecruisers into oblivion, and then the Zaltule battlecruisers were in and amongst the defending warships, making missiles useless.

Pulse fusion beams, particle beams, and energy weapons became the predominate weapons as space became lit up with their deadly fire. Energy screens glowed brightly from impacts causing cascades of uncontrolled energy to flash across space.

-

"Damn, I wasn't expecting that," groaned Fleet Admiral Kelly as the Armageddon shook violently from the impact of several Kleese pulse fusion beams. "Order all ships to gradually pull back toward Centerpoint. We may need the station's heavy weapons to win this. How many Zaltule ships did we get with the missiles?"

"Eighty-seven in the first wave and another eighteen with the second," Commander Makita reported as he studied the data on a computer screen. "Another forty-two ships are heavily damaged."

"Concentrate on the damaged ships and let's finish them off," Kelly ordered.

"Battlecruiser Trident is down," spoke Lieutenant Fullerton as she saw the friendly green icon disappear from her sensors.

"Light Cruisers Sundance, Victor, Pallas, Gemanoid, Starla, and Kestrel are down."

"We're losing assault ships too rapidly to keep track of," added Commander Makita, turning pale as the losses quickly grew. "Only a few ships are still firing missiles, we're having too much trouble locking on at this close range."

Fleet Admiral Kelly looked at the viewscreens and could see dying Human and Delton ships, but the Kleese were suffering losses as well. "Order the assault ships covering Centerpoint to move to the Moon and cover Luna City," Kelly ordered as his fleet slowly pulled back. There were thirty additional assault ships based at Luna City as part of its defense force, and along with the ion cannons that should give the habitats adequate protection unless the Kleese mounted a major attack.

Fleet Commander Achlyn grimaced as another Delton battlecruiser died under the powerful pulse fusion beams the Kleese were employing. He'd lost eight of his battlecruisers since the battle began, but his ships' powerful bow energy weapons were making the Zaltule pay a heavy price in exchange.

"The battlecruiser Ascendant is reporting heavy damage," Baylith reported with concern in his voice. He knew that every ship they lost was irreplaceable.

"Have them pull back to Centerpoint," ordered Achlyn as he watched the tactical display intently. "Order the Crescent and Balton to advance and engage the Kleese ship at coordinates C-22 by X-15. We will coordinate our own attack with them to take it out."

Achlyn felt his flagship tremble from Kleese energy and pulse fusion beams striking the ship's energy shield. On one of the viewscreens, he saw a number of heavy energy beams strike a Zaltule battlecruiser, causing its energy screen to erupt in a cascade of light before two of the beams penetrated, blasting deep, glowing holes in the ship's armor. Almost instantly, a multitude of beams tore through the weakened screen, drilling deep into the Zaltule ship. A massive explosion lit up the screen as the Kleese ship blew apart.

"For Delton," muttered Baylith as he watched the scattering and burning debris on the screen.

-

Admiral Layton gazed in fury at a viewscreen as one of her light cruisers disintegrated. Her biggest advantage were the new missiles, and the unbelievably close range this battle was being fought had neutralized that weapon. After considering her options, she knew there was only one way to bring the missiles back into play.

"London, New York, and Freedom," she said over her com, which connected her to the other three heavy battlecruisers. "Standby to accelerate to full power on X axis seventy degrees for twenty seconds then do a complete turnover and fire a full spread of missiles." By doing this maneuver, it would take them briefly out of the melee and far enough away to lock onto the Kleese warships.

Admiral Layton waited a few moments and then spoke into her com. "Implement maneuver!"

Instantly, all four heavy battlecruisers accelerated away on their subspace drives from the battle. For twenty seconds, they hurtled past the Kleese ships before turning one hundred eighty degrees on their center axis and firing full spreads of their multi warhead missiles. Ten Kleese ships were struck and blew apart as forty-megaton antimatter explosions tore through their hulls. The Kleese, seeing the danger, instantly sent twenty of their warships after the heavy battlecruisers.

"They'll be ready for that next time," Admiral Layton said grimly. "Head back to the fleet and let's show them our new plasma weapon."

-

The Phoenix was dropping down near the outer atmosphere of Mars, the rest of Second, Third, and Fourth Fleet were close by. They'd managed to get off two full spreads of the new missiles before the Kleese warships closed the range and nearly over ran the defending fleets. Even so, they had managed to take out forty-eight of the attacking ships and damage another twenty.

"The battlecruiser Starlight is under heavy attack," reported Ensign Sullivan from his sensor console.

"Order the light cruisers Queensbury and Drake to assist," Sanders ordered as the Phoenix shuddered violently and warning alarms began sounding.

"General Sanchez reports the Kleese ships are nearly within range of his ion cannons," Lieutenant Brassels reported from Communications.

The Phoenix shook violently and the lights in the Command Center flickered. Sanders looked questionably at Commander Carey Vickers.

"We've lost Secondary Engineering," she reported, grimly. "Energy shield is down to sixty percent and we have several fires burning out of control. A damn Zaltule pulse fusion beam penetrated our shield!"

"We have four Zaltule battlecruisers bearing down on us," warned Sullivan as he watched the four nearing red threat icons worriedly.

The ship suddenly shook and seemed to cry out in pain. Sanders could hear screams of fear and yells for help. The lights in the Command Center went out and then the emergency lighting came back on.

"I can't contact Main Engineering," reported Commander Vickers as she wiped blood away from her face. Her forehead had a wicked cut on it. "Energy screen is at five percent. The next hit will take us out."

"Contact Admiral Rivers," uttered Sanders to Lieutenant Brassels with an understanding look upon his face. "Tell him he has command of the fleet."

"Message sent," Brassels reported a moment later in a nearly toneless voice.

"Sir," began Vickers but her words were never completed as a pulse fusion beam tore through the Command Center.

A moment later, the Phoenix exploded as the four attacking Kleese warships riddled her hull with energy beams and pulse fusion beams. A scattering of debris and glowing gases was all that remained of Second Fleet's flagship.

"Phoenix is down," Lieutenant Jarvis reported on the Independence as the flagship's green icon suddenly expanded and then vanished.

"You have command, Admiral," Commander Greerman stated as he looked over at Admiral Rivers.

"This is Admiral Rivers," he spoke quickly over the fleet communications channel, not allowing himself any time to grieve over Admiral Sander's death. "The Phoenix is down and I am taking command. All ships continue to drop down to the edge of Mars' atmosphere. At that point, we will hold our position and the ion cannons will fire. They will continue to fire until the Kleese fleet has either been eliminated or the cannons have been destroyed. We shall see to it they are not."

"Fifteen seconds until ion cannon range," reported Lieutenant Wesley Jarvis.

"General Sanchez reports cannons are going hot," reported Ensign May Simone from Communications.

"Light cruisers Thrasher and Antarctica are down," reported Lieutenant Jarvis as the Zaltule ships continued to blast away at the fleet.

"Ion cannons are firing," reported Commander Greerman as hundreds of white beams of energy leaped up into space from the surface of Mars.

-

Zaltule Overlord Tetus gazed in shock as hundreds of deadly beams of energy erupted from the planet's surface and smashed into his fleet's shields.

"Report!" he demanded his triangular shaped head shifting to his second in command.

"Ion beams," uttered Minor Overlord Grafton. "The beams are neutralizing our energy shields."

Even as they watched, the weapons fire from the Human ships suddenly became far more deadly. Without energy shields to protect them, the Zaltule battlecruisers were suddenly very vulnerable. Human particle beams, pulse fusion beams, and even energy weapons were now ravaging the Kleese fleet.

"Spatial anomaly detected," reported the Kleese standing in front of the ship's sensors. "Numerous ships dropping out of Fold Space."

"Who are they?" demanded Tetus, feeling concern. The reserve fleet was not due for two more weeks.

"Sensors detecting Alliance ships," reported the sensor operator. "They are heading for the third planet and War Overlord Harmock."

"Disengage," ordered Tetus. He needed to go to the War Overlord's aid.

"We have twelve ships with inoperable Fold Space Drives," reported Grafton.

Tetus thought for a moment and reached a fateful decision, he could still teach these Humans a valuable lesson. "Contact those ships; I have a special mission for them."

The Kleese fleet began to rapidly extricate itself from the Humans, suffering even more losses from the deadly fire of the ion beams and Human ship weapons. As the fleet withdrew, it left twelve badly damaged ships behind, which suddenly began accelerating toward the surface of Mars.

"Get those ships!" ordered Admiral Rivers worriedly as they entered the planet's atmosphere. "We can't let them get too close to the surface." He had seen the arrival of the Alliance fleet, but it was too far away to be of help.

Pulse fusion beams and particle beams smashed into the Zaltule battlecruisers, which were without shields. In moments, eight massive explosions and falling debris littered the upper Martian atmosphere. Then two more ships were wiped out by heavy energy weapons fire from the surface. The remaining two Zaltule battlecruisers were glowing cherry red as they began to heat up from their swift passage through the thin Martian atmosphere. One of them was hit by multiple pulse fusion beams and broke apart just above Mars Central. The final one smashed into the huge dome, which covered the largest city on Mars. Instantly, a dozen antimatter warheads, which had been set to explode on contact, detonated. Mars Central was instantly flattened, and the massive blast wave moved out across the surface, damaging even more habitats. A huge cloud of red dust began to rise up into the planet's atmosphere.

"Confirmed detonation of antimatter warheads on the planet's surface," reported Lieutenant Jarvis his face turning pale.

"I don't know if even the deep bunkers could have survived that," spoke Commander Greerman his eyes wide in shock.

Admiral Rivers forced himself to turn his attention away from the viewscreens and back to the fleeing Kleese warships. "How many of them did we destroy?"

"One hundred and forty-seven," Lieutenant Jarvis answered in a shaken voice. "They're headed for Earth."

Rivers nodded as he turned to Ensign Simone at Communications. "Inform Admiral Johnson he is to remain here at Mars with Third Fleet and help with rescue operations. The rest of us are heading to Earth."

"Detecting Alliance ships!" reported Lieutenant Fullerton, excitedly. "Ten million kilometers."

'How did they get here?" asked Commander Makita, relieved to see them. The Kleese had nearly pushed them back to Centerpoint Station.

"I have Admiral Adamson on the com," added Lieutenant Jones.

"How many ships are you detecting?" demanded Fleet Admiral Kelly, reaching for the com button and gazing in stunned amazement at the horde of friendly green icons, which had just appeared.

"Two hundred and eighty Alliance ships, plus Seventh Fleet," answered Fullerton, her hazel eyes showing the excitement she was feeling.

"That's over three hundred and fifty ships," spoke Commander Makita with relief spreading across his face.

Kelly activated the com link, which put him in instant touch with Admiral Adamson. "How did you get here?" was the first thing he asked.

"A couple of Waltarn scout ships picked the Kleese up as they passed through a brown dwarf system," Adamson replied. "The Waltarn deployed several hundred small scout ships as well as some special buoys which can detect ships in Fold Space if they pass close enough. Once we had their course plotted, we knew where they were heading. I brought the Alliance fleet with me. They know they can't allow the solar system to fall to the Kleese."

"Bring your fleet up and hit them from the rear," Kelly ordered, crisply. "Between us, Centerpoint, and your fleet we should be able to crush the remaining Kleese ships."

"We're on our way," replied Adamson.

"Sir, I'm getting some bad news from Admiral Rivers," reported Lieutenant Jones from Communications. His face was nearly white. "The Kleese attacking fleet has been driven away from Mars, but they launched a suicide attack toward the end and Mars Central has been destroyed. Admiral Rivers reports ten to twelve antimatter missiles detonated on the surface, wiping out Mars Central and heavily damaging the surrounding habitats. He expects the loss of life to be heavy. He also reports the loss of Admiral Sanders and the Phoenix."

"Damn!" uttered Commander Makita, feeling as if he'd been punched in the stomach. "What else can go wrong?"

"This battle," answered Kelly, grimly. "We can't let the Kleese get to Centerpoint."

War Overlord Harmock gazed at the tactical screen, which showed the new arrivals. Most of the new ships were battlecruisers and being from the Alliance would be armed with technology dangerous to Zaltule warships. Not only that but the four large human warships were using plasma weapons, which were blasting right through his ships' shields. They were even more devastating than the Humans' particle beams.

"Overlord Tetus is on his way to our position," reported Minor Overlord Gareth. "He will be here shortly."

"This battle is over," Harmock spoke in a cold and nearly emotionless voice as he watched several more Zaltule ships explode on the viewscreens. "Order all ships with inactive Fold Space Drives to make to the trading station and land their warriors on it. If they can capture the decks containing the Fold Space Drive, they can activate it and fly the station out of the Human's system. Once out of the system, we can send more warriors aboard and take full control. Without the station, the Humans will not be able to rebuild. The fleet will cover them until they have docked and then we'll withdraw to repair our battle damage."

"Tetus reports he has wiped out the Human colony on the fourth planet."

"That will greatly reduce their population," uttered Harmock pleased that at least one of his objectives had been accomplished. Now if he could just take back control of the trading station he would consider this battle a victory.

-

General Mitchell looked grimly at General Pittman. "Governor Scott is believed dead and General Sanchez is reporting the casualties may reach over one million." He'd spent the last several minutes speaking with General Sanchez about the situation on Mars.

"We won't know until we reach the deep bunkers," replied General Pittman. "Communications are out to most of them due to the residual effects of the antimatter explosions."

Mitchell turned his gaze back to the main viewscreen. With the arrival of Seventh Fleet and the Alliance, the battle was rapidly turning in their favor. The Kleese were no longer pressing the attack but seemed to be fighting a holding action.

"Sir, we have twenty-two Kleese battlecruisers that have broken away from the main fleet and are making a run for the station," reported Lieutenant Bryan Vail, worriedly.

"They're going to ram," spoke General Pittman grim faced as he stared with worry at the tactical screen.

"No, they're not going to ram, they're going to try to board us," General Mitchell said as he leaned forward, gripping the armrests on is command chair. "Major Lest; don't let those ships dock to the station." Major Lest was the station's tactical officer.

-

The twenty-two Kleese warships sped toward Centerpoint Station, coming under heavy fire as they drew near. Particle beams and pulse fusion beams played over their energy screens, knocking them down and leaving them vulnerable to attack. Massive explosions spread across the hulls of the attacking Zaltule ships, leaving a number of them nothing more than burning wrecks. However, for all the firepower Centerpoint had, three managed to make it to the station and dock, sending hundreds of Zaltule warriors on board.

Human light cruisers fell back from the main battle and blasted away at the docked battlecruisers trying to destroy them. While docked, the ships couldn't operate their energy screens. In only a matter of a few minutes, all three had been destroyed, causing some damage to the station as well. Damage that would take weeks to repair.

-

"We have Kleese in the station," General Pittman reported as he listened to the reports coming in from the docking stations. "Three docking stations have been overrun by Zaltule warriors and the marines at those stations are no longer reporting."

"Their fleet is beginning to withdraw; there has to be a reason why they sacrificed so many ships to get their warriors on the station," said Mitchell as he tried to figure out the Zaltule's strategy.

"I know what it is," Pittman said with a horrified look spreading across his face as he received word of more contacts with the invading Kleese. "They're headed for the Fold Space Drive."

"Crap!" uttered Mitchell his face showing sudden comprehension. "If they can start up the drive they can take the station out of the system to where their fleet will be waiting. We won't stand a chance."

"I'm sending orders to Colonel Nelson and Major Winfrey," Pittman said. "I'm ordering them to intercept the Kleese and either turn them back or kill them."

"Send marines to plant explosives on all the main power plants' energy couplings," General Mitchell ordered. The station was powered by sixteen fusion energy plants. "If we cut the power to the drive, the Kleese can't activate it."

"I'll send the orders and have the command sequence to initiate the blasts set up on the main command console in front of you. If we have to, we can set the explosives off from here." General Pittman shook his head in worry; this situation had suddenly gotten very serious.

Wade looked over at Beth, deeply concerned. "The Kleese have managed to board the station and are headed for the Fold Space Drive; we have to cut them off."

"Captain Stern, Captain Foster, the Kleese are on board, it's up to us to stop them."

"Lead the way," Jamie said as she took her RG rifle down from her shoulder looking at the colonel.

"To reach the Fold Space Drive the Kleese will have to pass through junction eight from transit station fourteen," Wade said as he called up the schematics of the station on his HUD. "It's the most direct route for them to take. "If we take the shuttles in station four we just might beat them to the transit hub."

"Let's go, then," Beth said, turning and jogging down the wide corridor with the two marine companies following close behind.

It took then nearly forty minutes, but after boarding the shuttles and passing through thirty kilometers of tunnels, they reached the junction, which connected with shuttle line fourteen. The marines jumped out of the shuttles, sending them on so the shuttles behind could unload their complements of marines.

"It looks like we made it," Wade said as he surveyed the large room they were standing in. It was over one hundred meters across and several transit lines met in this location. It served as a transit hub for many areas of the massive station.

"They need to get through that hatch to get to the Fold Space Drive," Beth said, pointing across the room.

"There's no cover in here," Wade said as he looked around trying to decide how best to defend the transit hub. "Let's move our two companies over against the far wall next to the hatch, and when the Kleese arrive we can try to pick them off as they disembark from the shuttles."

"I wish there was some cover in here," moaned Sergeant Russell. All he could see were a few tables and chairs and some crates of supplies.

"Just shoot fast," suggested Sergeant Dawson. "The smoke will hide you."

"Yeah, right," responded Russell, shaking his head.

It took a few minutes for everyone to set up. RG rounds and RG explosives would be the primary weapons used. Only ten percent of the marines held energy cannons.

"I hear the shuttles," reported Sergeant Dawson, who was standing with his squad a few meters away from Captain Foster.

"Stand by," Nicole ordered as she unshouldered her RG rifle and clicked the safety off. She had already set it to explosive rounds.

The first shuttle suddenly appeared and came to a stop, the doors slid open and heavily armed Kleese swarmed out. Behind it another shuttle appeared and then another.

"Fire," yelled Beth as she saw the first Kleese.

Instantly, the area around the shuttles was covered in explosions as RG explosive rounds began going off. A few hit the first shuttle, reducing it to a pile of scrap.

"Keep firing!" Captain Stern yelled as she fired her RG rifle on full auto, spraying RG rounds into the mass of Kleese, who were now charging across the floor.

"They're coming out of the tunnel," warned Sergeant Russell as a swarm of Kleese suddenly appeared out of the transit tunnel firing their weapons into the marines.

The fighting grew vicious as the battle ebbed back and forth. Marines were going down as well as Zaltule warriors. The Zaltule continued to come out of the tunnel, and the marines were soon heavily outnumbered.

"How many are there?" yelled Sergeant Dawson as he fired several explosive rounds into the Kleese.

"Too damn many," grunted Sergeant Russell as he continued to fire his RG rifle at the enemy.

"They're getting too close," warned Dawson as he shot a Kleese that had nearly made it to the line of now desperate marines.

"I'm hit," yelled Sergeant Russell as a series of RG rounds struck his battlesuit.

Beth turned pale when she saw the green icon representing Sergeant Russell turn amber and then red. Sergeant Russell had been with them from the beginning and she couldn't believe he was gone. It had happened so suddenly.

"We can't hold them," Captain Foster said over the command channel. "There are just too many of them!"

Wade fired two explosive shells at a pair of Kleese, seeing one fall and the other stagger and then continue toward them. "We have to," he said, savagely. "We can't let them get past or the station's lost!"

"Looking at his HUD, he saw that over half of his marines were either injured or dead, if something didn't change soon they were all going to be wiped out.

Wade felt a sudden pain in his leg and fell to the deck. An RG round had penetrated his suit, going all the way through. He felt as if he were going to pass out and then the suit began injecting meds.

"Colonel's down," yelled Captain Stern as she rushed over, standing in front of Wade to give him covering fire.

Beth felt frantic, seeing more marines falling. Wade was injured and she could see no way out of this situation. "Keep firing," she ordered, taking command. "Keep them away from the hatch. Switch to explosive rounds only."

Several more minutes passed and the room was full of smoke and exploding ordnance. Nearly every marine was now injured or dead. Nicole had been hit in both the leg and the upper body and was lying immobile on the deck. The surviving marines gathered around Beth and Wade, who was now in a kneeling position firing his RG rifle nonstop at the advancing Kleese. The room was littered with the torn and broken bodies of both marines and Zaltule.

Just when Beth thought it was all over, the hatch they were defending suddenly swung open and Major Winfrey charged through. Behind him were marines in Type Four battlesuits.

"Need some help, Major?" he asked as he took up a defensive position just in front of Beth and her surviving marines. Major Winfrey had brought two full companies of his Space Marines backed up by Captain Brandon Perry and his company of Type Threes.

The tide of the battle quickly changed as the marines in the Type Four suits charged the attacking Kleese, pushing them back toward the transit tunnel. The Type Fours were more nimble and their armor more resistant to Kleese weapons fire. Captain Perry was in the thick of things with his company mixing it up with the Kleese as well.

For ten more minutes, the battle raged as the marines finally reached the transit tunnel and began clearing out the Kleese still inside of it. At last, the weapons fell silent and no Zaltule were left standing.

The transit hub was a wreck. Jagged holes were in the walls, the floor was torn apart, and pieces of suit armor were scattered about. It was a very morbid scene and more than a few marines got sick inside their suits. There was so much smoke in the large room that seeing without using suit optics was nearly impossible.

Major Winfrey returned to where Beth and Wade were standing. Captain Stern was helping Wade to stand on his two metal feet. "The Kleese have been eliminated," he reported.

"Where's Captain Perry?" asked Jamie not seeing him anywhere.

"He didn't make it," replied Major Winfrey, sadly. "He was killed in the transit tunnel but he took a hell of a lot of Zaltule with him."

"He was a good marine," Beth said, knowing he would be greatly missed. "How's Captain Foster?" She knew that Nicole had been badly hit.

"Hanging in there," reported Sergeant Dawson, trying his best not to think about Sergeant Russell. He couldn't believe his friend was gone.

"We need to get her to the med bay," spoke Jamie with some urgency in her voice.

Beth nodded in agreement. They'd lost so many marines in the fighting. Captain Perry, Sergeant Russell, and many others she had known for years. Looking at her HUD, she saw that out of the two hundred marines who had entered the transit hub with her and Wade, only twenty-two were still showing green and another thirty-two were amber; all the rest were red. For a moment, Beth felt herself sway on her feet as she realized everyone who had been lost.

"Let's get our wounded to the med bay," suggested Major Winfrey, nodding at Captain Stern who was picking up Nicole's limp battlesuit. "The threat is over."

Wade nodded. He felt numb at the losses they had suffered today. After they had time to recover he fully intended to see if he could talk Beth into resigning her commission and taking a civilian job, perhaps in Vesta. If she would have been killed today, he didn't know what he would have done.

"It's over," reported General Pittman, drawing in a sharp breath. "Colonel Nelson managed to stop them at the transit hub but it was touch and go for a while. If Major Winfrey hadn't made it when he did, we might have lost both companies of marines, including Colonel Nelson and Major Williams."

"At least we won," replied General Mitchell in an even voice. Looking up at the main tactical screen, he saw Admiral Rivers had arrived and the last Kleese warship was gone.

"What now?" asked General Pittman.

"Now we rebuild," answered General Mitchell in a soft voice. "We rebuild and try to replace what we lost today. This was a brutal battle, but there are more ahead of us. The important thing is that we survived and still have a future ahead of us."

Chapter Nineteen

In deep space, War Overlord Harmock looked at his shattered fleet. Out of one thousand battlecruisers, only six hundred and twelve remained and many of them were heavily damaged. In another week, the reserve fleet would arrive with their five hundred vessels. Once they did, he intended to withdraw to the trading station in sector twelve and repair his battlecruisers. It would take several months for that task to be completed with the resources of the station.

"What of the Humans and the Alliance?" asked Gareth. He was still shaken that a vermin species had repelled the Zaltule.

"The Humans may not be Vermin," spoke Harmock as he thought hard and deep about the enemy. "They fight like Zaltule and their ships are very powerful."

"Surely you can't compare them to our race?" objected Gareth, not believing what the War Overlord was suggesting.

"It had to happen someday," Harmock answered as he descended from the Command Pedestal. "The Humans, while they are not Zaltule, are clearly not an inferior species. I found it hard to believe myself, but the proof is in the battles; we have yet to defeat the Humans."

"Then they are a grave threat to the Empire," uttered Gareth. "We should gather the entire Zaltule fleet and destroy them."

"We must learn more about them first," Harmock replied as he thought about what needed to be done. "We shall repair our fleet and then capture a number of Humans to interrogate. We'll learn their strengths and their weaknesses. Once that has been done, it will be necessary to return to the home world and speak to the Council of Overlords. Our ships must be updated with new and more powerful weapons. It may take time, but someday the Kleese will rule the galaxy and the Humans will be no more."

Gareth bowed his head in acknowledgment. If the Supreme Military Overlord said it would be so, there was no doubt that someday his prediction for the Kleese and the Humans would come to be.

General Mitchell was in his office meeting with General Pittman and Fleet Admiral Kelly. They'd been discussing the losses incurred during the Kleese attack.

"We lost forty percent of the fleet," stated Fleet Admiral Kelly with a dismal look upon his face. "It will take two years to replace the losses, let alone the personnel."

"We're already moving the damaged ships into the station's bays," replied General Pittman. "Vesta is moving ships out of her spacedock to make room for the damaged battlecruisers."

"We're fortunate the Alliance fleet made it here in time," Kelly said, shaking his head at how close they'd come to being defeated.

"The Alliance fleet is headed home," commented General Mitchell. He had personally thanked the commanders of the Alliance fleet for coming to the solar system's aid. "Seventh Fleet will remain in the system until further notice."

"The Kleese fleet suffered heavy losses," Kelly said his eyes looking intently at the other two. "They won't be a threat to anyone for a while."

"The Defender and her small fleet will soon be in Alliance space," added General Mitchell. "For now, they will have to represent our people to the Alliance."

"They don't even know what happened," pointed out General Pittman.

"The Alliance worlds will tell them once the Alliance fleet returns home," replied General Mitchell.

"It will be a shock, particularly when they hear about Mars Central," Kelly said. He wondered if anyone in the small fleet had relatives on Mars.

"I spoke to President Steward a short while ago," Mitchell continued. "Mason is going to take over running the cloning program with the goal of doubling the number of clones being produced over the next several years. We can't fight this war without them."

"There will be problems over that with the civilians," General Pittman warned. "We were already having near riots before."

"Cheryl Robertson will shortly be starting a new campaign to help the clones become more widely accepted," Mitchell said. "A lot of clones died in the fleet and here on Centerpoint. She will be pointing out how they died to protect regular Humans."

"People are stubborn," said Kelly, feeling dubious that any type of campaign would help considering the deep rift in public sentiment toward the clones.

"We can try," Mitchell said, leaning forward. "We need to rebuild and after this battle we can say one thing for sure. The Alliance is real and with some luck and good negotiating on the part of Hyram and his people, about to get much larger. We're not in this alone."

"To the Alliance," spoke Fleet Admiral Kelly in agreement. Perhaps there was hope for the future after all.

Wade and Beth were standing in the training dome, gazing at Charring Mountain. They had gone to the dome to talk and decide their future.

"It's hard to believe that Eugene and Brandon are gone," spoke Beth with sadness in her voice. Sergeant Russell and Captain Perry had saved her life more than once.

"Not only that, but so many others," replied Wade, reaching out and taking her hand. "A lot of those we lost have been with us for a long time."

"Even from the days when we were Kleese captives," answered Beth her eyes glistening with tears. "Wade, I don't know if I can do this anymore."

"You don't have to," answered Wade, understanding her sorrow. He felt much the same way.

"I think I want to return to Vesta to take care of my mom and raise a family," she said her eyes focusing intently on Wade.

"Do you want out of the military completely?"

"Yes," answered Beth slowly nodding her head. "I think I've done my share and I've seen enough dying."

Wade looked up at Charring Mountain thinking about all the changes made over the years. He could still remember his first attempt on the mountain as a conscript of the Kleese. "Would you be interested in helping with the cloning program? General Mitchell mentioned to me that President Randle is going to be in overall charge of it now."

"I think I would like that," Beth answered. It would allow her to stay inside Vesta and give her something productive to do. Vesta was also the safest place in the solar system to raise a family. "Do you think General Pittman will be aggravated when I turn in my resignation?"

"After what we've been through, I don't think he will be upset at all," responded Wade, turning his gaze away from Charring.

"What about you, Wade?" asked Beth, looking deep into her husband's eyes. "What are you going to do?"

"I can't resign yet," he sighed, giving Beth's hand an affectionate squeeze. "There's still a lot more work to be done getting the Alliance established and ready to fight the Kleese."

Beth nodded, wishing things could be different, but she strongly suspected that as long as the Human race was threatened, Wade would be there defending it. After all, that was the kind of man he was and why she loved him so much.

—

Ryan was standing next to Casey in the small observation room on the Defender, watching the passing stars. They would shortly be at Lanolth and their new mission would begin. For once, they had the room to themselves.

Casey thought over what Lauren had told her the previous day. She was encouraging her to be more forthcoming in telling Ryan how she felt. Taking a deep fortifying breath, she reached out and took Ryan's hand. She was relieved when he didn't pull his away. That's the first step, she thought. Now for the second.

"Ryan, what kind of future do we have ahead of us?"

Ryan was silent for a long moment surprised at Casey's question. "Do you mean you and me?" He turned and looked deeply into Casey's beautiful hazel eyes. He felt his heart beating faster. It was amazing the effect Casey had on him at times.

"Do you love me, Ryan?" Casey asked in a soft voice.

Ryan took his hand out of Casey's, seeing the panicked look in her eyes when he did. He smiled, put his arms around her and pulled her close. Tilting his head downward, he kissed her long and passionately. Then he drew back and replied. "Of course I do; I have for a long time."

In the back of the room, Lauren smiled. The two hadn't heard her come in and she was pleased she had witnessed this moment. Being quiet, she turned and left not, wanting them to know she'd overheard. Some things were meant to be private.

-

Mason Randle left the Control Center still feeling shaken about what had occurred at Mars Central. A massive rescue operation was still in progress with Kivean, Delton, and Talt technicians trying to repair the surviving habitats as quickly as possible. Dozens of assault ships had been sent down to the surface to help provide power and a place for emergency personnel to stay. Even marines in battlesuits had been deployed to help shift the rubble in the search for survivors.

President Steward had just finished speaking to General Sanchez, who was coordinating the rescue efforts, and the civilian and military casualties on Mars were estimated at between six hundred to seven hundred thousand people. Considering the entire surviving Human population was only around nineteen million people, which was almost five percent of the overall population.

Taking a short transit tube, Mason stepped back out into the Smithfield habitat and took a deep breath of the fresh air. The people were out of the deep shelters and everything seemed normal. However, the Kleese attack had been devastating. The population loss, the damage to the fleet, and even Centerpoint had been eye opening. There was also the loss of Governor Scott, who was going to be very difficult to replace. Some major changes must be made. The cloning program would have to be greatly stepped up and a new campaign launched to encourage normal Humans to accept the clones. It was now obvious the Human race could not survive without them. President Steward had asked if Mason would be willing to oversee the cloning program and the new ad campaign. Knowing how important the program was to the survival of the Human race, he had agreed.

Mason spent some time walking through Smithfield, thinking about everything that had changed since the mining operations center came into being. Smithfield was no longer the city his grandfather and father had envisioned. It had grown until it now represented much more. The brightest people in the system now lived inside Vesta in the large habitats. Kiveans could be seen everyday working with their Human counterparts. As long as Vesta survived, the Human race would also.

After a while, Mason reached his home. It was on the outskirts of Smithfield and the long walk had done him some good. Going inside, he saw Adrienne sitting on the couch with Lara.

"Mason," said Adrienne, standing up and walking over to him. "Is it over?"

"For now," replied Mason, taking Lara and holding her protectively in his arms. He looked down at the innocent face, wondering what type of world his daughter would grow up in.

He'd thought his duties were over, but holding his daughter, he knew there was much more ahead of him. Walking over to the couch, he sat down and began rocking back and forth, seeing the happy and contented look upon Lara's face. There were some things that would always be worth fighting for.

The End

If you enjoyed Galactic Empire Wars: Rebellion and would like to see the series continue, please post a review with some stars. Good reviews encourage an author to write and help books to sell. Reviews can be just a few short sentences describing what you liked about the book. If you have suggestions, please contact me at my website listed on the following page. Thank you for reading Rebellion and being so supportive.

Galactic Empire Wars: The Alliance

After the defeat of the Zaltule fleet, the Alliance has become a reality. Twenty worlds now stand opposed to the Kleese and their desire for a Galactic Empire. In the solar system, new and more powerful ships are being built in preparation for the next attack.

The Kleese have other ideas. In a daring raid on the Alliance, they kidnap part of a Space Marine platoon in order to better understand Humans. These Humans will be taken back to the Kleese home worlds for study and interrogation.

Ryan, Casey, and others find themselves captives on a Zaltule battlecruiser. Can they find a way to escape the dreaded Kleese and return home?

Find out in Galactic Empire Wars: The Alliance, coming in the summer of 2015.

For updates on current writing projects and future publications go to my author website. Sign up for future notifications when new books come out on Amazon.

Website: http://raymondlweil.com/

Other Books by Raymond L. Weil
Available at Amazon

Moon Wreck (The Slaver Wars Book 1)
The Slaver Wars: Alien Contact (The Slaver Wars Book 2)
Moon Wreck: Fleet Academy (The Slaver Wars Book 3)

The Slaver Wars: First Strike (The Slaver Wars Book 4)
The Slaver Wars: Retaliation (The Slaver Wars Book 5)
The Slaver Wars: Galactic Conflict (The Slaver Wars Book 6)
The Slaver Wars: Endgame (The Slaver Wars Book 7)

-

Dragon Dreams
Dragon Dreams: Dragon Wars
Dragon Dreams: Gilmreth the Awakening
Dragon Dreams: Snowden the White Dragon

-

Star One: Tycho City: Survival
Star One: Neutron Star
Star One: Dark Star

-

Galactic Empire Wars: Destruction (Book 1)
Galactic Empire Wars: Emergence (Book 2)
Galactic Empire Wars: Rebellion (Book 3)

-

The Lost Fleet (A Slaver Wars novel) spring 2015
The Star Cross spring 2015
Galactic Empire Wars: The Alliance summer 2015

Turn the page for an introduction to The Star Cross a new military science fiction novel that will be published in early 2015.

The Star Cross

Chapter One

The Earth's 800-meter heavy battlecruiser Star Cross slid silently through empty space, the ship's powerful sensors scanning everything ahead and around it. Her four light cruiser escorts were in screening positions protecting the massive battlecruiser from attack. The 600-meter light carrier Vindication followed closely behind, protected by six small destroyers. Each ship was on high alert and tensions were high amongst the crews. Everyone glanced anxiously at one another, wondering what was awaiting them at Earth.

In the Command Center of the Star Cross, Admiral Kurt Vickers watched the main viewscreen focused on the light carrier as four fighters left the flight bay to patrol ahead of the fleet. The light carrier had twenty fighters in its flight bay as well as twelve small bombers.

"CSP has been launched," Lieutenant Lena Brooks reported as the four friendly green icons appeared on her sensor screen.

The twenty-eight year old young woman let out a quiet breath, hoping they would remain undetected. She felt her pulse racing and knew she wasn't the only one in the Command Center that was worried. Lena focused her hazel eyes upon the admiral, awaiting further orders. She trusted him to bring them through the coming ordeal.

"Current status?" asked Vickers in a steady voice, turning to his XO and commander of the battlecruiser, Captain Randson.

The captain checked several data screens before turning toward the admiral. "Long-range sensors are indicating no unusual movement from the enemy ships. I don't think they detected our hyper jumps." Randson let out a deep, ragged breath, feeling the tension running through the Command Center. Everyone's nerves were on edge.

Admiral Vickers nodded as he turned his gaze to the primary tactical screen on which information from the long distance scans was now appearing. He took in a sharp breath as he contemplated what his next action needed to be. He felt a tremendous weight of responsibility upon his shoulders, knowing his next few decisions could well determine the future of the human race. The crew in the Command Center were waiting for his orders expectantly. Everyone wanted to know what had happened here in the Solar System and if their friends and families were still alive. He knew they had good reasons to be concerned.

Two weeks back, a mysterious and hostile alien fleet had appeared out of hyperspace and annihilated the two human fleets permanently stationed around Earth for protection. The majority of the ships had been destroyed before their shields could be raised or a single weapon fired. Only a few had managed to fight back and then only briefly. This wasn't surprising as no aliens had been detected by any of Earth's long-range exploration ships and no one had been expecting an attack, so the ships had been at a low level of alert.

The Star Cross and her fleet had been in the Newton system practicing maneuvers and testing the new particle beam weapons the battlecruiser and the light cruisers had been equipped with. The Newton system held a thriving human colony of nearly eight million inhabitants, along with a large orbital station designed for deep space exploration and minor ship repair. The colony had a number of large scientific outposts, as ships sent out on exploratory missions were required to report to Newton before being allowed to return to Earth. Newton was also the only true Earth-type planet to be discovered so far in their explorations. There were other planets humans could survive on, but none could compare to Earth or Newton.

A heavily damaged light cruiser had jumped into the Newton system to report the shocking news of the attack on Earth. The ship's commander had barely managed to escape and lost over half of his crew in the brief battle above the planet. The report of the attack had shaken the colony and after conferring with the colony's leaders, it had been decided that Admiral

Vickers would return to the Solar System. His mission was to determine the current condition of Earth as well as the number of alien ships still present.

"What now?" Captain Randson asked as he stepped closer to the admiral. Upon the tactical screen, a large number of red threat icons were visible. "There are twenty alien ships in orbit above Earth. Four of them are approximately the same size as the Star Cross, and the rest seem to be similar to our own light cruisers."

Vickers nodded. "From the reports we received from the captain of the light cruiser, the alien ships are heavily armed. I don't want to risk an engagement with them at this time if we can avoid it. We need more information." Kurt had spent hours with Captain Owens going over the tactical data recorded during his light cruiser's brief battle above Earth.

"Our new particle beam weapons should give us an advantage," Randson carefully pointed out. "None of the ships we had over Earth were equipped with them."

"Can we detect any transmissions from Earth, the Moon, or from Mars?" The Moon and Mars both held sizable human colonies. Kurt didn't like the fact they were going into such an unknown situation and the Solar System was so quiet.

"No, and all the scientific outposts are also silent. There's not a peep coming from the asteroids or the moons of Jupiter and Saturn," Randson replied with growing concern in his eyes. His wife was on Earth just outside of Houston. He hoped she was okay; he didn't know what he would do if something had happened to her. They'd been married for fourteen wonderful years. They also had a twelve-year-old daughter about to enter those rebellious teenage years. "We could send a couple of the destroyers in to check on some of the outposts. It's just too damn quiet! I can't believe they've all been wiped out."

"Not yet," replied Kurt, shaking his head as he thought about the communication silence. "They might be detected. Right now, our biggest tactical advantage is that the aliens don't know we're here. I want to keep it that way for a while longer."

"Sir," Ensign Brooks spoke her eyes alight with fear. "The long-range sensors are picking up elevated radiation levels from Earth." Styles had been working at her console fervently, trying to get better readings on the home planet.

Captain Randson stepped over and studied the data, the frown on his face deepening. "There have definitely been a few nuclear weapons dropped on the surface," he stated, taking a deep breath. "The level isn't dangerous, but it's four times higher than normal. I'm not sure we can afford to wait. What if they drop more bombs?" He gazed at the admiral, his eyes showing his deep concern over the radiation readings. He was itching to find out if his wife and daughter were okay.

"The bombs may have been dropped in the original attack," Kurt said evenly, struggling to stay calm.

He knew if the radiation levels were correct millions of people could be dead on the planet. He felt anger growing inside him at an enemy who would nuke a planet from orbit. This said a lot about the temperament of the aliens they faced. He'd never married, though he did have a sister working at Houston. Both of his parents were deceased and he and his sister, Denise, were very close. She was married with a six-year-old son.

"You're correct," responded Randson with a curt nod. "What are your orders?"

Admiral Vickers studied the tactical screen for a few more moments as he tried to decide what the best course of action was. It was obvious the enemy ships could not be allowed to continue to orbit the planet; they had to be driven off before they nuked Earth again. The presence of an elevated radiation level changed things considerably. Vickers was afraid to even guess at how many people had already died. He wondered if the aliens had landed ground troops to occupy the planet.

"It looks as if the shipyard is relatively intact," Kurt said as he looked at the large green icon on the tactical screen. Earth's only shipyard orbited forty thousand miles above the planet.

"It is, Sir," Ensign Brooks spoke, nodding her brunette head as she studied one of her data screens. "My scanners are showing only minor damage to the shipyard, and its power systems still seem to be operating."

"I wonder why they spared the shipyard?" asked Captain Randson with a questioning look upon his face. "You'd think it would've been one of their first targets."

"Unless they want if for themselves," Kurt responded as he thought about the two thousand men and women who operated the station. He wondered if they were still alive or had been killed by boarders. There were just so many unknowns facing them.

"The first alien race we encounter and they are the ones to find us," Randson spoke as his eyes narrowed. "Why did they attack us in the first place?"

The higher officers in Earth's space fleet had always expected to eventually encounter an alien race as the planet's exploration ships ranged deeper and deeper into unexplored space. First contact protocols had even been set up, with linguists and other specialists assigned to each exploration mission just in case another exploring spacecraft from an alien civilization was encountered.

"We may never know," replied Kurt, brusquely. "Ensign Brooks, are you detecting anything else on the long-range sensors?"

"No," responded Brooks, shaking her head.

"What about communications?"

"Nothing," replied Randson, shaking his head. "There are no radio or video broadcasts of any type being picked up from Earth, the Moon, or Mars. Everything is silent."

"I've managed to get some additional information on the radiation in Earth's atmosphere," Lieutenant Brooks added her eyes indicating growing worry. "It's originating from twenty-two different sources. All points of origin are where major cities are located."

"Formerly located," Randson said his eyes widening in anger. He hoped Houston wasn't one of those sources. His eyes shifted back to the admiral. "We need to get into Earth orbit. What if they drop more nukes?"

"Get me Captain Watkins on the Vindication," ordered Kurt, folding his arms across his chest as he thought about his options. He knew he didn't really have any but one. The knowledge that some of Earth's cities had been nuked changed everything.

"Captain Watkins is on the com," the communications officer reported after a moment.

"Henry, we need to drive those alien ships away from Earth. From our scans, it's obvious Earth has suffered a nuclear bombardment. We can't afford to allow them to bomb the planet again."

"I was afraid of that," his long time friend replied. "Our scanners are showing the same thing. What do you have in mind? We're outnumbered by nearly two to one."

"I'll jump in first with the light cruisers. We've spotted what looks like four enemy capital ships. We'll try to take them out with the new particle beam weapons. Once we're engaged, you and the destroyers will jump in. Launch your bombers and target the smaller ships with tactical nukes. Hopefully, we'll have enough surprise on our side to carry this out."

"It's risky," Henry replied after a moment's pause. "But I don't see that we have any other choices. I just hope everyone's families are still alive."

"Get your bombers ready," Kurt ordered decisively. "We make the jump in twenty minutes."

Lieutenant Brooks stepped over and handed Kurt a list of cities hit by nukes. He noticed with relief Houston wasn't included. However, Chicago, Washington, Paris, Cairo, Moscow, and numerous other cities scattered around the world were. He felt his heart grow cold as he looked over the list. If this was correct, there could be well over forty million casualties from the orbital attack.

"It's not too late to turn back," Captain Randson reminded Kurt in a quiet voice. "We could return to the Newton colony, load everyone up, and head out for parts unknown. We could find a new world to start over on."

"I thought of that," replied Kurt, somberly. "But what do I tell all of our crews? Most of them have family on Earth or one of the outposts here in the Solar System. I think we'd have a mutiny on our hands if we didn't at least try to find out what happened. For all we know there could be a lot of survivors depending on us to drive these aliens off. It would also take us too many trips to move everyone off Newton. We don't know of any other inhabitable planet we can go to."

"You're right," Randson conceded with a sigh, his shoulders drooping. "Let's just hope this is a battle we can win." He was also relieved that they were going in. He didn't want to leave his family stranded on Earth.

The tension and anxiety in the Command Center had increased considerably as the time for the attack neared. All the ships in the fleet were at Condition One with their crews at battle stations. This would be the first time any members of Admiral Vickers' fleet had actually gone into combat.

"Ready to jump," Captain Randson reported as he listened to the readiness reports from various ships over their short-range coms. His eyes focused on the admiral, who was still studying the large tactical screen on the front wall of the Command Center.

Kurt nodded. There was no point in waiting. "All ships initiate jump in sixty seconds," he ordered. "They are to fire upon targets as soon as they exit hyperspace and don't need to wait for orders from the flag."

"Message sent," responded Captain Randson as he activated a counter on his console. "Helm; prepare for hyperspace insertion."

Randson buckled himself into his chair in preparation for combat maneuvers. He knew the hyperspace jump would only last a few seconds. He wondered what they would find when they reached Earth.

"Tactical, ready the main particle beam cannon," ordered Kurt, seeing the increased activity in the command crew as they prepared for combat. "Lock on the enemy's nearest capital ship and fire as soon as you have a confirmed firing solution." The cannon could only be fired once every forty seconds due to heat buildup, so they needed to make every shot count.

"Jump!" ordered Captain Randson his hands gripping the armrests on his command chair.

High Profiteer Creed stood in the Control Room of the pirate ship Ascendant Destruction. He was bipedal and slightly taller than a human. His skin was a light blue color with coarse white hair on his head. His face, while humanoid, had larger than normal eyes. The last few days had been quiet as he waited for the return of the rest of his ships. They were escorting a large fleet of ships to carry detainees as well as heavy cargo ships.

"We'll make huge profits from this planet," gloated Second Profiteer Lantz as he gazed at the main viewscreen on the front wall of the Control Room and the blue-white planet beneath them. "Their people will sell well in the slave markets on Kubitz."

"Their world is rich in many things that will bring us great profits on the black markets," added Creed, recalling his last trip to the bustling black market world of Kubitz as he folded his powerful arms across his chest.

Hundreds of alien races could be found on Kubitz either selling or buying, some of it openly and some done in the back rooms of the pleasure palaces. It was also a very dangerous place for someone unfamiliar with the workings of the black market system. People were known to vanish quite routinely and the local authorities always seemed to look the other way.

"We were fortunate to find this world in these backwater systems," Lantz spoke as he thought greedily about the five percent profits he would receive as his share. "There have been few ships which have ventured out into these areas where the stars are so far apart."

"We can thank the Kreel for that," Creed said. "Several of their cargo ships have reported unknown ships appearing on their satellite marker buoys in a number of systems they have laid claim to. It wasn't difficult for the computers on Marsten to correlate the data and extrapolate the most likely location of those ships' home world." It hadn't been quite that simple. The computers had given them an area of space nearly thirty light years across, which had contained quite a few stars, even in this sparse region. It had taken the Profiteer Fleet two weeks to finally pin down the system they were seeking.

Lantz nodded in agreement. Marsten was the capital of the Gothan Empire, which was a loose Federation of one hundred and eighteen star systems that routinely raided many of the civilized races of the galaxy. It was a dangerous living, but the huge rewards from the bounty they collected more than offset the danger. Lantz was already thinking about how he would spend some of his share in the pleasure houses upon Kubitz. Any type of pleasure one desired could be bought for the right price.

"It is good we found this system when we did," Lantz spoke with a nod of his head. "They had a sizable fleet and in a few more years would have been too powerful to overwhelm without major losses. Even now, they are hesitant about obeying our demands, despite us having destroyed their cities. More examples might need to be made."

Before Creed could reply, warning klaxons began sounding and red lights started flashing in the Control Room. His eyes instantly went to the sensor operator.

"We have ships exiting hyperspace," reported Third Profiteer Bixt as red threat icons began appearing on the sensor screen in front of him. Then, after a moment, he looked at First Profiteer Creed with astonishment on his face. "They're human!"

-

Admiral Vickers felt the familiar gut wrenching feeling as the Star Cross dropped out of hyperspace within close proximity to its intended target. The tactical screen quickly updated, showing the alien ships in orbit around Earth.

"Target lock!" yelled Lieutenant Evelyn Mays as green lights flashed on her console. "Firing particle beam cannon." She reached forward and pressed several buttons in front of her, activating the deadly weapon. Beside her, two ensigns were targeting the ships' KEW batteries and preparing to fire the ships' missiles.

From the Star Cross, a deep blue beam flashed across space smashing into the enemy battlecruiser they'd targeted. The cruiser was still in the process of raising its defensive energy screen, which failed to stop the beam. A massive explosion tore into the cruiser, leaving a gaping hole forty feet across in its hull and blasting a huge fragment off into space. The ship seemed to stagger as valuable systems inside were compromised and went down. Several secondary explosions rattled the ship, sending waves of fire through shattered compartments and corridors. Frightened crewmembers slammed bulkheads shut, trying to stop the growing destruction.

From the bow of the Star Cross, the two KEW cannons fired, sending a pair of two thousand pound rounds toward the reeling enemy cruiser at ten percent the speed of light. They impacted the alien ship, tearing completely through it and setting off secondary explosions. The energy generated was like twin nuclear explosions going off. With a brilliant flash the battlecruiser exploded, sending debris in all directions.

"Enemy battlecruiser is down!" Lieutenant Brooks reported excitedly as the red threat icon swelled on the sensor screen and then vanished.

"We caught them before they could raise their shields," spoke Captain Randson, jubilantly. "We've got them in the same position they caught our fleet in when they attacked Earth."

"Switch to secondary target," Kurt ordered as he intently watched the tactical screen, seeing what success his other ships were having.

"The enemy battlecruiser the Hampton was targeting is down," reported Brooks elatedly as she saw another red icon vanished from her screen."

"Vindication is jumping in!" added Captain Randson as he saw more green icons beginning to appear on the tactical screen.

First Profiteer Creed picked himself up from the deck, looking around the Control Center in anger. "What's happening?" he demanded as his eyes shifted to the ship's tactical screen. He could see numerous red threat icons appearing close to his ships. Too close!

"It's a human fleet and they're attacking," reported Second Profiteer Lantz, breathlessly. "We've already lost the Warriors Pride and the Addax. The enemy is using a powerful particle beam against us as well as kinetics."

"Particle beams and kinetics!" roared Creed in disbelief his eyes growing wide.

He knew that for most warships particle beams were impractical as they required a tremendous amount of energy and needed a long cool down time between firings. Most Gothan ships were armed with ion cannons and missiles, which were cheap and efficient. Kinetics were a thing of the past and had been given up to be replaced by more modern weapons.

"One of the new arrivals is a carrier of some kind," Third Profiteer Bixt warned, feeling worried. "It's launching smaller warships toward us."

"We've lost four of our escorts," spoke Lantz, seeing the ships drop off the tactical screen. He groaned, seeing his profits from this venture rapidly dissipating. His fantasies of the pleasure houses were rapidly fading. "All of our ships have their shields up and are returning fire, but I fear we've already lost too much. The Glimmer Fire is reporting heavy damage and they're asking to withdraw." The Glimmer Fire was their only other remaining battlecruiser.

Creed looked at the viewscreen showing numerous explosions in space. He could even see the path of a few beam weapons. "Order all ships to jump!" he grated out, knowing he had no other choice but to withdraw or be destroyed.

They were in this for profit, not to lose expensive ships. He would return to Marsten and come back with a much more powerful fleet. This planet was too rich to allow a single human fleet to keep them from it. The humans could have the planet back for now, but he would return with a far larger force and take it back. He would also have to contact the detainee and cargo ships and have them return to the Marsten system.

"Destroyer Brant is down," Lieutenant Brooks reported grimly as the friendly green icon representing the small destroyer vanished from the screen.

"We've taken out two of their light units," Captain Randson added as two more red icons fell off the tactical screen. He began to breathe a little easier. At this rate, they would win the battle and then as soon as possible, he intended to take a shuttle down to Houston and evacuate his family. He knew others would be doing the same thing.

"Enemy ships are showing an energy spike," Lieutenant Brooks informed them as one of her sensors indicated a rapid buildup of energy emissions from the alien ships. "They're activating their hyperdrives."

Kurt switched his gaze to one of the large viewscreens just in time to see one of the two remaining enemy battlecruisers jump away. On the tactical screen, other red threat icons were also vanishing.

"Their last heavy is too damaged to jump," Brooks reported as the enemy ship turned toward them with its weapons firing. "They're attacking!"

Kurt felt the Star Cross shudder slightly as an energy beam struck the ship's energy screen.

"We're being hit by some type of ion beam," Lieutenant Brooks reported as she looked at the data on one of her sensor screens.

"The shield is holding at eighty-four percent," Captain Randson said as he quickly checked the status of the ship's energy shield.

"Particle beam is recharged," Lieutenant Mays spoke as she targeted the alien battlecruiser. "Firing!"

The deep blue particle beam smashed into the enemy ship, flashing right through its weakened defensive energy screen. A huge hole was blasted into its bow and the ship seemed to lose all power. Two KEW rounds from the Star Crosses bow cannons plowed into the Glimmer Fire, traveling nearly its entire length, and then the ship detonated in a blaze of light as too many vital systems were destroyed.

"All enemy ships have either jumped out or have been destroyed," reported Lieutenant Brooks, breathing a sigh of relief. "We have control of Earth orbital space."

Kurt nodded, allowing himself to relax. The battle had gone better than expected. "Get me Captain Watkins. I'm going to have the Vindication check out the shipyard; they may need their marines to secure it." Kurt turned his attention back toward one of the viewscreens showing Earth.

"Now let's see if we can contact someone down on the surface and find out just what in the hell is going on."

-

To be notified when the Star Cross becomes available please sign up for book notifications at my website.

Website: http://raymondlweil.com/

ABOUT THE AUTHOR

I live in Clinton Oklahoma with my wife of 40 years and our cat. I attended college at SWOSU in Weatherford Oklahoma, majoring in Math with minors in Creative Writing and History.

My hobbies include watching soccer, reading, camping, and of course writing. I coached youth soccer for twelve years before moving on and becoming a high school soccer coach for thirteen more. I also enjoy playing with my five grandchildren. I also have a very vivid imagination, which sometimes worries my friends. They never know what I am going to say or what I am going to do.

I am an avid reader and have a science fiction / fantasy collection of over two thousand paperbacks. I want future generations to know the experience of reading a good book as I have over the last forty years.

18141050R10177

Printed in Poland
by Amazon Fulfillment
Poland Sp. z o.o., Wrocław